SEARCH FOR Wise WOLF

R á ð ú l f r

James Hendershot

Order this book online at www.trafford.com
or email orders@trafford.com

Most Trafford titles are also available at major online book retailers.

Printed in the United States of America.

ISBN: 978-1-4907-3306-7 (sc)
ISBN: 978-1-4907-3305-0 (e)

Trafford rev. 03/31/2014

 www.trafford.com

North America & international
toll-free: 1 888 232 4444 (USA & Canada)
fax: 812 355 4082

Dedicated to

Dedicated to my wife Younghee, with special thanks,
and to my sons, Josh and John and daughters, Nellie
and Mia and publishing services associate Evan
Villadores (not pictured), and book consultant Tanya
Mendoza (not pictured). In memory of my departed
Trafford inspirations Stacy Canon and Love Blake as
their portraits, hang on the wall behind me.

CONTENTS

CHAPTER 01

The Exodus from Petenka

Names can disguise themselves as such a strange prodigy. Everyone has one, which others decided all calls us. Somehow, I learned to accept this phrase and act in response. Those, who allege to comprehend all things, claiming that our names decide our destinies; nevertheless, I realize that there are those who walk among us who share the equivalent names as those who no longer walk with us. Their same names did not benefit those who sleep in the dirt. The name whom my brothers and sisters call me is Yakov. Our father is a member of the hunting group that feeds our clan. We seldom see him. The longest that he stays with us is when they must bury those who died while hunting with the group. They replace those lost with the strongest young men. Our people could not live without the food they bring back for us. Those same people consider the hunters as foolish, as the hunters kill so they may live. I remember this as among my first memories, although I never saw or understood it, my older brother Kaus and oldest sister Olimpia would always complain about how the clan treated our family. The remainder of my siblings and I would sit and listen to them explain all the problems in our lives. Olimpia would sometimes tell us stories about our mother before she became sick. Olimpia swore that our mother, Perla was much more beautiful than she is. We agreed that our three sisters possess a beauty that no other women in our clan enjoy. Olimpia is our mother. She works in our home each day tending for her brothers and sisters whom, she cares as her own. She is a few years older than we are and therefore, except for Kaus, she witnessed each of us being born, and the pain that she suffered bringing each into her home.

Olimpia promised our mother as she was dying that her babies would be her babies. Olimpia took this as the purpose in her life. She has made our life so rich in that we are all still together. This is what we crave as much as she wants. I see my brothers obey her without challenge, so I also obey her, as do our sisters. She spends much time with Pava considering she was the last life to come from our mother. Olimpia tells us that this makes her so special. The important thing that I appreciate is that when I hurt, Olimpia can make the pain leave, when I am hungry, she always puts food before us, we never feel cold, as she makes us warm. If a mommy is supposed to do those things, then she is our mommy. I grasp one of the features we love about her is that she knows how to create fun. Even when it rains, she can make getting wet enjoyable. When darkness arrives, she floods the black emptiness with fun in the light. I feverishly believed during my early days that she was a magic woman. Later, I discovered that she was every inch an enchanting woman. Her magic kept the spirit and blanket of love rolling within our home. Many of my friends also verified with me, my early robust years of bouncing off everything and crying throughout the nights are only a distant vague memory. Olimpia tells me I had many friends at once. This was the age we could merely crawl, and could not talk. I remember things differently, somewhat dismal, and a few times rewarding. I loved my daddy and when he could spend a few days with us, he would play from early morning to late night. He was swifter than the fastest animal that I knew, and he was a tricky person. He would mislead us into running one way, and we wait for us as we zoomed into his arms. I reminisce that sometimes when we played; some other children would call him names. These were not kind names, yet he would ignore them. I kept an eye on who they were. After daddy left, these creeps became bolder and starting calling me those names. One day, I asked Answald if he taught me ways to fight. He knew of many ways from daddy, as he would always toughen him and Kaus up to defend us.

My day came one day when I had a wonderful club in my hand. I was going to use it to get some nuts from a nearby tree. The three of them surrounded me, and one of them knocked me to the ground. As I fell downward, I knocked down an old woman. I told her I was sorry, and she told me it was all right, since it was not my fault. This made me angry, and I came up with my club and hit the first one in his head. When I saw the blood come from his head and the shock in the other boys' eyes and new sense of confidence and urgency overtook me. I instantaneously hit the other two, both in the front of their heads and down. They went crying. The old woman immediately rushed to my side and ushered me into her house. The three creeps, who so boldly called me names, who were going to teach me a lesson, now ran to their mommy's crying about their unfair attack. I returned to my house and soon thereafter; a large group of villagers was beating on our door demanding that our family give me to them. Kaus refused as he and Panfilo rushed outside with arrows, threatening that if any remained on our property, he would kill them. The people refused, and Kaus shot one man in his arm. All the fierce members of this killing band immediately ran from our yard. They are such bigots and hypocrites. They are willing to dish this out, yet possess no ability to withstand some heat. Soon a group of the villager defenders came with the village's leader and told Olimpia that Kaus and I had to go with them for a trial. He assured her that they would treat us equally, and no harm would come to them if they were innocent. Olimpia had no choice but to agree. The villager's leader took us with him and told the protectors to guard us. I told them not to worry; that they were all cowards. The villager's leader was a good friend of our father, and he agreed with me. He also recommended that I do not voice my opinions, so freely until we solved this situation. The villagers screamed names and threats at us. Our leader stopped and warned them that he had to power to ban from our clan any who interfered with this justice. They soon regained their cowardly composure. We subsequently felt a soft shower begin lightly to soak us. My father's friend told me that these were the heavens crying because of the evil in this village. Kaus was the first they brought before the judges.

The people claimed that they were simply asking, exceptionally politely, that I go with them to the village leader. The village leader called two of the neighbors and asked them what they saw or heard. They told him the people were a raging mob, and that they had their arrows pulled, ready to also kill. The village leader ordered that all in the mob spend three days tied to the village's trees. Within an instant, the mob vanished. The leader sent his escorts to round them up and bring them back and to beat them if they resisted. The first couple resisted. They beat them in public. His escorts next called throughout the village for all those in the mob to come now, and serve their three days. Those who did not come must serve ten days, and then be beaten. About three out of four came voluntarily. At the end of the third day, the leader told them that unless all punished who was part of the mob. He would keep all until all received their just punishment. Names came flying out immediately, as the escorts rounded them up, beat them with twenty lashes, and tied them to trees. Once evidently no others in the mob had escaped justice, they released the original three-day prisoners. Many asked him why he was so hard on these people, and he told them that when you make the gods cry because of your evil, they must see the punishment, or we will die. He allowed me to go back to my home. The parents of the other three boys brought them before him to issue the charges. He warned the parents that if any, provided evidence these charges were false that he would hang the three boys in public. They still had time to speak to their sons and make sure they were telling the truth. The three boys swore that they were playing privately and that I rushed on them and began beating them. When the day of the trial came, Olimpia brought me to the hearing. The village leader told our family that he trusted us and would only intervene if any were to harm us. He told Olimpia that her brother would be with her that night. Each of the boys came forward and told so many lies I could not believe what I was hearing. As they would continue to testify, the villagers then sprang up and yelled to the village leader, "How can you hide this brutality?"

He sat there calmly, asked each boy three times, if he had been calling me names, and had pushed me to the ground. They each denied this, and all three sat down beside their parents. I could feel my heart beating so hard and sweat dripping from my head. Some of the villagers currently yelled to me, "Your evil will be punished, you little heathen." The village leader now called forward the old woman who had taken me into her house, with the group of women who were visiting her that day. The five women testified that they heard the boys call me names and threaten to beat the life out of me. They all witnessed as with the woman whom, I fell into the boys pushed me into her knocking her to the ground. These six women were the spiritual leaders of our village, and no one would dare to accuse them of lying for fear of their lives. When the second one was testifying, all those present left as I could hear them say, "The little boy was telling the truth, and the other three boys must now die for their lies." The reason they had to die was a rule in our village that if you falsely accuse someone of an offense in which death is the punishment, you must die as your punishment. When the third older spiritual leader finished testifying, the three mothers began crying and hitting their sons cursing them for lying. The village leader asked for some of his escorts to take these mothers to their homes and care for them until their mates arrived home. After the fourth woman testified, the fathers asked the trial end, and the punishment begins. The village leader told the fathers, "We must live with this day for the remainder of our lives so if there is any chance of saving your sons, we must endure until the end." The entire village was silent, presently, as everyone knew the sounds that would soon echo throughout our little piece of this giant land. The fifth woman and sixth woman testified. The leader called the father and boys to stand before him. As they stood before him, a cool breeze began to blow pass them. The leader said to the boys, "Today, you are lucky, for the winds are here to carry you into the dark land of the spirits."

One father asked how he knew they would go to the black lands. He told them that something bad would happen when the six spiritual women who represent the ghosts accuse you. You would go to the dark land. He next had his escorts give each father a rope and told them which tree to hang their sons. I watched while this unfolded and felt sad inside that I was rejoicing in their deaths. I watch each as their father put the rope around their neck and pulled them into the air from a branch on their tree. They gagged, and their legs and arms moved totally out of control. The last act is when an escort runs a long knife deep into them to ensure they are indeed dead. They did not move anymore. This was my first introduction to people dying, and even though they had been foolish enough, not to remember the old woman that I knocked down, that could fearfully been me on that rope. The fathers looked at me with hate in their eyes. The village leader then ordered that they give each father fifteen lashes. He next told them, "These are for you being failures as fathers. If I ever hear of any act against this innocent boy, I will ban you from this village for the remainder of your lives and give your wives to new men." I walked home now with Olimpia, who was also acting uneasy. We knew the evil and hatred in this village would find a way to resurface once more someday. Olimpia told me that neither our sisters, nor I would ever play outside our yard another time. They would build a fence around our home. Olimpia was special in that she took us with her every time she went into the neighboring forests and would find places for us to play while she gathered our food. Afterwards, she would return and then play with us. I remember her telling us that no one was going to chastise her little people for the deeds of bad people. The six elderly spiritual women would stop by, and take us playing or bring special food for us. They watched our house and anytime someone would start to poke around our home would walk out and warn them. During the weekly village spiritual meetings, which we no longer attended, they would announce the names of those who they felt were evil, who would be those who snooped around our home. Soon, everyone stayed away from our home. The women had our street closed and their young men in the village to build a large fence that surrounds both of our homes. Olimpia told us we were in the safest hands that we could be. Kaus began to complain that we were prisoners, because some dead bad boys. Many secretly held these black-hearted boys to be heroes.

The reason they held this secretly was the spiritual mothers had been the accusers, and if they made them angry, they were in danger of the spirits punishing them. Olimpia knew that we had to find somewhere new to live, yet she did not recognize where. The other main thing that was saving us was the village leader who loved us. If anything ever happened to him, we could face our inquisition. I remember the fear that flooded our young family. We were afraid of what we did not comprehend could happen. This was enough to take our happiness, from us. Olimpia and Kaus would kill anyone or thing that would try to kill their little people. They would not even trust the meat from the village, in that someone could easily poison it and thereby kill us without anyone discovering them. Our firsthand bonding with the six elder women dampened our paranoia some. The woman, who I fell on, was their leader. Her name was Guðfriðr, and we could all sense that she loved us fantastically much. One night a band of men from the village came once again to tear down the fence that surrounded their home. They volunteered to barricade in our home. Guðfriðr refused and put a curse on all who touched her enclosure. They reluctantly, left. Another night, while we were sleeping, we heard some screams coming from their house. Kaus and Answald grabbed their spears and ran to Guðfriðr's house. Two men entered the home to kill the old women. One woman was already dying as they entered. Kaus speared one while Answald speared the other. As they fell, Olimpia stabbed them with her knife. Guðfriðr asked for Answald's spear and told us to leave immediately and not to leave our home until morning. When the villagers came to investigate, they found the two dead men with the one dead spiritual woman. The four other women had bloody knives in their hands and escorted the village leader in the home so his assistants could remove the bodies. The next day, the women called a spiritual meeting in which they told the villagers that until they removed all this evil, the incorporeal mothers would no longer leave their small fortress. This resulted in an even deeper bonding as they would invite some or all our family to sleep over or eat with them.

They adopted Olimpia, as she became the only person in our village that they taught the mysteries of the roots and herbs. At first, Olimpia argued against this in that we now openly confess that she must take our family and leave. The spiritual mothers told her that they knew this, and that is why it was so important that she learn these great secrets. They took her down into their secret underworld. They had built their home over a cave opening that led into a series of small underground tunnels. Here the women would perform their rituals to the spirits and produce their magical roots and herbs that could heal many things and produce a mental state that could see into the world of the spirits. We avoided these roots, as the spiritual mothers told us to venture into the nonmaterial world without proper knowledge could be deadly. For two circles of the Cegi Moon, we only saw Olimpia when she came up to bathe. The 'we' were Acia and Pava of course. I stayed out of her sight, in case she found dirt on me, as she constantly found dirt on Acia and Pava. They did not care, as they wanted to be as beautiful as Olimpia, and she told them they could only be like her if she invariably cleaned their dirt from their skin. They fell for it, and I did not want to tell them differently, if it would make Olimpia angry with me. When Olimpia returned to be with us, we could see that she was different now. She had a stronger stare in her eyes, a glare of greater confidence and understanding of the world around us. Our master spent much of her first week back spoiling us. She hugged us constantly and slobbered all over our faces crying how much she loved her little people. Guðfriðr complimented her on this love and gave her a blessing that someday she would enjoy a pleasant family and new children. I heard Guðfriðr telling the other spiritual mothers that it was accordingly rare to find a woman; consequently, young being so devoted to her family. The mothers told Guðfriðr that if they had such beautiful little people to care for, they would also be as excited. I now felt obligated to feel thus, well. Another bad man, one of the three boy's fathers, came one night to exact his revenge on us. Guðfriðr threw one of her magical powders into his eyes that caused him to become blind and in great pain. She next slung her large cutting blade into his left leg chopping it off. One of the women rushed to bring the village leader, Cobus, and his escorts.

8

He took the man in the middle of the village, tied him to a pole, and had him burned to death. He did not speak throughout this process, being so angry at the continued foolishness of his people. At the end of the burning he asked, "Who will I burn next?" Actually, no one complained about this burning, as this is clearly a death offense to enter the spiritual mother's home without a legal reason. Many of the people were also sharing their leader's fear the spirits could turn against us. They strove so hard to rebuild confidence in Guðfriðr to return with her teachings and blessings and now this happened. This was not good. Cobus complained to the people that Guðfriðr had to carry defensive herbs in her pockets and not healing herbs. Bad times were ahead without any doubt. It was for me, good times, because these older mothers knew exactly how to feed little people. They even gave us a few treats, which they told us not to inform Olimpia. These special foods tasted so good we promised not to reveal this to Olimpia, who discovered it when she was cleaning our teeth that night. She essentially began to laugh about it. We wanted to understand why she was laughing. She explained the spiritual mothers were recognizing her powers as a mother for us, and that made her feel pleasant. Acia told me later that night that it was excellent when we get to eat a treat and Olimpia is happy because of it. I agreed with her. Olimpia told Guðfriðr and the other spiritual mother's one morning that we would soon must depart to see our father and asked them if they watched our home. They agreed to do so, and when we left the next morning, Guðfriðr gave each of us some food and special roots and cried as we left our small fortress. We ensured that no one else know, so danger would not follow us. I kept a few other memories that stick out in my mind as that day did. It just felt so wonderful, and I would now see what I believed to be the greatest site on our world.

This greatest spectacle was when I first saw the Lake on the Top of the World. This summer, which was a bit hotter and dryer, then most, my sister took all of us to the skinny peninsula where we would meet our father. This finger of land had tall, thin evergreens on its most extended part, into the beautiful many shades of blue covering the surface of this Lake. Olimpia spoke of how our mother told her that many times she would wait for our father on this rare cape. They had worked out a deal that he would always return this way, as the fishing was great, and they could add to the wide range of the wild game they had captured for our small village. The smallest game, they would kill and field clean. Many of the larger beasts, they would break one of their legs and lead them from rope back to our people. They secured the beasts, many by breaking another leg, which constructed it, to be dreadfully grueling for them to escape. The abundance of wolves that would patrol around our village also helped to keep these beasts beside the cut-dried grass, which our village fed them. We were people who would never waste anything. When we cleaned a large beast, anything that we did not eat, we gave to the wolves. We always worked truly hard to make sure no blood hit our soil inside where we resided. The old medicine men told us that if we spilled blood on the land the spirits of our nature would take that land from us. To solve this, all wildlife, except for fish, they cleaned outside our boundaries. The adults would build a small fire that would encircle them, clean the animal and exiting through a minuscule fire gateway that took them into our village. They would next place the meet inside our choking air building and ignite the bowl fires that would pack the building with choking smoke. This was so the meat would go into the world of the spirits. The spirits would enter because the dark smoke made in impossible for us to see and breathe. The spirits would next consecrate the meat and to show their blessing would paint the meat with the smoke to kill the little beasts who would give us plagues. They also put the lifesaving-bleached sand on it. We had a large cave nearby where our young men would dig within and bring up this white sand. When they put it on our meat, it would remain edible much longer. The sad side effect of this is that it made them less dependable on the hunters and therefore, allowed them to downgrade them even more.

They are such absolute fools. They forced my father into being a hunter. They made him be a hunter because he was so strong. My mother and father had to marry in secret and live in the wild lands. When she died, which was their fault, as she was giving birth to Pava, the village finally took us to exist with them. We hope that someday he will take us away with him, and the hunters will stop hunting, wait until they starve to death, and then come back to the village. This is our private hope as we smile at them in public, yet once inside our home, we curse them. Today we will be going through our mountains to the Lake on top of the world. Olimpia tells us it will only take three days, so we are excited. I am excited because Kaus tells me we will enjoy so much fun. I was, consequently, wonderful walking through the woods, as the branches snapped under our feet and the birds left the safety of their trees in roving flocks. I hear the wind blowing through the top of the trees, yet I cannot feel any wind where we walk, while we stay under the trees. We try to walk quietly, yet are not as successful as we should be. Kaus tells me that sometimes, bad people hide in the forest. He shows me his large spear, and explains how he will fight to save us. Answald also has a smaller spear and approximately mimics Kaus. Panfilo has the mission of protecting our two of my other sisters, Acia and Pava and I. He could be overbearing at times, especially since he has to hit something before talking to us. This stressed us, at first; however, now we simply laugh at him, which makes him even angrier. When he throws his temper tantrum, Kaus or Olimpia will rush to and yell at him. We want to laugh; at the same time, we realize if we do laugh, after that they will stop yelling at him. Therefore, we held fast until they leave, later we make jokes about him. Either way, the calmness in this forest continues to overwhelm my senses, because so much life is around me, yet remains hidden. They are afraid of us, as I fear everything. I am fortunate that they do not understand this. We walk through the day as Kaus and Olimpia gather things from the trees and the ground. When the late afternoon arrives, they pick a campsite for us.

They appear to understand that Panfilo needs a time-out from us, as we need a break from him. They understand that Acia and Pava, with me need some playtime. They always tell me to take care of my sisters. My sisters continuously tell me what we are going to do. I head off in my direction and tell them to watch out for the snakes, bears, or sometimes dragons. Soon they are beside me asking if they can play with me. I tell them that I would feel so sad if they gave up what they wanted to do, just to be with me. They assure me that what they fancy is to play with me. We produce fun, as I always tailor our activities so it will be fun for likewise them. I do not want their evenings to be like our day under the tyrant Panfilo. After about one hour of excellent playing, Olimpia calls for us. She is constantly so happy to see the three of us returning. She regularly sits down as each of her sister's land on one of her legs, and I stand in the middle while she hugs the three of us declaring her love and joy that we are still with her. She creates our feeling of her wanting us so much. I am just on that borderline that she can get me in with my sisters, as I like in addition them. The other brothers do not want to mess with the little kids. We help pull her up, as she at no time tries to appear perfect for us. She is not obligated to; because she cannot be once literary do wrong in our minds. When we get her upright, she guides us to our evening meal, which is consistently so amazing. The brothers unfailingly snap a few small animals on our hikes during the day. Olimpia grabs the special roots and fruits, and they make a little fire to cook it. After they cook our meat, roots, and vegetables, they immediately put out the fire. Daddy always taught us the smoke from the fires would tell the bad people where we were. He would not even allow a campfire, unless a moonless night, or while sleeping in caves. Anyway, we bundle together in our blankets that mommy and Olimpia made for our family and sleep in peace. Mornings can bring us back to reality, especially when we see a couple of snakes cooking on our morning fire. Kaus always tells us he got them beside our blankets, yet Olimpia hits him and orders him to stop scaring our little people. We do not recognize for sure who to believe, as we understand that Olimpia is overprotective and Kaus is more reality based; nonetheless, as our other brothers, do enjoy stretching the truth.

Either way, the snake does taste good, as we soon start the day number two of our walk. On this day, we will go down into some valleys and then start the steep journey to the top. The descending is easy and at the same time strange. The richness of the variety of trees heightens, as also do the actions of the wildlife, which survive within them. The wind begins to blow swifter and more destructive, as if angry for having to travel the lowlands. We seldom step on branches now, as the leaves from the previous, years' cover this ground. This helps our feet land softly on the ground as we walk.

It feels different, yet I would prefer the snapping branches up in the mountains. Olimpia tells us not to worry, as the mountains surround these valleys. We can tell by the hillsides that much water drains down, yet it only goes into little streams. Olimpia tells us daddy revealed to her the streams go into caves that flow out into many small streams to the west of our mountains. We see so many new species of animals and birds. I feel almost as if we are in another world. We stay close to the mountainside as we cross through this area. The people who live here do not like outsiders and will not bother us if we stay on the crossover path, which we will be on for a few short hours. We stop as we cross a medium-sized stream. Kaus wants to fish for a while. We join him, and soon he has about twenty fish, so we start to go up the cliff. Olimpia says there are some small plateaus that we can stop and eat our fish with a pleasant fire. We need not to worry about our security, as the lowland people will protect us. I asked her how they knew us. She explained, as she raised her eyebrows and released her heavenly smile on us, "Little people, they saw how beautiful you are and therefore, would never want anything bad to happen to us." We do not understand if we should believe her; however, Kaus and even Panfilo, looks serious when she is talking, so she must be telling the truth. I tell my little sisters that we need to clean in the nearby stream, so they will not see us dirty and then decide to kill us. I rush to the stream, as Acia and Pava, both fighting to keep their breaths are right behind me. On returning, we sat down to eat our fresh cooked fish, now extraordinarily clean, as Olimpia rushes to us slobbering kisses all over us. We never did figure out why this excited her until later in our lives. Nevertheless, we so much enjoyed making her happy.

Thus, we would stand there while she slobbered over us and pretend as if it was okay. We had to listen carefully, as she would say she loves us, and we wanted to respond with our passion to the same degree as quickly to such an extent possible. We knew that she enjoyed this, as we could see our words going into her mind and then to her heart, giving her enormous satisfaction. Acia questioned me once if this was our magic, and I had to confess that I did not know. I told her while Olimpia still fancied this; we need to keep feeding it to her. Considering how much she did for us, it was a small price to pay. Acia and Pava listen to what I say, as I never would say anything to hurt them, and saying scaring things to keep them with me is not hurting them. We are the three 'little people' and as such, learned to stick together. Olimpia always brags that I am the big brother to the minute sisters. Acia and Pava tell her, "He is our best older brother in the whole world." When the three of them put so much charm on a little boy like me, I simply become, mellow. I would become a perfect mommy's boy, if I had a mommy. I understand this is also tough on Acia and Pava, so I do not mind having two extra friends. They are my allies in that if Panfilo becomes too overbearing, they will help me sick Olimpia or Kaus on them. Kaus also treats his little sisters as his special pint-sized loves, so they stand strong beside me in my defense on anything. If Kaus is yelling at me, they rush to my sides and start crying. I am amazed how this giant turns into a midget within seconds as Olimpia, who has a special ear for her little sisters always comes running. They tell her that Kaus is going to kill me. Kaus denies the charge and retreats as my sisters hug me and Olimpia tells me that no one will kill me. This is when I started to sense the special powers of women. I remember seeing them boss the men in our village. Nevertheless, I attributed this to these men being weak. We eat our fish quickly as Acia has a new plan for us now. We will get close to Olimpia and tell her we are scared of the cliffs that Panfilo will make us fall and die. Olimpia buys it, thanks to the tears that run down our cheeks. We can make these tears appear when we really want something. She tells us to stay with her.

We actually avoid all the cliffs, as for the steep ones she knows of a nearby cave. After we go through a few caves, she feels secure in that no one is following us. We make it back to the top late on the second day. The brothers quickly capture some game for us, and Olimpia scouts for her herbs, roots, and plants and wood for our fire. The brothers also bring some wood and fruit back with them. We do the important job, and that is to stay out of trouble. Olimpia tells us this is the most important job. We also help to unpack the blankets and cookware plus tiding up around our campsite. We, of course, must zip up a few trees to make sure we realize what is around us. We climbed saplings, without any hesitation our entire lives. Our village teaches all their children how to become one with the sky. We learn how to feel the tree and listen to what it has to say. Nature has a message for us, as it truly wants all who obeys its rules to enjoy life. One rule is always to be watching, as other parts of nature also want to survive. At all times, we can become a meal for another creature. There is always that quiet warning that we must hear. We eat our evening meal as Olimpia divides some of her root paste, she prepared for our sore feet. She rubs it into her 'little peoples' feet. Tonight she wants us to sing songs. We sing so many songs and laugh all the way through them as Olimpia and Kaus act foolish while singing them. They are accordingly amazingly funny. Acia tells Pava and me that when she gets older, she will not be so foolish over the loving boys' junk. She only loves me. I confess to them that I love furthermore them. I then ask them, "What is this thing called love?" Acia tells us she does not know, except that love is a delightful thing to say to those who are your friends. Pava and I immediately declare our love for each other. Olimpia comes to take them with her, yet they now cry for me also, so she brings me into their special group. Olimpia tells me someday that all the girls will like me. I tell her I do not want that, I only want Acia and Pava. She tells me I can merely keep one, and I must pick just one. Acia and Pava start to cry. They are folding their hands over their hearts and gripping their feet into the ground.

The entire forest becomes quiet, as if the world wants to hear one cheer and the other to cry. I tell Olimpia, "I will take my sisters and you if you wish, into a new land, and we will live by our laws that say I can keep my sisters." Acia and Pava cheer and tell Olimpia, "We told you, he was the finest brother always." Olimpia replies, "I will definitely want to live with the best brother, whoever was. I will cook and clean for you." I told her, "You will only cook. I want you to rest for all the hard work you gave us. Your love will keep us happy." Tears start to run down her cheek as she begins slobbering on all our faces. Acia tells me not to get her so excited next time. I agree with her. Olimpia tells us one of her great nighttime stories. This story had a little girl who was unbelievably beautiful and when she became a woman, so many men wanted her to make babies for them. She wanted to stay with her parents and learn about the angels in the heavens. The men would ask the father if they could care for her. He told them no, she wanted to learn how to talk with the angels. One quiet summer night two men came and started a fire to burn down their house. They waited and waited for someone to come forward and revealed themselves. No one came out, so the men became afraid that they had murdered them and ran into the mountains to hide. While in the mountains, one fell over a cliff and broke his legs. As his friend ran down to get him, a large wild beast was eating him. When he saw the enraged beast, he ran away as fast to such an extent possible. Nevertheless, another beast saw him and chased him into a tree. He stayed in the tree for two weeks, while the beasts tried to shake the tree. Finally, some snakes that lived in the tree became angry that he was in their tree. They waited until night, went to him, and bit him, putting their poison deep inside him. When his dead body stiffened it fell to the ground, and the beasts ate him. Meanwhile, back at the old man's house that had burned, they had been on another mountainside with their daughter who was looking forward to talking with some angels. They waited until deep into the night when they finally gave up and returned to see their home burned to the ground. The father told his daughter that even though they had not talked to an angel, an angel had saved them from this fire, and that it was time they moved to a new land where bad men would not chase her.

They went to a new land and lived happily ever after. We loved this story, although I became worried and asked her, "How can I save my sisters from bad men. As my sisters are so beautiful and when they become women, shameless men will want you, and I want to keep my sisters just for me." Olimpia told me there are many good men, such as our daddy, and that when the respectable men come, and you approve of them. All your brothers and daddy will also be absurdly over concerned about this. Then our family will give our sisters into what we call marriage. Other families will give their daughters to our family so my brothers and I, can also keep a wife. I told her that I did not like this; however, if daddy likes it, then it must be okay. I am going to make sure they are moral and will be good to my sisters. Acia and Pava cheer up and say that if I say they are to be a worthy man's wife, then they will do this.

Olimpia smiles and says to me that even she will want me to verify whether her possible husband will be suitable and not beat her. When she talks about the beating, I rush to her and hug her crying, "If any man ever beats my sisters, I will kill him." Olimpia looks at me seriously and tells me that she believes me and will depend on me to save her. I ask her, "What if I am still little?" She tells me that I will grow to be big and strong just like our daddy. That makes me feel a lot better. She next confesses to me that our mother told her I would be the one to protect my sisters. I ask her, "How did mommy realize this?" She confesses that there are so many things that a mother comprehends everything about her babies. These things only the angels tell her so that way she knows how to care for the babies since they were living with the angels before they came here to settle. I disclosed to her that I did not remember ever living with angels. I wanted to understand why I would not recognize anything this important. Acia and Pava told our older sister that they did not remember. We thought that because Pava was the youngest, she should remember. Olimpia tells us that this is the way of things. I asked her how we knew these things. She tells us that some special medicine men, long ago, discovered these secrets. Acia asks, "How did they discover this?"

Olimpia informs them that they had special dreams, which some secret spirits told them, and now mommy was one of those wonderful spirits. We smiled at this, because, if our mommy was with them, then they were good things, and mommy could teach them everything. Our third day was smoother than the first two. We could take more liberties now in that the paths were so much wider. Kaus and Answald walked ahead scouting to make sure everything was safe. Olimpia was happier today, as the vegetation in this area was much richer. She could find my things with ease. She had predicted this, thus told Kaus and Answald; we would eat three times today, in the morning, at midday and our evening event. Lunchtime was without cooking, consisting of simply fruits, leftover fish from last night, and some roots. Since we were walking faster than the two previous days, she felt we needed some additional rest. I did not care because today would be the first time I saw our family's secret meeting place. I also saw some milky mountains. Olimpia tells us that these mountains stay bleached all year long and that the white was frozen ice. I looked at both of our suns and asked her, how this can be icy when the suns are burning directly on them, and they hold no trees for shading. She tells us that is the secret of the high places. This way, no one can build homes or villages in those upper parts of the mountains that are closer to the sky. The milky ice and the bleached clouds make it easy for the white spirits to visit when they wish. Acia thought this was smart. I also concurred and was so happy that Olimpia

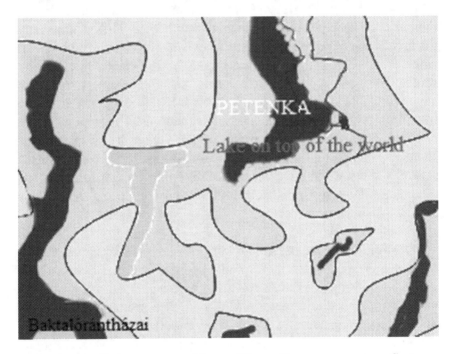

understood all these great things. We walk pass so many flowers. Some are tall, others little. Nevertheless, they share so many colors and strange shapes. I go to touch them; however, some flying insects that sting are hovering over these beauties. I do not want to be stung, so I enjoy their fresh smell from a safe distance. I am so puzzled that the same color of dirt can make so many colors of flowers. Even so, when I get dirt on me, I stay the identical color. Some things do not appear to be fair. Olimpia explains this by saying that mommy wants us to stay the same color that we were when we lived in her belly. At first, I did not believe that babies lived in the bellies until I saw some women in the village that had particularly big stomachs.

Then a few weeks later, their tummies would be little once more, and they would be holding their new child. It was therefore, important for me to start forgetting our old village, as Olimpia claims that if daddy does not join us, afterwards we will join him on his hunts. I so much already miss Guðfriðr and the other spiritual mothers. They had a funny smell to them. Olimpia told me that was from the special roots and herbs they covered themselves with reducing the pain that comes with advanced years. This compels me never to want to grow old. I do not miss Cobus, although he did so many good things for us. Without him, I would suffer a hanging on a tree instead of the three bad boys. I hope that spectacle never again to witness. I do not regret those boys having to lie with their false testimony against me. I still think that someone should question the spiritual mothers' way earlier. They finally did, and alerted those boys that they had confirmation they were lying. He somewhat led them into an ambush and then, by village law had the power to destroy them. I asked Olimpia about this later, she further inquired from Guðfriðr who revealed to her that these boys were destined to do more harm and evil to others, and therefore, they had to stop them. This was the advice that Guðfriðr had given Cobus. It all fits so well together when looking back, yet it was chaos when it was happening. Olimpia continuing to argue, cites this as one reason we can never live with stupid people who think they are smart. Their foolishness can kill us. We are lucky in that our father knows so much of the nearby land. Now that she has knowledge of the roots and herbs, we can be our own, medicine people. Each night, she shows us the roots and herbs she collected during the day and tells us how they can be prepared for our healing's. We still boast perfect feet even though we engaged in walking for almost three days now. Therefore, she knows what she is doing. Olimpia tells us she feels bad for not telling Guðfriðr that we were leaving. Kaus shows her some things they gave us as going-away presents. He tells Olimpia that they knew and did not say anything to embarrass her, for they knew we could never live in the village. Olimpia shares with us that she will inform our father the spiritual mothers told us we could no longer live safely in the village.

The two suns are passing each other over the top of our sky during our midday. This is when they shine into the forests and life therein begins to scramble. Branches are bouncing as various leaves are riding the light winds. Daddy is always telling us that living within settlements such as our village is taking away our ability to survive as his ancestors did. We are becoming weaker as a species. Someday, he predicts, that many people will spend their total days living in small villages as some in Petenka already were doing. Petenka would take its entire people into the forests for two weeks, three times each 300 days, so they can learn to live some outside. We knew that was a dying practice, as so many were bringing their luxuries in the forests with them. Daddy heralded this as the end of our species. He said the beasts had no homes, no clothing, and limited ways of preserving their food. They were also born in their clothes, as he believed we were, although no ancient tales spoke of this. Only those who could master all the skills for survival continued to live, unlike our village where so many did not understand how to hunt. He thought that this specialization in the skills needed to survive, even though risky, could produce benefits. The issue we faced is how they carried out this specialization, which resulted in some being lazy and having to do nothing for their survival. He hoped that a day would never come when large groups of selected people would not work, while forcing others to do their toil for them. He knew slavery; however, this was different. Slaves worked for fear of being beaten. The villagers worked in the hopes of gaining enough trading stones so they would not labor. Daddy is such a wise man, although so much that he spoke about he had witnessed in other villages or learned from their ancient tales. He told us that to keep from working by depending on your merchandising jewels you must control others who will help you protect these gems, with force ready to kill if need be. He compared it to the escorts of our villager's leader.

These escorts gave him his power. Therefore, those who had the wealth of the special stones would also need escorts to protect them.

Daddy, whose name is Pawka, told a tale about such a village that had the protected against the remainder of the clan. There came on this land a great famine. The vegetation turned brown because the rains no longer fell from the sky. When the vegetation withered, the wildlife made their exodus. The protected could buy no food, because there was so little food the working people kept it, for if they sold it, they would, then perish. The rich man became angry and ordered his servants to attack and kill those in the village. His protectors departed for the village; however, he stayed in his house having consequently, vast faith in his wealth. His protectors were much hungrier than he was, because the prosperous man did not share his last remaining food with them. When the protectors arrived in the village, some women came out and offered him food if they went back and killed the rich man. As evidence of his death, they wanted to see his head. They gave the protectors some herbs and roots to eat. A few of the protectors questioned what sort of roots and herbs they were eating, because they did not recognize them. The women told them that they had to search hard for these roots, as they were so valuable in stopping the pain of being hungry. They ate the roots and herbs. The villagers showed them the food they could eat when they returned. They had put all their remaining food reserves on display for the protectors, thus when they returned the protectors would eat all their food, leaving the villagers in deep danger of their demise. The protectors returned, passing through the forest on their special dirt path. They entered through the affluent man's secret gateway. They next entered the well-to do man's house, after placing guards at every exit. These protectors wanted to finish their mission and return to the village to eat their bounty. They rushed into the house and killed the rich man. Afterwards, they beheaded him. They all joined and cheered in excitement that soon they would hunger no longer. Even though temporary, they planned on harassing and torturing the villagers to find them more food. As they were cheering, a deep sleep fell on them. When they all fell to the ground, the villagers tied ropes around their necks and lifted them off the surface to hang. Fortunately, the rich man had plenty of rope.

They hung the ten protectors on different branches that circled the house. The villagers went into the rich man's house and collected all the precious stones that he had. They would use these gems to trade for food. His wealth was ample for them to purchase enough food until the drought ceased. Our daddy told us he feared this would happen one day in our village. A day when a person's wealth, would allow them to think they could kill or do as they pleased because of their riches. The main thing that had kept our village together was the power of the spiritual mothers. This power is under danger of execution nowadays. The spiritual mothers were currently living in a fortress and no longer having their weekly meetings. Daddy always told us these bad people forgot so much when something is between them and what they want. Olimpia calls for a meeting, as we are only about two hours from our peninsula. She wants to discuss our argument against living in the village. I am sitting beside Panfilo, who will soon be dethroned when we complete this three-day journey. Pava is sitting on my left with our junior dictator on my right. Acia is sitting in my lap. She never sits alone. Usually, there are many competitions on who gets her. Nevertheless, Kaus and Answald are taking a nap, so I am the only one she can sit beside during this conversation. If I ever ask her to join me, and she is with another brother, she will leave him and come to me. This does not work on Olimpia, for when Acia, Pava, or even if I am on her lap, we stay. She is our hero and mother. Olimpia tells us we can rest for a while, as she is going to search for some roots and herbs. Panfilo tells us he will keep watch for us, and that we may enjoy a nap. These short snoozes are so refreshing, as, 'we little people' doze, off every afternoon, except for the two previous days. When I lay on the soft yellowish-green grass, Acia and Pava snuggle beside me. The peaceful breeze that lightly ruffles their hair creates a soothing sound and compels me to dream about floating on the water. This is exceedingly quiet with each random sound, adding to the harmony of peace. Suddenly, I hear a loud scream and as, I am awakened, I see blood all over us. Acia, Pava awake, and I quickly put my hands over their mouths. I am now looking forward to seeing what is happening. I hear another loud groan and a thump.

A dead man's head has crashed onto our legs. Acia and Pava are shuddering. Sweat is soaking their bodies, and small moans try to sneak past my hands sealed to their mouths. My arms are hurting from holding their mouths. I remember Kaus once told me that the best defense for little people was to stay hidden and quiet. I cannot see what is happening, and therefore, only hope that I conceal us from this danger. If we stay quiet, later I think we will be safe temporary. After that, just in time, Kaus comes over and discovers us. He asks me if we are okay. I release my hands from Acia and Pava's mouth. They say hi to Kaus. He questions me, "How were Acia and Pava during this horrifying event?" I tell him that they were extremely quiet and calm. He leans over and gives both a kiss. They each still keep one arm against my leg and pinch me. I smile back at them. That is our little people way of saying thanks. Answald comes running up to us and tells Kaus he did not see any others in this area, so we should be safe for a while. Kaus rolls the dead man over and says, "His face does appear familiar; however, no one from our village would be this far away unless they were hunters, and this evil man does not come across as a killer." I ask Kaus, "Where is Panfilo?" Answald tells us, "We are sorry. This man drove a spear in his back and through his chest. I kicked the man's face to get his head away from my right leg. Acia, Pava, and I jump to our feet and see around. I see Panfilo laying on the ground just past a three-foot wide patch of weeds that not only separated us, but it also provided concealment. The killer stabbed him in his back. This is a serious violation of our ethics. To kill someone in his back is a sign of being a coward. Either way, Panfilo is dead. I shall miss him so much, as I see also that Acia and Pava will. I realize we flooded him with sarcasm and made fun of him too often. We discern that now a big sibling, most likely Answald is going to be our guardian. At least, Panfilo liked to play, when he was alone with us. Olimpia comes running into the camp and sees Panfilo laying sideways with an arrow in his back. Her face turns red as she asks Kaus what happened. Kaus explains that we were asleep and heard Panfilo scream. He saw a man pushing his spear inside Panfilo and then tried to pull it back through his body.

The spear was stuck in Panfilo's ribs. Kaus continued by telling her that he immediately grabbed his spear, in one move arose, and drove his spear into this killer. Olimpia raised her hand for him to pause and asked, "Do you recognize who the killer is?" Kaus said he did not know. She asked me, and I told her I had not looked at him yet, because I was more concerned with keeping Acia and Pava safe. They each pinched me again, which told me they knew I was making excuses. Acia then told Olimpia that I saved them and protected them. Olimpia looks at me with tears beginning to fall down her angelic cheeks and tells me, "Yakov. You will need to work twice as hard now to protect our little girls, as Panfilo is no longer with us." I shook my head yes. She went over and turned the man, over so we could see his face. Instantly, hers and my face turned red. I walked over behind her and asked her why this man tried to kill us. She tells me that in his own sick mind, he blamed us for his son's perjury. This was the third father of the three boys who had lied about me. The other two were already dead. I surmise that now we only need to worry about the mothers. Olimpia discloses to me that the mothers will not seek revenge because they must stay and care for their children. Widows in our village must live with each other as the children live together in another large room in this house. They work for the village, as the village provides them their community house and food. Olimpia believes that no mother would venture into these forests looking for us, as she would then risk never seeing her children once more. This is one argument that Olimpia will use with our father, that if we do go back, they most likely would beat her to death for endangering her siblings, especially with the death of Panfilo. Olimpia looks at us and swears she will never again live in the village of Petenka. If she must die, she will meet her death in the wild forests. We now knew that if daddy did not agree, we would venture off on our own. Kaus took some of the clothing from the dead father as Olimpia tied Panfilo to his back. Olimpia and Answald would pull the dead man. She was thankful the rest of our journey had a slight descent and as such; they would not be pulling these dead bodies up any cliffs. Olimpia wipes her feet on the ground, saying, "Petenka is no longer our home. We will now search for our new home."

CHAPTER 02

Journey to the lake on top of the world

Each step, although we are going downwards slightly, is taking so much time. Olimpia hopes that daddy will arrive later in the week. She had planned our trip, so we would arrive in plenty of time. Even though I am not carrying any dead bodies, we must all stay together. This slowed walk is boring Acia, Pava, and me. We are sticking light together and avoiding Kaus. They tied Panfilo's body so his head points backwards. His eyes remain open. Olimpia left them open, so he could see us taking him to daddy, and therefore, he could witness of daddy one last time before he goes to the land of the lights. This perhaps may be good; however, we do not want to allow him to watch us. Acia complained that even while dead, he was watching us. We, therefore, remained close to Olimpia and Answald. What normally was a two-hour trip was turning into many more hours. We usually finish each day around the sixth hour past the two high Suns. Olimpia tells us that today we will endure until we can see the peninsula. She remembers a large ledge that is about thirty minutes from the peninsula. We continue to clomp what seems to be forever inch-by-inch. My feet are beginning to hurt. It is easy to see Acia and Pava also struggling. Nevertheless, I put on my strong face and comfort them, which for now are merely peaceful words. Olimpia observes me talking with our sisters and congratulates me for my great hard work. I think this odd in that she, Kaus, and Answald are pulling the dead bodies. We are now in the cool part of the day as the Suns are hiding behind the high trees. I notice the birds are starting to leave their trees and making some strange noises. Olimpia notices this too, and alerts Kaus. Kaus tells me, and his two younger sisters, to hide in the bushes on our left. We run into the bushes without argument. I understand that when in situations such as this, the best thing to do is obeying.

They are trying to prepare to defend against a possible danger and must concentrate on organizing. Olimpia told me they could not arrange their defense, unless they first knew we are okay. I get behind some bushes that allow me to snap enough of their thin branches, so we can see what is happening. I always share my view with Acia and Pava. They need some knowledge of the situation, if we must create a break for it. I find it better not to hide things from them. I can detect if they are disturbed. They trust me and I trust them, because, if they fashion a noise, I could also die with them. They came to close a couple of times even though they were trying hard to hold themselves back in their little bodies were trying to take control of them. I learned early that if I wanted them to depend on me presently, I had to build that trust and respect during our free times. They love to play with me during my play times, so I let them tag with me and prepare the necessary modifications to fit them into my game or adventure. The stillness of our area escapes us, as four men with spears come out and surround Olimpia, Kaus, and Answald. This is when I realize that I may need to help save them, against their wishes. I can stab them in their back, as I am a child trying to defend my family. I motion for them to be still and pull out my little knife that I use to play and tell them that I may also be required to join this fight, as they are outnumbered. This plan died out extremely fast when three more men joined the ambush. They question Olimpia about why she is bringing dead people into their lands. She tells them the one man killed her brother. They accuse her of bringing the dead bodies into their land to spread death and suffering. He then puts his spear into the skin on Olimpia's neck, and tells her if she yields even one move, she will die. He tells Kaus and Answald to put down their spears, or she dies. When they drop their spears, the other man takes them and ties them to two trees. Their leader tells Olimpia the fighting men must die because they raised their spears against them. Olimpia tries to talk; however, when she moves her mouth, the man and jabs his spear at her neck, creating a small cut in which blood begins to pour.

He tells her to be quiet. They will let the spirits test if they are innocent or guilty. The two men will do this by throwing three spears from seventy feet at them. If all three spears miss, then they are innocent. If one hits them, causing their death, afterwards they are guilty. Even I am having trouble holding my fear inside me. Kaus and Answald are great brothers who must remain as part of our family. I can only hope now that our time with the Spiritual Mothers caused some of the spirits to like us. The killers line up and throw their first two spears. The spear aimed at Kaus bounces off the tree about three inches above his head. This killer is going for a strike on Kaus's head. A minor adjustment and he will kill Kaus easily. The killer throwing at Answald hits him in his leg. Blood is gushing, as his leg still holds the sword. He will die unless treated now. I cannot take a chance on another round of spears, as I retain no doubt that two more throws will kill them both. I place my knife back into the special pocket Olimpia had sewn for me. I tell my sisters not to move. I now come running out screaming, "My father; Pawka will revenge you. You will not live more than a few days, as even my sisters currently fly through the forests to alert him." The man with the spear to Olimpia's neck brought down his spear and motioned for the other two men to stop. He then looked at me and demanded, "Prove you are the children of Pawka." Our mother and father had made identical necklaces that they wore as a sign of their love. When mommy died, she gave her necklace to Olimpia. She had now reached down the front inside her shirt and pulled up the necklace. The leader looked at it and argued, "I do not recognize this." He called for the other men to identify it. One by one, they confessed never to seeing a necklace like it. Finally, the last man came running to see the necklace and comments, "Wow; Pawka has one such as this." The leader asked him how he knew this.

The young man said, "Because my mother once offered him three horses for it, and he refused, saying it represented the love of his wife." He then looked at Olimpia and commented, "Strange, I always pictured his wife to be older. You appear young to be the mother of seven children." Olimpia told him that our mother had died and before her death, she gave this necklace as a sign of eternal love for her children. The leader then asks, "If he has seven children, why do I only count four?" Olimpia reminds him the fifth one lies dead as she points to his body. She looks at me and I tell him, "Remember, two of our sisters are riding the winds to find Pawka, so he may save us." The leader afterwards orders the two brothers to be untied, and that they treat the one boy's leg. Olimpia tells them that she will treat her brother, as she knows the secrets of the roots and herbs, and that she must gather them now. He sends one of the men to help her. Meantime, they placed some large leaves on the wound after cleaning it with some water they had with them. Olimpia returns quickly, and as she does she walks by Acia and Pava and motion for them to join her. She tells the ambushers, "See who I found flying in the forest." The leader looks at the three of them and comments, "Your mother must have been beautiful to produce three such pretty daughters." He tells Olimpia, "Your brothers tell me you are going to the peninsula. We can carry the bodies for you if you wish." Olimpia tells them that we would appreciate their help, and that she has a special ledge, about thirty minutes from the Cape to camp tonight. She does not want to arrive on this strip of land without first preparing some defenses. The man tells her that they will escort them to the ledge, and two will stay with them tonight, since Answald is injured, and will need help to finish this part of his journey. The remainder of the group will go to the promontory with the dead bodies and camp there until they arrive in the morning. Meanwhile, some of the men will do some hunting and gathering and enjoy our evening meal prepared for us on the ledge. Olimpia agreed and therefore, told them the ledge she wanted to camp. The men knew of this ledge, as it was popular among the hunters. We, in reality, arrived at this place within twenty minutes, as we were moving fast.

Olimpia came back to me and gave me a big kiss and powerful hug. She then tells her sisters, "Today, Yakov has grown into a man as he has saved our lives. Kaus and Answald would be dead, and I would be a slave somewhere, never to see you again." Acia and Pava tell Olimpia, "Yakov is the bravest man in the world, which is why we will always live with him." Olimpia gives each of a fast kiss and tells them she will also live with him forever. Kaus comes over to me and congratulates me on my bravery. He tells me that I, without any doubt saved his life, as the next two spears would have been in his head, leaving him no chance of surviving. Kaus then tells me he is proud to be my little brother, because today and all our remaining days I will stand ten feet tall. I did not comprehend how to respond except to thank him for all the charming words. I did not want any praise; I just wanted to keep Olimpia, Kaus, and Answald in my life. They represent the world to Acia, Pava, and me. I take my sisters now to walk beside Answald. He is sleeping, because Olimpia gave him, a root that put him to sleep faster. We can see some smoke rising in front of us. The leader tells us, "We shall soon eat some good food children." As we arrive, we find plenty of meat and fish, plus vegetable ready for us to start eating. Olimpia rushes to Answald, uncovers his wound, and begins grinding some roots and herbs together. She washes his wound and applies her potion inside his wound. One spot continues to bleed, so she asks for one of the small logs from the fire and presses the burning end again the part of the wound that is bleeding. Answald begins screaming and trying to move. Kaus and the leader hold him in place. Olimpia afterwards rubs some salve she keeps in one of her pockets inside the bag the Spiritual Mothers gave her. After this, she then pulls out some hair from another part of her bag and a tiny metal nail with a minute hole in its head. She begins to sew the wound so the no larger gash is visible. Finally, she takes some water and mixes it with the fresh roots and herbs she ground with the rocks, after that she rubs it over the outside his wound.

Olimpia asks for three sturdy wide sticks and some rope. She subsequently tied the three sticks to his leg, leaving his wound open all that she could. She wanted the sun and air to help in the healing, which was a new idea for us. Then the young man who remembered the necklace came to sit beside her. He had a small wet cloth that he began to clean her face. She did not resist, which surprised Acia and me. His name is Joggeli and they soon begin talking about so many things. We could hear her laughing, and pretending not to realize certain things. She kept complimenting him on things, as he would also compliment her. Acia told me she would now do the love test. I asked her, "What is a love test?" She told me to watch as she went over beside Olimpia and asked if she would tell her another wonderful story. Olimpia promised to do this later tonight and told her she wanted to be sure Answald was recovering first. Acia came back and told me that Olimpia liked this Joggeli. Acia recommended we play some fun games, as no one would be watching us for a while. As we began to walk out of the camp, their leader Kristoffel asks us where we are going. We tell him we are going to do some exploring. He yells back at us to say we are still prisoners, and a magistrate has not decided our punishment yet. I ask him, "We are just little people, what crime did we commit?" Kristoffel, their leader tells me he is examining that maybe I lied about my sisters flying in the forest. When little people lie about such a thing as this, then the Justice for the Pain in Children must decide. I gaze at Kaus and he asks me, "Did not I tell you this one hour earlier?" Acia, Pava, and I tell Kaus that he never told us. Kaus looks at me with a serious stare and says, "Sorry." Kristoffel looks at us and discloses, "Since your two little sisters are so beautiful, I will allow them to play with you if you stay in the open area on this ledge so Kaus, and I can see you. You need to play fast with your games, just in case this is the last time you play together. The three of us rush to the side of our small plateau to talk.

Acia begins by crying, "I do not want you to die." I think to myself and realize that they could hang me as the three bad boys were back at Petenka were for telling a lie. What was I thinking about when I told this lie? I did not want my two little sisters who are crying now to die. Nor did I want my brothers to die and

Olimpia to be a prisoner. I so much hope the Justice for the Pain in Children understands this. Yet again, what if he is an evil judge, as daddy told me once these sometimes-honest people suffer for the actions of their actions from evil judges Even so, a person is better to suffer for doing what was more right than doing what was wrong. I never thought I would die this young because I was not bad. I wonder how this evil magistrate will kill me. He will most likely stand above everyone and laugh. I so much hate to see Acia and Pava crying like this. I tell them, "You must be strong for me now as I approach my execution. Always remember that I did love you and want so much to keep you with Olimpia and me." Acia asks me if she and Pava may give me a good-bye kiss. I tell them of course, and they, each give me a slobbery kiss on my cheeks. I do not complain about the slobbers, because I appreciate they are also hurting so much inside. Suddenly, we hear Kaus calling for us. As we begin to walk back, Joggeli comes out to us and asks us if we are okay. We each wave our heads showing we are not hurt. As we approach Kaus, who is standing beside Kristoffel, who both seem somewhat pale and Olimpia, who appears, to be angry. We walk up to Kaus, as Acia and Pava are holding tight to me. Kaus tells us that Kristoffel has some news for us. As we glance at Kristoffel, Acia begins crying out, "Please, do not let them kill my favorite person in the whole world." Pava begins crying and saying, "I need him additionally." Olimpia jumps down to the ground and stretches out her arms for them to come to her. They stay put, as Acia tells her, "I am sorry, but we want to hold Yakov as much as possible until they kill him." Olimpia looks at Kristoffel and points her finger at him asking him, "Are you happy now?" Kristoffel tells us that while we were playing and having fun, the Justice for the Pain in Children visited and said that since you were a hero, he would set you free. You are a freed man and may play wherever Olimpia says you can. We ask Olimpia if we can play in the corner grass where we just came from.

She gives us her permission, and as we start to run, I can hear a loud slap, as someone's hand just belted something. We turn around and witness Olimpia is now slapping Kaus. He just stood there and did not try to defend himself. Acia tells us that they must have done

James Hendershot

a bad thing. We can see Kristoffel holding his face, yet he also is not moving. We currently hear her saying, "You never talk to my babies again, both of you." Now, this scares me, because what if he is a friend of the Justice for the Pain in Children. We rush back and I say to Olimpia, "Please do not hit him, because he may be a friend of the Justice for the Pain for Children and tell him to order me to be beaten to death and killed." Acia and Pava now begin crying aloud. Kristoffel then asks me, "Where did you get the idea the Justice for the Pain in Children would hurt you?" I told him, "In Petenka, if you lie, they can hang you." Kaus clarifies this, "No Yakov, only when you lie in a trial will cause someone else to die, and then you must die. This is for fairness to the innocent." Kristoffel tells us that the worst punishment the Justice for the Pain in Children ever gave was that he forbids a kid from playing for two days with his friends. He has never given a punishment that hurt a kid. I then asked him, "Why did Olimpia slap both of you?" Kaus answers, "We were teasing her about kissing Joggeli. I think that we really made her mad." Acia looks at Olimpia and tells her, "If you want to kiss him, you may; because Yakov let me Pava, and I kiss his cheeks." Olimpia looks at me getting ready to say something; however, I understand I must respond fast, or she might slap me, because, if her slaps can freeze Kristoffel, I am a goner. I tell her, "Olimpia, we thought I was going to die. How could I cheat them from doing a silly woman thing?" Olimpia looks at me and says, "Once again; I am so proud of my little gentlemen, for you, did the moral thing in placing the needs of your sister's hearts over your comfort and pride." Pava and Acia each grabs one of my hands and tells me that now is the time to play. As we are running, Pava falls down.

Acia and I stop and turn around to see if she is okay when we see something that shocks us so much, we freeze. Pava looks at us and then turns her head fast and says, "Oh no, we should not have told her we kissed Yakov, because that made her want likewise a kiss." Joggeli has his arms wrapped around our Olimpia, and they are kissing a lot. They keep on kissing and do not realize we are watching. Being somewhat dark now, we can only see them because they are in front of our campfire. Acia is worried that Olimpia may be in trouble. I tell her that Olimpia just belted

Kaus and Kristoffel; she could belt Joggeli if she wanted to do so. Pava confesses that she believes Olimpia does not want to. I watch Joggeli as he is beginning most of the kisses. I think that he is nuts for slobbering inside Olimpia's mouth. At least on the side of your face, you can wipe it with your hands. Acia wants us to go to the fire and see if Olimpia is okay. We walk up to the fire while they remain interlocked into another long kiss. Acia asks Olimpia, "Sister, what are you doing?" She breaks loose and turns to the three of us as her face turns red. She tells us that Joggeli was having trouble breathing, and she was trying to put some air back into his body. I ask her, "Olimpia, why is it taking such a longtime and so many tries? We have been watching you for almost one hour now." She asks us, "How do you recognize if it has taken a longtime, for this is the night currently?" Pava tells her, "You are standing by the fire. Everyone can see you. I never thought you would be one of those bad girls who let men do to you what they want." Olimpia picks up Pava and tells her, "I am not a dreadful girl, remember the times I told you some day you would meet a polite man who would be kind to you? Joggeli is that warmhearted man who is caring for me." I ask her how spitting into your mouth for such a long time can be generous. Joggeli tells me that someday I will understand. Acia asks Olimpia if she can sleep with her tonight. Olimpia tells her she is sorry; however, Joggeli and she is going to sleep beside Answald to ensure he is healing properly. I tell her that Answald will be sleeping.

He will not be worried about healing at night. She tells me the work of the healing is her job, and the defending Acia and Pava are my job. Acia looks at her and says, "You are going to be a bad girl tonight. The Spiritual Mothers told me all about when good girls fall to the temptations of strange men." Kaus joins us now and says, "Acia, do not worry. They will watch Answald from beside the fire, as we created the fire to help him heal. Kristoffel and I will be watching them. Accordingly, you take our two princesses and find a delightful place close by, in case we need your help." Kaus and Kristoffel move Answald closer to the fire and wrap him with some animal skins the hunters had with them. My sisters and I sat down in front of nearby trees where we could watch Olimpia easily.

Acia yells Goodnight to Olimpia, who yells back. She loves us. This is indeed strange, because any other time she would come to us and give each of us a kiss. They are all around the fire and leaving us in the dark to fend for us. I do not want to alarm my sisters; however, I think we may be in trouble, as they may want to be free of us. I wonder if we should carry out our break for it tonight. I am somewhat reluctant because I do not grasp where the other men who were with Kristoffel are camping. I fear that if we run into them in the woods, they may kill us, so there will be fewer witnesses to daddy. These could be dangerous times for us, especially if Olimpia decides she wants a man more than her family. I am incredibly much surprised and starting to get angry. I yell out, "When are you ever going to stop kissing and making all those strange noises?" She breaks loose from Joggeli's tight hold and begins walking to us. I get up, run to the next tree behind mine, and lay flat on the ground. Olimpia comes over and asks Acia and Pava where I was. They tell her that I am hiding because we think she is going to kill us because she no longer wants to enjoy a little brother and little sisters. Pava closes her eyes and tucks herself tight, and a small voice comes out of the ball. She is saying, "Kill me fast so I can be with the spirits who love me." Olimpia drops to the ground beside her, reaches her hand up under Pava's armpits, and begins to tickle her.

Pava starts laughing and tells Acia that being dead is so much fun. Pava's laughing overtakes her so much that she comes out of her ball, sees Olimpia, and starts to scream, "Why are you hiding your knife?" Olimpia falls down on her and having her pinned starts slobbering all over her face. Acia complains that with all the practice Olimpia had tonight, she did not learn anything. Olimpia explains that whenever the woman kisses a man too much, they forget how to kiss the correct way. She wonders if anyone would let her practice the right way again. Acia and Pava remain silent. Olimpia now rolls over releasing Pava and says in a loud voice, "I cannot believe that my little man and two princesses would think that I do not love them more than anything." I then speak out, "What about Joggeli?" Olimpia explains that this could be like a love that mommy and daddy had when mommy was still alive, yet mommy still loved all her babies. You three are my babies forever. Remember, I explained that our family would give away our daughters to the men of other families, as other families will give their daughters to us for our three remaining sons. Joggeli will not want to be a part of this family if you three do not like him. I think that he truly likes me, and that we can begin as great friends. I came walking out and asked her, "Why did not you come over to us and tuck us in tonight?" Olimpia explains that since I was such a big man now, we did not want her to slobber on us, especially with so much of Joggeli's slobbers in her mouth. Acia and Pava tell her that they think Joggeli is handsome and that if she accidentally puts some of his slobbers in their mouths when she kisses them Goodnight, which it will be okay. I, in turn, tell her that I do not want any of Joggeli's slobbers in my mouth, and that I will wait until first thing in the morning. She next asks us where we want her to sleep. Acia questions, "I thought you were going to sleep beside Answald." Olimpia explains that if we are going to accuse her of not loving us, then she will sleep here. I tell her that since she came to tell us that her love for us was still alive, we can give her leave for a few nights. Olimpia then looks sad and tells me, "You would send me back to a stranger without giving me a hug?" I run over and give my older sister and the only mother; I ever knew a giant hug.

I tell her that this is strange in that she is our only mother, and we are going to see our daddy, yet she loves another man. She tells me that she understands this is a complex situation; however, her oath to our mother outweighs any other new loves. She continues telling us that only because we are meeting daddy, and the death of Panfilo, combined with the near death of Kaus and Answald that she feels now is the time to add some more defensive power to our family. Acia asks our mother, "What if he takes you to his family like you told us the men did?" Olimpia tells us, "I already told him that if we get serious, we must always live with our family." Then I complain to her, "You said I would be the one to take care of you." She kisses me and discloses to me that I will need some help with taking care of three women, plus the one I find to love. Pava yells at her, "He is only allowed to love us." I shook my head yes, not understanding what she meant, but simply for the power in which she used in expressing this. I then agreed with Olimpia and said, "I think she is right, in that two men taking care of three women would be better than one man protecting three women." Acia looks at Olimpia and says, "Our brother is so smart, almost as wise as you." Olimpia smiles and says, "Sometimes, I think he is even smarter than I am." I disclosed to her that no one could ever be as wise as she is. Afterwards, I tell Acia and Pava time to sleep, and I tell Olimpia that we cannot get to sleep until she leaves us alone. She kisses and states, "If that is what my number-one man commands, then I shall see you three angels in the morning." She tucked us in and away she went. This time, we slept in front of my tree, as Acia and Pava jumped to my sides. Off into our dream worlds we went. I was completely exhausted today, with all the walking, though not as strenuous as our first two days, yet we walked easier and much farther. We also had many stressful events today. Within what felt as minutes, I felt something dragged me toward a tree.

I looked around and saw Kaus laying on the ground with two spears in his back, and Olimpia's head removed and laying on top of it. I continued to search for my visions, yet I could not see our new friends until I saw Kristoffel laying on the ground with a knife in his neck. Something is terribly wrong. I cannot see who is dragging me as something has put out our campfire. They continue to drag me as we pass through an opening in the trees and the lights from our moons. The thing that is pulling me is not a person; it must be some sort of large beast. It takes me to a tree and begins to tie me to it. As the beast is tying me, its face turns pale and blood shoots out of his mouth. When it falls to the ground, I can see two spears jabbed in its back. I glance around and feel my ropes losing as soon I can break free. Subsequently, two people come rushing to me, Acia and Pava. Acia wants me that we must hurry and escape. As we are fighting through the forest, I can hear much noise around us. Something surrounded us. It is simply a matter of time before they capture us. Acia points up; therefore, we spring up into three trees. As we are going up, Pava slips on one of the branches and begins to fall from twenty feet. When going down to meet her unwelcome landing, she is screaming for help. As her body hits the ground, we hear the thump and stare down to see her not moving. I motion for Acia to stay in place and then to continue up. Pava is gone, as with

Panfilo, they will move no more. If she were to create one noise or movement, I would chance a rescue. There are now drums beating in our background. We hear the thumping on the ground, as if an Army was marching toward us. The noises they created by breaking the brush was crispy and cut through the night air as if they were the glass. Usually we can hear small animals jumping around in the trees, yet tonight they are silent. Even the air is feeling chilled. Soon the invisible enemy is visible below us. We climbed exceptionally carefully, and made no noise, except for Pava's fall to her death. I suppose that is what has drawn them to our position. We remain as quiet as possible. They soon begin chopping at Acia's tree. I motion for her to climb out the sturdy branch, which hides her. We have her scoot one move each slash of the ax. This way, they will not hear the noise or notice the movement, as the ax shakes the tree. She is now as far out as she can get. I possess no rope or way to pull her to me. We will need to wait until her tree begins to fall and have her jump over to my tree.

This will be dangerous; however, she is enormously skilled in the trees as we play with them extremely often. We wait patiently, as I slow move down a few branches, so I can retain more time to catch her when she jumps to our tree. This branch is special in that it lets me move farther out from its trunk. This will be tricky for me, in that when she jumps, I must guess where she will come through, and sit down, bracing myself on this branch, so when I catch her, we will obtain support and yield less noise. The tree begins to fall to our right. Acia jumps perfectly at a sturdy branch that she is gripping with both hands. The branch is three rows above me. Nevertheless, I slowly move back to the trunk staying in a position with her. I must stay prepared to catch her. Ordinarily, I would not worry; however, today I understand that stress could be dulling her senses and reactions. The loss of Pava must be weighing on her mind. She makes it to the trunk, and we both position ourselves for a rest. We watch the beasts as they inspect Acia's tree. They are bringing wild wolves to the tree. I never witnessed wolves being tied to a string and obeying a master. This could present danger. The wolves rush to the part of the tree that Acia was hiding. They begin to howl as the beasts run to this area. They take the wolves out in the opening the leads to the back forest. I think that they are trying to determine if she landed in the tree and ran into the forest. We must be too far for them to smell. Therefore, I motion for Acia that we must begin climbing higher, but must not form one noise or the wolves will hear us. We are lucky in that the next tree is much larger and has branches that overlap our tree. The beasts are now assembling beside my tree. I hear them beginning to chop with their giant axes. Our tree is beginning to waive and release a crackling sound. We both jump for our next haven. Acia lands faultlessly, without making a noise. I jump and grab my branch perfectly. To my surprise and disappointment, my branch snaps. I guess a bird or insects whittled away at it. I am now dropping fast. My leg hits another branch, as both the branch and my leg crack. My luck is changing temporarily, as I can grab a branch.

I am still over ten rows high, so the issue now is the noise. I hear no noise below me, and can only hope that these hunters are concentrating on my former tree as it goes crashing down. The noise did disguise my disaster. Only if I could climb back up to where I was, and could I have a feeling of security once more. My leg is shooting pain throughout my entire body. Any movement hurts too much; therefore, I possess no choice but to hope for the best where I am hanging. My self absorption in my pain ends when I hear the wolves below me howling. Then arrows begin flying past me. Fortunately, Acia is high enough to evade the arrows, as most cannot reach her because of the fifteen extra rows between us. She must stay close to the trunk with its decreasing circumference, so the arrows that succeed pass by her. The arrow hits my broken leg. I do not even flinch. So many arrows are going up at me. Soon the arrows stop. A few minutes later, they begin again, now coming in toward me from my front. I wish that I could swing around to the other side of my trunk. Within seconds, three hits me, one in each arm and the other in my right leg. No moving around this tree for me, as I do not even comprehend if I ever touch the ground once more. It was impossible to maintain my balance. Now I am going down fast, as I have no way to maneuver I take a few more hits to the head and roll in a tumbling fashion down through the branches. I crash onto the land, yet surprisingly land on some brush that is now here. I still take a good thump, and looking around only to see wolves staring at me. They must be waiting until I die before they rip me apart. Each second I am fighting so hard to stay awake. To my astonishment, I hear intense growling as I experience the jaws latching into my shirt and pants, and my body begins to move amazingly fast. I soon find myself under another brushy bush. The wolves retreat quickly to the tree and mosey around as if bored. The beasts come to them and found most sleeping as if they were babies. They return and restart our campfire and begin eating their fresh kills. I can see this as the wolves drug me to a higher elevation on our moderately sized ledge.

The wolves wanted me up higher so the beasts would not smell me in any crosswinds. They now stroll over to the beasts for their share of the bounty. I find myself slowly falling into a deep sleep. This sleep will get me away from all this pain for a while. Unexpectedly, I sense someone shaking me. I wake up and see Pava staring at me. The first thing that I can think is that we are in the land of the light, as I see light covering all the surrounding land. Next, Acia hits me and tells me to get up. How did Acia get to here before me? I peek over and see Olimpia and Kaus playing with Joggeli. I in no way want to tell them how I watched their bodies eaten. Acia asks me why I kept kicking them last night. I asked them how I could have kicked them as we were in different trees. Acia calls for Olimpia, who rushes over. I gaze at Olimpia and say, "Someone did a good job of putting your head back on you." She looks at me strange and reaches her hand out to pull me up to her. My legs appear scratched, and she asks me what happened to them. I tell her I got these scratches jumping from that tree to that one. I then notice they are standing up now. I guess the land of the light gave them back to us. Acia tells her that I hit them in the middle of the night and ran to that bush on the hill over there. I tell her the wolves drag me to that bush. Olimpia breaks the news to me now that I was only dreaming. I ask her how she knows, for I saw the hairy beasts stab Kaus, Joggeli and cut off her head. I also saw Pava fall from a tree, and the beasts take her lifeless body to their campfire. Olimpia tells me I had a bad dream about all the things that happened to us yesterday. I tell her that I just cannot believe it was a dream. She tells me wolves do not drag people to bushes and that she has never seen beasts with long hair create campfires. Kristoffel, that is with us now reveals the beasts who live in the wildernesses are afraid of fires. He asks me to tell him some more things that they did. I told him that they chopped down the tree that Acia was in, and then chopped down the tree that she and I were hiding. Kristoffel asks me how they were chopping the tree, and if it were from their teeth.

I told him they were using large axes and swinging hard at the trees. He tells me, "Yakov, I have never seen a beast in all my travels that could even carry an ax, must less swing one. I think you had a rough day yesterday and experienced some dangerous dreams last night." Acia and Pava told him that I had kicked them, although not hard, and took off into the woods last night. With this, Olimpia told us that if I ever go into the woods at night to come to get her fast. She looks at me and reiterates, "We are on a ledge, if you took a wrong turn, and you would be in the land of the lights, now as we speak." She afterwards tells Acia and Pava that at night, they need to care for me, as I care for them during the day. She hands us a rag and points to a small spring pouring out of the rocks on the cliffs behind us and tells me that since I was hiding in bushes and dragged by wolves that I must clean extra. I complain to her that she told me it was only a dream. Olimpia tells me that until I inform her that, I will clean extra hard. My mind questions how cruel this woman has become since she stays up all-night kissing on Joggeli. For now, I hold my peace until daddy arrives. I wonder what he will say to the way Olimpia and Joggeli are acting so strange. Acia and Pava come with me and volunteer to help me. I let them, because when Olimpia discovers they helped me, she always approves the cleaning. I believe this is a loyalty thing among girls. We reemerge after my morning baptism and sit down in the opening of our family circle around this campfire. With Pava sitting on one side of Acia and me on the other, Olimpia does not inspect me. This must be an honor thing between them. I often wonder how they share these great secrets of established behaviors. I would ask them; however, I believe some things men should not know, or are not worth the vast effort in trying to rationalize. Olimpia gives each of us a kiss.

As she kisses me, I can hear her sniffing. I gaze at her as if she was strange, and she tells me, "I just love the way my big man smells." She expects me to smile; therefore, I do. Any fool would realize who her big man truly is. He is working his way inside her on all these little rituals.

She does appear happy because he is beside her, so I pretend also to be pleased. Olimpia deserves to enjoy the things the other growing women have. I remember seeing many girls her age kissing on boys behind trees and other hidden places where adults cannot go. Acia showed me all these secret viewing spots, which totally bored me; nonetheless, peculiarly excited her. Joggeli oddly shakes my hand as Kaus likes to do. I do not recognize if he is babying me or respecting me. This is a question for Kaus. I glare around and cannot see where Kaus is; as a result, I ask Olimpia where he is. She tells us that he is standing on the hill above us looking at the lake. Acia immediately asks, "Can we go also?" Olimpia tells us that she has some work to do cleaning our camp and packing our things. Kristoffel discloses to her, "Olimpia; I would be proud to take them to see Kaus." For some unknown reason, I am uneasy about him. Nonetheless, I really do want to see this famous lake, thus suppressing my fears at this time. We quickly finish and follow Kristoffel up to the top of this small hill. We go up from one of its sides, as the cliff between us and the top is not that stable to climb, and the risk is not worth it, since it merely saves a tiny quantity of time. Kristoffel walks strong going up the hill. Acia yells at him, "Hey bad man. You are supposed to be guarding us." He apologizes and sits down to wait for us. I marvel that a girl of any size can yell at the men, and they surrender. If I yelled at him, my teeth would be flying in the air. The astonishment of this does not end with the apology. As we walk pass him, he asks for his forgiveness. She informs him that she will think about it. He thanks her and then gives me a dirty look. Pava is behind me, so I tell him to stop looking at me that way. Kristoffel quickly denies looking strangely at me, as Acia is turning around to see what is happening. Pava tells Acia, "He was looking mean at Yakov." Acia plants her feet and yells for Olimpia. Kristoffel quickly puts his hands over her mouth and warns us that he will not take us to see the giant beautiful lake, unless we are good. I shake my head yes to Acia, who, in turn, shakes her head yes to Kristoffel. He turns his face from me and does not observe me for the rest of our short trip. I hold the winning stone in my pocket, as I will tell daddy when we meet.

We arrive at the top of our hill, and I glance over and see Kaus, lying on the ground sleeping. He is up here hiding from Olimpia. I run over to him and accuse him of hiding from Olimpia. Kaus denies this by reminding me that she now has Joggeli and does not need him anymore. I sit beside him and ask, "What are we going to do about him coming into our family and stealing her?" Kaus tells me there is nothing we can do, as everyone calls this love. If she wants to be with him, and he wants her, we must let her go. Kaus reminds me that mommy's family let her go so she could be with daddy. I tell Kaus that she made Joggeli promise to stay with our family, so she could finish raising her babies. Kaus asks me how we talked her into this. Acia tells him that it was simple; we just told her we wanted to be someone else's babies. Kaus looks at us and says, "A threat like that would scare anyone." He opens his arms as all three of us jump into them. I can experience his loneliness now that Olimpia is ignoring him, and Answald is injured. I ask him what this wonderful smell is, thus he reveals to us the fresh air from the giant lake in front of us. Turning around, I expect not to see much; however, to my shock, I see the grandest thing that I ever yet beheld. Before me are two long walls of rocks sloping to the clouds. Small patches of grasslands spot the sides. Deep in front of us, these stony mountains form their circle. Behind them are giant white colored mountains that spire far into the clouds. Before me, I see a valley filled completely with water. The water is as beautiful as daddy said it was. It truly is jutting out into the famous peninsula with its yellowish-green grass and cluster of tall pines toward its end. We see two men standing in the open. Kristoffel waves a white cloth that he tied to the end of a stick for them to see. The men below us do the same thing. Kristoffel tells us that our daddy has yet to arrive. Kaus tells him that our daddy always stops here in remembrance of our mother, as they used to camp nearby often. Kristoffel agrees that he will soon be here. He tells me that we are safe to go to this cherish land, so we should head back and get the lovers. I ask Kaus if they are lovers already.

He tells me that love is strange in how it hits people. To think she would love the man who shot Answald in the leg is weird, yet not a problem. I ask him why this is not a problem. He tells me because Joggeli was doing what he thought was right to save his people. We would also do the same thing if we thought people were trying to bring the plague to our families. I looked at him and realized he was right, so I shook my head. Kaus further tells me that I will need some help to defend this family. I ask him if he is going somewhere. He tells me that Kristoffel tells him that his village has many fine beautiful young women. Acia asks him, "What about Pava, and me?" Kaus confessed that these women were not that beautiful; however, his sisters do not let him kiss them all-day and night. Acia and Pava glare at Kristoffel who instantly agrees the village women are not as pretty as they are, and that he thinks our dad would get angry if Kaus lie around kissing his sisters all-day. Acia asks him that if she tells Olimpia to lie around and kiss his all-day and night would he stay. Kaus reveals to us that if he did such a thing with Olimpia that Joggeli would try to kill him. Acia answers Kaus that she does not understand about these things and will ask Olimpia and Joggeli. Kristoffel starts to laugh and spouts out, "I want to see that." Acia decides not to ask Olimpia because Kristoffel wants to see it, so it could mean more trouble for us. I ask Kristoffel if that lake in front of us has many fish. He tells me that one could fish for a large family in this lake and eat for the rest of their lives. Looking at this giant lake, I tell them that it must contain all the water in our world in it. Kristoffel tells me that once he saw a huge sea in which he could not see the other side. He walked for three Cegi Moons, and the sea was still beside him. While hiking, he ran into an old magic man who told him that he could walk half his lifetime until coming back the where he was and that the sea completely surrounded our land. I asked him what a Cegi Moon was.

He told me that was what the magic man called the first moon, which appears at night. Kristoffel then shares with us that this is the largest lake that he has ever seen; although another one, not as large, rests at the bottoms of these mountains at the other end of the river that flows from the east end. We go back to collect our group and head for the lake. I cannot wait until I jump in it. This will be so much more enjoyable than swimming in streams. As we enter the camp, we notice our fire is burning high now. Olimpia is on the ground next to Answald crying. Joggeli is packing our things. We run over to Olimpia and ask her why she is crying. She tells us that Answald's leg is badly infected. Olimpia cut his wounded area again and placed strange leaves on it. Olimpia now asks us to step back and give her one of the burning sticks when she asks. She has some water boiling in one of our vases and asks Kaus to bring this to her. Our medicine woman pulls off the leaves and presses on his wound forcing some ugly junk up out of it. She then pours the boiling water on it. Answald begins to scream as Kristoffel holds him fast in place. After this, she sprinkles some added herbs and crushed roots covering his reopened wound. Olimpia sprinkles her leaves in the wounds and begins to sew him up once more. She takes the special tool that she has to stitch with, and sticks in into her burning log beside her. She hems his wound tight again. This time, she wraps the wound with some of our extra clothes we carry with us. My oldest sister looks at Kaus and Kristoffel and tells them that he cannot walk on this leg until she can get the infection out of him. Olimpia now opens his mouth and fills it with selected herbs and root chunks. Kaus gives him some water to wash it down his throat. Answald does not appear well, as his leg has a red rash covering it with some spots that is a darker black. These dark areas, Olimpia made a new cut through them, just deep enough to get some blood seeping through the tissue. Kristoffel calls for the remaining two of his group to be flesh carriers. They use these when killing a large beast. I watch as the cut two thick branches and begin zigzagging rope between them, keeping the logs about three feet wide. Afterwards, they place Answald on the ropes, while he is lying, lift him up. Joggeli brings our other equipment to our campfire. Olimpia and Kaus are putting out the fire.

Joggeli asks Olimpia if she needs some help. She turns to him with an angry glare and screams, "No. I must care to my brother now." I am stunned at what just happened. Acia tells me they are having a lovers quarrel. Thereafter, I walk over to Kaus and ask him to explain why Olimpia is yelling at Joggeli. He tells me that sometimes when the woman loves you, she will change and hate you for a little while. In those situations, you must be calm. Joggeli joins us now and confesses to me that if a man truly loves a woman, he will be patient during these times when a woman is crazy and wants to fight. I reach up to hold his hand and ask, "Are you being patient with my sister currently?" Joggeli tells me that he is trying extremely hard, and wishes he could now go somewhere and cry. Kaus tells him not to worry that he can walk with us. I tell them both I do not grasp if I could handle love if that is what love is. Joggeli and Kaus tell me that someday I will search long and hard for it. I gawk at them and say, "Yucky." Looking around, I see Olimpia talking with Acia and Pava. Our segregated trip to the lake has boys in one group, girls in the other, while Kristoffel leads the way, and the remaining raiders carry Answald. All this is because my sister has to be crazy. I wonder if Acia and Pava plan to give me headaches such as this when I am taking care of them. If they are, they need to start looking for other men to share their craziness. Olimpia looks back at me, and I turn my head to Kaus. She yells for me to come to her now. I tell Joggeli, "She is going to beat me for standing beside you." Kaus tells me to stay close to him as we both walk to her. Kaus tells her, "I do not understand what your problem is; however, you cannot take it out on the boy who saved our lives yesterday." She tells Kaus to shut up and go back to his friend. Kaus tells her that he is her friend, and if she does not like him, he will tell him to leave. Olimpia tells me to hold off on this, and that she is not mad at her little man. I looked at her and told her I was not a little man anymore. She smiles and agrees, telling me that I am still her protector. Acia comes to us and confesses that she is the one who wants me to join them because she missed me so much and did not deem herself safe. Kaus then smiles and says, "Anything for my princess."

He now complains that he only has Joggeli to protect him, and that he is in danger. Acia tells him not to worry because Yakov can run fast to run to and correspondingly save him. Kaus hits his head and exclaims, "How could I have forgotten that?" Pava tells him this is okay, because even she forgets things sometimes. Kaus looks at Olimpia and asks her, "How could be ever lived without our three bundles of love?" Olimpia tells us we need to catch back up with Answald. Kaus runs to the rear to Joggeli and tells him the news. I am the only one looking back out of curiosity. I see Joggeli hugging Kaus; therefore, I can see that Joggeli has new hope in his relationship with Olimpia. I ask Olimpia, "My mother; you confuse me so much, in that yesterday I hated Joggeli, and now I like him and you hate him." Olimpia tells me, "I do not hate Joggeli. I am only making him work harder for my love before daddy gets here. I need him to be strong and beg daddy relentless, because daddy is a tough one to fool. Therefore, I want you still to love him. Any ways, why do you love him so much suddenly?" I told her this was because I appreciate he honestly loves her so much. Olimpia bows down and kisses me on my head saying, "Where would I be without my big man telling me all these secrets?" I told her I hated keeping secrets when it makes people sad to do so. Acia then looks at Olimpia and asks if that means the girls win. Olimpia tells her that no one wins in love fights. This was a fight to help her keep his love, so if she can keep his love, then we win. I examine Acia and ask her if she understands this. She shakes her head no, and we laugh with Olimpia. Olimpia pleads with me to do her a favor and tell Joggeli that she hurt her foot and needs carried for a while. I tell her that Kaus, and I can carry her. Acia yells at me to do what our mommy said to do. I notice that Olimpia is limping some now. This makes me feel awful that her injury occurred while I was supposed to be protecting her. My heart now feels bad that I could not protect her. She probes me wanting to see if a can keep a secret. I tell her for my mommy, I will.

Olimpia tells me she is playing a game to help her and Joggeli to reunite and that her leg is okay. I am much better now, so I run back to Joggeli and tell him that our Olimpia hurt her leg, and that she is too big for me to carry. He volunteers to carry her. Looking at him, I tell him he had better hurry fast. Joggeli thanks me and shoots toward Olimpia. Kaus also thanks me and says, "I should have known that you can do miracles." I told him it was a simple process of making women do what you want them to do. Kaus requests that

I teach him that art someday. Subsequently, I tell him that I will think about it. We glance and see Joggeli examining Olimpia's foot, and then she gets on his back and holds on as our crazy bin begins to march again. I wonder which one is smiling the greatest, Olimpia or Joggeli. I tell Kaus that I surely hope daddy lets them stay together. Kaus reveals to me that this is an area that he is an expert. He will be working hard on daddy to approve this new relationship, especially since Olimpia will still be living with us. We walk a few minutes more and soon are standing on the peninsula that I heard so many things concerning. I run over to touch the water. Kristoffel tells me to be careful because there are many dangerous things that live in the lake. Olimpia looks at him and yells, "You are going to cause him to suffer from bad dreams tonight." Joggeli tells her there really are dangerous things live in the lake, and that they never go that close to it, without first tossing in some rocks to scare these things. I jump back as the two raiders that came here last night rush over to me and toss in a few rocks. They explore around and go to the water, splash their hands in it a few times and then tell me we are okay. Olimpia expresses joy that Joggeli was telling the truth and to Kristoffel, she is sorry. Olimpia questions Kristoffel if there are any other dangers in this narrow place. He tells her, that while they stay on the yellowish grass, they will be safe. Kristoffel additionally adds that if anyone wants to walk on the small dirt beaches, one of his men will be glad to escort them for safety reasons. My face is now frowning as Kristoffel is giving the rules.

He looks at me and says, "These are the rules that your daddy gave us, use the buddy system when playing on the shore anywhere on this lake." I examined him by questioning what the buddy system was. Besides, since I do not possess a partner, what would I do? He laughs and then reveals to me that we are all friends here. Kristoffel volunteers to be my pal and escort me around our little private sanctuary. I scan our group and notice two of his men are missing. Consequently, I ask him where these two men are. He points to two spots on the surrounding mountain ridges and tells me they are up there guarding us. The mountains trapped us on this Cape, and we need to recognize if anyone is approaching, so we can find secure positions. I confess to Kristoffel that he appears to be extremely wise in the wilderness. He tells me those who are not clever, die early. This land injection into the lake looked so large from the hill. Nevertheless, now that I am on it, it looks small. The water is so near, although the evergreens are tall and spread out enough that we can lay on the ground below them protected from the Suns and still sense a cool lake breeze. Kristoffel and two of his men hold a rope with a rabbit on its end that they now cut his neck and throw him out into the lake. He tells me to watch and see something new. They hold the rope in their hands as they rock it slightly. After about one hour, when I am laying under our evergreens, I hear the man yelling for help. Two of his friends rush over to him and all three pulls on the rope. I run out to see what they are doing. Kaus joins me as the men fight hard on the rope. They pull back, and then walk around the first pine tree to loop the surrounding rope. Next, they tie two knots to secure the rope. I can see as the tightrope yanks, the tree shakes. They next pull on the rope more while walking along the trees. Soon, to our surprise, a giant fish begins to emerge on the shore. Kristoffel takes his spear and begins stabbing it. The men continue to pull it onshore. Kristoffel then grabs his ax and chops off its head. He rushes over and drives his spear all the way inside the fish, thereby preventing its headless body from bouncing back into the lake. Afterwards, he picks his ax back up and chops of the fish's large back fin.

The other men come forward, remove the rabbit from the fish's jaws, and fling its head into the water. They cut off the rabbit's head, give it to Olimpia, and begin to clean it. Kaus and I rush over to the large headless fish as I ask Kristoffel, what this is. He tells me this fish is a lake carp. They can get to be ten feet long in this lake. Kaus and Kristoffel begin to clean it. They are pulling out tremendously large chunks of fish meat. He cuts most of its skin off and cuts it into two pieces. One he lies beside him where he puts all the extra parts of the fish that we will not be eating. He places all the large pieces we will be eating on the other coat. They finish fast as the slices are so big. Kristoffel and Kaus carry the meat we will eat under the pines beside Olimpia, as the raiders already started a big fire burning. These two men then carry the parts of the fish that we will not be eating away, going down the shoreline. I ask Kristoffel why they are taking that part off when we could simply throw it in here. Kristoffel tells me this is not wise, for there are many large predators in the wild and under the sea. We do not want to invite them for dinner. He takes his ax and chops at the ground that has some fish blood on it, working it into the soil. Next, he collects some long branches with fork like endings. I follow him, while we give everyone a branch. He tells us to sit around the fire. He pokes his branch into a large piece of fish and lowers the fish over the fire. Afterwards, he invites all of us to do the same, and then tells us, "This is how we cook lake fish." Olimpia forks a big piece and cooks it for her, Acia, and Pava. Kristoffel explains that if anyone gets hungry, just come over, and he or she may prepare a piece of the fish. If you do not finish it, put it on the fish hide and someone else will eat it. Burry any bones or parts you burned. I sat here contented that one mission in my life was complete, for I now see the Lake on top of the world. This will help keep the pests away from us. I began to wonder, what did he mean by pests?

CHAPTER 03

Journey to the other side

The word pest continues to ring through my mind. I can barely move from all the fish I eat. The faces of the other members of our family show the same distress, except for Answald. We gave him pieces from our servings, as he ate what he could. He is not looking well at all. Olimpia cleaned his wound again today; nonetheless, she tells us his infection is growing. Kaus asks Joggeli if he had anything at the end of his spear. He swears his spearhead was clean, yet when he took it out of Answald's leg; insects from the tree covered it. They would push the spear forward and try to wipe it; nevertheless, the spearhead would fill up at once, as they also were invading his wound. Joggeli said they had no choice but to yank the spearhead through the wound expeditiously. The wound has been swollen to the point that they could not see how to pull it back the same way that it inserted itself. They pulled it backward through, and immediately took him to the fireplace where Olimpia met them. I asked them why they did not break the spear in half and pull it out on each side. Kristoffel explains that their law of the wilderness is never to damage your sword, as this is the same as entering the land of the dead. They spend years working on their spears, as one spear usually lasts them for a lifetime. Kaus tells me the same is true for our daddy, as he never hunts with a different spear. We are fortunate that our father relies on the bow with his arrows. He only uses his spear when killing a beast who is near him. If it gets too close, he used his long knife. Answald's leg is turning black under his wound. Olimpia has tried placing slashes in them. Nevertheless, now the dark places are too many. Olimpia knows what they must do. She hopes that our pa will arrive here in time to do this. She refuses to tell me. Suddenly, Olimpia jumps up and asks, "Where are Panfilo and his murderer?"

Kristoffel takes her where they have covered them with dirt. He tells Olimpia that if they leave them in the open, predators will come after them and us in the process. Kristoffel also reminds her of the smell. They will place the bodies in water for a few hours before taking them to their burial site, which must be close. The Suns are now peaking over our horizons and shooting their last light of the day. The rays are arriving sideways as we can see more in our forests. We glance around our horizon as the birds are settling into their trees for the night. I see an occasional fish jump out of the water and dive back into their world. There is now much green colored water as it steals the light reflecting from the trees. This creates a picturesque dynamic view. I wonder why people do not build homes around this lake. Subsequently, I ask Kristoffel if he knows the reasons that no one builds homes around the lake. He explains the wildlife uses this lake for their drinking water. Many that come to the lake are both thirsty and hungry. These large animals would feed on those who would live around this lake. I ask him if we will be safe tonight. He tells me that all his raiders are with him now, and tonight they will concentrate on guarding the neck of our peninsula. Early in the morning, two will return to their lookout locations. We will sleep under these evergreens tonight and have two large fires burning all-night. I asked him why we needed two fires. He explains that this will cause it to appear that we have a large group and possibly ward off the invaders. Most invaders do not come near this place anyway. I ask him why, as he looks around for Olimpia, who is kissing with Joggeli. Joggeli was extra friendly to me today for helping get them back together. To me, I just seemed so foolish of the way they were acting. That weird thing called, love is rearranging their minds. Kristoffel tells me that I must promise never to do anything that would allow Olimpia from finding out he told me this great secret. I ask him why he is worried about Olimpia. He reveals to me that she is so pretty, and he does not want her to get scared.

Since I am such a strong fighter, he knows I will not be afraid. I think about this for a minute, and then I promise to keep it a secret. He begins by telling me that once many years earlier, he and my father were hunting and planning to camp out on the patch of trees on the mountainside to our right. They originally planned to camp on the peninsula; however, their only beast was behaving erratic. Therefore, they decided to camp by the small cave on that ledge. Because they had just one beast, they tied him to the mouth of the cave, so they could sleep in the cave. They knew that any intruders would alert the beast and thus alert them. They cut selected high grass and sprinkled it on the ground in front of the cave. My father did not want a fire in the cave because the smoke going out could scare his beast. He merely remained on the hunting trip to help Kristoffel find a beast. Pawka believed the thick low trees in this area could help them capture Kristoffel's beast. As they still had a little dried meat to eat, they decided to finish that off first and on the next, day did the fishing. While resting on the neck of the cave that night, snakes began appearing from the sky. At first, it was simply a few. One landed on the back of Pawka's beast, took a large chuck of flesh in its mouth, and flew away. The beast began to ask crazy and making loud stressful noises. Snakes soon covered this animal as they began to eat him alive. Kristoffel and my father hid inside the cave just slightly back, to where they remained in the dark. Pawka wanted to go forward and free his beast; however, there were too many snakes. He thus stood up in the dark, put an arrow in his bow, and hit his beast on its head, forcing it to fall and smash those greedy snakes who were on the wrong side. Shortly thereafter, so many snakes appeared in front of their entrance that no sunlight came into their cave. The snakes made such a loud hissing sound that at times Kristoffel and Pawka had to put their hands over their ears. They had long jaws with sharp teeth on the upper and lower maxillae. Their teeth were long and cut like razors.

They would swoop down, bite off a chunk of the presently dead beast, and lash back into the sky. My father was impressed with how they could maneuver to pass one another with speed and ease. They are all the same lengths, which was extremely long. Kristoffel adds one thing that caught him off guard were they had no wings yet could travel the sky as if they were moving across the land. The snakes revolved around the lake, as they could see that they dive straight into the water and fly back out of the water with a fish in their mouth. They would eat these fish in midair, for when they clamped into the fish, the unsecured parts that broke free of its jaw would float in the air. Another snake would flash by, and eat that loose piece of fish flesh floating in the sky. Pawka's beast completely disappeared. The snake devoured every part of it to include its hide and skeleton. Nothing remained except a small hole in the ground underneath it where the snakes had also clamped down on the dirt. While the snakes were concentrating on small game and fish, Pawka and Kristoffel departed their cave to see what was happening. Pawka looked over to his left a saw dark black clouds appearing as soon as possible. He alerted Kristoffel as they ran back into their cave. This was a flash summer storm. This area is bad for that because of all the water. The sudden cool air appeared to be fighting with the hot dry summer air. As with so many of these flash summer storms, they released much thunder and lightning. The lightning from this storm was more intense than the average storms. The winds funneled into this mountain valley, and this time felt as if it were pushing toward the ground. About one-half an hour later, the storm disappeared and what they saw next shocked them. These blue snakes completely covered the lake. Kristoffel tells me that they waited a few minutes to see if they would get up and fly away. They could see a small group of them flying over the next mountain most likely returning to where they lived. Kristoffel and Pawka went back into the cave to sleep. In the morning, they discussed what had happened and dismissed it as an illusion from a wizard. After that, they walked down to the lake to fill their water bags and clean themselves.

To their crowning shock, these dead sapphire fish covered the shores. Kristoffel tells me that ever since that day, the lake is always as bright ultramarine, unless it grows tired at night and allows selected parts to be green. I asked him what color the lake was before, and he tells me that it was green as the other lake in the valley below us. Pawka told him many times the reason he always spends a bit of time on this peninsula. He feels this lake protect all who are kind to it. I told him it did not help Answald. Kristoffel tells me that Answald was not at the lake when he was then hurt. He also reminds me something saved Kaus and Olimpia from the doors to the land of the dead. Kristoffel tells me that if one were to dig a few feet out from the shoreline, they could find skeletons of these snakes. Meanwhile, he decides to go to check Answald. On seeing Answald, he yells for Kaus and Olimpia. They form a private huddle and argue extensively. Finally, Kristoffel leaves the huddle angry and goes to the mouth of our peninsula. A go to see what is in error with Kristoffel, he asks me to give him a little time, and he will take me on a hike. Sensing that something is in error, I go over to Kaus and Olimpia and see that Olimpia is crying as Joggeli is holding her. I question Kaus, "What is wrong?" He asks me to take a walk with him. Acia and Pava appeal also to join us. Kristoffel tells them it possibly could be dangerous and that until we are sure that this is safe, they should stay in the camp. He calls for a couple of his men to join them and play with Acia and Pava. They pretend to be large beasts and growl at these little girls who at once attack them. I growl at them for not doing what I said to do and that is when in danger hide. They tell me these men are familiar and trying to trick them. The men laugh and pick them up and talk to one another about the little girl toe soup for lunch. Acia and Pava begin gently attempting to break free from them. Nevertheless, as that does not produce the results, they want, they begin kicking and biting. The men currently hold them out in the open so their legs kick in the air, as their mouths are not close to anything to bite. Acai and Pava resort to plan B.

This is when they become limber and laugh, saying how fun, this is. The men reveal that they also have youngsters in their village and are aware of all the tricks. I realize that they are good men who live around families, so I begin walking toward Kristoffel who is waiting at me at the mouth of our peninsula. He tells me of a special place where my parents would always spend a few weeks when they were camping in the area. We traveled alongside the lake to where it became narrow. Kristoffel explains to me that this is where the lake form into a long winding river, which flows into another large loch in the forest lands below. They both, high and low, branch off into two rivers. This makes it possible for a person to cover large distances by traveling these watercourses. Kristoffel tells me that he has traveled alongside these waterways for months at a time. One time, he traveled five Cegi Moons on the river that flows north from the lower lake. The trees had so many color leaves. He was lucky to find a small tribe to stay with during the dark days. Kristoffel noted that the stars and moons did not appear as bright in the lowlands at night as they do up here in the mountains. That spooked him some. On his return trip, one of his guides revealed to him a shortcut from the river; he was one a river east of him, which led back into the mountains. Kristoffel told me not to worry, because my father had furthermore traveled these paths, and promised someday to show his sons. We passed back into the high hills around us and followed a crispy small stream that had little fish and toads jumping around in its waters. Next, we arrived at an unusual flat grassy area with one tree in its middle. This place surprised me by seeing such a large area that was level. The low cut grass was somewhat smooth. I asked Kristoffel what this place was. He told me the only thing that he knew was what a few of the older villagers in this area told him. I looked at him and smiled, as if to question that he cut the drama and answer my question. They finally get the hint and continue telling me how the villagers claim in the days long ago that the lights would drop from the sky here, and gods with their goddesses would play here. I asked him if anyone had seen them recently.

He informs me that there have been no visits in his lifetime. Afterwards, I ask him how the grass stays so perfect. In response, Kristoffel shares with me that the legends claim that these gods planted a special grass here that is nowhere else. It stays low enough as not to attract grazers and high enough to present a scenic landscape. Kristoffel tells me that sometimes in life we must accept what our eyes are telling us. The grass here stays green, even during the dark days. Extremely few people are aware of this place, as many get lost attempting to find it. I glance around and ask him if he knows any games, we can play on this ledge with one tree. Curiosity starts to take control of me as I head for the one tree. Kristoffel tells me not to touch the tree, as the legend is that anyone who touches the tree will die. I notice that never before had I seen a tree such as this. Nevertheless, I find this so strange indeed. It probably would be best not to touch it, so after examining it from a safe distance to turn toward Kristoffel. All the dead birds under it take away any special meaning for this tree, except for death. I asked him why they would put such a deadly thing in a wonderful place. Kristoffel tells me that he believes someone else put the deadly tree here, and he does not understand why. He is glad they have not planted any elsewhere that he is aware. We walk next to the side of the cliff that dash down its front toward the remaining mountains. Kristoffel shows me a small path that cuts into the cliff and tells me he will walk down first carrying a rope that once he gets down I am to tie around my waist before I start down. This cliff has selected small trees growing out of its sides, so he, therefore, tied his rope around that tree. Once he is in the cave's opening, he immediately unties himself to give me a little slack in the rope. I scoot down the path to the tree as he told me not to stand until I have my smaller string secured around my waist and then about his knotted rope. I cannot loosen his tight knot, thus he allows me to attach my rope connecting his line and me. Down I go, a little faster than he wants me to. Therefore, he yells for me to go slower and be careful. He does not realize that by me being smaller, this path is larger and easier for me to navigate. Once I arrive at the entrance, I hesitate in disbelief. I see before me a window into another world.

My eyes behold beautiful small green trees growing from green stones. The lights from our Suns sweep in with a vision of warmth, chasing most of the dark from it. A small stream flows both ways over three walkways that connect each side. I ask Kristoffel how water can flow both up and down. He explains that not only does this water flow both directions; when it reaches the small pond at the bottom, it returns to its mouth and flows once more. Before

I can ask him how he knows, he tells me one time he threw a small cloth into the stream, carried it to the pond, and the next morning, the cloth was laying on the ground beside the top mouth of this stream. He adds that one time he and my father were in here when it began to rain, and the rain did not enter. They stood at the entrance and watched the downpour stop just before touching them. They also marvel at how the water is so white in the streams, as if it were carrying the bubbles to the pond. I could see deep into the crystal blue pond from where I was standing. There were so many strange creatures swimming in this liquid. I saw a fish that not only had a long, thin fin flowing from his lower back. He also had a large fin, twice as wide as his body that smoothly flowed from his lower torso. I also witnessed many colors covering his body. I had difficulty identifying any other life in this pond, as all I could work out resembled stones. Nevertheless, occasionally one of the stones would move and give a bolt to my heart. I can see a deep hole directly in front of us. Kristoffel tells me that if I sit here for a while, I will see many types of sea life come forward. My magical fish escapes through the deep dark hole. I now wait to see what else comes forward. Kristoffel asks me to sit beside him as he now wishes to talk to me about something important. He wants to explain why he was arguing with Olimpia. Answald's leg is turning black. If they do not remove that leg, he will die. I tell him that if they remove it, he will die, because we will not be able to move when attacked. He would be helpless. Kristoffel adds, "However, he would be alive to see your father. Olimpia does not want your father to see him like this. Even if we cut the leg now, he would only live for a few days."

I sit back and try to fight back the tears. This is a big problem for me as well. Our father will find Panfilo dead, and if he were to see Answald dead that may devastate him. I cannot realize how much worse that would be, compared to see him dying in this pain, without one of his legs. Next, I tell Kristoffel that Answald should give a decision such as this. I then ask him if we can return, because I feel bad about being in such a special place when one of my brothers sleeps under the dirt and my other, one will soon join him. Kristoffel nods his head signifying that he understands. This gave me a boost of confidence in knowing that a feeling this terrible was justified in acknowledgement. I have a hard time trying to comprehend was going on inside Olimpia's head and heart. Before long, we decide on returning to our camp. I leave this place in this case much divided in knowing I have been somewhere special, yet at an extremely difficult to me. Soon, I would discover the sanctuary that I had just departed was protecting from more than I thought I was to face. When I arrived at our camp, everyone was kneeling beside Answald. He was barely breathing and was crying in pain. I asked Olimpia what was happening. She had given him a couple of strong herbs and was waiting to see what they would do. I asked her to speak privately with me. Olimpia told me we had to speak fast, so I simply told her in front of all, "Why do we not let Answald determine the road, he is to travel?" She looked at me strangely as Kaus, Acia, and Pava quickly agreed. Olimpia then told Answald that his condition was mortal, if she cut off his leg, he could have a chance to live, however, and most likely, he would die within one week. If he keeps his leg, and she gives him selected new roots, he may have one-half of a chance to live, yet if he did live, he would have his leg. She asked me to request from him what he wanted to do. I gave the choice to him, and he told us, "I want to die as a man." Kristoffel queried him, what turned out to be the most important question for our future as a family. He asked him if he wanted to avenge the man that did this, or even the man that gave the order.

Answald told them, "No, we were in your land and should have followed your rules. As outlaws, we earned our fate." He continued with, "Those who do wrong should not punish those who obeyed their laws." We looked in amazement, waiting for more words, which never came. He joined Panfilo as so many in our family were with our mother currently. The only thing that I could say is that, "Mommy has two big boys to take care of her now." Olimpia came over, picked me up, and hugged me tight. This time she did not give kisses. Instead, she gave tears, and so many of them. She looked at Acia and Pava, which meant for them to follow her. After that, she walked over, gave both Kaus and Joggeli, kisses, and said to Kristoffel that she could not kiss him because he was so ugly. Kristoffel returned an especially respectful bow and when he became vertical again, Olimpia had taken her three babies walking toward the inlands. She told us she was taking us to her favorite place in the world. Looking at her two younger sisters, she sat down so Acia could get on her back, then standing up; she put Pava on her right side and me on her left side. Acia then commented that this was just like the old times. Olimpia tells us that she will work hard to prepare our new times much like our old times. We are traveling the opposite way that Kristoffel took me earlier today. This one felt as if we were almost going straight to the top. After a few minutes, I asked her if I could walk because we were too heavy. She stops to catch her breath and says, "My babies will never weigh too much for me. I could sense that she was hurting inside and needed the extra physical pain to give her a sense of balance. Next, I turned my head back to Acia who I could tell felt the same thing. Our mommy was hurting. Her life was going through so many changes so fast that she was spinning. She had decided to leave our village, and even before we met our father, two brothers now slept in the dirt. I would not try to guess what she thought, and instead we would overemphasize our love and willingness to die for her if need be. We may hold back a little on the last offer if we are able to do so. She pounds away and soon we are walking into a small ledge that is flooded with flowers. She sits us down under particular trees, as we are now able to survey out across the deep valley in front of us.

To our left is a white mountain, yet this is not much higher than we are. I ask Olimpia about that, she enlightens us that sometimes we cannot believe what our eyes are telling us, for the mountain is actually much higher, it just sloops so slow and long that it appears not to be that elevated. Afterwards, I ponder to myself how today was a day in which I could not believe what my eyes were telling me. I almost hope to wake up and see Panfilo and Answald playing in our camp. Pava and Acia start picking the flowers when Olimpia calls them to her. They wonder if they may be in trouble; nevertheless, Olimpia takes a few of the flowers from them and fits them into their hair and remarks, "Now I have my flower girls." They do that entire strange girl hugging and sit down junk, while I keep control of my senses. Acia looks at me and I shake my head no,

I do not want to play with the flowers. I do want to pick them just before we leave to place them above Panfilo and Answald's body. Maybe we will be lucky and they will have dirt over Answald when we return. It hurts me to peek in Olimpia's eyes, yet I believe that is why she is with us, so she can regain her composure with a more forgiving group. The three of us immediately tackle her, as she went down easier than normal. It could be the ledge that is nearer than we thought. Either way, we are safe for now so we begin to crawl over her, trying to blow our bubbles on her. She always enjoyed this and before long, we have her laughing. Olimpia laughs for a while and then a somber expression comes over her face as she grabs us and we move closer to the flowers. We glimpse back near where we were and an avalanche of snow is flowing down the cliff that would have been behind us. I ask Olimpia, "Where did that snow come from?" She looks at us and shakes her head confessing that she may have been laughing too loud. After this, she recommends that we travel back pass the flowers these little ways where the ledge is wider. I reveal my desire to bring these flowers back to the camp. She reassures me everyone's shares this intent. I am having a hard time accepting this, as I do not think Acia and Pava thought about taking flowers back with them.

This time, I will let this slide, as I do not want to argue with the only real mother, I ever had. Olimpia wonders aloud to us now if she made the correct decision to leave the village, as we just missed another attempt for the land of death to take us. I tell her that we will have to get tougher if we are to live in the wilderness, and if the choice to return would bring her harm than we will get stronger. The babies stay with their mommy. She smiles as she releases a sneeze. Acia tells her she needs to dry her wet dress from all the sweat from carrying us. We collect our rags and give her enough to create a temporary outfit, one that she may only wear around her babies. We then lay her pants and shirt in the Suns, which are high above us now. They should dry quickly. Olimpia now asks us how we will live without Panfilo and Answald. I tell her she will have to allow Joggeli to join our family and because we will be living with daddy currently, the numbers will be the same. Acia next adds that since I am a man now, we will be plus one. Olimpia then smiles at us and asks us why we love her. We tell her because she is our only mommy. Olimpia further tells us she feels so bad for Answald and wonders if she should have cut off his leg. I reveal to her that Kristoffel told me that most men, who have their legs removed because of the black skin, die any ways. Olimpia tells us that daddy will be extremely angry when he finds two of his sons dead. Acia tells her that he will find five of us still living. If he is, even so mad, then we may have to find a new daddy. I tell her that he will not be mad, for he knows the ways of the wilderness, and we got the man who killed Panfilo and the ones responsible for Answald are his friends. He should have told his friends more about us. Acia and Pava are laying on Olimpia to protect her from the Suns. Her clothes are drying swiftly as I flip them to the other side. I cherry pick through the largest varieties of flowers, selecting the white cones with a light pink tint. I select a wide assortment of the orange flowers and avoid the yellow ones. Olimpia asks me to add the yellow ones, and I tell her yellow is not a good color for boys.

Olimpia confesses to me that this is why they are so lucky to have me with them. Therefore, I can teach them these things. She asks me to select extra for Kaus, Kristoffel, and Joggeli. It hits me now how easily in life; old names go away, and new names come to stay. I try to think what the name Panfilo meant. He took his responsibilities serious and was not afraid to fight for what he believed was the right thing to do. Kaus and Answald more or less kept pushing Panfilo to watch us, thereby excluding him from the big kid things. We could see that he no longer had a desire to do little kid things. He was stuck in the middle, in trouble if we did something wrong and having to work double time as we were always working around him. Any mistake or action we did not approve we went straight to Olimpia, who most times gave in to us. The main thing that Pava, Acia, and I agreed on was that we did not want to be Panfilo. His life was now waiting until we got bigger, so he could do many of the things he wanted. That day never came for him. Answald followed Kaus every minute he could. I seldom saw them apart. Answald was determined to be skilled as much if not more than his older brother was. This forced Kaus to work harder. We will always be able to see Answald in

61

the actions of Kaus. I realize that he will miss Answald so much, especially considering that Answald also worked hard to be his friend. Answald treated Kaus as a hero and always gave him the honor for any of his accomplishments. I grasp there are many things they did that annoyed me, especially Panfilo. Nevertheless, now that they are in the land of the dead I cannot remember those things. I notice that Acia and Pava have also only expressed the happy things they remember about their older brothers. Their older brothers did all they could for their little princesses. I cannot complain, because they often would include me in their games. They worked hard with me on the throwing the spear, shooting arrows, and cutting with the long knives. Olimpia's clothing is dry now. Acia slipped through to the side of the avalanche and brought her back the snow so Olimpia could clean herself to this extent.

Olimpia found a few flowers that she rubbed on her skin to cause her to smell pleasant. Acia teased her about doing this for Joggeli. She informed Acia that she had to keep him interested until he had his talk with daddy. Olimpia jumped into her outfit; we collected our flowers, and this time we walked back to the camp. I think Olimpia is feeling better now, and does not need the additional physical challenge to keep herself together. She has rebuilt a small oasis around us. She will use this comfort zone in her return to accept responsibility. We slowly walk back into the dismal looking camp, to find Joggeli, Kaus, and Kristoffel all sleeping around the dying campfire. They have lain Answald beside Panfilo and covered him with dirt. Interesting how Kaus is sleeping between them. Answald ensured our new extended family would stay united after his death. To blame and hate for something did in a spirit of an established morality is foolish. He must have already climbed to a higher level before dying and realized that we would need Joggeli to move forward in our struggles before we rest in the dirt. Kristoffel's men have another batch of fish cooked for us. They motion for Olimpia to wake the men. She goes over to Kaus as her old self and kicks him telling me to get up. He bounds out of his sleep with a smile and welcomes her back. Joggeli springs into action as he shakes Kristoffel. They inspect her, and she points to the campfire. Enough said, they go directly to the campfire and begin loading the fish on their eating rocks. Although many villages produced excellent pottery for eating, we never took it with us when going to the wilderness, as it would break, chip, and be heavy to carry. Olimpia brings us over to the fire and carefully selects our fish and certain vegetation the men gathered for us. Once she has the three of us settled in, she asks if anyone needs anything. Everyone shakes their head no; therefore, then sits down and prepares her rocks. Kristoffel then compliments Olimpia on how well she smells. Joggeli begins to sniff, and afterwards lowers his red face in embarrassment. Kaus hits him, asks him if he has anything to add, and then begins laughing. Joggeli lifts his head and fires back with, "I am so embarrassed; I thought that was an angel."

Olimpia smiles at him and says, "Okay. You get off the hook with that one." Acia asks why. Kaus tells her, "Acia, it does not matter why; she let him off the hook. That is the important thing." Olimpia picks up another piece of fish, while smiling at Joggeli and goes to stick it in her mouth. Suddenly, the arrow splashes into her fish, slowing it down just enough for her to catch the end of it before hitting Acia in her head. Kristoffel yells for the other two men to prepare for a fight as someone is attacking us now. He grabs me and tells Olimpia to get under the pines. Our two escorts are firing arrows into the forest where the attacking arrow came. Kaus grabs Pava and Joggeli grabs Acia. Two more arrows come flying at us, although not well aimed. Our two raiders notice the location and slowly slip into the woods to work their way into the land behind our peninsula. Kaus, Kristoffel, and Joggeli have set up their positions behind the trees and are scouring the hills looking for any movement that could give away a location. Olimpia is protecting her three babies. Kristoffel looks back at her and comments, "Olimpia, life is nothing but a series of fates, a few fates we lose, others we win, today fate gave you back Acia, only by a few scary inches and not even one second, or breath." A few more arrows came firing down at us; however, these were missing our peninsula and hitting the surrounding water. Kristoffel comments that they must be retreating, yet our foolish for wasting their arrows. This is almost as if they are making a final attempt at maybe a kill. He warns us to stay under the pines until he can get all his men back. Kristoffel walks out into the open with a rag and starts making strange signals with the smoke from the fire. He does this for about twenty minutes. He tosses more wood on the fire and then comes back under the pines for about thirty minutes. Afterwards, he returns to the campfire and once again makes the signals. The last two men, who rushed into the forest, returned now with four heads each. They tell us the remainder of the raiders has fled to the other mountain.

Kristoffel asks them if they have seen any signs of the first two guards he sent today. They deny seeing anything. He tells them not to go too far apart from one another, place the skulls along any entrance paths, and find the other two men and return. When he returns to the pines, Joggeli asks him why he is recalling the guards. He tells him the enemy must be able to work around them and as such; they are only sitting defenseless targets that we could better use to defend ourselves here. He then recommended that we eat much tonight, because tomorrow we will go on a hike. Kristoffel afterwards looked at Joggeli and told him to go along the upper lakeshore and find the hollowed log and bring it back. Since this is such an important job, he wants me to supervise. Joggeli stands at attention and salutes me telling me he is at my service now. I motion him off to the side and tell him that since I do not understand what a hollowed log is and as I have never been on the upper lakeshore, the second we get out of range, I want him to take charge. He tells me it will be our secret. Subsequently, I tell him that it will be delightful having him as a brother. Joggeli tells me he will try to live up to the greatness of Answald. I gawk at him strangely and tell him, "Answald was still a kid weirdo. You have him clobbered by two moons. Any ways, with you around keeping Olimpia busy, Acia, Pava, and I will have more time to play, and I will have to clean less." Joggeli looks at me and winks, then tells me that I will have to teach him a few tricks on how to slip by the cleaning. I tell him not to worry, just stick beside me. He recommends that we go to finish our meal. Olimpia looks at us and asks Joggeli, "What have you been say to my man?" Joggeli reassures her that he was only asking for the best way to find the hollow log tomorrow. Olimpia then shakes her head yes and says, "If anyone can find it, my men can." Joggeli grabs hold of my hand with a big smile on his face and escorts me to our fire. Kristoffel now advises us to take our food and finish our meal under the pines. He shares with us, "Fate is a lady whom, you are not wise to tempt after she has given her warning. She is a lady who decides when to give and when to take. We do not want to lose when she is trying to give."

We sit around under our pines and begin to chat about another warring day. Olimpia tells us that daddy never talked about this much killing. Kristoffel tells her he always begins his trips with ten men. She next asks why daddy never loses men. He tells her that he does, he is merely making sure you do not hear about it. I ask him why he is always talking about fate. He tells us that fate is something we all must take seriously if we are to enjoy happy lives in the wilderness. He looks at Acia and tells her, "Fate gave you another life today. There is no possible way that the arrow did not go into your head and for you not to be lying beside your brothers. I have been saved by fate so many times that I do not even recognize for sure if I am truly alive or am a spirit." I walked over and kicked him. He yells back, "That hurt." Olimpia yells at me to tell him I am sorry and to stand in front of the tree facing its bark for being bad. I looked at Olimpia and told her I was not being bad. I just wanted to ensure that he was real and not a spirit." Kristoffel laughs on this one saying to Olimpia, "I guess I did set myself up for that one, let him off the hook on this one. I will take the blame." She agrees, and I go over and shake his hand. We smile at one another as Kaus remarks, "To think that a few days ago, he was my little brother, amazing." Kristoffel tells a story about an old man who lived in a small village of three families. Each morning, each family sent out a son to join that day's hunting trip. Each day, they would all return. One of the fathers would grumble about each thing his sons would do. Life in his family was sad, as even their mother would cry most days. One day, as a son from each family went to hunt and returned, they were missing one of their members. The crabby father lost one son. He protested to the other two families that they must give one of their sons to help him, so that all the hours would be fair. Reluctantly, they gave out their sons for a small quantity of time roughly just to stop his endless murmuring.

These boys would return to their homes after a grueling work for what they called the evil man and tell their families how horrible it was to help him. Then about one week later, another son did not return. The whining father once again demanded extra help. The other families refused to help him anymore. They told the old man that his only remaining son, and he would have to hunt for his family, as the village would no longer share with him. This made him incredibly angry; consequently, he threatened to burn their homes while they slept. The other families refused to talk with any of them and shunned them. Then one morning, the wicked man woke up to find his wife and only remaining son gone. He was now all alone. He took this vengeance out on the other two families by poisoning their drinking waters. Fortunately, several of his neighbors' animals drank the water first, dying immediately. This angered his neighbors so much that they sent their sons to hang him. Three moons later, when his family had learned of his death, they returned to their home farm. The sons brought their new wives who were pregnant. The small village lived happily ever after. Kaus asked Kristoffel what this tale meant. Kristoffel likened fate as the sons who left. Those who continually mistreat fate will lose her. She will depart from them. When one casts fate away, they will find themselves in much more misery and will cast all from themselves. You will never win complaining about fate, for fate will defeat you in the end. Those who trust fate and follow her ways will live much happier lives. The three sons did not avenge their belligerent father; instead, they followed fate and even saved their mother. Fate rewarded them by removing the unthankful and replacing them with the thankful. Kristoffel reveals to us the only reason he told this story was, so we would believe that happiness could still be in our future. He confesses that each day now when he sees Acia he will believe that something great happened here today. Our family lost Panfilo and Answald. Something saved Acia and we gained Joggeli. Kristoffel tells us that when fate saves someone, there is usually for a reason. We will need to live our lives in thanks for what we received and not for what we lost.

Acia is too precious a gift to waste. I distinguish that I was not the only one in this family that felt guilty now. Each of us was feeling guilty. I walked over, kissed my best friend, and asked her, "Now that you are so famous, are you still my best friend." She told me that I was her best friend forever. Olimpia asked her where she stood. She looked at her strangely and said, "You are my mommy, which is the most important person in my life." Joggeli asks where she stands. She tells Joggeli and Kaus that they are her giant brothers. Acia further tells Kristoffel that he is her favorite uncle. At this time, his two raiders returned with particular bad news. They found the bodies of the two scouts. A beast killed the first one we found, and the other had knives in his back. The strange thing that they reported was the knives were not from the same tribe as the ones from the other attackers they had chased away. Kristoffel asked him if he saw any other strange marks on their stabbed comrade's back. They told Kristoffel that he had a reddish rash around his neck, his eyes were still open, and little blood poured out his wound. Kristoffel subsequently tells us that a rope hanged his man first, most likely with a hood of various sorts over his head. That would explain the rash around his neck and eyes open, as he was trying to see through the hood. Because he was hitherto dead, when they stabbed him with their stolen knives, little blood would pour. I asked Kristoffel why they would waste stolen knives on him if he were already departed. Kristoffel tells us the knives were an attempt to get us to revenge the wrong tribe, thereby do kill their enemy for them. This is one reason Kristoffel always collects all the weapons from his men who die on the missions. Presently, the two men give him all the weapons they retrieved, to include the stolen knives. Kristoffel confesses that he also uses the knives from other tribes to keep the raiders off his trail. Accordingly, many warriors use this trick. Therefore, weapons are the least category or item used to identify potential enemies. Kristoffel asks which one of the invaders stabbed. The warriors told him that it was his son. Kristoffel began to cry fell on his knees.

Joggeli quickly explained to us that the guard the enemy killed was Kristoffel's oldest son. Olimpia asked if he was going to take the body back to his family. Joggeli asked that we remain at peace until he tells us what to do. Kristoffel, overhearing our conversation, tells us he has no family remaining. Acia and Pava ran to him and began hugging him. Unexpectedly, this elicited more tears to my eyes. I went up and asked Kristoffel if he wanted to be a part of our family, as our uncle. He shook his head yes and then began telling us his story. His family had four daughters and five sons. One of the five sons was dead on the ridge above us. He was the only remaining one, and had been on hunts with him for years. The other sons were still too young as their mother refused to let them travel with the hunters. One day a giant Army that was raiding through the mountains stumbled on his village. They hung his wife as a sign of mercy before they beat and killed his four sons who were there protecting the family. All in the village had fled for their lives, as this Army did burn the complete village and searched for inhabitants, finding a few in caves and beat them in public handing them high so all could see. Many of the villagers committed suicide by drowning themselves in the local rivers. They rounded up as many women as possible, as they used these women to service their soldiers. Olimpia's face turned red when he said this Army used the women to service the soldiers. I thought this to be strange, as she services us by cooking, bossing, and washing. Her healing skills are extra services for us, so I guess we could say she over-services us. I was more interested in Kristoffel's story than worry about my sometimes-strange older sister. When returning home that year, he noticed other something had destroyed many other small villages. He listened to many tales of how this large Army was collecting women and beating men. Not any knew where they had come from or even why they were here. The puzzling thing was that they were not taking any booty, except to feed themselves. They would select twenty women each five miles they marched, rape them, and then tie them to trees. The ones, who took part in their punishments willingly, they gave a swift death by an arrow in their head. Those whom, they punished were left to die while guards ensured they eventually died. One area local people reassembled, killed the guards, and freed the women.

When the guards failed to rejoin the Army, the Army came back and spent one month flushing out everyone, recapturing the women and this time beat them alongside the men. They allowed a few of the men to go free, after a severe beating, to warn others of the punishment for killing their raiders. This produced the opposite effect, as the villages that now lie in front of them fought harder for their survival, although none could match this great Army. They did; however, able to delay the Army. Their commander had not prepared for the long winter that came while they were attacking, followed by the dark days. His raiders starved to death, as the predators fed at will on their weak remains. The villagers had destroyed all food and poisoned the water in the lands that lay before and behind them. Many of the women could escape, while others released them, hoping they would guide them to food, during this bitter winter, knowing the dark days were just ahead. They did not have to worry about which way to go, as they would end in a village in any way they went. The wilderness people could fight in the dark days much easier, as they would simply hide and wait. Kristoffel worked his way back to his village, checking the killed women every five miles. He discovered two of his daughters, which told him they were resisting as hard as they could. He worked his way back to the Army, not reaching it until deep in the winter. Unable to find them, he returned to the main trail and prepared for the dark days. Kristoffel hoped his daughters would return to this path. Once the long cold days of winter and the bitter cold that reigned the dark days had finished, he prepared to search once more for his daughters. He rummaged for weeks through all the scattered lifeless bodies finding nothing. The enemy commanders through the dark days had led their Armies into dead end, deep valleys, which they could not escape because of all the monstrous cliffs that surrounded them.

One dismal day he found a special prison for women among the highest commander's empty tents. His remaining two daughters, they trapped inside this fortified prison left to greet their death through starvation. The raiders had abandoned the camp, as he found many had tried to negotiate the nearby cliffs to no success as their crushed bodies scattered the valley's floor. He decided to leave his daughters' bodies there as they had died fighting for their freedom and while caged, would not be eaten by the predators that made this area accordingly dangerous now. He could bypass these predators and return to his normal territory, having the peace of mind that this Army met its death and would raid no longer. Kristoffel devoted the next three years of his life searching for the homeland of these raiders and never could properly identify any area they may have come from. He did notice that many of the northern areas was sparsely populated and eventually found an old wise man that told him about how many sons from this area were searching for new wives, so they could produce a great nation. This project was one where men from a vast area had united. They formed a great Army, and went in search of wives. What did not add up was all the beating and killing every five miles. He asked the old man about this. The old man knew nothing of any beating or killing and could only suspect that this evil came from men of another area who had gained control of the Army. They must have foolishly believed that this would deter the locals from fighting back and leave them in total fear. Kristoffel told him it had produced the opposite effect. The old man told Kristoffel that power was a dangerous thing and that when many gets it, their greed turns them into servants of the dead. The innocent die of this, as they gave their sons much booty to trade for these wives. In worse case, they were to pay double the local dowry for a woman they had to capture. Now the old people have so few sons to sustain and protect the population left behind. As raiding villages who did not participate in this raid currently invade their dying neighbors, killing them in mercy to free them from a long painful death and spreading diseases.

Kristoffel felt sorry for these old people; however, they were too many for him to save, and if they were starving, they had to kill them before they began spreading these diseases. He, therefore, returned to his hunting lands in the south, where eventually he joined with our father. I asked him, "If you have joined with our father, then why he is not here now?" Joggeli tells us that he wanted to trade several furs he had for any special garments that select villages along the great sea were selling. I went over to give Kristoffel a warm hug. Olimpia beat me to him, as I paused wanting my mother to share her warmth first. She was slow to accept Kristoffel blaming him for Answald's death. Olimpia cried on his shoulders. He gave her a rag, and as she wiped one of her eyes, he wiped the other. Joggeli then slowly pulled her back as Kristoffel now wiped his eyes and thanked her for the wonderful emotional hug. He continues to break our hearts as he tells us the one special thing he misses about having no family is the exceptional hugs his daughters gave him when he returned from his hunting trips. Olimpia tells him she will always give him a hug when he returns to his new family. She asks him if he can forgive her for the way she has mistreated him. Kristoffel laughs and remarks, "I did not understand if you were mistreating me, I thought you were simply being a woman. It shows you how long it has been since I was with my family." I asked him why he had not started a new family. He tells us that he feels too old to do all that again, and was instead planning to help his last son raise his family. That made, sense to us, as we have seen many other elders do this in our village. Kaus tells Kristoffel, "Fate has really given you many hard blows." Kristoffel tells us that he was not the only one to lose his family, for so many did. Justice punished those who did the killing along with their loved ones. Fate also collects from those who were doing the taking. Kristoffel admits he lost his family, yet hopes now he has found a new family.

He afterwards tells us that when those who have lost will join, all win. I scrutinize Kaus and I can see we both agree that Kristoffel will be a perfect addition to our family. He knows so many things, yet most importantly, he knows how to survive. Kristoffel turns his attention to me and asks, "Young man, do you expect the hollowed log to appear by magic, or do you think we would get a lot faster if you went searching for it?" I looked at him and smiled, then looked at Joggeli and told him we needed to go up the shoreline. We subsequently went over and collected the back bags that Olimpia and Kaus had prepared for us. After that, we began our search. Joggeli taught me how to walk along the lakeshore. We walked about ten feet in the forest, enough to be in the dark for those who could be watching for us. He also taught me that before each step, we would glance around and every time we moved our feet, we would be looking down. We could produce no noise. A noise could mean our deaths. We tried to stay close to trees, so we could walk on their roots if possible. This was turning into an adventure and was exciting me. The adventure ended when an arrow went flying past my head. Joggeli slipped around his tree, moved a few feet inland, and released his arrow straight into the head of our assassin. One direct shot and he was down. I did not recognize this stranger. Joggeli tells me this man may be a part of those who attacked us yesterday, and most likely left behind and was waiting for them to signal for the rendezvous. Our men must have killed the ones who were supposed to call the retreat. He suspects there may be a few more. Joggeli wants to walk about twenty feet inland and have me walk about ten feet in front of him along with our original path. If anyone spots me, they will be bracing their arrow for the perfect shot. He will be able to kill them while they are watching me. I am the bait at present; nevertheless, I trust Joggeli's abilities, as he knows how to survive in this type of terrain. He tells me this is important that we flush them out currently, before we get into the hollow log and float back, as then we will be sitting ducks. Joggeli notices a strange ring on this man's hand and pulls the ring off, as we will allow Kristoffel to study it.

He is starting to appear better as the forest is beginning to come back to life. This is giving him a feeling that we may now be alone. So long as we remain alone; we remain alive. We are coming on another bay, though they are not that deep. We move long our shoreline as if nothing is wrong until we meet with a small stream. Joggeli looks at the trees around it and then notices several strange rocks in the stream. At this time, we change our direction and follow the new stream until we find another smaller stream. We travel up it for a short distance and walk over to a few dead trees. Joggeli pulls out the hollowed out log, which they packed with branches. We remove the branches and afterwards shoot it to the small stream where he tells me to hop in and stay low. He scouts around the area and subsequently returns, grabs a rope he tied to the front and pulls it out to the larger stream where he jumps in. Afterwards, he shows me special sticks they fabricated to row the boat across the lake, and soon we are on our way back. Joggeli first rows us out in the middle section of the lake and then we row back to where we line up with the peninsula and row straight back in. I ask him why we did this, and he says this makes it easier to protect us this way, as we are moving in and not beside the shore, we can see what is in front of us and prepare to defend against it. When we return, Kristoffel tells us to go to our new campsite, secure it, and afterwards scan the lakeshores on the way to draw out any hidden surprises. We row out about 100 yards into the lake and subsequently move parallel to the shore. Joggeli keeps his eyes searching the coastline looking for anything that might not be normal. The Suns roast us, as Joggeli and I rotate diving into the lake to cool down. We failed to bring any extra fabrics to protect our skin, so we soon both wade in the water beside the boat, which is actually not dreadfully bad in that it makes us smaller targets. The lake supports a steady cool breeze, which is chilling me. Joggeli goes under and moves around keep enough under to where it does not affect the surface waters. He then smoothly resurfaces. I was tempted once to go back into our hollowed log, yet Joggeli warns that to do so can cause to be to burn from the Suns. This presented certain light difficulties and only ended making my return to the dry land much more rewarding. Joggeli finally guided us to our new camping area.

We scouted their area inside the fortified wooded walls that had been constructed, which added more security to this area. Joggeli tells me that Kristoffel and my father built this fort as a safety zone if they needed to use it, such as, we did now. After we checked everything out to ensure the area was safe, we both waded in the water, and later we rolled in the sand until we covered our bodies with sand and dirt. We after that went back into our boat to find the remainder of our family. Kristoffel was leading them along the ridge that surrounded this valley. This provided him with the ability to explore both sides of our range. Occasionally, Joggeli would fire an arrow high in the sky so it would land about halfway up the mountainside that faced us. This was to see how the animals responded. He said it kept everything awake and moving around. Kristoffel soon had our family running about on our new beach as Joggeli and I rushed to meet them. Although this separation had been for less than one day, it felt as if an eternity. I jumped from our log before we reached the shoreline. There could be no way that my mother could catch me this dirty. Olimpia would listen to none of my heroics if I had one-piece of visible mud. When I reached our shoreline, Acia and Pava were waiting to ensure I would not get into any trouble and to welcome their hero from the lake. They wanted to comprehend everything that I had done during the day. I told them about the man who tried to kill us. Acia said that Kristoffel had to shoot arrows and kill two men along the way. This is starting to bother me in that every day someone is dying, and I am so afraid the next one may be your turn to pay. Kristoffel explains to me why he and our father fortified this station. The hollow log can get us back to our peninsula in extremely little time, as we are also able to see what is happening behind it. They cut down many trees and pilled them in the water along our shoreline to prevent invaders from the lake, from being a threat, although seldom would we ever see a force from the water. Most would attempt to attack from the land, and this is where their wooden walls produced a great defensive tool. We could leave our hollow log in the water in front of us with the other trees that floated partially in the lake. Kristoffel unpacked the remainder of our fish as we have finished it this evening.

He told us that tomorrow his two men would get more fish for us, and that we would eat much fish until our father came, as this would help cause us to become stronger for our trek to the new home, this family would have to discover. The two remaining of our protectors builds us a pleasant campfire as sit around and slowly seat ourselves into another provisional place to stay. I ask Olimpia if we are always doing to temporary dwellings in fresh places, or if we plan to settle in one place. Kristoffel tells us that our father has selected many spots that he would like to raise his family. We will examine those first to see if one rallies our fancy. The trees on this side of our lake have a rich variety of colors as they appear to blend from yellow to green while they are saying, 'enter here, and as we will show you what life is.' I ask Kristoffel why this site creates such a different feeling. He explains the peninsula is in the open, whereas here our world is enclosed. We must use our imaginations to fill our world. Considering that we are comfortable with what we know, we fill the unknown with what brings us ease. I stare at him strangely and respond, "I think this is closer to such as I like this more than I like that over there." Joggeli laughs and remarks, "That is another way of saying this big guy."

I direct this next question to all in our group, "Why are we having to kill every day to stay alive, and when we are not killing, we are putting dirt over those we love?" Olimpia and Kaus shrug their shoulders. Kristoffel looks at Joggeli, I think because he is afraid his answers are somewhat complicated for me to comprehend. Joggeli explains, "Yakov, I ask myself that same question every time I release an arrow or spear into another person who is trying to do the identical with me. Such as in the case with Answald, I have often dreamed that we would have a way to talk with each before we immediately kill. Someone has to be the brave one, stand alone in front of the others, and talk, as you did for Kaus and Olimpia. I so wish that someday, our different people would appreciate one another. Knowledge and understanding one another would bring a halt to all this endless foolish killing. I hope that someday, a great Army that serves a virtuous king and queen will unite our people. That may be more of a foolish dream than a possible reality, as this world is too large for such a power ever to control. Until then, we either kill or were killed. Panfilo is proof of that. This is a wonderful question Yakov, and I hope that someday you find the answer to this for us."

He sat down in front of our fire noticeably in a philosophical trance. Kristoffel added his part now, although more focused and not as elaborate as usual, "We think about this question each time we place dirt on one that we have killed. I gaze at them and imagine a family who will have no provider and can merely wonder if they will survive or starve. This death of their dreams torments me the greatest. Each time I think of my lost family, I remember our shattered dreams. Our home no longer provided the spirit or desire to greet our next day. Alone and trapped forever only to dissolve in the air that was their home. Therefore, I now realize how important this exact minute truly is, for our next minute has a chance as being our last. We recognize only one thing, and that is our time to cross over will come. No one escapes this journey. The fittest simply postpone it for a while. My new dream is to see how long we can postpone our inevitable deaths and live each day as happy, yet not careless as far as possible." Acia joins the conversation revealing to us that she does not like to think or even talk about death because it makes her sad. She hopes to remember Answald and Panfilo by the pretty flowers she put on the dirt that kept the Suns out of their eyes, thus they could sleep in peace. Our group shows signs of smiles emerging, as the thought of these flowers shifts us from what is below them. I cannot help but to examine across the lake at what is our family reunion place, a place in the open with no hidden secrets. These hidden secrets; nevertheless, are still there and waiting for their time. The difference that is they hide not as close, compared to this new place. All who live today must keep at least one eye on them and the other to travel their appointed path. In this respect, we are never in truth alone because death is beside us, with her leg stretched out waiting to see if we jump or fall. I have never enjoyed thinking about this, as I am still young. I take my role in protecting Pava and Acia seriously and I understand this is what creates that special feeling in me. I like it at this spot, maybe because I do not have to wade in that cold lake water. My mind currently is asking me, 'how much pain do I need to be happy.'

CHAPTER 04

Mommy, please wake up

Talking and thinking about death is making my legs tingle; therefore, I decide to stroll around our new small secluded area. Often I find myself amazed at trees, because they all appear with so much sameness. Only after carefully studying them can we find the minute variances. When done, the few differences represent many distinctions. I have noticed that about the people likewise I recognize. When I first meet them, they appear the same, yet after talking or just being around them for a while seems to bring these small special differences out into the open. These differences lose their negativity as the more positive features take root. Even though these trees do not present a danger, what they hide does. Behind each one or even in their branch's death could be waiting to deliver her move. When gazing at these trees and trying to understand if all this has a purpose, a series of crackles pulls me back to reality. This time, I was lucky, because in front of me is Acia. I tease her about scaring, me. She tells me there is nothing in the world, which could scare me. Can there be any logic to her unsound faith in my abilities? I ask her, "Acia, examine me; I am just a small kid like you are. How can you think of me having so many abilities, when we recognize that even Panfilo exceeded me?" Acia glares at me and responds, "It is comfortable, because that is what I believe, and if you do not stop this foolishness, I will have to tell Olimpia to give you a thumping. Why are you always trying to cause easy things to be so hard?" With merely a short pause, she continues, "Why are we looking at the trees?" I smile at my sister and tell her, "They remind me of people, except that they can live beside each and not kill. Any somehow, they can share the rain and energy from our Suns." She smiles at me and says, "That is what I thought." I ask her if she wants to explore inside our fortress.

Acia agrees; however, tells me that we cannot be out too long because Pava will wake up soon. While walking through our small forest, I notice that the tiny stream wiggles its way in our little part of this world and then runs parallel with the lake. It also has many respectable sized fish swimming in it. I tell Acia that if she jumps in the stream over there, I can jump in upstream. Then we can grab a handful of fish, throw them pass these trees. When done, we simply collect them and take them back to camp. She jumps in as I ask, and I start to grab these confused fish, actually two at a time, and tossing them about ten feet from this stream. We are lucky in the area I am throwing the feet is sunken; therefore, the fish flap into each other and remain pretty much, where we throw them. Acia is tossing the fish as well now. Within minutes, we hold at least a two-day's supply for our family, and we have more to collect. These are solid fish also, and they seem healthy. We continue for ten-minutes more. Then we go to inspect what we have captured. One thing is obvious. This is too much for us to carry back. I send Acia to get us for a little help. She returns with Olimpia and Pava. I ask her where the men are. Acia reveals to me these men are laughing; saying little kids cannot catch big fish with only their hands. I stare at Olimpia and inquire, "Why did you come?" Olimpia says, "Because I understand if Acia tells me my man caught big fish; he will need help with them." She brought all her special root bags, as they are empty. I question her, "Olimpia, where are your healing roots?" She tells me, "They are safe, in Joggeli's bags." I laugh and ask, "Olimpia, why did not you just take Joggeli's bags?" She discloses to me that he would not let her take his bags. Olimpia and Acia can be exceptionally industrious when they want to be. One thing is for sure, and that is our mother believes in our abilities. Olimpia looks at the fish and says, "Oh no. These are too many for us to carry; I will get us some help. Now, I want you three to lay on the ground on the other side of this small pit. Pretend you are hurt; nevertheless, create no noise and do not move." Once we are in position, she screams for help. As her second cry for help bellows out, "Kaus, Joggeli, and Kristoffel are on us."

She points to us. They run straight for us, falling in our fish pit. Joggeli now asks her, while fighting to regain his breath, "Why she was screaming for help." She blinked her eyes and said, "The fish were jumping at my babies. I was afraid they might bite them." Kristoffel crawls out of the pit, looks down at it, and then stands up. He walks toward me and shakes my hand, saying, "Good job hunting young man, and Acia." He then tells Kaus, "We will take what we can eat tonight for our first night here feast and the remainder we will cover with selected dirt to keep the predators away. We need to get on the move before they start discovering these fish's scents." Kristoffel looks at me and asks, "You think you can take our women to an open field up to the bay on our left. It is about 100 of your steps back from the bay's mouth, and then about thirty of your steps inland, over a small hill. In that meadow, are had many good vegetables for us to eat." I ask him how he knows they are there. He tells me that our father and he planted them accordingly; if we camped here someday, we would have plenty of food. Afterwards, he looks at Olimpia and tells her, "We planted several roots in the forest between us and that meadow, so simply come straight back. Before returning, I examine the movement of the clouds. Walk in the same direction that the clouds are moving. You will come to this lakeshore. Then follow the smell of our cooking fish. Now we need to hurry because tonight we will celebrate." I dash off with my sisters. The pacing is easy as Acia and Pava count each of my steps, and we arrive at this meadow. The meadow is much larger than we expected. As each year's harvest reseated, the garden packed itself with so many vegetables. The seeds additionally spread throughout the area. Olimpia tells me that before we leave this place, she will return and pack an entire bag with these seeds, so we can start a large garden wherever we decide to settle. I ask her, "Why do not we settle here, because we consider this to be the place of our roots?"

She promises to ask Kristoffel about this. I continue to question her about what we would do if Kristoffel tells us no. Olimpia explains to me that she will phrase the question to formulate the final decision that our fathers. I glance at her and shake my head saying, "You sure are a wise mommy." She smiles at us and says, "I have to, because my babies are so smart." Her compliments are one of the things we enjoy about being around her. She continuously looks for ways to say good things about us. We are so much better being around her. She explained her rules, and if we stay within these rules, we will have no trouble. This is why death is so much on my mind, because it does not fit in anywhere, yet hovers over everything. Hating by everything possible, it swallows all into its bosom. Death's greatest power is its patience. It is in no hurry, because the faster that you run away from it, the weaker you will become. Once death gets hold of us, no one escapes that I know. I wish that I could get this death, fear away from me, because I hope to have more years than Answald and Panfilo. Nevertheless, perhaps when we resettle and life slows down once more. My mind will give me back the peace I need. I am so happy that we have Kristoffel in our family presently, because I can see us escaping those nasty attacks from death with him in our camp. If only I could have the confidence, that Acia has. Her confidence is important in that she and Pava are this family's true babies. Notwithstanding; I understand I am also considered a baby; even so, this family appears to treat boy babies different from girl babies. Thinking about how many brothers, I presently slept on the dirt, I can understand why they would want to rush my development. An issue that I am having is that too many big things are falling on me. I am, nevertheless, happy that someone is beside me helping to carry this load. My mind is alert enough to comprehend that Kristoffel put me with Joggeli, and the hollow log, to provide me various experiences in doing men's missions. Only a fool would not be thankful for this, as my fear tells me that within minutes, we could lose Kristoffel. I even question if I have the right to complain about death, as my hands must kill to keep me alive.

The fish, which I took from their world today most likely should have something to say about their right to live. Kill to live; live to kill most who appear within our world. Can we ever clean our hands from this blood? Is the blood from one life worth more than the blood from the other lives? Olimpia walks by me and snaps my ear. I regain my conscience and ask her if everything is okay. She smiles and informs me, "Big man that is what you are supposed to tell me." I smile at her and then complain, "All this hard guarding is taking away all my energy. I need a mommy hug and kiss to save me now." She stops what she is doing, drops to the ground, and opens her arms as all three of us rush for our hugs and slobbers. I can experience the excitement in Acia and Pava as Olimpia squeezes us tightly together. She then looks at Acia and Pava and asks them if they are going to help her keep me out of trouble. They give her a serious glare and shake their heads yes. Fortunately, for me, they like the same things I like so this should not present a problem. Olimpia is tying us closer together as we must; watch each other's backs if death is going to pass us for now. Here I go again, going back to dwell on death. I guess if it were not so fast and permanent, I would be able to have a better grip on it. A deep danger that I am currently feeling is that this preoccupation with death could be pulling me away from my family and making me isolated. Alone is where death wants me, because when we are alone with death, death can cheat and then play by its rules. Acia and Pava offer me this protection, as I also offer it for them. Everything that Kaus, Joggeli, and Kristoffel teach me, I want equally important to instruct them. It cannot hurt to offer death a few surprises when it tries to trip us. There are so many reasons not to worry about Olimpia. She is smart, can think on her feet, and appears always to have a backup plan. She knows the surrounding people. She is a master at getting them to do what she wants them to do. I did not really appreciate this gift until I saw the surprise she had for this family tonight. We finish our gathering and begin to flow with the clouds back to our camp.

The only delay, we experienced was climbing over our fortress. I found a tree that we climbed and crossed over its branches to our side and then carefully worked our way to the weaker sections that would slowly droop down toward the ground. Olimpia was not able to go out as far as we could go. We, therefore, had her drop her bags and carefully to hang from the branch using her arms to navigate toward its breaking point. Luckily, when it broke, she only dropped a few feet. As we collected our vegetables, we assured each the next time we returned it would be up the bay to our camp. Kristoffel appeared to be slightly surprised to see us come from the forests; nonetheless held his comments. Olimpia took her sisters and quickly started to prepare our food, almost as if she had a secret agenda for this evening. The food was prepared extra special and with many of her tastier herbs. We ate a fine feast and finished with the Suns still comfortably in the sky meaning at least two more hours of daylight. Kristoffel suggested that we had specific family time as she used to have with his family where everyone simply sits around and talks about anything on their minds. Olimpia raised her hand quickly wanting to be the first to talk. Kristoffel liked this, as he knew if Olimpia talked willingly, everyone would chat openly. She stood in the middle of our circle and began by asking Kristoffel at what age would he had approved his daughters getting married. He told her is a slow and peaceful tone that all his daughters were younger than she was, yet their mother was already searching for qualified husbands. I could see that liked this answer. Olimpia then asked him, "What makes a man, a qualified husband?" Kristoffel told us that each mother decided this, for his wife the man could not be a hunter and had to have a home already built for her to live. Olimpia afterwards asked, "Should a woman give herself to a man who has no home and is a hunter, as my mother did?" Kristoffel then told her, "Olimpia, I will be honest with you; she would be a fool to do so." She next asks him, "What if the man promised merely to hunt nearby for food to feed his family and vowed never to leave for long periods of time?"

Kristoffel then told her, "Well, maybe he has pledged it. You could give him a chance. My wife also swore that no man would marry any of her daughters, unless he first begged her father on his knees." Olimpia agreed that would be a good condition. She then asked him how he knew that he loved his wife before he married her. Kristoffel told her, "Olimpia, my precious little angel that is something that you both just grasp beyond any doubt. When you are apart, you are miserable. You want to share everything. You consider nothing to be yours, but for the relationship, all things to be ours. Your heart sings each day." Olimpia then asks him, "How long does that last?" Kristoffel tells her the time varies with different couples. He then tells her, "Olimpia, such a beautiful woman, such as you must have so many strong men from your previous village who want to marry you. Do you want me to start questioning them and select the top five for your father to decide?" She adds, fuel to this fire by confessing that so many boys like her, she was just hoping someone close by might want her. Kristoffel looks around and says, "Olimpia, I will send Kaus and Yakov out to search in the morning, unless someone steps forward tonight to declare his love for you." We are all staring at Joggeli currently, as his face is red, and he is starting to tremble. He slowly stands up, walks over to Olimpia, and declares his love. She winks at him and then reveals to him, "Joggeli, you have to speak to Kristoffel first." He turns around, walks in front of Kristoffel, then drops to his knees and starts to speak, saying, "Kristoffel, I do truly love the angel we call Olimpia." He raises his hand and then talks, "Joggeli, I have heard that you promise to stay with this family if you may receive Olimpia as your wife. Is this true?" Joggeli answers, "As with you, I also have no family, except for those around us presently. Her family will be my household, and I will be one within her clan. I swear this with my life." Kristoffel next tells him that he can love no other women and must stay faithful. Acia jumps up alongside Pava as they scream out, "He must love us also, or we will say no." Kristoffel changes his last condition, "You may love no other women, except for Acia and Pava, and must stay faithful." Joggeli tells our family that this will be the easiest rule; he will ever have to obey. Kristoffel tells him, "You will be responsible for feeding, protecting, and caring for her and your family to the best that you understand how to. This is where your hunting present the greatest problem, as hunting slaughtered my family and has started killing in this family. If this is any consolation to you, my hunting days are finished. The only hunting I want to do now is for a new land for us to build this family."

Joggeli then confessed, "I am so tired of risking my life to capture large beasts so those who are fat in their greed can feed on my dangers. I am ready to work for something of a greater value, and the love inside my Olimpia is that thing of the greatest value." Kristoffel tells Joggeli, "I have known you for many years, as also has Pawka. I share this in secret and if any ever tells it, I will deny saying it. Pawka did tell me once that he felt you would be a fine husband for Olimpia. He confessed that he had to find a way for a meeting as one of his greatest priorities." Joggeli looked around our family and asked, "What if they do not forgive me for the death of Answald?" Kaus jump from his position, rushed to Joggeli, and told him, "We have forgotten that as Answald asked that we do. His wishes are our greatest responsibility. If Olimpia adores you, and then we love you, so never mention your guilt to us again." Joggeli looked at Olimpia. She simply stood there, speechless. I walked over and pulled on her hand. Our mother turned to us and asked, "Do you think I should believe him?" Acia said, "If you do not want him, I will take him." Pava joins the bid by saying, "Me too." Olimpia smiles and looks at Joggeli with slow tears rolling down her cheeks saying, "I hope you recognize the answer my future husband." Kristoffel currently warns Olimpia that we must first ask her father, and that sometimes fathers do change their minds. He also swears that he will plead with all his heart on their behalf. Joggeli and Olimpia run to him and hug him as tight as they can thank him so much. Kristoffel afterwards says in a serious tone, "I have no idea where Pawka could find a better man for you. I understand you both have many things to discuss, so take a few of our fabrics and ropes, and prepare yourselves a tent just a little ways back of us, as I still think, we need to stay together. Have you thought about what you can give for a ring?" Joggeli's eyes seem sad as he asks, "Where can I find a ring in the forests?"

I tell him to use the ring we found today. Kristoffel asked him if he found a ring today. He thinks for a minute, then sticks his hand into his pocket and subsequently says, "Yes, here it is," and hands it to Kristoffel. Kristoffel looks at it and says, "Oh, do you realize what this is?" Joggeli stares at him speechless. Kristoffel explains to him that this is the ring worn by the killing pirate's number one son. These Pirates raid these lands without mercy. He takes and throws the ring far into the lake. He tells us that, "They are an advance party so the main force is most likely a few days behind. Considering we came from the peninsula and up over the mountain range, and you came from the lake, which they cannot track. They most likely will not blame us, unless they have a witness. Tomorrow, we will load the fish and start crossing back the lake in our hollow log to our peninsula where we will wade in the shallow parts of the river with our babies riding in our temporary boat. We do not want to give them an idea that we left from here, as they will most likely believe we are hiding in nearby caves. Tonight we will rustle up five large fires in our area so it looks like a small Army is camping here. We will also prepare as many arrows as we can. Olimpia, it may be a better idea if we stayed closer to each tonight. Even if they do not blame us for this carnage, the turpitude of living is enough justification for them to kill." Suddenly, with this unexpected chaos, my mind gave up the temporary serenity, I felt from watching Olimpia, and Joggeli confess their love for each other. Acia, Pava, and I truly enjoyed this. I told Olimpia that we were lucky to have Joggeli with us, and that I believe he will give her a good life, for she so much deserved to raise her babies rather than her mother's babies. She looked at me and while crying, told me the greatest gift that our mother left for her was three babies to love and to have three babies love her. Acia told her that sometimes it was not easy for us; however, we always kept our love for her. She looks at us while laughing and says, "You are special people, and our blood will keep us together forever, especially because we now have two men to care for us. We will be extremely rich."

I told her, "We cannot get that rich if we keep throwing magnificent rings into the lake." Olimpia clarifies for me that sometimes when things appear beautiful on the outside, they may be ugly on the inside. That ring was filled with death and evil on its inside. Consequently, I asked her if this could be why I have been so worried about death recently. She tells me that we are all on the edge over this death. I ask her what we are going to do about Kristoffel's son and our brothers' bodies. Olimpia agrees this to be a good question and walks toward Kristoffel to ask him. He tells her that we will leave the brothers on the peninsula and simply bury them deeper, considering that place holds family value. He will bury his son's head between them, so he may also be a part of this new extended family. Kristoffel now modifies his plan by deciding to cross the lake in the dark. Joggeli will take the hollow log across each time, with several fish and family members. He wants Kaus to go first with much fish and me. When we get there, Kaus is to start digging deeper graves for his brother. Do not move the bodies, as he will help do that to assure they transferred the bodies in a respectable fashion. I am pulling guard duty. Joggeli will take the supplies with Acia and Pava on the succeeding trip. Olimpia and more fish will compose the next trip across. He will pack all the remaining fish, supplies, place additional large logs on the fires and return with Joggeli on the ensuing trip. When he arrives on the peninsula, Kaus and he will properly bury the bodies while Joggeli takes Olimpia and the babies, with our supplies up the river in the shallow areas. Once the burial is complete, he and Kaus will load up as much fish as possible and begin wading up the river to catch up with the family. Before leaving, they will spread the remaining fish over the peninsula, so predators will come to eat it, thereby packing the area with their tracks. He figures the vegetables we have on hand will be enough to keep us fed for the next few days, as we should be able to find various fruit trees along the way. We most likely will be in the river for a couple of days, and then will ascend the stream our father always travels. He will leave certain special marks on selected trees, which are symbols that our father understands, and therefore, will be able to track us with ease.

He explains that we can travel to the top of the western mountain stay in the stream for at least another two weeks so no one will ever be able to find us except for our father. Our trip up the river begins smoothly, as we have the three moons, all in different quarters and providing enough light that we are not totally in the blind and at the same time have this concealment. Kristoffel places a stone on each of the graves and with his knife carves a special symbol on each stone. The symbol represents a place where they met his wife, and he knows that when Pawka sees this, he will understand where we went. Kristoffel likewise, leaves one of Acia's necklaces under the rock so as when our father lifts the rock, as it is their standard practice to bury things under a grave rock, he will realize his family is also with Kristoffel. Kristoffel is pleased that by early morning, they have made it to the part of the upper river where the skin-deep area is closer to the river's banks, so they will not be wading in the open as much. He knows of a cave about one hour from where the shallow waters move close to the bank where they can rest during the remainder of the day. They will travel at least two more nights before moving during the day. This is to ensure that few, if any spot them. Once he gets us in the cave, he and Joggeli go back out to snoop for any scouts who might be following us. They return in about one hour confident that no one is snooping around in the surrounding forests. We are completely exhausted as our wrinkled skin needs this time to air. While sleeping someone enters our cave and yells, "Wake up." In absolute shock, we awaken in total fear. I examine closer and see it is our father with one of his friends. At first, I think the other man could be one of our two guards, which we have not seen since we began our escape. I say hello to our father as he is hugging Acia and Pava. Looking at Kristoffel I ask him what happened to our two guards. He tells me that he released them, so they could return to their families. The silence in our cave is shattered as our father yells, "Who is that sleeping beside my daughter?" Kristoffel then calmly answers, "Oh, you do not remember that fine young man you call Joggeli?"

My father begins throwing stones at Joggeli saying, "I understand who he is; I just want to see why he is lying beside my daughter." Joggeli, now with two bruises tells him to stop throwing the rocks before he hits Olimpia, as he is getting up presently. He stands up, as my father throws another stone, this one hitting Olimpia in the head. She begins to cry. Kaus yells for him to stop. Kristoffel runs over, grabs him, and shakes him, saying, "Do not hurt your daughter. You should be thankful you still have three daughters as mine are crying from their graves now in anger over your actions. Why are you being so irrational, you fool? I hope

I do not have to knock this sense into your empty skull." Daddy goes over to Olimpia, who immediately hits him, saying, "Get away from me." Then Daddy says that he is sorry and never meant to hurt her. It was just that Joggeli moved so fast without warning. Kaus screams out now, "Daddy; he warned you and asked you not to hurt Olimpia." Our father apologizes, saying that the shock of seeing his betrothed daughter beside another man overshadowed his comprehension. Kristoffel asks him, "Who said they were betrothed?" Our father answers, "Not I, anyway, I am not talking about her and that hunter. I am talking about the fine husband; I found for her in our village. I brought your friend Bastiaan with me. He eagerly wants to take you back to our village and begin his new life with you Olimpia." Olimpia reveals to our father that Bastiaan is deceiving her and only wants her to return with him, so he can collect the bounty for her public beating to death. Joggeli immediately attacks Bastiaan as they begin fighting hard. Kristoffel picks up a club and while our father is not looking hits Bastiaan in the head, weakening him for Joggeli. Kaus stares at our father and asks him, "Why do you think we are here? Bastiaan is seeking revenge because his cousin falsely accused Yakov of a hanging offense and the village thereby executed him and his two friends. We also had to kill his uncle who attacked us on our way to the peninsula. They killed Panfilo and were enormously responsible for Answald's death. You lead the enemy into our sanctuary. Even the Spiritual Mothers should have warned you."

Our father raises his hand and says, "The village burned the Spiritual Mothers for their association with the wicked spirits." Kaus informs him that we are the evil spirits they are telling you they associated, and that corrupted them. If Olimpia or any of us return, we will die, as the only one who would save us is Cobus." Pawka raises his hand once more and says, "The also burned Cobus for his failure to enforce justice and association with evil." Joggeli, after defeating Bastiaan, rushes over to Olimpia and screams, "She is not responding. What do we do now?" Kristoffel asks Pawka, "Did anyone follow you?" He told him, "Some did up to the peninsula; however, once I saw Acia's necklace, I put them on another track. I told Bastiaan we had to stay low because there was a giant pirate

Army close to us. He slipped out that night and warned the villagers as I could hear them retreating." He hands Acia her necklace. Acia then comments, "I wondered how I lost this." Kristoffel told her, "Young lady, you need to keep an eye on the old men who sit next to you." She laughed and told him thanks. Kristoffel after this tells Pawka, "The boy must die, if what Kaus says is true. In addition, I hope you do understand there is a pirate Army heading to the peninsula. Without question, they will, wipe out that evil village of yours. This will fulfill the number-one warning to all villages that, 'if you kill your Spiritual Mothers, you will die a worse death. We realize the Pirates have tortured much more dreadful than burning. The only thing that is saving you art your family was not with them. You will be pleased to be aware that the Spiritual Mothers passed the secrets of the herbs and roots to your pure daughter." My father looks at Kaus and tells him to put the head of Bastiaan along the wall of this cave. We surround Olimpia trying to wake her. Kristoffel stands up, grabs my father by his hair, and hits him in his mouth as hard as he can. My father drops to the cave floor offering no resistance. Kristoffel asks him if he is going to fight him. My father looks at him and tells him, "I will not fight you, for I deserve this. If you believe this will bring my daughter back to us, then beat me until I never move again." Kaus now goes to Kristoffel and tells him that one member of our family who cannot move is more than enough. Kristoffel agrees and extends his hand, helping my father to stand once more. My father asks where Olimpia's roots and herbs are.

We show them to him. He rummages through them and then hands two to Joggeli. He tells me to feed this one to her and to take the second one and rub it over her head wound. His instructions are to rub in slowly and to keep it moist. He looks at Acia and Pava and tells them to sing Olimpia's favorite songs to her as close to her ear as they can comfortably get. Our father tells Kristoffel to clutch one leg while he grabs the other and to elevate it about one foot. He additionally instructs him that we will massage her feet and lower legs, making sure they stay warm. He looks at me and instructs me to keep kissing her belly telling her how much I love her. Daddy tells me to keep my head under her shirt, so she does not get cold. Kristoffel looks at daddy and then comments, "I did not understand you were familiar with the roots and herbs." Daddy tells us that the Spiritual Mothers had taught our mother about the roots and herbs. She in turn taught him a few that could come in handing in the wilderness. Fortunately, as she knew our father had a temper. She feared that he would be hit in his head, or hit someone else in their head, and kill them. Rather than risk his execution for murder, she believed that if he kept the victim alive, they would set him free, eventually. Kristoffel looked at Joggeli and told him, "Whoever you marry, remember to share both your strengths and weaknesses. If the woman loves you, she will work around your weaknesses as Perla did with Pawka to keep you." Daddy looks at Joggeli and asks him if he has anyone special. Joggeli reveals to him that he did have someone in mind; however, they have certain family problems; therefore, he is not in the mood to work around them. Kaus, while wiping his bloody knife in the cave's dirt begs Joggeli, "Come on; you are strong enough to overcome that obstacle, and if you were ever to need help, I recognize someone who would fight to her death to protect you." We remain in the cave all through the next night, as daddy does not want to move Olimpia until she awakens. During the following night, Kristoffel builds a fire inside the cave in one of the side tunnels that leads to the surface. He knows the smoke will go out that tunnel, and with the darkness should not give away their position.

Kristoffel with Kaus's assistance cooks all the fish, which he feels will feed us easily for at least ten days. He hands our father the first piece he cooks. Daddy looks at it and says, "Wow; this is a large chunk of fish. Who caught this?" Kaus tells him, "Your little belly blower and older ear singer." Daddy looks shocked and asks Kristoffel if this is true. Kristoffel tells him the hands of Yakov and Acia caught every piece of fish that we will be eating for the next week and a half. Daddy tells us, "My family has changed so much, I do not recognize if they need me anymore or not." Kaus looks at him and pats him on his shoulder and shares with him, "We will always need you. It would be virtuous if you did not try to stone us to death; nevertheless, I think we can help you in that small imperfection. Anyway, you control three daughters you must give away." Joggeli looks at our father now and then confesses, "Actually,

Pawka I do possess someone fantastically special that I love so much and want to build my future around her. I am willing to give up hunting. I will stay with her and our babies. I will care, share, and protect her with every part of my strength and my passion. I will only love her as a woman. Her family will become my family, as I boast no family." Daddy raises his hand and then comments, "Unless you are talking about my Olimpia, I do not want to hear anymore." Joggeli discloses, "I am talking about your wonderful daughter Olimpia and her three babies. I promise to care for the four of them, even if I must work from the early morning until the last night. I am begging you for her hand." Acia yells out, "Joggeli, you fool, ask him for every bit of her." Daddy begins laughing and answers, "Just for Acia, I will give all her body to you. You enjoy my blessing. Now, all we must do is wait until she wakes, which should be sometime early the following week." Kristoffel asks daddy why he thinks it will be next week. Daddy has him stop massaging her foot for one minute. He instructs Kristoffel to count the number of heartbeats he can sense in her feet. He tells daddy he counted ten. Daddy then revised his estimate and says, "She will be awake in about eight days, give or take a day. Her brain is slowly regaining its control over her body. Tomorrow, she will turn up her heat. Then each day thereafter, she will start kicking her feet and swinging her arms. The important thing is she has more than five blood thumps to her feet, so she will be back, maybe a little meaner than previously."

Daddy tells us it is just a waiting game now, and that he needs to warn our village's other hunters not to return. Even evil, if starved, will wither from us. Kristoffel argues that we need his skill of the roots here, and he has much catching up to do with his family. He will gather them and offer them a chance to form up with his village. Kristoffel asks if any other these hunters possess family in our village. Daddy tells him that our village forbids families; nevertheless, many hold families spread throughout the region's villages. Kristoffel shakes his head and says, "I should have been listening to you throughout all these years. If I had been, I would have belted you long ago and brought your family to my village. I am so sorry." Daddy then confesses that he was trying to hold a long tradition for our family. Kaus tells him, "That prolonged tradition would have made me a hunter and a stranger to our greedy village." Daddy then tells Kristoffel that he may need to lead several false tracks, as our village has a few overzealous retired hunters who are looking for one more day of fame. Off into the dark went our Kristoffel as a spirit of sadness currently wrestled with the damp chill of our cave. Our father currently asked Kaus and I to help him carefully scoot Olimpia deeper into the cave. As he was settling Olimpia into her new resting place, daddy told Kaus to keep an ear on the outside for anything out of the ordinary. He was concerned that with all the chaotic scattering through the wilderness from our village could confuse the Pirates just enough that they would accidentally discover us. Once we had her settled and bundled extra tight, he told us it was a waiting game now, and if we simply wanted to talk with her that would be wonderful. Thereafter, he believed that this cave had a delightful warm room deeper down, so he would go search for it. After he slipped away, I looked at Kaus and Joggeli as we realized we were responsible now. Joggeli volunteered to clean the entranceway to the cave. Most Pirates will not search too deep inside a cave when the entry is undisturbed.

He then went outside to the stream and filled Olimpia's water bags, dumping the remaining water and refilling every bag with freshwater. After verifying that no tract identified our area and our hollow log laid upside down beside a few other loose branches and decaying logs, he returned to us. We were restless, knowing that we should be in the wilderness running for our lives, yet instead we were here for a greater cause. Without Olimpia, nothing seemed to fit together any longer. Food was simply food. Sleep was boring, although not as boring as being awake. Even the thought of love and playing was disturbing. How could one person mean so much too all us? She stood her ground and if it was good for her babies, they were going to get it. She was responsibility and loyalty. Even the Spiritual Mothers told me how much they respected her and how lucky our mother was to have her as a daughter. I used to watch the other mothers with their children screaming and hitting them to gain their obedience. They would gawk at Olimpia with envy as she would calmly call for us, and we came running without hesitation, stopping for nothing. As our sweaty, rapidly breathing bodies appeared before her, we each received our reward kiss and grabbed each's hand as we went our way, which of course was Olimpia's way. She would watch the other children; we were playing beside, and tell us stories about how bad youngsters suffered. I remember the story about the children who decided to hide from their mother to see if they could cause her to cry when they did not return. The children saw the hole that their mother had told them never to play. Something bad would happen to them if they went inside this hole. One day, these kids saw other youths playing in the hole. They sounded as if they were having so much fun. They now decided that their mother had lied to them, and that they would punish her. They hid inside the hole and refused to answer when she called for them. She walked all over their play area calling for them. The children laughed quietly inside the hole. The remaining mothers became afraid for their youngsters and took them home immediately. The village guards came to search the play area.

They stuck their heads inside the hole and called for the offspring, yet no one would answer. Finally, they believed the children went into the forest and became lost. Therefore, everyone left the play area and began searching in the woods for them. The juveniles believed the adults were hiding in the play area waiting for them to exit the hole. As a result, they remained quiet and decided to wait until the night until they left the hole. Nighttime soon arrived, and as they were preparing to leave the hole, they heard a strange noise. Nevertheless, scared, they remained silent behind several rocks. The next week, when a few other kids went to play in that hole, they discovered these children's shredded clothes and saw bloodstains throughout the walls inside the hole. They immediately exited, the pit screaming. The village guards inspected the hole, filled it with wood, and burned it. After they finished burning, it, they crammed it with stones. No one ever again played in that den or recreation area. Olimpia had so many stories such as this. We never went anywhere she told us not to go. I believe that we obeyed her not from fear of her anger, but from the hurt of causing her sadness. She would cry when we disobeyed her. That hurt us much more than any public whipping. Olimpia's dedication and hard work warrant

love and obedience. Acia is taking this hard, so I realize it is, time
to help her. I walk over to her and Pava and ask them if we can talk
for a little while. Acia asks me if I think Olimpia will become better.
I tell her, "We appreciate that our daddy knows how to survive in
the wilderness. I do not believe this to be a serious condition, which
should compel you to worry or became sad. If Kristoffel and daddy
believed this to be grave, they would have still been here. Olimpia
has worked hard for many years and therefore, deserves a temporary
rest. Remember, she lives in our love, so keep pouring your love
for her, and she will once again stand tall and strong." Pava falls
down on Olimpia. We can hear that minute puff of air exit her lungs
from Pava's weight. Although her face is not showing it to us, I
understand she is smiling inside. Acia lifts one of her eyelids and
waves at her.

I do the same with the other eyelid. Kaus discovers what we are
doing and tells us to stop. I tell him to concentrate on the things he
knows, and leave our mother to us. Initially, he appears angry about
my response and comes over to take us from Olimpia, who in her
cloaked anger kicks her foot. Kaus drops me when he witnesses her
foot kicking. Acia goes to him and asks him if he stays back, and
leaves the hard work to us. He smiles, in shock, and steps to the
rear. The three of us start to wallow her. She always enjoyed this so
much. We sing her favorite song that she loves accordingly greatly. I
hold her hand and begin kissing it. She wiggles three fingers. Kaus
witnesses this and jump for joy in his excitement. He confesses, "I
do not recognize what it is about you little guys; however, Olimpia
does and will live for you. She knows how lucky she is to have your
great love, dedication, and hearts." While he is talking, she kicks her
other foot. We elect to calm things down for Olimpia now and allow
her to rest. Our boring day rolls into a boring night. Joggeli returned
just after dark telling us that the villagers are scouting this area.
He additionally gives us a bag of fruit that he picked throughout
his scouting. Our father left yesterday and has yet to return. I
start to worry if something could be wrong. Kaus volunteers to
begin looking for him. Joggeli overrides him explaining that he
understands our fathers tracking system, such as Kristoffel's system
where they leave signs so when they return they will not get lost.

Joggeli rushes deep into the cave. I inform Kaus that we must force our father to teach us these skills even if we are not to be hunters. We still must be survivors. Late the next morning Joggeli and our father return. We explain to our father how Olimpia is responding to several our questions. After congratulating us, he explains that we must go deep into the cave to a warm spot he discovered that has a lighted large cavity in front of it. We will be warm and have plenty of air to breathe. More important, we should be much safer, and even if danger finds us, we will have more exits. He tells us to pack up our belongings and for Joggeli to tie Olimpia to his back. Within a few minutes, we are trudging deep into this dark cave. Although stepping down continuously, I ask my father if we have to climb back up to get out. He shares the great news with us that this cave has an entrance not far from where we will be staying for the remainder of Olimpia's recovery.

That is the pleasant news; the not so delightful news is the entrance leads to the bottom of a nearby pond. It is not that far of a swim to the surface, yet in exchange for this inconvenience we should not worry about the villagers invading us. We reach the appealing warm place that actually has a small stream bleeding water from a wall. It is oddly shaped. I guess that I could not expect perfection this deep into the ground. The cavity has a ledge that runs along its northern wall, with a small hole that two people could sleep in if they scooted in body crawling on your elbows. The ledge that forms the lazy 'U' in front of it will give us enough space so all can sleep on this side. We immediately tuck Olimpia feet first into our private hole. Daddy does not want to chance her waking up and banging her head once more. He also wants her babies playing with her. We have selected area to walk around, and an acceptable open area in the middle to eat and store our supplies. Daddy tells us not to worry about hiding things, for if something comes this far down, they already realize we are here. While we are standing in a circle, a small rock hit Kaus's shoulder. He spins around telling us that something just hit him. Kaus tells our father that he is going to go up and see if anyone is watching us. Daddy asks Kaus if he wants Joggeli to join him. Kaus tells him this is something he must do. Up to our entrance, he quickly ascends out of our view. I hear a small thump, as if someone were falling. His spear comes flying into our cavern. I run over and grab this spear positively identifying it as belonging to Kaus. Daddy and Joggeli stand calmly. I yell at them, "Did not you hear that thump? Something is wrong. This is Kaus's spear. We need to save him." They sit down and begin eating several of our cooked fish. I complain to them and demand that we do something. They continue to ignore me. Therefore, I tell my father that if they do nothing, then I will. He tells me I cannot go unless Olimpia approves it. I run over to Olimpia and ask her to wave one finger if I can go to save Kaus. She does not respond.

This calls for certain creativity, so I decide to ask her to move no fingers if I can go to save Kaus. She moves all her fingers. Joggeli subsequently invites me to join them for this lunch. I tell him that I will save Kaus. Daddy gazes at me and tells me, "Do not you think it is wrong to disobey your mother?" I tell him that she does not understand how terrible this situation is. Daddy tells me to sit down and try to remember a few of the things he taught me. After that, Kristoffel returns with Kaus's hands tied behind his back. Kaus's face is red because of his embarrassment. Kristoffel guides him to my father and reports, "Here is your dead son, Pawka." Daddy thanks him and tells me to stand beside him. He then tells both of us that we have two choices. If we want to do as we please, we may leave this clan forever now. Go through the pond and never gaze back. The second choice we have is that we may remain and be his sons. As his sons, we will obey him and not go off on our wild attacks as Kaus just did. He continues by explaining to us that he saw the two graves that hold Panfilo and Answald. He is not in the mood to place additional sons beside them. Staring at us, as we dwindle in size he adds, "I have shown you the rock trick every time I played games with you, have I not?" We shook our heads yes. After this, he reports that if we are to live in the wild, we must think before we jump. If we are to jump into the easy traps to glorify the villagers, and then we might as well surrender now. Daddy surprises us by asking Kristoffel if he has anything to add. Kristoffel verifies that what our daddy is telling us will keep us alive. He also discloses that many villagers are roaming around this cave, and he removed our markers and reset them to a few tunnels, which end with cliffs. Daddy asks him how the villagers became so smart at this fast. Kristoffel leaks that several of Pawka's hunters had joined the villagers before he found them. He discovered half of them or four and sent them to his village. Daddy looked at me and asked that I untie Kaus and remain here. He then told Kristoffel, "This is a hard thing that I must do now and that is to kill four who served me so well." Kristoffel told him, "You are wrong. This is a tough thing we must do, and I think we can get two of them inside this cave if we get to it instantly."

They grabbed their long knives and went up our entry hole. I wondered why they left their swords behind. Joggeli explains these swords are of no value in a cave and the risk of them hitting the walls and making noise is greater than their offensive benefits. Kaus and I stare at each other. Joggeli comforts us by saying, "Do not worry; we will teach you and within a few years, you will be as ghosts roaming the wilderness." Daddy and Kristoffel captured two of his scouts, executed them, and moved their bodies to the other side of the river. They left the group signals to show the scouts intended to cross the river. Kristoffel tells us that they will most likely waist one week on the other side and return in time to greet the pirate invaders. We should be up to the stream and moving east by then. Each day, we waited, in this belly of the world. Olimpia continues to sleep. Our hope rests in that she has moved ever so much more each day. This family rotates as we have someone massaging her hand and talking with her each day. Day nine will arrive in just a few hours. I could not sleep as if by more or less a form of magic that my father could forecast this recovery with such accuracy. I must be aware of every little part of her face and almost started to count her hair once, nevertheless, when the number got more than my toes and hands, I had to stop counting. She has done a fine job at covering up the hard knocks she has received throughout her young life. This final one from our father could leave a mark; however, we will trade that mark in thanks if she returns to us, or I guess when she comes back. I just wish she would tell me to do something. The days and nights are so boring when I do not have anyone to order me to sleep. I understand that Kaus and daddy are trying hard; nevertheless, only Olimpia's voice puts us to sleep. We pretend to snooze, only to get them out of our hair. Life at this moment is different. This accident is taking its toll on our family. We grasp that danger is around us, and we are almost as sitting ducks in a helpless position. Daddy keeps reassuring us that we have many benefits going for us now. His two deserters would plan that we will go north, as he always talked about living in the Northlands. Daddy kept his dreamland a secret. It is a land called Cvetka. He appreciates it because it has no mountains. This land is composed of small rolling hills with minuscule streams to fish. He plans for us to live in the northern part of this land close to the people known as the Jožefa.

They are nations that travel the seas and are most times at war with other tribes. He has a treaty with one of their chiefs to live in peace. Daddy enthusiastically pulls out a small coin, which confirms this treaty. By having strong nations to the north and south of them, they should not have too many dangers. There are the sand lands to the west and these mountains to the east. He brags about the wide variety of plants and trees that grow within this region. Daddy tells us that large herds of grazing animals roam these lowlands. This translates that there will be no long hunting trips. We will not live in a village at first; however, through the years, he suspects that other families will join our small settlement. Kristoffel returns with a bag of fish and fruit. He tells us the Pirates are moving to the river to face the villagers. We will have to sit tight for at least another week. Daddy pulls out several pirate rings he has collected. Kristoffel then smiles and tells us, "I have a strange thinking that your villagers may be in for certain hard times." Daddy adds that he will have to place these rings extremely carefully, or his defectors will find them. If they find a ring, they will realize we are still in this area. Kristoffel also reports to us that he sank our hollow log in our pond. He fears that his action may not have been in time, as a few footprints were in this area around the log. He rearranged the area by appending several rocks and additional broken branches so the area would not appear as it did before. We can only hope that when the scouts return, they will not recognize the area. If for any strange reason, we need our log again, we can swim out into the bottom of our pond and roll it to shore. Daddy then predicts the scouts will move ahead of their people and verify if the log remains. If we can get those scouts, after that this group of killers would be traveling blind. The trick is to kill them, before they enter our bay, which will be difficult, as they will most likely bring their Army up the river. Kristoffel asks daddy if they could hide in the trees at the upper bend.

Daddy tells him the weather has been dry lately, and the leaves are crispy and will fall into the river. The scouts may notice this. He then smiles and says, "We might be able to use this to our advantage. We will shake the leaves and afterwards pick them off from the rock ledge above it, which has the rock stream behind it." Kristoffel smiles and says, "That is perfect. We slide in and out like ghosts. We can leave a shirt I took from your ex-scout as a welcome card from the villagers. These am sure the Pirates will enjoy that." Daddy then projected the Army would come over the dirt paths on the ridge and that extra dust in the air would tell them when they were coming with plenty of time to set the trap. I enjoyed listening to how they would set the plan. Kristoffel tells Joggeli that he should take Kaus with him to set the leaf trap on the river. The villagers left plenty of logs tucked against the trees that they can use to navigate the river. Daddy looks at me and tells me to take care of our womenfolk. I smile and shake his hand. They go to the mouth of our cave, as daddy tasted the dust in the air, so they jumped into action. Meanwhile, I study Olimpia while she is sleeping. We move her legs and arms exercising them so when she awakes, they will be easier for her to control. Pava asks us if we have knowledge of when our mommy wakes up. I tell her that she will soon, at least she is still breathing. Joggeli and Kaus return within the same night. Joggeli brags how well they set this trap. While Joggeli was bragging, Olimpia made a strange noise. We stared at her as she wiggled her fingers. Kaus tells Joggeli that his woman is proud of these great achievements for our defense. Our joy is short lived, as the next day, only Kristoffel returns. He complains the scouts had a protective platoon with them, and they ended fighting over twenty-five of them. They battle hard until the exhausted all their arrows. They still had about half of them remaining. They ended in a rock fight in which they killed another four; however, our father became hit with a rock. Daddy fell over the rock ledge they were fighting beside, and into the flowing stream. Kristoffel could collect those hit by rock's arrows. With these, he killed five more. The remaining three began to run. He got two of them with spears; nevertheless, one remained.

Kristoffel dived into the river and could flip the boat and hold the lone survivor under the water drowning him. When he returned to the tree site, one of the men hit by a rock was recovering. He immediately took his knife and finished off those they previously crippled with rocks. Kristoffel, knowing he had a little extra time as a scouting party, this large is usually far before the approaching Army. He now looked over the cliff to his side that our daddy went over, in hopes of discovering him. Our daddy was not in sight anywhere. He decided to assemble the dead bodies belonging to the scouts into a formation facing the river to create the appearance of an attack from the sea. He retrieved all our arrows and replaced them with the scouts' arrows. He did not recognize how to set this scene as so much had happened during this chaotic battle. Kristoffel decided he had another mission of a higher calling, and that was to find our father. He searched under every rock and behind every tree, until he could smell the Army in the air, and then he slowly worked his way back to us. He suggested that we waited until this massive Army pass through, as large Armies must move through fast to keep their soldiers fed and focused. We will then search hard for our father. The remaining part this continued to haunt me. Death was flirting with us now, by taking us slowly. Olimpia would not wake up. Our father was lost in front of the Army that wants nothing more but to kill anything that moved. They were even famous for killing that which was deceased simply to ensure it was dead. We do not realize if our father now suffered from the injury all his fall. So many questions are bouncing in our minds. Why did our father hide from Kristoffel? He had to have hid from him, because he knew exactly where Kristoffel would search. Something was not adding up in this crisis as our family dwindled. I almost felt like taking Acia and Pava and freeing them from this nightmare that would not end. Somehow, I naturally ended beside Olimpia's head and began to cry. This cave feels cold and empty, as if it is making a wall between me and everyone else. Kaus, Pava, and Acia also appear to sit around dazed at what is slowly destroying us, giving one kick at a time.

We pound the word hope so hard into our heads that our foundation begins to crumble. Now, instead of walking we crawl on sharp rocks that cut without mercy. I cannot hold this back. How can I pretend to walk straight, when walking on air? We were supposed to be building a new life. Instead, we are already in our grave deep under the surface and losing each step we take. Olimpia only sleeps. Daddy just returned maybe permanently to destroy Olimpia's life. Everything is so confusing now. If only mommy woke up, she could fix everything. I glance at Acia and Pava as I can see they sense my sadness. How can I pretend to be strong when my mind and body are betraying me? Why have hoped, if you only hang on to hurt more? I can see no way the Army could bypass us, even though we have hidden ourselves so perfectly. There must be a leaf we forgot to flip on this mountain's other side, which has the road map straight back to us. Bad luck seems to enjoy hanging around us. Kristoffel comes over, sits beside me, and tells me it is good to cry and let it all out. I tell him I am a man now and should not be crying. He tells me if am going to be a man, I must never forget to cry. When he tells me this, Olimpia hits me with her hand. It actually hurt. I jumped so happy now and asked Kristoffel if he saw that. He told me that he not only saw it, but he felt it. That was a solid hit. Your mommy will be back soon. You had better give her a kiss before she forgets she hit you. As I turned to kiss her, I heard another voice say, "You had better save additionally one for me." I looked around and saw my father. He looked ragged, but he could hop on down into our little cavity. Everything really turned around fast for me. I had a tough decision to make. Should I become joyful and take a chance on getting hurt again, or ought I to stay in my self-absorbed pain? This time I would be happy, as Olimpia depended on this, and I suspected mommy was going to wake up before too long. As I went to hug Olimpia, daddy started his story. I yelled back to him to hold the story until I got there beside him. My face went down quickly to kiss and hug my special mommy. Astonishingly, both her arms embraced me.

Joggeli yells for all to see. I am in a total haze. Fate puts me so close to breaking down, seeing my end in sight and having no hope to continue. However, the new hopes are flying as if an Army were unleashing all their archers on me. No time to think, I simply keep telling Olimpia, "Mommy, come back, mommy came back . . . mommy came back." Within seconds, Acia and Pava are holding on to Olimpia's arms and begging mommy to come back. Our father decides to postpone his new tale and alongside Kristoffel, Kaus, and Joggeli slowly slide Olimpia out into our lighted open cavity about ten feet from where she was resting. Daddy looks at me and relays, "We need to give her enough room to return, right?" I glimpse at him with a smile and return to my chanting. Papa opens Olimpia's herb bag and sprinkles a few herbs on her face. She sneezes and then yells for someone to get her a rag. Kristoffel spreads a thin rag over her face. She begins to kick slowly. Afterwards, her arms release me and grab the rag, wiping her face. Daddy next tells us that she will be back soon and suggests that her children feed her. At first, I wondered why he gave such a great honor to us. Afterwards, I saw the mess we made on her face. We went to clean it when dad shook his head no. He wanted this on her face. I went over and asked him why he needed that we leave her appearance in such a mess. The old man just looked at me and smiled, saying, "Because she hates it. I want to force her to be mad. Now, you keep working on being kind to her and let me be the bad guy in this one, okay son." I shook my head yes and instantly returned and began tickling her feet some. She always loved this. I knew not to overdo this as too much laughing without the muscle control to release it could cause her one or two difficulties. Daddy sat on a rock nearby and began to tell his story. Kristoffel and I were dropping them evil raiders as if they were flies. As I began to run short on arrows, I decided to hide in a few rocks. The rocks behind me would stop a handful of my enemy's arrows and therefore, give me a chance to retrieve a little additional firepower. I shot all my arrows and those lying around me. While continuing to search, one of the raiders leaped over the rock in front of me. I pulled out my long knife and stabbed him as he dropped over me. Next, I rolled him over to the cliff nearby me when I noticed a few arrows lying on a small bush only about two inches from my grasp.

I scooted my dead counterpart's body out over the ledge and while stepping on him reached for the arrows. While reaching, this body began slipping over the edge taking me with it. We floated in midair toward the stream below us. I knew enough to lie on his body and use it for my impact to soften the blow as much as I could. We hit the stream as I could hear the splash whack his body to an unusual extent. The stream slapped his body with only three feet deep of water to cushion the impact into the rock bed that absorbed the remainder of the crash. I broke free on the small rebound from his crash and swam the stream for a short while, wanting to get out of the view from our hilltop point. I thought about going back up to help Kristoffel; nevertheless, with no arrows, I figured to be more of a burden than any help. In addition, with less than a dozen remaining, he should easily be able to handle that. While relaxing, enjoying the sunshine and preparing to start singing I noticed company was approaching. Another squad of about twenty men was approaching. I slipped under a nearby bush and grabbed the last man, cutting his throat and taking his arrows. This was such an easy kill; I did it five more times. Now the group merely consisted of fourteen men, and they were beginning to ascend the cliff that had fallen. One by one, from the bottom up, I started picking them off, as soon there were only five remaining. They were getting close to the top, so I changed my firing pattern and started popping the ones on top. The first two, I shot in the base of their neck and while falling grabbed the companions taking them to their inevitable death. One remained and as he went to reach the last rock to the top, I placed an arrow in the back of his head. As he fell, I rushed to the site where the two without arrows lay and stabbed all to ensure they were dead. While stabbing them, I noticed they had their head choppers (axes) with them, so I chopped every head I found and collected all the arrows. The next hill over offered a fine lookout point, so I began transferring all their weapons to that lookout point. I laid all the heads along the bank of the stream, while piling their bodies at in the open field beside it. The only chance I could have is if this looked as a fight those in the top or a surprise raid from the sea. Ending my first delivery to this new station, I noticed that Kristoffel still had five warriors against him. Therefore, I loaded the raiders' long arrows into their bow and picked off the remaining five who were hiding behind rocks waiting for him to walk by.

He looked at Kristoffel and complained, "You need to be more careful. After retrieving all my additional arrows, head choppers, water bags, food bags, and spears and placing them in my new lookout point I noticed more trouble. To my shock, Kristoffel was searching for me on the wrong side of our previous station. This worked to our benefit as another squad ascended to this point. I picked them off one my one, as they were hiding in the brush below me, which I could see them easily, and they could not see me. Subsequently, I figured out now that three squads on a single area were a sign of big trouble not far behind and that each squad had a bit of time behind them. I took my head chopper and transferred most of their bodies to the other side of the stream where I chopped their heads. After consolidating all their equipment, I carried it up the little stream that ran from a spring inside my defensive position. This took about one hour. I then noticed that Kristoffel was fighting warriors from the sea. Quickly, I loaded the long-range arrows and began dropping them one at a time. Shortly thereafter saving him again, I noticed yet another squad coming through the identical pass as their predecessors. Easy picking again, and continued the same routine. I noticed that Kristoffel had departed from our area. This gave me a little relief in that now I only had to defend myself and pluck away at this inflow of danger and death, without also having to save him." Kristoffel flowed with the story, as I believe we knew it was slowly emerging into a tale that was a little too much to believe. He rose and offered his hand in thanks to my father, who shook it while also rendering a slight wink. Kaus asked him where the arrows and head choppers were. Daddy told him that when the large Army appeared, they forced him to retreat through the trees as quickly and quietly to such an extent possible. He was able to bring the field food.

He then went up our entranceway and began dropping four Army bags packed with field food. Kristoffel examined these bags and in shock told my father, "My goodness, Pawka, this is enough food to hold us for at least two weeks." Kristoffel helps distribute the bags in our open cavity to concoct them easier for us to stockpile for our meals. Daddy tells us that we might as well relax, because that Army will take a couple of weeks to move through if we include all the stray scouting squads. I can hear Kristoffel telling Kaus that this is about three squad's field food. I gaze at my father with a new sense of pride. He was out there and will always come back to us. I may have found certain solid ground to rebuild my young confused mind. The life of a thirteen-year-old in the wilderness is not going to be easy, as I also have Acia and Pava to protect. I have my sisters because I want them. It begins to become clear that Olimpia has us because she wants us. Daddy must have us because he wants us. Why would he struggle so hard to keep us safe, to any extent considered possible from the soldiers that are destroying the world above us? His disappointment is how the Army and our villager sorcerer hunters have not met yet. Kristoffel agrees that additional planting evidence of the villagers before this militia will only distract them and lead them astray. It is, time to allow the villagers to generate their own blunders. I ask daddy how he knows the villagers will cause these slip ups. My father looks at me and comments, "Because I have never seen them do anything right nor have they ever listened to me, so why would they listen to my scouts? Knowing your enemy is equally important as fighting him. If they will hang themselves, why give them the rope?" I smiled at him, as I always do, and then told him, "This will all fall into place with me when my mommy wakes up." I noticed a twinkle flash in his eye when I said mommy. We never actually called Olimpia our mother when he was with us. This to a certain extent slipped from my mouth as my self-control is waving. Notwithstanding; I force myself to appear in control and smoothly walk over to sit beside Olimpia's head. My father has told us many times that someone who loses his or her self-control is dreadfully dangerous. The last thing I want to do now is muddy the water running over the new strong foundation I am trying to build with my father.

He follows me and joins us beside Olimpia's sleeping body. My heart is pounding, and sweat begins to pour from my head. I understand this must stop, as daddy can sense fear from afar. He begins to speak. I am convinced that he is going to put me in my place without hesitation. She is the powerful force that has controlled our family for so long, slowly and calmly, absolutely completely. I appeal to her, "Mommy, you need to wake up. The babies want you." Olimpia wiggles all her fingers, and a smile emerges from her beautiful lips. Our papa takes her hand, gently kisses it, and once again starts speaking, "I so wish Perla was here now. She could see how hard you are keeping your promise to care for the three little ones who love you as much as Kaus and I do. I have told your mother so many times what a wonderful job, you are doing. Of how Yakov, Acia, and Pava are the happiest, most dedicated children in our village. More important, they have the love and respect of the Spiritual Mothers, as you so much wanted them to possess." Olimpia's eyes are rolling under their eyelids rapidly now. I can sense strong vibrations rolling around her body. Daddy continues, "Your babies belong to you, and I think they need cleaned and fed. I would appreciate it if you helped us." Her eyes flash open for the first time since daddy accidentally hit her with a rock. Our father motions for us to swarm her with kisses. Acia and Pava join me as we slowly pounce on her and flood her with, "Mommy wake up, mommy wake up."

CHAPTER 05

Trouble with women

Not surprisingly, minutes move slower than before; however, I suspected that we are progressing to something better, so I can endure the extended, prolonged wait. Excitement sends a signal to the Suns to stop and slow everything to a halt. Even in the few short years, I have been dodging arrows, I now that excitement invites carelessness and therefore, control inessential. This almost feel as good as when the dark day's end and the time to play outside once more arrived, after helping to replant our gardens of course. This time, I am going to release, because I must pull Acia and Pava back into our little circle. They tried to get my attention many times, which I kindly ignored. I judge myself bad that when they needed me; I was falling apart. There must be a way that I can work this out for us. By it, I walk over to them and ask if they want to play. They look at me as if I am a stranger and turn away. My young wisdom with girls told me that on this first try, I should retreat and look unhappy. Notwithstanding; I sit in my corner looking sad. My misfortune awards me be presenting our father before me asking me if I want to play. This is too good of a deal to pass, so I agree, and we begin playing. Kristoffel joins in, and they start wrestling me around as if I am with my air, which I am to them, either way I am screaming in total fear and fascination. When we finish, I find myself so exhausted that I am immediately falling asleep. I wake up about one hour later to see two sets of inflamed eyes staring at me. Acia and Pava are so furious; I can sense it from where I am sitting. Because I am the boy here, I must go to them and see if I can seek a compromise. When I approach them, they turn their faces from me. This is the time for stage two, so I begin to use my advance skills. I explain to them how I am so sad without them and want them to forgive me.

They turn around and start throwing dirt at me and in my face screaming, "You looked happy when you were playing with Daddy. You keep Daddy just for yourself." Daddy yells over, "Acia, do not throw dirt in someone's face. You could hurt their eyes. Now be pleasant." Oh, this was not a good thing for me. My little hearts decided it was time for me to learn not to get younger sisters in trouble. I never paid much attention to what they carried in all those pockets that Olimpia sewn onto each of their dresses. I simply knew it was, so they could do things I did not want to do. Acia invites me to sit down beside her. She now tells me I have been a dreadfully bad boy, and that I am just like Panfilo. In fact, so much like him, they are going to start calling me Panfilo. I look at them, sad of course and masking my desire to hit them, and tell them that this is therefore, unfair. Acia takes something thin and long from her pocket and stabs in my leg. She smiles and says, "If you scream, we will get you every time Daddy leaves." I asked her what she used to stab me. She tells me she merely poked me with a needle, and that she has the little ones. Pava smiles and says, "I got the big ones," and into my other leg, she injects her needle. I look at them and report, "I never thought my sisters would be so evil. Lucky for me, I discovered this before I must take care of you when you grow older." Acia smiles and pokes me once more while sighing and declares, "We will tell Olimpia, and she will force you. So prepare for a long life of bitter pain." They are pushing me beyond my ability to control myself, so I blurt out, "Not if I tell her first." Acia and Pava rush to occupy each of Olimpia's sides and growl at me, "Try it." My happiness is beginning to take a few serious hits here. Acia and Pava swore their loyalty to me for all the days of our lives. Our days ended before I realized it. They are different. I used my best cards on them, so now is the time for me to join with Daddy and Kristoffel and try to fill in the open gaps created by the loss of Answald and Panfilo.

I walk over and sit down beside Daddy with a stunned look on my face. He asks me what is wrong with me. I tell him that two ghosts just visited me, and they came as Acia and Pava. He puts his arm around me, and requests that I tell him the whole story. "Daddy," I begin, "the change in Olimpia has shattered everything that I once stood on. She was constantly there, most times before. I always had her at my side to lead Acia and Pava. When Olimpia went to sleep, I did not comprehend how to react with Acia and Pava. The pain they were releasing scared me, and I ran from them. They want revenge presently. I was so afraid that I would hurt them. I was only protecting them until I worked everything out in my mind. How could they turn therefore evil so quickly?" Kristoffel, who has joined us looked at me and said with a serious stare, "Son, I would sooner wrestle with thirty Pirates than one angry woman." Daddy quickly added, "Make those thirty five Pirates for me to one woman with your mother's blood in her. Let me go again and talk to them." Daddy walks over, sits at Olimpia's head, and says to his daughters, "I was so preoccupied since I returned to verify how my little angels are doing. You think there could be something we could do together?" Acia tells him, "Daddy, we are girls and do not do those boy things like we did when we were babies." Daddy looks at Pava and asks, "Are you still my baby?" Pava shakes her head no and says, "I am a mommy's baby. She is the one that is here with me all the time." Daddy looks at them and says, "Well, unfortunately because she is sleeping, you only hold a Daddy for now." Acia tells him, "Olimpia will be returning real soon." Daddy after that suggests, "I guess she will want to see Yakov when she moreover wakes up." Pava tells Daddy, "No, she only likes good boys. When she went to sleep, he did not do what he promised her he would do. When she wakes up, she will be extremely mad at him?" Papa asks Acia, "What did that bad-boy promise Olimpia he would do?" Acia tells him, "He promised to be strong for us. When Olimpia went to sleep, he started being cruel to my sister and me. He did not protect us, while we were in this dangerous situation." Daddy asks her, "Honey; Daddy came home, and Daddy's job is to protect his family."

Pava asks, "Daddy, when did you put Olimpia to sleep?" Our father explains to her that this was an accident, and that he is trying hard to wake her up once more. He additionally tells them that since we are in a wonderful, safe cave and possess our food, she can rest now. Acia complains, "Or she could be having fun with Joggeli. Yakov is also trying to get us in trouble with you by saying we are terrible." Daddy then asks Acia, "Were you girls bad to him?" Acia defends herself, "Father, we told you he was a liar and an awful boy. We are good girls. Do not you believe us?" He looks at her and says, "I believe that all my children are good, my little princess. I will return and talk with you in a little while." Pava cries, "You will come back after he tells you those bad things and beat us. I know." Daddy looks at her and says, "He only says good things about you, and how much he truly loves you. Anyway, you realize I never hurt my little girls." Acia responds with, "I am sorry Daddy; I cannot trust you until Olimpia wakes up." Daddy walks back to the men, when Kaus asks him how it went. Daddy tells them, "They are scared and confused. We need each to spend some time with them and let them vent. Meanwhile, we must build some defensive plans if things turn bad for us. I saw some Vandens vines in the trees above our pond. I think that we can cut the ends to maybe eight or nine of them and pull them into our pond opening and use them to breathe when the Pirates smoke out this cave, as they do too often." Kristoffel calls for Joggeli and confirms that we need to get this done quickly, because we also need to rock in our entrance, as loosely at possible, we go away to seal it when the smoke begins. Daddy looks at Kaus and asks him to chat with our little girls and see if he can loosen them up to some. Our father grabs a few regular knives, and away they go jumping into the pond and swimming to the surface. Vandens vines grow, wrapping themselves around trees and will drop into ponds and lakes and resurface elsewhere to climb another tree. They are hollow on the inside, use this space for moving moister, and with such a wide-open internal flow, area creates perfect breathing underwater tubes. They are flexible and take much time, sometimes even months, to wither. They grow just about everywhere; therefore, most people ignore them.

Once they get the open ends into our cavern, Daddy grabs some rope and goes back into the water to tie these vines to some underwater tree roots. This will keep them from moving, as is common knowledge that they anchor themselves extremely secure. Kaus goes over and sits down with his sisters. Acia looks at him and remarks, "You are only here because everyone else is gone." Kaus tells her, "Yakov is still sitting solely in his corner." Acia discloses, "He should be alone; he is not brave and does not protect his friends." Kaus asks Acia, "Are you still his friend?" Acia laughs at him and cools Kaus a fool. Kaus then asks her, "Must Yakov also be brave when our clan has Daddy, Kristoffel, Joggeli, and me?" Acia and Pava both respond with a yes. Kaus next asks them, "Does your Daddy let him fight beside us, or would Daddy get mad?" Acia answers, "We do not want him fighting beside Daddy; we want him fighting in front of us. Does he think we are not good enough?" Kaus answers, "Acia; you realize a son must offer to fight beside his father first. That is the law. And if I thought he was better than you, would he be looking so sad in that corner?" Acia asks Kaus, "When someone cannot be trusted, it should be better to shun them. I heard one of my friend's mothers tell her this." Kaus responds, without hesitation, "Remember. Those people will all die because they killed the lovely Spiritual Mothers. If the relationship were based in love, then understanding why would be better than shunning." Acia tells Kaus that they will wait to see what Olimpia says before they punish me. Kaus returns to me and tells me what they said. I ask him for some recommendations. He tells me that he has never really had to deal with anything like this before, because he never argues with Olimpia. I question him about why he always obeys her. He tells that when he does, Olimpia offers to inform some of her friends, he is a fine and kindhearted boy. Therefore, he has received a few special kisses from them. I tell him that this is more serious than that stupid kissing stuff. Olimpia gives us all the wonderful kisses in the world, so you are foolish for wanting that so much. Kaus tells me that he is too old to kiss Olimpia and if they were to do such a thing, they could get into big trouble.

Arguing with him, I tell him that family kisses are forever and different, except for mommies and daddies. Kaus once more recommends that we stay here until Daddy gets back and while waiting move some rocks toward our side entrance so they can work on sealing it for us when they return. We start moving around a few rocks, and then he helps me as we go into our entrance to look for some loose rocks. We must be careful so as not to leave any signs for the Pirates. When we depart, Acia calls for Kaus to return and protect them. Kaus tells them that Olimpia said Yakov was their protector and that Olimpia did not allow him to protect them. He adds, "Any ways, Yakov is smaller and can kill those long black snakes that are hiding in that hole where Olimpia had her feet yesterday." Acia looks over in the hole and says that she cannot see any snakes. Kaus tells her that is because she does not possess boy's eyes and then adds, "Nevertheless, do not worry, Daddy has herbs that will wake you up after the snakes bite you. I sure hope he did not use up all the pain herbs on Olimpia. Oh well, you two stay out in the open and listen for any strange noises." They sat beside Olimpia and remained extremely quiet until we finished. When we came back down, they ignored us, as if they had everything under control. Acia calls me over to them. I think maybe that we may be friends again. She tells me, "I just want to tell you how sorry we are for trusting you, and that we will never trust you anymore. If you think you can get others to scare us, so we will like you again, you are foolish." I am completely flabbergasted and stand there before them silent. I do not want this fighting to continue, so the only thing that I see to do is to retreat. I simply answer, "I am so sorry to hear that. Tell Olimpia, if she ever wakes up, I will help her find some herbs for your new sores." I solemnly turn around and return to Kaus. As I am walking back, Daddy pops his head out of our small pool and asks for my help. I begin pulling vines up. He tells me to pull them slow and no more than five feet inside our cavity. Kristoffel and he keeps popping their heads for some air, then back down they go. Kaus joins me as Joggeli pops up out of the water.

Within just a few minutes, all the vines are out of the water. Kaus is draining them, so we can use them for breathing. Daddy pops us and tells us that no one may talk any longer. We may only whisper, because these vines, likewise, carry noise to the surface. Once the Pirates start smoking us, we must leave these veins attacked to our faces, because the smoke can also go up to the surface. He calls us all into a circle and begins his speech, "Family; they are on their way, as we saw much extra dirt flowing in our nearby stream. I cannot figure out why they are so determined to swing this way. We believe that they are avoiding the hill where we killed so many of their scouts. That could also suggest that they would totally clean that area. Strip every leaf from every tree. We can only hope they find enough signs from our village, as I left so much. The main force may be more concerned with getting across the river. If that is the case, then a small squad will smoke out this cave, and we will be breathing through these vines for only a few days, as they will do other caves in the area similarly to smoke out. When they begin to smoke several caves, smoke will seep through the surface in many places. That is when I unplug the extra vine, I hold here to pull our smoke out when the Pirates leave the area. We all will be under much stress so please, no fighting among each, another. Life and living are our hope now, and that game just became harder. We will sort our food out so that everything is close to each of us. Eating will be harder, as no noise, and you must keep your vine sealed. Take one bite, chew slowly for a long while then swallow. There can be no burps or any unusual noise. These scouts boast ears like the birds. Kaus, help me with these herbs, we must knock Olimpia out for about four days. I hope that will rest her sufficiently so she will be strong enough to come out of her sleep, because once the scouts are gone, we wait one day for the trailing scouts, then we go without delay. Everyone must catch your breaths for a few minutes, and afterwards we will finish sealing our entrance. We can do this." We all scatter around as I help Joggeli sort out our field food and distribute it in small piles. He asks me if I am having any girl problems. I tell him that I did not grasp that little boys like me could possess such big girl problems.

Joggeli reminds me that I must be patient. He elaborates on how Olimpia put him through that trouble earlier and how I saved him. If I can save him, then I should be able to save him. I tell him this is different because, "They are new people and own so much hate. Who are they?" Joggeli tells me they are growing women. I tell him that, "I can now understand why so many men want to be hunters. They are getting away from all these women headaches." He tells me to be extensively patient, as they understand how to cause him to be angry, and they will go for the weakest first. If you are truly someday to be a father, you must learn how to control your anger. He reminds me how patiently our father is handling this situation. I glance over and see Kristoffel sitting down beside them. Notwithstanding; I motion for Joggeli to be silent so I can hear what I will be trouble for next. Kristoffel begins by telling them, "I sure do miss watching the way you little guys would play and be so happy. Bet you we cannot count all the little scars on your legs from all those trees and ditches you use to battle to save our family and Olimpia. Acia explains to him that this was when they had a brother, which loved them, cared for them, and had not abandoned them. Kristoffel tells them that just yesterday their Daddy abandoned him and left him searching in dangerous territory for him while he relaxed and had all the fun fighting the squads. He asks them if he should forgive our Daddy. Acia tells him she would not. Pava says she would. Kristoffel tells Pava that she then still has a Daddy, and I guess the family must find a different Daddy for Acia. Acia tells him that she does not want a new Daddy, for all daddies are bad. Kristoffel calmly smiles and says that one time they had to kill the evil father they found. They were hunting in the northern lands when the sound of children crying began to flood the air. It was such sad crying, and they could hear a loud cutting whip snapping in the hot air that evening. They ran quickly to the place and saw ten children, five girls and five boys all tied up to trees and their backs beaten. Daddy threw his spear into the back of one man who was beating the little screaming and bleeding girl.

As he threw his spear, two additional ugly men who had no teeth and no ears, came running at them with head choppers wanting to kill them. Kristoffel tells how he quickly pulled out two arrows and shot them hitting both in their heads. When he shot the second one, an arrow came flying past his head. He could not see where it came. The children were bleeding so much that they knew if they did not stop their blood loss soon, they would die. Daddy ran around to the back of the house and started a fire to burn the house. The house soon began to burn quickly. The front door came, open and three women came running out with long knives. They were running to the children. He did not understand what to do, so as Daddy came back around, they put arrows in their bows. One of the girls began yelling for help from these killing women. As she was yelling, one of the women cut her head off with one swing. Immediately, Kristoffel and Daddy killed the three women. They walked over to untie the children and try to save them. All five of the boys were already dead. Only two of the little girls still lived. As they uncut, the girls they ran to their brothers begging them to forgive them for telling lies to their parents about them. Her remaining sister died while trying to get to her brother. We kept the last sister alive for the rest of that day; however, the next day, she was dead. She kept telling us through the night how sorry they were. They had been fighting with their brothers when their father tried to stop them. They accidentally killed their father, and the neighbors came to punish them. The law of that land was that if children killed a parent whom the child would die. The sisters hated the brothers, so they told the parents the brothers did it. They strung up the brothers and beat them to death. They watched all their brothers die in so much terrible pain. As the last brother died, two of the sisters confessed that they had been a part of this. The village then beats them to death and decides to thrash the other three sisters for not telling the truth that they knew the innocence of the brothers. Kristoffel, who has tears flowing from his eyes, tells them, "I sure hope your hate does not get your family killed." I ask Daddy if that story is true. He tells me it was such a sad time for them.

I tell him I want to go and attempt to solve our problems now. He tells me they could get angry and yell at him; therefore, rather than take the chance, we should wait. Kristoffel picks up Olimpia to lay her in the back part of this cavity, the one with the dark hole. As they are tucking Olimpia in there, Pava complains there could be snakes, and they might hurt Olimpia. Daddy tells me to go hide in the dark place, and if I see any snakes to kill them. I run into the dark hole. They planted Olimpia in front of me. Pava complains to Daddy that this is too dangerous for her brother to be alone with all those snakes. While she is talking to Daddy, I sense something moving beside my leg, and I sling my little knife as if my life depended on it. I squeeze around Olimpia and pull what I just hit outside into the cave's cavity. Daddy tells Pava not to worry, "Yakov already got one of the little ones, and he will kill the other twenty by early morning." I pulled both halves of the snake out and laid him in a straight line. He was longer than Kristoffel. Daddy orders me back into the hole. This time I went in a lot more vigilant. I am terrified, yet if Daddy told me to do, then I must do it. Pava cries for Daddy, "What if he dies?" Daddy tells her, "Then Acia will be happy, and we will entertain no more family fighting." Acia looks at Daddy and says, "Yes," turns her back and sits beside Olimpia. Our father tells her that she cannot sit there because it could be too close to the snakes, and if she yells, the Pirates could capture us. Acia tells dad that I am moreover a big coward. Daddy tells her, "He will not scream, as he has just proven. Nevertheless, I will hold you and Kristoffel will hold Pava. Like it or not, young lady, I am your father and your mother gave you to me." Acia did not even want to challenge this because Olimpia told us so many times that our mother gave us to our Daddy, and that he is the boss. That is why I am sitting in this snake bowl waiting for the snakes to eat me or for me to eat them. Pava whispers back to me, "Yakov, you must be careful. If you do well when we are finished, I will hit you hard anywhere you want me to." When I hear this at first, I am confused, and then I remember that Pava is still dreadfully little, so I believe she is saying something good to me, so I tell her thanks. When I give her my thanks, Acia hits her in the face. Daddy grabs hold of Acia and tells her no noise and that if she must make noise, they must drown her now.

He adds, "If you must hate, then you will hate in the land of the dead alone. Like it or not, I am going to keep the rest of my family alive." I am surprised in that I was not happy to hear this, because I do not want her to drown. So I whisper out, "Acia, if you be good and do not drown, I will let you beat me with our Daddy's whip." Acia smiles and whispers, "Okay, Daddy, I will be quiet. I am so happy now. Ensure you do not lose your whip." Daddy looks at her and says, "If that is what you want Acia, and if Yakov agrees, I guess I must let you harm one of your mother's babies." I sink back into my darkness. I never thought Daddy would agree to this. The only hope I enjoy now is maybe a snake may bite me. So much, trouble, because I wanted to keep our family together. If rewarded in this manner for every good deed in my life, then why should I be humane to others? What would my sisters do if I were as those Pirates or notwithstanding our villagers? I am not even cruel enough considerate ever to hope such a thing for them. I can only hope that each time I become overloaded the remainder of my life that I do not suffer such as this when I try to recover. I separated myself from those whom I love so they would not be hurt. If only my real mother had remained alive. If's do not solve our problem now. I understand that when Olimpia returns and Daddy gets us to our new home, things will be so much better than. Patience is a thing that I hate because it just makes things so much more out of place and confusing. Daddy and Kristoffel are finished with our seal and as the first trickle of smoke enters our shaft, they work on the final sealing. All their work and the smoke continue to enter. We recognize that if the smoke is settling this deep the scouts will not be able to drop down and search this cave in person, as so many side tunnels will backlog the smoke. We sit here hushed as possible while the smoke slowly continues to pour into our cavity. This is somewhat like fog except that it smells so strange, and it makes us cough. The comfort is that all is quiet. Daddy prepared us well for this what is actually a boring experience. The only excitement is an occasional mouse running in front of us. We sit like statues and follow them with our ears.

I cannot see the excitement in being smoked out in a deep cave while breathing air through a vine that runs through a pond. Did I mention the Army of Pirates is moving through and the village of killers on the other side of the river that want to see us dead? The icing on this cake is that soon, we will be carrying my sleeping sister through the wilderness trying to escape from all this excitement. I enjoy the most excitement as a few snakes tried to zip past me, as they do not like the smoke and are moving among the rocks and through their secret tunnels. The smoke is flushing all the life from the immediate soil below the surface; therefore, they should be having some excitement in the world above us. Almost wish I could be there to enjoy it. Nevertheless, I appreciate that disruption will still abound when we return. It just may not be as exciting, yet more than likely will be more enjoyable than handing from one of the nearby trees with a Pirate knife in my back. I guess I need to rethink this because according to Daddy who is only for the lucky ones. I notice that Kristoffel and Daddy create a new mark on the ground each time they wake up from a long sleep. I made it a practice to pull out the snakes; I had been splitting. Their senses are dull, thus making them easy targets. We hold the belief that this hibernation will soon end. Silence abandoned us as screams and pleas for mercy highlighted by Pirates' cheer shot arrows of fear into our precious souls. I could sense people beating against the cave walls as their bodies met the rock walls without either compromising. Our only consolation was that they sounded as if they had died at once. Daddy, who makes his rounds to check on everyone about once each hour tells me this could mean they are in a hurry, or expecting a big fight, thus must clean up fast and move on to their next point. One morning, what I would suppose as a few days later, as sometimes this is hard to distinguish if a new morning has arrived or a long nap during the current day when I awoke, I noticed a fresh partner lying beside me. It was little Pava. This reminded me somewhat of our previous times.

Soon, this temporary partial truce dissolved when Acia rushed between us, slapped me and pulled Pava back to her designated sleeping place. Daddy pointed at us to be quiet, so I watched little Pava be pulled away while holding my peace. The hope I now enjoy it there may be a small division in their iron curtain. The final resolution must rest with Olimpia's return. Joggeli has worked hard and silently caring for her during this smoke time. The smoke is starting to thin out a little, which I can see some relief beginning to reemerge on this clan's face. Daddy and Kristoffel slowly drop into our caves pond, and then thereafter swim to the surface. After scouting for a few hours, Daddy returns and tells us to prepare for our departure. We are returning to the real world. He has Kaus carrying me as he takes Acia and to the shore, we go. Once there he tells us to hide between the two trees on a small hill hear the pond. We are watching each other's backs, which gives us a 360 view. We are close to a stream, which he tells us to look at the clarity of the water. Any changes, brief him or Kristoffel when we return. Kristoffel was on our lookout point and is now dropping into our pond. He goes and has Joggeli help him bring Olimpia while directing Kaus to bring Pava. Daddy is now occupying our lookout point as the remainder of our stole ways begins to emerge. Kristoffel sends Kaus up to relieve Daddy who is watching our northern side. At this time, he journeys to a lookout point on the southern side of our position. Daddy and Joggeli now go back in the pond to recover our hollowed out log and roll it close to the shore. Once in shallow waters they emerge and lift it out of the water and onto the shore, hollow side down to release as much water that they can. They roll it into an open meadow about thirty feet from this pond. Daddy tells us the Suns will dry it out quicker this way. I ask him why we need the hollow log. My father tells me that we will be following streams all the way to our new homes and as such will want to carry our supplies and Olimpia in the log. He stresses that Olimpia may be too weak for walking the first two weeks she awakens. Acia refuses to talk with me while we are watching the low hills that surround us. Everyone appears to be busy preparing us for the journey before us. Kaus and Daddy are catching fish and cleaning them. Many streams of smoke drifted into the sky, from the cave openings the Pirates ignited. Even Daddy did not realize there were so many caves in this area.

These smoke streams will allow Daddy to cook our fish as long as the wind is blowing east to west. The smell of cooking fish with a westerly wind could alert some lagging scouts. He plans to cook enough fish to feed us for a couple of weeks, so when we begin to move we can move rapidly. Last afternoon our father motions for everyone to join him. We sit down and begin eating our food. Kristoffel tells us he now believes that another Army is moving toward the Pirates. The Pirates appeared to form a defensive line on the other side of the river. This will give us an advantage by moving west, as their positions on this side of the river are solely to hold their flank. If they retreat, they will do so by going back north, which will suck their enemy not far behind them. Daddy senses the apprehension among us and tells us to relax, as soon we will hide in the green of the forests. Our log dried out within a few days. Daddy returned from his scouting. Kristoffel rushed out into the green forest, returning the next morning. Our family met that afternoon as Daddy and Kristoffel explained that we would be leaving late this night traveling the stream beside us, so as not to leave any tracks. The cool air that night felt as if it was blowing in our freedom. This excitement overshadowed my current struggles with Acia. Pava now bounced between Daddy, Acia, Kaus, and me. Pava was proving to be much smarter than we originally had given her credit. She did not want to be in the middle of any family struggles, so if Acia and I were to get in too deep with our fight. Pava unfortunately, has seen how family members die, or go to sleep and she wanted people to hold onto for the long life she needed to be awaiting her future. Acia's separation intensified as she clung closer to the sleeping Olimpia. Our first morning back on the surface soon released the moons and invited the two Suns to brighten the sky and warm our damp bones. The brightness from our Suns gave us another surprise in this morning. Our fortitudes gave up their walls, as we believed our eyes were deceiving us. Olimpia sat up in the boat and began crying, holding her head. As if she was still living at the time, the rock hit her scalp.

Daddy stopped us immediately as he and Kristoffel pulled Olimpia from the hollow log and pulled her out on the ground, ensuring that she remain quiet. Even though we are a safe temporary distance from the Armies, those who live in this area were apprehensive for fear that, dislocated people from the other lands would try to resettle in their areas. This is why Daddy wants to travel during the nights and stay in trees, or thick forests during the days. Olimpia begins by striking and kicking Daddy and Kristoffel. She is behaving as a wild animal. Acia rushes beside her, yet Olimpia also pushes her aside screaming, "Stay far from me, you kidnappers." Daddy looks at her and quickly ties a fur strip around her mouth as Kristoffel labors hard to tie or feet and arms.

Acia begins to cry. I rush to help her. She almost for a minute let me help her, before pushing me away. Kaus then grabs her and tells her to relax and stay calm. Pava asks Acia to be quiet. All this rumbling and struggle from within almost took away our appreciation for the land beside us. Next to us is a large meadow covered with yellow flowers as if an ocean of waving yellow. This yellow is so powerful that it even colors the rays from the low sun as they flood this meadow. The heat rushes in beside it, causing the yellow flowers to stand and us to place our hands above our eyes. We soon reform with our backs to this powerful array of light beams. Olimpia looks at each of us with hate in her eyes. I start to think that we may be facing another Acia on our hands. Olimpia responds, "Who are you kidnappers and why did you take me from my family?" Daddy asks her who her family is, and where can we find them. She looks at him strangely and says, "You poisoned my mind," looking around at each of us once more, "that little one beside you art mine." She was pointing to Pava who remained halfway hidden behind our father. Daddy pointed to Acia and asked if she meant this one. Olimpia tells him, "No, she looks too much like you and that tall boy over there." She was pointing at Kaus. Acia begins to cry. Daddy motions for her to join him, now that Olimpia is holding Pava.

I am so sad for Acia, even though I realize she would have used her relationship with Olimpia against me. At least currently, I am not the only one that someone hates within this clan. The big boys are now trying to decide how they will control Olimpia. They begin by agreeing to tie her to a high branch and to keep Pava separated from her during the days. We will keep her a few branches higher so that Olimpia can see that she is okay. We will let Pava ride in the hollow log with her at night. For now, Pava is giving her a big hug and saying, "I love you so much mommy. I am glad you woke up." She continues by telling Olimpia that a rock hit her head, by accident and has been asleep for two weeks, and that we are running from some bad Armies while hiding from the black-hearted people who live around here. Kristoffel tried to explain to Olimpia the danger they could be in, and if she made any noise, these people enjoyed killing little children. We slept through our days and would begin on the stream in late evening when poor visibility ruled the lands. Olimpia continued to deny knowing us and if any went to touch her, she would hit them hard. Acia was now enormously withdrawn. She mimicked Olimpia's hostility. It was as if we had a big Olimpia and little Olimpia to fight. Daddy was wondering how we could keep our family together. He decided that it was too dangerous to continue under these conditions, so he decided when we passed a cave that he knew was a few hours ahead; we would unpack and settle there until we worked out our problems. If we cannot become friends again, then he will remove a few members of our family. He was serious. If he takes Acia, I can figure she deserves it, as she did not suffer from an injury. I believe that Olimpia is innocent. She did not request Daddy to throw the rock at her. Our family is both hiding our hollow log and moving our supplies into our cave. Kristoffel at first ties Olimpia to a rock in the cave yet keeps Pava with him. Acia sits inside to watch Olimpia. Olimpia asks her to untie her, so they can escape. Acia asks her, "Why would you want to escape with me, as Pava is your daughter is she not?" Olimpia explains that she just said that so they would think they had control over her.

She knew all along that Acia was really her daughter. Acia rushes to her and unties her. Olimpia takes her hand, grabs a bow, knife, with arrows, and travels deep inside the cave. She has no idea where she is going. Olimpia believes that because there is a draft, an air vent or opening on the surface can exist. They wonder as soon they see a small light above them. They negotiate the stones and work their way to the hole at the top and slide through it onto the surface. Olimpia looks over the area and decides to run from the stream deeper into the mountains. Meanwhile, our clan after settling into the cave discovers something is not right. I ask Daddy where Acia is. He looks around and then asks Joggeli, "Where is Olimpia?" Kristoffel and Daddy search around our cavity in the darker corners and discover nothing. Then Daddy tells us he feels some footprints leading into a tunnel in front of us. Kristoffel tells our Daddy, "We can always follow those tracts; nevertheless, we recognize the best she can do is to find an entranceway and escape into the mountains. We would do much better to rush to the top of the mountain behind us and try to spot her running. Something will give her away. I believe that we should be able to set up four lookout posts." Daddy agrees and out, we go. He tells Pava and me to stay with Kaus at his lookout point. This plan actually works out well for us, as within about one hour, we spot them. We had not only spotted them, but we also notice something we did not enjoy. Some hunters were tracking them. Daddy sent Kaus back to our cavern with Pava and me. Kristoffel, Joggeli, and Daddy went forward to figure out a way to save Olimpia. The problem for them was if they saved her too fast, she might not believe she was in danger. Her private journey with Acia through the woods ended abruptly as they stepped into a rope trap that pulled them into the sky. The men surrounded them and after leashing a rope around Olimpia's neck cut her feet loose. They ignored Acia. Olimpia fought with them trying to get back and free Acia. As she raced toward Acia horror crippled her to the ground as Acia's blood dripped down on her. These killers had shot three arrows into Acia, killing her instantly. Olimpia turned toward them and slung the knife she had hidden in her pants.

The knife hit one of the men in the head. By now, Daddy and our clan were in position and unleashed their arrows, picking these killers off with ease as the remaining six dropped to the ground. As they fell to the surface, Olimpia took her knife and cut each of their throats and the leash around her neck. Daddy came over, without looking at Olimpia, and cut down Acia where he held her and cried. Kristoffel and Joggeli joined the group. Olimpia held her knife pointed at them. Kristoffel tells her, "You can put that knife down, because we are not here to hurt you. If we wanted to see you suffer, we would simply go back to the stream and float off without you." Olimpia asks them, "Why would you want to save me and my daughter?" Daddy tells her that she is a daughter, and Acia was her sister. She calls him a liar and says she knows Acia is her daughter, because she has so many memories with her. Daddy asks her if she has memories with the other little boy and a little girl. She confesses to be confused over those two. Daddy then explains to her how their mother had died long ago, and that she was raising those three as their mother, so in that sense she will always be their mother. Her father looked her in the eyes and said, "Olimpia, I am your father, and this is your clan. Nevertheless, I will not lose Yakov or Pava to your foolishness. If you want to go on alone, I will not stop you. If you want to stay with us, we will care for you. You must tell us your choice. Just remember one thing, if you take another of my children away into this danger again, I will be the one who shoots the arrow in your head. We are the same blood and only kill each to save ourselves." As he finished, he took Kristoffel and Joggeli while holding Acia and walked back to the stream. No one looked backward to see if Olimpia was following. She actually was following, yet trying to avoid detection. When Daddy brought Acia's body back into the cave, we began to cry. Olimpia was hiding at the entrance as she had stayed close to them. When she heard them crying, she entered the cavern and told Daddy she was sorry for killing Acia. Daddy lay Acia down and then turned to Olimpia and opened his arms. She dropped her weapons and slowly walked toward him.

Olimpia stopped walking when still just out of reach from Daddy's arms. Daddy dropped his arms and then told her, "Olimpia, it was an accident. We cannot expect you to understand that those killers were waiting to ambush you. Move around as you please and eat as you wish. If you need any help you, let me know." Olimpia notices that Pava and I are crying over Acia. She walks over to us and asks me, "Why are you crying over her, as I never saw you talking to her?" Pava explains to Olimpia that Acia hated him because he was so sad when she was injured. He then withdrew from everyone. I inform her that I was being patient with her, for I knew that we would once again become best friends. Olimpia looks at me and asks, "You were best friends?" Pava reveals to Olimpia that Acia, she, and I was the greatest best friends ever and promised to live together forever. Olimpia asks us if she is our real mother. We explain that our actual mother died, and that she promised to be our real mother. She asks us why we do not hold a home. We tell her that she took us to be with our Daddy because the people we were living among wanted to kill us. She then shakes her head and comments how everyone seems to want only to kill. After this, she asks us to explain who everyone in this group is. When we explain that she and Joggeli were to get married, she becomes irritated. I ask her what is wrong, and she explains that she is not ready to be with someone. I look at her and reveal, "Mommy; we understand that." She looks at me with a strange temporary glare then smiles. It was almost the same as she remembered something. Daddy and Kristoffel take some Acia into the dark tunnel and cover her with dirt and rocks. I cannot believe that she is dead. I wonder if she died hating me. Consequently, I ask Olimpia if Acia told her she hated me." Olimpia tells me she never talked either way about me. I guess this will be a mystery that will remain unanswered until I ask her when I venture to the land of the dead. Daddy calls us together and explains to us, "We will be back to the streams again tomorrow, this time as a clan, even though some things are forgotten, we need the patience to endure." In the late afternoon, Joggeli goes up to his lookout point to see is any danger is around us. After watching intensely he determines the area to be clear, and motions for us to start loading our boat. Once more, we begin walking as the evening becomes darker.

Olimpia wades in the water this time, as she puts Pava and me inside the boat. She wades beside Kristoffel, which she later explains was because she felt safer beside him. Daddy tells us that within two weeks, we will be in the low hills. Kristoffel and Olimpia chat about so many foolish things. I can see her becoming more at ease around him. She tells me each day that some more memories are returning, such as the roots and the herbs. I tell her this is a significant one as healing is important and that if Daddy had not known about this, she would not be alive now. Each day, she is spending more time caring for Pava and me. Pava follows me everywhere currently, and I do not even hint at resistance. I realize never to withdraw again. The last thing I ever want in my life any longer is a sister who hates me. Olimpia surrenders a restrained cry as she slips and hits her head on a rock that was sticking out of the water. She was so preoccupied with Kristoffel's story that she was not paying attention. Into the water, she drops as Kristoffel quickly secures and moves her body to the shore. Daddy takes some fur strips and wraps them around her head. They laid her back into our hollow log. Pava and I remain as our supplies are dwindled currently. Daddy tells us to keep her warm and tell him if she moves. When morning arrives, she remains sleeping. Kristoffel finds some trees for us to sleep under, so the Suns do not burn us. Just as we are about to sleep, Olimpia jumps up and calls out, "Who are you and where I am? Why did you kidnap me?" Daddy looks at her and answers, "Oh no, not all this trouble again." Olimpia walks over to him and says, "You evil man, is that the way to talk to your oldest daughter?" Kaus rushes over to her and asks, "Do you remember me?" She answers, "Which one, the last time you did what I asked you or the last time you got into trouble?" He rubs his fists on her waist as she begins to laugh. Kaus looks at our father and says, "I think we got the mouth back." She swings at him as he ducks and begins to run while laughing. She chases him and reminds him that he can never escape her. He trips as she lands on him, grabs his arm, making a painful L behind his back, and easily marches him back to camp. She asks Daddy what she should do to him.

Daddy laughs and recommends that she let him go because we should not hurt someone so ugly. Olimpia starts laughing at this recommendation as Kaus flips himself around breaking free. He immediately sits down and says, "Uncle." Olimpia tells him that Kristoffel will not save him now. I tell her that Kaus is really giving up or surrendering. She laughs at me and tells me she knows that. Olimpia now struts over to in front of Joggeli and informs him, "The children told me that I possessed something you want. Do you understand what that could be?" Joggeli looks at Pava, Daddy and me gazing at him. His face turns red and he stutters, "I do not remember." She looks at him, lightly pinches his cheek, and says, "Oh well, that is so sad, because I had something for you, yet if you cannot remember, it was not that important to you." She now looks at Pava and me and says, "Your ears had better be clean or your behinds will be red." We immediately grab water bags beside us and start cleaning as fast as we can. Daddy smiles at her and says, "Welcome home mommy." Kaus and Kristoffel also welcome her back. Joggeli is sitting with a confused look on his face. Olimpia tucks us in and gives us our goodnight kiss, a ritual we missed so much. We both told her repeatedly how much we love her. She goes over, sits down beside Kristoffel, Daddy, and they begin chatting about what plans they made for our new home. They ask her for her opinion. She tells them that she does not really care, while we are all together. Joggeli confesses to her that he now remembers what he wanted from her. Olimpia grabs Kristoffel and our father's hands and tells Joggeli, "Sorry, whatever your name is, if you forgot so easy then I could not have been that important to you." Kaus asks Olimpia to give some mercy to him. She tells him to shut up or she will pound him until he no longer talks. Joggeli looks at Kristoffel and asks whether he will help him. Kristoffel tells him that he agrees with Olimpia, to why she should give her life to a man who forgets her so easy. After this, Daddy wraps his arm around Olimpia and says, "Oh, you poorly abused brokenhearted woman. How can I ever mend your broken heart after this?" Joggeli, trying to defend himself asks, "What was I supposed to do, say I wanted to be your lover in front of the little kids?"

Olimpia looks at him and crying says, "Oh Daddy; he only wanted my body to be his toy." Kristoffel looks at him says in an extremely angry tone, "How could you lie to me and tricked me into thinking your intentions were honorable?" Daddy looks at him and shakes his head. Joggeli trying once more exclaims, "You are all causing what I say to sound bad." Kristoffel tells him, "We do not need to do that Joggeli, because you are doing this for us." Olimpia now cries out, "Papa; I cannot believe I loved him so much." Joggeli asks Olimpia, "What must I do to win you to me once more?" Olimpia tells him, "You can begin by leaving and never return." Joggeli, now overtaken by anger stands and replies, "I will not be treated this way by any woman. I am out of here, good-bye!" He gathered his things and vanished into the woods. They were somewhat surprised at how he rushed away to easily. Olimpia asks Daddy if she was too hard on him. Daddy comforts her by saying, "If he leaves that easy, let him go. It would simply be a lot more trouble for you in the future." Kristoffel agrees with our father and tells her there will be many new boys who will come along her way. Olimpia asks him how he knows this. Kristoffel tells her the boys always find the girls, and they never miss, any in their searches. Olimpia remarks how our family is growing smaller each day. Kristoffel tells her that this is the way of the wilderness. He next recommends that we enjoy some much-needed sleep. That night we load up and begin floating once more. The streams are beginning to lose their depth. Daddy tells us that most likely tomorrow night, we will hide our hollow log and continue by foot. While wading once more through the night, Kristoffel notices someone hang from a nearby tree and goes over to explore it. He returns, warns that now is the time for us to prepare for some trouble, as we should hide our log here by sinking it. We must start our walk through the forests when possible. Olimpia asks him what he saw hanging from the tree. He tells her that Joggeli was hanging from the tree, and if they can catch him, we are in too great a danger to continue in this stream.

Our father looks at him and agrees. Olimpia volunteers to carry Pava as Kaus volunteers to carry me. Kristoffel offers also to carry me as Daddy offers to carry Pava. Olimpia tells them not this time, as we need their scouting skills to stay alive. Kaus and I can carry our little loves. I look at Kaus and ask him if he loves me. He tells me that this was supposed to be a secret. They all laugh at this. Pava and I wonder why they are laughing. Daddy tells us that we will go straight south from our current point to confuse any who attempts to track us. While walking along toward morning during the times when it becomes hard to see anything, Pava begins to cry that something bit her. Kristoffel looks up and sees a long snake. He immediately swings at the snake cutting his head off as we watch it hit the ground. Daddy instantaneously cut her bite and starts sucking out her blood. Olimpia grabs the snake's head and squeezes something out of its big teeth and then mixes it with some of her herbs and water and pours it down Pava's throat. I ask Kaus what they are doing. He explains that Pava was bitten by a hanging snake, and because we do not recognize if this is poisonous or not, they are drawing the venom out of her wound. I ask him if it was the poison, why Olimpia had her drink some. He did not see the answer, so we went to Olimpia, who was pounding some roots to produce a salve to put on Pava's wound. I asked Olimpia why she gave Pava the snake teeth's juices to drink. She explains the herbs she added to it diluted its power and that Pava's body would start making little fighters to fight this poison. She could be sick for a few days, and we must wait to see how fast she recovers. As she looked around, she told us to follow her. We came on an old campfire. She gathered the burned black remains from the logs and put them in her bag. I asked her what she was doing. Olimpia told me she was collecting Pava's lunch. She could not give it to Pava until the herb and snake water had time to soak into her body. Kristoffel comments how large the campfire was and explains that one tribe must rule this area, as they obviously are not afraid to camp in the open. Daddy now tells us to follow him, and we begin walking once more. Kristoffel tosses the dead snake into a bush so no one will find his body split.

Kristoffel is looking for a small brush area that we can hide in and get some sleep. When we lie down, Pava's body begins to move out of control. Her face is strange and legs kicking the ground hard. Pava is slapping her front with her hands and trying to roll around on the ground. Olimpia asks Daddy to hold open her mouth and begins to push the burned murky wood from the campfire as deep as she can. Our older sister gives her youngest sister, a small drink of water to help slide the black crushed wood into her belly. Pava coughs and then fall to sleep. We watch intensively as her chest expands and contracts, which tell us that she once more breathed. One by one, we each slowly fell asleep. I fought hard to stay awake, yet could not do so. If I had known, what awaited me when I awoke my battle with my sleep would have been more combative. As my eyes began to focus on our clan, I noticed something was missing. Tears start to flow down my eyes, for I could not find Pava. Olimpia's face was red and swollen, as if she also had been crying. I asked Kaus where Pava was. He put his arm around me and confessed that she was now with Acia, Panfilo, and Answald. Counting Joggeli, we had lost three people since we reemerged from the cave. I am having great trouble in deciding if we were wise to fight for our survival, or were we simply postponing something that had to happen, that being our deaths. The fear of dying now filled my life, as I could not understand any joy in living. What were we trying to accomplish? If Olimpia had offered me to our village as a sacrifice, so many in our family who were now sleeping in the dirt, would instead be playing in the dirt. She thought that saving one was worth the gamble. I must now live with the fact that my life has too much blood sacrificed. Our faces all reveal that this family member was too much to lose; she had not had a chance to live yet.

We were hurting for this one. She was in all our hearts being too little to walk, as we had to carry her. Everyone in our family wanted to carry her, except for me. I did not believe myself wise enough to protect her, as I was too afraid of physically hurting her. She was the vessel that we poured our love.

My future would not include my two sisters. I was truly working hard to become a great protector and thereby give them long lives. The bodies of our family members are now scattered to where we will never be able to find them in the future. I remember how in our village, families would be buried beside each, another. Many in our family will spend eternity alone, which I think is so sad. I can only hope the land of the dead has a way to find all these dead bodies spread everywhere. Kristoffel alerts us to how the dark clouds are forming, and that we need to move forward now, because when the rains begin to pour we will seek shelter. I ask him why we do not walk in the rain. Daddy tells me because we will leave deep, long lasting tracks, which will alert others that we are in this area. Kaus picks me up and off, we go. The only supplies we carry now are Olimpia's herbs and our weapons. As we exit, I realize that I did not get to say good-bye to Pava. Thus, I will keep a secret as I grasp the time is critical for us now, and we must keep moving. Our father leads us halfway up to a hill and then along the side of these hills. The winds are beginning to blow harder and the air is chilled. The dark clouds are now controlling all the sky above us. Our father stops walking and begins to motion for us to join him. He points to a cavern that we can enjoy as some shelter during the hard rains that will soon fall. He also points at some fruit trees that Kristoffel rushes collect a bounty. Not long after that, he comes rushing inside with a large collection of fruit branches packed with fruit. Daddy tells us to eat much, as this will return energy to our bodies. We will need extra energy to fight the damp weather. He also leads us into a tunnel saying that others may try to seek shelter in this cavern. I ask him what we will do if others enter. He tells me that we will wait until they are vulnerable and then kill them. Before, I may have questioned this; however, I now consider the time has arrived for some others to suffer from all this dying. Kristoffel tells me that many times shelter seekers will pretend they do not realize we are in here and then once the rains are finished to seek their friends and return to kill. This makes sense, to me. Just as they had predicted, not long afterwards, a group of four men entered our cavern's open area. They started a pleasant fire and unpacked the game; they had caught that day, and then began to cook them on their fire.

We patiently waited until they finished cooking. The fire, at the same time, was warming the open area and chasing the dampness from this rain-free area. Kaus, Daddy, Kristoffel, and Olimpia each loaded their arrows and on Kristoffel's signal fired at once. Each hit their target except for Kaus. The man who he shot at immediately loaded his bow and shot at him. As he was shooting, Daddy got him in the face. Kaus could duck and avoid the arrow, which hit the rock in front of him. Daddy told me to cut their throats, which I cut two and Olimpia cut two. We next moved the bodies back into the dark tunnel. I helped Olimpia carry the smallest man. Daddy broke the Pirate arrows; we had used to kill them and tossed them deeper into the cave. We could find a side tunnel to place these bodies, hoping this would buy some extra time if; we needed it. Afterwards, we rushed back out to the semi-open area and put out the fire, tossing the smoldering logs into the rain. Next, Daddy told us to eat the meat quickly, before the smell made it any deeper into the forest. We collected their weapons and supplies. Daddy did not want to use his Pirate arrows unless necessary for fear the locals would believe a Pirate invasion was in process, and thereby form a fighting force to chase them down. The 'them' would unfortunately be us. By using local arrows, they may think it to be outlawed among themselves. The large quantity of meat and fruit that we ate proved beneficial as the rain continued for one week. Daddy told us that when we left, we needed to find a little stream and walk on the rocks. The small streams would be high because of all the rain. This week was long as my heart longed for the two Suns to share their light on my body. We also did not understand if another group entered, so we spent much of our time in one of the tunnels. This cavern actually had four tunnels that ran into the darkness. We stayed jointly as one, as Daddy told us that we must keep our killing force together. I thought it odd that no other hunters came into this cavern. Kristoffel explains this as the side hill of our being well hidden, and that only experienced hunters in the area would understand about it, as evidenced by what the hunters who we killed had with them.

Daddy heads out to the area in front of our hideaway and after a few minute's returns with what may be good news. He explains the hard winds had removed many leaves from the trees, and this should allow us to walk without creating long-term tracks. Kristoffel volunteers to walk last and hide as many tracks as he can. Daddy tells us not to walk the same tracks as the person in front of us, as that will form those tracks deeper and harder to hide. More tracks beside each, another help to spread the weight evenly and push more down, thereby helping to hide the tracks. Either way, he wanted me to walk so Kaus would not be heavier and my tracks should fade away quickly. Hiding that we were here so we can be somewhere and in the process be alive confuses me to no end. We walk for a few hours, long enough for our Suns to be riding in the middle of our sky as pass some fruit trees. Daddy tells us to collect some fruit and try to render as least noticeable noise that we can, as he is going to do some quick scouting. He returns in an hour and tells us that he could see no danger in front of us. The streams were flowing strong, so we should be able to jump from one to another and continue for the remainder of the day. He wanted to travel during the day now, as he had seldom been in this area to hunt because the locals forbid others to hunt on this land and had the killing power to back it. If we continue to pack fruit, do not hunt game for us, and continue to move on, they may ignore us. The minute we begin to hunt, the invisible will become visible. He hoped that by having a woman and little boy with them, they should view us as a family heading for the rolling hills beyond the mountains. Our father emphasized that this included many maybes. Daddy said the best way to stay away from this trouble was to avoid, as best, starting it. He would get a better idea of our situation tonight, as these locals enjoyed forming into larger groups for their night camps. When nighttime arrived, we went into the trees to sleep. Daddy said this would keep us from the damp ground and any night beasts or hunters who would be passing through. We did hear some hunters pass through, as this made Daddy happy, because they were leaving their tracks, which we could follow.

We saw the campfires speckled around us. Daddy decided that we would also need to travel at night now. Notwithstanding; we would wait until when the third moon appeared, which unusually was the sign for hunters to sleep. If anyone were tracking us, we would boast a chance to change our position and perhaps lose him. I just wanted to get away from all the campfires, which appeared to be on this hill. We could climb two hills pass our original sleeping tree, as we did not see any large campfires. Our father cautions us that this does not mean they are not here, for sometimes their fires burn out during the night. However, for a positive note, I believe it strange that none of them continued to burn. As the day hours were appearing, we once again climbed a tree. This time Daddy was looking for anyone who was cooking a morning meal. The wind would be helpful in our detection. The surrounding hills appeared to be safe. Daddy wanted us to move forward as far as we could and keep all those who were a few hills back away from us. We continued traveling the streams as Daddy now changed our direction from going south to go west. Early that evening we went into some trees and prepared to sleep until the third moon rose. We slept extra well this evening, as we had found a berry patch and loaded up on some berries. When the darkness permitted us to see the small campfires from faraway, Daddy confirmed they were going south and away from us. With our wading in the streams, which were now becoming shallow once more; nevertheless, had plenty of rocks to walk on and hide our tracks. Kristoffel revealed to us that with all the circling tracts of renegade hunters, and our tracts disguised it would take those enforcers' months to figure out where we were going. Moreover, once they did, they would not care, because we would be on someone else's land. I was naturally listening to all they told us and trying to discover how they figured these things. If I were to survive in the wilderness among killers, I needed to learn how to figure furthermore these things. We were in the middle of these killers yet slipped through their hands, by changing the habits they were using to predict our behavior. We were guessing their habits also, the difference being. We predicted this correct. This day was one of the few days one of us did not die.

CHAPTER 06

Hurting, healing, and the Bezdroża

As we are walking in this maze of a forest that has everything, except a surface to walk on, Daddy raises his hand. That means, we are to find a place to hide. We are always supposed to keep our faces pointed toward the path. He wants us to see what is happening in front of us. We will not allow someone to stab us in the back. We must go down with a fight. I am almost sorry for anyone who makes a move at Olimpia because I can sense the tremendous quantity of frustration. We watch as the long groups of people pass by us. They are mixtures of women, children, and a few elders. A real family moves before us. We stay frozen as the children toss rocks and play along the path. They soon pass completely by, and linger down the path. We rejoin in the path, and Daddy tells us that we will follow this family, while we may do so. Kristoffel tells Daddy that we must be in another territory. That night, we can see no campfires along our southeastern ridges and a few small-scattered fires before us. This is more like family land. The sight of the children today hit Daddy and Olimpia rather hard. Daddy consistently looked forward to this time with his two youngest daughters as they consistently glorified him as a great hero. That time had finally come into our lives as he was to reunite with us in a new place, and we live happily ever more. His eyes tell a different story now. Our father's story is of a man who gave his life so his village could survive, and how that village tried to take everything from him. He blames them for the deaths of Acia and Pava, as they should not have been in this dilemma. He will carry this revenge, until he dies, as I realize someday he will tell us he must go away for a little hunting and instead go back and destroy whatever may remain from our village.

Olimpia was no better as the hurt on her face, revealing disappointment in so many things going wrong for those who did not receive the ending of his or her life as she planned. All the days were filled with love and long 'sometimes just slightly on the fictitious side' stories to brighten little Acia and Pava's days. We were all so much larger than we really were in actual life in their warm hearts. Even I was a mighty warrior and savior of women from all the beasts one could ever imagine. I leaped higher than the great mountains; nevertheless, in a few situations saved our Daddy. Acia never spared the grandeur in my daily roles for me to assume. So many of the roles, I had no idea what they were; however, neither did they know. I ponder now how many images of things are in their minds that in no way exist in reality. At least, they took those grand illusions into the land of the dead with them. They packed them with so much imagination, that even as a little boy I never really wanted to play with the other dull boys, who merely wanted to brand me the bad person, or the victim who went down in defeat. Especially, the last time I ever played with other little boys, and they knocked me into the helpless Spiritual Mother. I will never play with other boys another time for the remainder of my life. I can see that, until I settle down again with other non-hostile, people, the solitary way, I will ever be touching another male will be with a weapon, with the intent of making them sleep in the dirt. Olimpia has always been the foundation for everything in my life. Even when I was saving the world for Acia and Pava, I was holding onto Olimpia's hand hiding in her shadow. She could duck back just in time, so Acia and Pava could not see her. I was so important in the design for her relationship and style of life she wanted for Acia and Pava. I was the one next to them that was always there. We had our personal concerns and complaints that stayed private. I was the chance for them to vent their frustrations when they thought mistreatments had engulfed them.

In addition, if I explained why an action, or rule was important, and the right thing to do, then that was the way of things. There was no need to verify it because a big kid who they trusted said it was the thing to do. Moreover, if Olimpia said it was the thing to do, and then I immediately wrote it in my book of rules never to test or defy. Olimpia would, in the same way, threaten to punish me for the actions of Acia and Pava, which would bring them back to Olimpia's way of thinking without any form of delay. For such a longtime, when my heart would beat, I could hear two others also beat. I constantly told them repeatedly that it was no more than a little boy was. The single reason I became what they wanted me to be for them, for their hopes and dreams. That was the thing so important to me. When Olimpia fell into her sleep, her foundation was always under me, and never departed from me without warning vanished. I searched for it, yet could not find it. Now, instead of standing tall and strong I was floating in circles spinning with no control. Fear blinded me, and took away my hearing. When Acia called for me, I could not hear her and when she came to me, I was not there. Pava did not matter, as she simply tagged after Acia and waited for one of us to say something. If someone occasionally said something, she was happy, especially if it did not mean she was in trouble. Pava at no time was in trouble in our family, because someone was always watching her. The poor little companion never had a chance to be adventurous, as she was the pot of gold, we held fast. She was the last living creation of our mother. We never told her, as she was still too young to understand, that her birth was the event that took our mother away. Daddy always told us that something on the other side gave Pava to us, so we could enjoy our mother's love for a lot longer, and that she would be a strong love for all of us when we were much older. Olimpia kept everything together for me. That is why I was so ashamed when Acia and Pava told her I became weak when she went to sleep. I was extremely relieved that she had not expressed anger with me. We rather view each other, a tad bit on the precautionary side. I am scared, as I now grasp firsthand how a woman can force my life to be miserable.

Nevertheless, as I discovered with Pava, they can also be pardoned, if her forgiveness counts because of her young age. I believe it should count as she knew what she was doing, as Acia was warning and threatening her to no end. She just casually did what she wanted to do and that was it. She was not ready to lead, yet she could decide whom she would follow, and she wanted to be a part of our whole family. Pava did not recognize Daddy well, so she was still feeling her way around him. He was so busy in trying to keep us on the move. Our father has decided that he wants to rest in this area for a few days. We are not far from a stream, and he believes we should be able to catch several fish there. He is still worried about hunting, as he noticed the family that passes; we did not possess the standard hunting spears that most families carry with them. He also suggests that they could be locals and were simply visiting neighbors. Daddy does not like to guess; therefore, this is why he and Kristoffel will do their standard snooping and tell us what they discovered. Away they go and we carefully sneak to the stream and begin hunting. Olimpia searches for certain roots and herbs, while Kaus gathers the fruits and keeps a general view of what is happening. I witness various children jump into the stream on the other side and play. At first, I worried that they may come toward me. Nevertheless, they had their own area that they swam and splashed. When Olimpia heard the splashing, she rushed to where I was ensuring that I was okay. When she surveyed the situation, she grabbed me, pulled me back under a nearby tree, and gave me a big hug and her slobbering. I told her it had been a longtime since I had received several of her slobbers. Next, she reveals to me that she knows the suffering I went through, and can barely imagine the pain I felt when Acia turned cold against me. I told her that Acia was hurt and that pain changed her, yet I do not think it would have lasted much longer, as she did promise if a got a big stick, she would beat me. Olimpia wants to comprehend how that is a sign of her liking me. I told her I had enough faith in her that when she saw she was hurting me and I was in pain; she would stop and become my blood sister once more. Olimpia pats me on my head and tells me, "I believe she would have changed much earlier than you think, as she told me that after three hits, she could do more. I could see you in the back of her eyes, and that by your remaining patience; she was rebuilding her love for you inside her heart. I knew that Acia just needed a little more time with me. She complained to me for being barbarous to everyone. I stayed cruel, so she could see the foolishness of this type of behavior."

Now, I asked Olimpia how she is dealing with the rule that they are gone forever and must always sleep in the dirt. Olimpia looks at me and informs me that this time we are going to be who we really are with one another. Therefore, she confessed that she was still hurting awfully inside, and that she did not discern if she could keep this pain hidden much longer. I then asked her, "Mommy, since I am a boy, is it okay if I also hurt inside like this?" She grabbed me as a mother does and hugged me tight tells me that I can hurt while I want, just if I were honest with her about this hurt. Olimpia elaborated that will always be things the people do or say that Acia and Pava once did or said. Those are the times when the memories come back not simply to hurt us, but also to ensure we never forget them. I told Olimpia that they would live in my mind until I die, with Answald, Panfilo, and Joggeli. She asks me if I were fond of Joggeli. I told her that I was and will always be. Notwithstanding; I added that he was not all those bad things we said he was. Kaus had now slipped into our conversation. He added that Joggeli told him he would scout ahead to ensure things were good for us and check with him from time to time to see if his love had forgiven him. Olimpia tells us that she was not mad at him, that she had informed him he must beg Daddy to get her hand. She was just making the water hot, so he would dance a little livelier. I told her that he told me he knew this, and that he wanted you to dance as well. Olimpia hugs me and says, "I would have danced also, because I do want a man who knows how to draw certain lines and stand strong. It is so sad that they caught and hanged him. With our luck, they may have thought he was going to hurt us." Kaus discloses to us that he hopes that was not the reason.

Olimpia speaks in a moderate voice for security reasons, saying, "Joggeli, I will always love you. You should be good in the land of dead and do not confuse those girls' minds." Kaus picked up a soft leaf and wiped the tears that were beginning to roll down her cheeks. Our solitude eroded as six children circled us and asked who we were. The group had four boys and two girls. One of the older boys tried to act tough with Kaus and swing at him. I grabbed him from behind and threw him to the ground, jumped on him and hit his face with my fist. I now stood up, looked at the other boys, and said, "Anyone who touches them must fight me." One of the boys and the smallest of the girls came to stand beside me and said, "No; you must fight us." Kaus came over on the boy's side, and Olimpia sat on the girl's side and said, "No; you must fight us." The four children on the opposing side complained that they were outnumbered and had to get more help and rushed away. Olimpia asked the little girl if they were in danger. She told them that if they stay with her and her brother, they would be okay because her father was their tribe's chief. Olimpia then asked the tiny girl, her name, and she said, "I am Andreja and he is my brother Gerlach. We want to be your friends because you were being so warmhearted to your little boy." I tell them, "Olimpia (pointing at her) and Kaus (pointing at him) and Yakov (pointing at me). We have seen so much death and hurt in the wars and evil behind us. If you wish to be friends, then we will be your friends." Olimpia looks at Andreja and asks, "Do you realize where I could find a little girl to help me clean these fish?" Andreja responds while overflowing with enthusiasm, "I will." Kaus asks, "Do you understand where I can find a little boy to help me gather a handful of fruit and vegetables?" Gerlach answers, "I will; however, we just pick the best-tasting vegetables and not the unpleasant ones the girls enjoy." Andreja yells at him, "I will tell mommy." Gerlach, then questions her, "What about the ones we enjoy?" Andreja smiles and says okay. I then ask, "What can I do?" Olimpia tells me, "We need a strong boy to guard us and catch the big fish."

Gerlach, then volunteers yet Andreja yells at him, "You cannot, because you already promised Kaus you would help him, so keep your promise." She then waves her fist at him. He complains, "These are not fair," turns to Kaus and says, "We can go now." I went back to my fishing hole and started catching fish again. I did not mind the new kids got Olimpia and Kaus because I was doing something that Gerlach wanted to do. This gave in great value. Things were not going as well for Daddy and Kristoffel. While they were scouting the village, a few guards caught them and took them to the village elders who asked them why they were spying on them. They did not answer. They next asked them if they were alone. This closed Kristoffel and Daddy's lips even tighter, as they refused to say anything. After this, the elders told them that every person has their breaking point and that they would find theirs. The elders explained that they were not evil people and simply had to understand if their families were safe. Daddy had heard of people who trusted elders such as this and had lost their families. He told Kristoffel to tell them a lie and lead them into a place that he could escape. Kristoffel told him that he could do no such thing, as the village would keep Daddy as a hostage and then return to kill him. If anyone had to go, it was Daddy so he could gather his family and move to their new home. Our father told Kristoffel that it was not fair, he dies for our family. Kristoffel reveals that his family had already died so he was giving his life to keep another family together and so he could join his family in the land of the dead. Daddy asked him for a bit of time to think about this, as there may arise a chance they both could escape. Meanwhile, the villagers would untie them one by one and whip them with three lashes before tying them up once more. An elder came out to tell them that they would receive no food until they talked and three lashes each day. They did not mean for the lashes to kill them, but instead to give them ample pain that they would be unable to ignore it, as they would hurt for the remainder of the day and enough to cause sleep to be difficult if not impractical. The steady dose of three each day would soon begin to accumulate to the point the pain would be too great to dismiss. The long days and nights would give them plenty of time to confess. The Suns were climbing once more and beginning to burn their stripped-down bodies. The villagers tied a garment around their man parts because they wanted all in the village to be able to see this chastisement.

The elders told Daddy that all could see this as the punishment they were receiving was the same for their people, although they based the intensity and duration on the crime. Kristoffel tells Daddy that he wishes the rains would return, as much cool water would be good now. A few children begin to throw little rocks at them. The elders call for men to come to punish the children. They tie them up and whip them with a leather whip, which they apparently designed for children. Kristoffel next suggests to Daddy that this may be a sign, they are good people, and it may be possible to trust them. Daddy says that he needs more time, because a mistake now could leave him, for the first time in almost twenty years without a family. The elders come once again and sit behind a few tables the villagers brought out for them. The villagers then brought food to the table as the elders began to eat. The chief elder began to talk to Daddy and Kristoffel, "My name is Hæge and I am the chief elder of this tribe. We hear that two great Armies are fighting higher in the mountains. Do you recognize anything of this?" Kristoffel tells him, "We share all that we comprehend to our friends. Any who are respectable and kind to us, we are kind in return. How can you expect us to worry about your safety when you take our clothes, beat us in public, a feast in front of us while we go without food?" Hæge answers him, "When you prove to us that you are not as the killers who roam these forests and kidnap our children and rape our wives, and then we will treat you with kindness." Daddy tells him, "You do not fool me, for I understand that those who are evil can do no kind thing and those who are kind can do no evil thing." Hæge responds, "We do not force you to go without food, for I invite you to eat with us. We enjoy plenty of extra food. Nevertheless, we must realize why you were spying on us and who you are. The lives of our families are in danger." Daddy looks at him and says, "If you were wise enough to be worthy of life you would see that we are not warriors. You die because you let the killers roam free and just torture those who you recognize are of no threat." Hæge asks Kristoffel how a warrior is supposed to appear like and how they understand such things.

Kristoffel tells him, "You ask foolish questions now, for you cannot live as long as you have without knowing what a warrior look as. I understand these things, because I realize how killers appear. The reason we were scouting your village was to search for such killers and avoid them." Hæge asks him why he would want to avoid such killers. Kristoffel accuses Hæge of being friends with the killers and repeats how he is not friends with the killers. Hæge accuses Daddy and Kristoffel of evading his questions and reassures them that as they become weaker and hungry, they will tell him all he wishes to know. The elders continue to eat their food, in front of Daddy and Kristoffel, while four children come running into the village screaming for help. They rush up to Hæge and scream, "Chief Elder, they control your son and daughter and plan to kill them." Hæge asks the girl how she knows them. Moreover, how does she realize they plan to kill his children? She tells him that they possess strange arrows, long knives, merely fish for their food, and hide in the brush. They also ignored her pleas, to get Andreja and Gerlach released. After her pleas, they threatened to fight them. This is when they escaped for their lives, being afraid of the long knives. When they reached the hillside and looked back, she could see them holding Gerlach and Andreja. I could see the third one going to hide under the trees by the stream, most likely waiting for his next prey. We need to hurry, because I miss Andreja already. Hæge looks to the other members and orders, "Assemble the warriors." They rush off as the village prepares to rescue their children. Daddy looks at Hæge and reports, "I knew you were warriors, and you tried to fool us." Hæge tells him, "I do not have time for your games now; I have my children to save." Daddy tells him, "You are not the lone one with children to rescue." Hæge responds, as he is leaving, "I will confess, you are doing a great job at hiding your children." Not long after that, the village became quiet, as just little children and the women remained. They selected two large, fierce women to guard them. Daddy looks at her and comments, "I can see why this village has so few people. It is because they suffer from too many ugly women."

The woman walks over to Daddy, hits him in his mouth, and discloses to him, "If you desire to run your mouth, and then I will close it for you." Daddy shuts up and turns his face slowly away from her. The warriors rush to the hillside the children lead them.

They see Andreja and Gerlach lying on the ground with the three strangers. Carefully, they form a circle completely around them. They are afraid that little Gerlach and Andreja are dead. They slowly work, their way in toward our weapons. One of the warriors cracks a small stick by accident and wakes Gerlach, who is sleeping on the outside under Kaus's arm. He awakes and yells, "Help; we are being attacked." Andreja, who was sleeping on Olimpia, because she was afraid to sleep on the outside and I wanted to sleep between Olimpia and Kaus, yells for Olimpia to wake. Two warriors leap to grab Andreja and Gerlach. As they do, Olimpia grabs Andreja trying to pull her to safety yelling, "I will save you." Kaus does the same for Gerlach. The warriors are also yelling they want to save them. By this time, two warriors, stick their spears close to my chest and motion for me to rise. I ask them, "Why are you hurting our friends?" The warrior reports, "They are your prisoners." I ask him, "Since when do prisoners sleep on top of their captives." By now, the warriors all hold spears covering each of us and their leader yells out for everyone to stop moving. He tells Kaus and Olimpia to, "Release our children." They then point for Andreja and Gerlach to step away from their captors. Wisely, he next asks Andreja if they had been hurt. Andreja discloses to them, "These are our good friends. We were sleepy from eating too many great fish." Gerlach, then adds, "We also ate the children's vegetables that I picked. It was so much fun." Their leader is now motioning for everyone to drop their spears. He walks over to Kaus, extends his arm, and tells him, "My name is Bälz, we mean you no harm. We were worried about the little girl and boy from what the other children told us." He lifts Kaus to her feet. Another of the warriors reaches down to lift Olimpia, yet Andreja screams and rushes to Olimpia giving her hand to lift her. Olimpia cleverly works it so it appears that Andreja is lifting her to the ground.

Andreja yells out, "No one touches my best friend, or I will fight them." Bälz looks at Olimpia, who has me on one side of her and Andreja in front of her and tells Kaus, "I do believe little people loved that woman." Kaus tells her that the children worship her for certain strange reasons. Bälz shares with Kaus, "Children put together a way of seeing past what we see. Well, certain children do. We hold several children who need whipping." Bälz yells for the four children to stand in front of him and shouts, "Do you realize that almost caused two innocent people to die today?" He tells the warriors to take the children back to the council of elders and tell them what they did. He will walk with our new friends. Bälz explains to us that the children told them Andreja was in great danger. Andreja tells Bälz that they were supposed to get a few more people in a fighting game that they were going to play. Bälz then shakes his head and remarks, "I think they wanted to play the real fighting game. Moreover tell me, about the great tasting fish and children's vegetables that kids pick and eat. I need a little of that in my house." Andreja reached out her hand for me to hold. Subsequently, I gently grabbed it and told her thanks. She tells me, "Oh no, thank you for being my friend." I told her, "I do want to be your friend, because my two best friends and little sisters died on our way here." Andreja tells me that this is terrible and that we can stay with her until all the hurt goes away. Her hand is about Acia's size, as Acia had large hands for a small girl. Andreja's hand has more flesh and protection over her bones. Her hands are also soft from the flesh and warm. She has a solid grip, as I believe she will not let go. I always tried to give Acia and Pava solid grips so they would also think I had a fine hold on them. Andreja held Olimpia with her other hand as I held Kaus with my remaining hand. We walked alongside each in a row as Bälz walked ahead of us. We entered the village as all the people were standing waiting to see the new people. After we entered, they surrounded us as we slowly made our way to Hæge who welcomed us. Behind him were the four children tied to newly erected poles so they would not interfere with the other children who they had punished. Bälz reports to Hæge, "Here are your Andreja, Gerlach, and their new friends."

Hæge smiles at me and asks for my name. I tell him who I am. Andreja tells her Daddy, "Yakov had two sisters die recently from the bad men who roam the land, so I am going to be his two sisters until the hurt is gone." Hæge looks at Olimpia and remarks, "You are too kind looking to be living in such danger." He looks at Kaus and says, "You appear as if you could be a good fighter. You will stay with my family, and I until your hurt depart. We found two bad men today who were preparing to harm our loved ones. These forests are too dangerous for good people like you to be in the killing woodlands that imprisoned us." I just stood there with my head facing down and began to cry. Hæge apologizes if he said something to hurt me and then tells the villagers to return to their duties, as our new friends will meet with them all soon. They cheer. Hæge hands me a children's whip and invites me to hit each child once for the evil they did to us. I told him that I could not do this, as hurting people, for good or evil, causes more pain and the hurt I retain I do not want any other to have. He hands it to Kaus, who tells him, "They are children. I hate to punish children when I do not recognize if they were not properly educated to avoid doing what they did. I too want no more hurt unless necessary. If they broke your rules, then should not you be the one to punish them?" He looks at Olimpia, who begins to cry, "They are such pretty little people. I promise that they will never do this again." She runs to them, with tears in her eyes and asks them if they are well-behaved children from now on and not try to hurt people. The children, now sensing a chance to avoid their punishment, try to explain that they were simply playing a fighting game and wanted to scare Gerlach who is always bragging about how tough he is. They would never let these wonderful new friends, get hurt. Hæge looks at Bälz and complains, "I at no time should have offered the whip to that woman. That is the same as giving their mothers', a chance to save them, which they will always do without fail. If I punish those children now, I will be the cruel monster who hates children. The best I can do is getting the empty promises out of this, and I might own something else that will work just as well in the long term."

Hæge walks over in front of the children cracking his whip. Olimpia is completely covering the other little girl named, Ermtraud. Kaus now shields, two of the boys and I cover the smallest boy. I must cover him because I do not think that Kaus can lean over this far. Hæge now pretending he is angry tells Olimpia, "I will not beat them merely if you promise me they will be well-behaved. If they do something bad, I will beat you instead. Do you agree?" Olimpia goes over in front of him on her knees shaking and garbles out, "I promise. You may beat me instead if they do wrong once more." Hæge turns around and whacks the whip on a tree without someone tied to it. He then turns to the children and says, "You must still be punished, yet maybe not from my whip. Do you agree to this?" Olimpia, still on her knees, begs, "I beg that you first tell me about this new punishment." Hæge then reveals, "If they are so eager to send people to the land of the dead, then they should sleep three nights in the place where our dead sleep in the ground. Do you think this to be fair, so at the same time that they can learn about the terrible thing, they almost caused to happen? If you do not, then I guess you force me to beat them with this whip." He afterwards hit the tree hard once more. All the children cry out, "This is fair. We agree." Olimpia asks Hæge, "Can you promise these warriors will protect them from any bad living people?" Hæge smiles and says, "Yes, I can. I am curious, how many children do you have?" Olimpia tells him that her womb has yet to produce a child. Hæge asks her if she is married. She tells him that she has no husband. Hæge tells her, "I can promise you that one of our warriors will be begging you to marry them. I can promise you that he will be begging with all his heart." Olimpia tells him that would be as a dream to come true because she so much loves children and that on the journey here she had to bury her lover, two brothers, and two sisters. She confesses to have much empty space inside that needs love. He motions for the warriors to untie the children. Ermtraud comes running and jumps on her, forcing her to the ground and then begins kissing her and crying out, "Show me those empty places, and I will fill them with my love."

I glance at her and say, "I enclose many empty places as well." Andreja comes and hugs me telling me she will fill those places. Her dad asks her to do the filling in front of her mother, if she needs extra help. Andreja looks at her father and tells me, "Daddy, this is a good idea." The four boys surround Gerlach and I and ask if we can be friends once more. We shake hands and present our promises, to be friends forever. I then turn to Hæge and ask him if I can stay with them when they sleep with the dead. Gerlach cries out begging his Daddy, "Me likewise Daddy, please." Hæge asks me why I would want to be with the bad children while they received their punishment. I tell him, "So I can see when they turn well, and because we are friends and friends are supposed to stay with you during good and bad times." Hæge looks at Kaus and Olimpia and tells them, "You hold a fine young man here. You both may suffer with your friends." Andreja now asks if Ermtraud and Olimpia can suffer with Ermtraud. Hæge tells her that just she can, and that Olimpia cannot because she is a woman and all the boys will sneak out here and try to kiss her even in front of you innocent children. Andreja answers, "Oh, sorry father, I was not thinking. She is too beautiful for the dead because they might also try to kiss her." Hæge smiles and says to her, "I never thought about that my daughter, I am fortunate to boast such a wise daughter as you, am I not?" Olimpia wraps both girls in her arms and says, "I am in luck to enjoy such wonderful friends. You think you can show us the fun games or places to play." They all scream, "Yes, hurry, follow us." Olimpia looks at Hæge who waves his hand for them to go. Olimpia is paying so much attention to her new friends whom, she runs into the tree that has our blindfolded father tied to it. She hits the tree hard enough to fall to the ground. Kaus and I rush to her side as all our friends surround us. Afterwards, I hear a familiar, "Ouch." I stop what I am doing and standing up, investigate where we are.

I see two men tied to trees behind us with blood splattered over them and their skin red from the burning sun. Afterwards, I call for Kaus to join me. He comes to me, and I point at what I believe is our father and Kristoffel. He also shares my need to explore in more detail. As we walk toward them, Hæge yells for us to stay away from the bad men. I tell him that we might recognize these men. Hæge tells me to stop and he will order his warriors to remove their facemasks'. I bellow out, "Daddy, is that you." He crackles back, "Yes, Yakov. I am too weak and thirsty to talk with you now." I yell back to Hæge, "This is my father and Kristoffel. They are not bad men." Hæge brings the water and asks two of the women standing nearby to wash their faces and give them the water so I can identify them. I yell at Kristoffel to wake up and say something. Olimpia is now rushing to Daddy and hugs him crying, "Daddy, do not worry; I will heal you." Hæge asks me if I understand how Olimpia will heal her father. I tell him with her roots and herbs in her bag. He asks where her bag is and I tell him that Andrea has it tied to her back. With this, Hæge orders his warriors to release my father and has many wonderful soft furs brought to lay under them. Olimpia begins to work on the whip cuts. Fortunately, they are not deep cuts, as their design is for skin pain and sting and not for tissue destruction. Olimpia's primary concern is the way our Suns burned their skin, as we have spent much time in caves and traveling at night recently. She moves them under the nearby trees. Hæge offers to give her a hut for him to sleep. Olimpia tells him that she wants him in the open so the air and the Suns can help in their recovery. She looks at Andreja and Ermtraud and asks them if they will help her. Their little faces light up so bright that Olimpia was afraid they would burn the surrounding people. She gave them several of her mashed roots that were mixed with water and showed them how slowly to work it into their skin. I asked her if she would let me help her. Nevertheless, she told me that this healing had to have a woman's touch. I remember a few times when she, Acia and Pava had to care for me as there are things that just a woman's touch can heal. I always thought that was weird because I do not see much difference between a boy's touch and a girl's touch. However, I do appreciate there are pronounced mysteries with this advanced heeling, so I am not going to interfere with our great developments. While advanced minds such as Olimpia are among us, I will count myself to be lucky.

I walk over and from behind begin to run my fingers through her hair. She likes me to do this, although I will never be as experienced as Acia. Olimpia likes her hair untangled, so this helps straighten it out. The people around us smile as they see me working hard to do a good job. Even though she cannot see me, Olimpia tells me, thanks as she moves slowly so I can keep up with her. A short while later, she speaks out, "I hope that big strong man behind, he will massage my shoulders. If he would, I would love him and maybe even marry him." Andreja and Ermtraud begin laughing and say, "Olimpia, he is your little brother fooling you. You cannot marry him." I am laughing also as I massage her neck. Many warriors are standing around us, from a safe distance watching every move of my fingers. Olimpia teasing Andreja asks why she cannot marry him if she loves him so much. Ermtraud begins to laugh and tells her, "Silly woman, you are supposed to love your little brother, so this is excellent that you love him." Olimpia then starts to pretend cry and says, "If I do not marry him, where will I find a good wife for him?" Andreja shouts out, "I will marry him and be a great wife for him." Ermtraud repeats the same thing. Olimpia laughs and asks, "Is it okay for him to have two wives?" Andreja solves this mystery for Olimpia by telling her, "If my father says it is okay, then we can do it." Olimpia, playing with their minds now, asks, "But I thought you had to have love if you are going to get married." Andreja and Ermtraud respond quickly, surprising Olimpia by saying, "We love you so is love because you love him; therefore, everywhere we have love." Olimpia looks at me and says, "Yakov, it looks like I found you two wives." I stare at her and ask, "Mommy, do you think I am old enough to get married?" Olimpia looks puzzled, then looks at Andreja, and says, "I guess we probably should also ask your Daddy." Andreja agrees that would be a good idea. I then confess to her that I do not understand what a husband is supposed to do. Additionally, I wondered that if I made a mistake would they hate me as Acia did.

Olimpia tells me that I cannot produce a mistake with girls, or I will suffer. Andreja asks Olimpia, "Do we have to cause him to suffer, because I do somewhat like him?" Ermtraud follows with the same answer, although she says she really rather loves him. Andreja asks her why she told Olimpia that she loves our husband. Ermtraud tells her, "My mommy told me that if I ever got married, I had better love that boy or she was going to give me a big whipping." Andreja appears puzzled for a minute and then tells Olimpia, "I believe Ermtraud is right, because my mommy is always telling Daddy that she loves him, so I really love Yakov." I tell them that this is good because I would be mad if someone gave my wives a whipping. Hæge comes walking over to comment and tells us how great a job we are doing with our healing. Andreja asks him, "Daddy can Yakov have two wives?" Hæge asks, "Well, that depends on who the two wives would be." Andreja tells her father that it would be her and Ermtraud. Hæge answers, "Well, in that case it would be okay, once he asks your fathers if he can have your hand." I focus on him and say, "I am sorry; I forgot all about that. I think that

I forgot everything. Can you tell me everything a husband must do?" Andreja and Ermtraud also ask him, "Will you please tell everything that a good wife is supposed to do?" Hæge asks them, "Oh, so you want to be good wives do you?" Andreja and Ermtraud tell him that they want to be great wives like their mothers are. Hæge then smiles and says, "I think I can identify a few mommies who will be happy when they hear this. Okay, for you Yakov a good husband must always first love his wife or in your case wives. He has to find particular work that he can trade to earn his hut and the food, clothes, and other things for his wives. He must also always be charming for his wives and tell them he loves them and kisses them when they want to be kissed." I appear a little pale and then confessed that I did not like to kiss girls, unless she is my mommy. Hæge continues by adding, "When they say kiss you had better kiss long and hard. Do you want to show me your hut now and where you are going to get the rocks to feed them and buy them new dresses?"

I ask him, "Why cannot they sleep in their houses, and their mothers feed them?" Hæge says, "Oh no, once you marry them, they belong to you and merely you." He looks next at his daughter and tells her, "Once you marry Yakov, you have to leave our house and live in his home that he makes for his family. You have to reproduce babies for him. You must also cook his food. He is your boss." I gaze at Olimpia and begin crying, "I still want to be a little boy and perhaps get married next year." Andreja cries to her Daddy, "Daddy, is it okay if I wait until next year to get married? Ermtraud looks at Olimpia and asks, "Can I wait until next year." They answer us at the same time, "If that is what you want." We looked relieved as I say, "Oh, it is wonderful to be a kid once more." Hæge smiles at me and leaves. Olimpia looks over and sees and elderly woman messing around in her herb bag and yells, "What are you doing?" She jumps back, yells at a few of the boys to follow her, and walks away. Ermtraud tells us not to worry, because that old woman will not hurt anyone. Therefore, we get back to our work. Daddy and Kristoffel begin to start coming around. I ask him why they were so weak from a few whips and the Suns. They say that various old woman gave them water and that was all they remember. Out they went. About this time, the boys returned with little bags and handed them to Olimpia. She looked at them, touched and smelled each bag, then started blending them with her herbs and roots. She told the boys to tell the old woman that she was thankful. Olimpia looked and told me to, for the first time she can remember, to play with the other boys and have fun. The boys grabbed my hand and said, "We can go play several games." I was so surprised and scared. Olimpia told me, "Honey, it will be okay; they will be kind to you. Go ahead." Kaus offers to hang out close by me and be there if I need a little help or support. I consent, even though I want to do this so much; fear is gripping me subsequently hard that I can barely breathe. I ask Kaus to teach me how to play with the other boys. He tells me not to worry, most games children play they create the rules as they play. Andreja tells me not to worry, because my two future wives will help me. They each grab one of my hands and guide me with the boys.

Olimpia calls for Kaus to return to her saying, "Kaus, his wives will take good care of him." Kaus then complains, "Why do I always have to be married last." Olimpia offers to find several little girls for Kaus. Kaus grabs her and starts tickling her. She is laughing hysterically and for the first time I ever remember, she is letting him win and control her. I stand here in disbelief. Andreja pulls at me to join her. Kaus stops tickling and stands up while lifting Olimpia. He asks her why she let him win for the first time in his life. Olimpia tells him there are many reasons for her new outlook on life, she no longer has to be the big strong mother and father because currently we have a father. Therefore, now she can be a funny, silly young woman like the rest of the girls her age. She next pinched Kaus's cheeks and shook his head telling him that he should give up on the little girls and start playing with the big girls like her. Kaus reminds her that she is not merely his sister, but also his mother. Olimpia slaps him lightly and tells him she did not mean her. She told him it was time he started to search for a woman in his life and begin the road that our father walked. Daddy looks at Kaus and says, "Do not be afraid son, Kristoffel and I will guide you." When I heard this my heart started to beat again. Hope was flowing back into our family. Andreja and Ermtraud are not the same as Acia and Pava. They are; however, vessels that can love and share our happiness. I did not have to be the big boy, any longer, as Olimpia did not have to be both mommy and Daddy, and Kaus did not have to be the muscle and rock that Olimpia walked on when the ground was muddy. We had lives once more, as even Daddy had a new life ahead of him. Olimpia planned for us to endure a serious talk with him, because we must remember, he lost not just our mother, but also four lives that came from them, lives that he wanted to guide, provide for, and build into future families in our clan. Our hurt would never go away. Notwithstanding; my hurt over the loss of Pava and Acia would give me the extra energy to work harder so Andreja and Ermtraud would not have to hurt that way. This time, I would appreciate the little things consequently much more. I was also determined to be as I am now, jumping into new challenges holding on to them. I am not going to hold back anything, except for them. Trust will be the power to kill this hurt and drown any hate.

Each minute now is so important. We shed too much blood to get us here, and we must take that death and recover it to life. Consequently, I realize the tears will always come from my eyes filled with Acia and Pava; therefore, as they depart from under my wings, I will now learn to fly under Andreja and Ermtraud's wings. At last, I am comfortable again being around other people. Andreja and Ermtraud do not appear to be dominant and flow with whatever looks to be fun. They warn me about this first game. We stand one at a time in front of the other team. One at a time, two of them will throw rocks at one of us. If they hit one of us, they get one point. We will play this until the first team gets four hits or the side with the most hits after everyone has sat twice. We have five people on each team, as the other team also has two girls. They tell me I must be smart in this game. I must never dodge a rock the same way, twice. She also adds that I must keep my arms close to my head so if I go down, I can protect my head. They volunteer to go before me. Andreja goes first. She stands in front of them calling them names and making daring faces at them. The first one comes charging at her, stops at their line, and throws his stone at her. She calmly steps to one side as the stone flashes by her missing her by less than one inch. My heart almost explodes. Ermtraud laughs at them for throwing so wild. I have never seen something pass someone who is accordingly close and the person to survive. Ermtraud now sits in front of them. I ask her why she is sitting. She says because no one on the other side knows how to throw stones. The two biggest opponents grab their stones and move into the line to toss their stones. She remains frozen, as the first stone comes flying to her. She does not move as the stone comes flying to her right and misses her. The next boy stands up and throws at her, and once again and throws the stone. She remains frozen. She does not move, once again, as the stone comes flying to her right, for the second straight time and misses her. I behold Ermtraud and ask her why she did not move. She smiles and tells me that she knows how to play this game. They told me I must move because I am learning this contest.

Notwithstanding; they brag on how no one has yet to hit them. I tremble out in front of the other team. I hope to receive a boost of faith as I see their two girls stumble forward with smaller stones than the boys threw at our girls. I stood in front of the first girl, and she threw her stone, which I went left as it flew by my right side. I was a tad bit impressed with the speed of the small stone. Andreja smiles at me and reminds me about our plan. This time as she went to release the stone I went right as the stone hit me straight in my head. I perfect shot and down I went. My head feels as if a head ax hit its head. That tiny girl hit me perfectly, and that stone came fast. The little girl came to me, and to my humiliation, apologized her hurting me so bad. The pain was great; however, with what little pride I still held onto, I did not want to compel her to sense the bad ambiance and allow everyone to see that a little girl defeated me. I asked her how she knew which way I was going to go. She laughed and confessed that it was so easy, because Andreja was the one who taught her. Andreja looks at me and apologizes claiming she forgot, because she has trained so many other children. Ermtraud escorts me back to Olimpia for my healing. I am now ugly, as these bruises cover the front of my forehead and has my pride smashed over it. Andreja and Ermtraud rush to me as after their game had finished telling me that they won four to one. They also cried on my head wound and begged Olimpia to tell them I would recover. They then bragged to Olimpia how brave and strong I had been after

153

they knocked me that hard. Andreja told my Daddy and Kaus the accident was her fault. She confessed to give me the wrong advice. She emphasized how proud she was that I trusted her, even to my possible death. They kept telling us so many wonderful things the people in this village liked to do. Olimpia tells her, delicately of course, that throwing rocks at each is not really a fun game. Andreja says that she has never had any fear in this game. If the player stays away from the flying rock, everything is okay. She did not want to go too far into this for fear of hurting my pride. Andreja told Olimpia and my family that she and Ermtraud would care for me now, so they should go to explore the village and see how they live.

As they leave, Andreja gives Kaus and Kristoffel a kiss, as Ermtraud kisses, Daddy and Olimpia. I notice how they simply kiss Olimpia in repetition, yet for the males; they always rotate. I tell them it does not matter; nevertheless, they tell me it is their custom to treat all equally, and the 'woman master of the group' special giving her the greatest honor. When they departed, leaving us alone Andreja told me that neither Ermtraud nor she would ever say or do anything that would allow others to think poorly of me. They promise always to fashion me to come across as charming, especially because their mothers have already linked them with me. I told the girls that I was the stupid one that they hit in the head with a stone and no matter how we disguise this; I will still have the big bruise on my forehead. This tells everyone the girl from the other team not just hit me, but also hit me in the place that is supposed to be the most protected. Andreja pleads with me not to worry, because she explained to everyone that my tribe did not play this game. This is subsequently special, allowed to be weak and protected for two strong girls. I trust Andreja and Ermtraud and everyone in this village is so unique. I have never felt like I belonged anywhere in my life, except for our trip from Petenka toward our once free peninsula, until the death of Panfilo. That was when death took the heart from me. Now Andreja and Ermtraud are working so hard to give me a life again, yet I became scared when they talked about being married. Many thirteen year olds were married in Petenka. I believe the overload on responsibility tripped me, although I had responsibility my entire life. It was shielded responsibility, which, if I failed, they would rescue me immediately. I apologize to Andreja and Ermtraud for my fear to marry. They tell me that fear besides grabbed them. Ermtraud then stares me with a serious glare and informs me that they can throw stones with more speed and accuracy than the little girl can in the game. If I explore for love from others, after having promised myself to them, I will enjoy pain at a level never before imagined. They tell me that our love must be honorable and have a bonding that holds us together and prevents others from degrading it.

I think about what they are saying then wholeheartedly, agree. Next, I tell them about how so many hated me in my previous village; therefore, I had to distrust everything that I saw or heard. This will be hard for me. They snuggle on each side of me and tell me that because of my weakness, I will need two of them to keep me standing. I explain to them that I have never heard of a man having two wives. They tell me they have no such marriages in their village either. Bezdroża allows lopsided engagements such as two wives or one wife with two husbands. They do this because of the constant raids from other clans. When they raid, they either kill or take their slaves as victims. The couples rearranged the engagements based on who is still living in the village, thus it is better not to focus on the one-to-one relationships. After this surprising revelation, I asked her why everyone around here is so happy and full of life. My women tell me because they have no tomorrow; we live life merely for today. I ask them if they have any arrows the invaders left behind to take. Andreja tells me her father collects them. She also tells me the open huts from those who the raiders captured or killed, they will give the village to the first who pledge themselves for them. Therefore, if we pledge ourselves soon, we can have a pleasant hut, and we do not have to marry until we are ready. Ermtraud told me not to worry about a job, because her father and Andreja's fathers were extremely popular in this village, and they would ensure I had an excellent position, so their daughters could give them strong grandchildren. I told them I wanted two daughters first, so I could relive my times with Acia and Pava. They both agreed that would be great, as daughters do need the careful guidance from their fathers to live in this place. I told them that my father and Kristoffel were inordinate hunters and would be able to teach the village many tricks. Andreja reveals to me that it will take the village time before they can honor my father and Kristoffel considering how her village could capture them. Responding, I asked her how did the village catch my father and Kristoffel. She tells me that they fell into one of their hidden traps, built especially for spies. I reassured them that they were just concerned about our safety.

They wanted to ensure that we could pass through without harm. We are running from the great Pirate Army and killers from Petenka. Andreja grew a pale red color, and then asked me if the Army was following them, and if so, how far are they from us. I told her not to worry because a considerable Army from the west came to fight them, and they met to fight on the other side of the great mountain, with the evil killers from Petenka caught in the middle. Andreja consequently, wants me to explain why my father was scouting for danger if the Armies were fighting so far away. I explain to her that sometimes these Armies send scouts who trail their main force and explore all the areas around them for protection and greater exploitation opportunities. Fortunately, we did not find such scouts, but instead found many other villages, a couple united, who began killing us. I explained to her that she was the first kind person, and this was the initial friendly village I ever was so lucky to have in my life. My days are ones filled with hurt. Notwithstanding; my short time with Andreja reveals that she also has lived a life of hurt, yet they are always happy. They apparently have mastered the skill of chasing hurt from themselves. I ask them once more, how they can ignore the death around them. Andreja smiles and says, "We bury our dead. That, which lives in the dirt talks to the others who are in the dirt. Those who exist above the surface speak to those who breathe above the ground. Crossing that line is, hope to join those on the other side. Therefore, if you wish to live with the dead, afterwards you will seek them. If you want to live with others who are also alive, after that you will seek them. Happiness could exist with the living. We do not understand how the dead exist, except for tales of the land of the dead. I agree with them that their concepts are the best ones and ask them for help in adopting them." We talk about selected wonderful people in our lives. Subsequently, Olimpia returns with the men in our clan. Hæge takes us to a large open hut with tables covered with food. It is not extremely elaborate, but conservative. Actually, this is refreshing as it shows us these people are so natural. We sit around and talk for hours.

I can hear so much laughter. Kaus has a couple of pretty girls he is talking to, as Olimpia is adulating her eyes and releasing a phony laugh at the stories, the boys are telling her. Fortunately, I am the solitary one who knows her laugh is fake. Each time she catches me looking at her, she gives me a 'mind your own business' stare. Hæge additionally invited a few widows to sit at the table with them. Daddy and Kristoffel are behaving as conservative men, as if they have a strange rock wall around their hearts. I can see that we will need to talk with them about loosening up and moving on in their lives. Everything appears to fit in place now, as I can see us blending in with this village with ease. So many others have gathered around us. They are chatting and playing with each as if we were not even beside them. This allows us to be so much more at ease and similar to not being on stage for display. The greatest event of the evening occurred when various people came out with special music tools they had created and began to play music for us. It was unique in that a few had strings that they plucked. Others blew into a piece of wood, and yet others hit these empty round coated skin pieces. Hæge finally stands up and motions for all to go home. We follow him and Andreja's mother back to their hut. Next, we each collect a few soft large fur pieces and several garment bags filled with feathers, go outside behind their hut, and prepare to sleep. I asked Andreja why they sleep outside. She tells me they do this because it is so much better for them. They also want to remain strong if the village must flee from invaders. During the cold months and raining nights, they sleep inside. I am rather surprised that as I go to sleep beside my mommy, Andreja and Ermtraud jump in beside me. I end with my head on Olimpia's belly as Andreja and Ermtraud also place their heads on her belly. I see a smile come over Olimpia's face as she scratches each of our heads and wishes us sweet dreams. Olimpia is reliving Acia and Pava, as am

I. Something makes me bear guilt about this, so I tell Andreja and Ermtraud that my sisters and I used to sleep like this on Olimpia's belly. They laugh and explain to me that this is wonderful, that they can be a part of restoring happy memories. Olimpia pats me on my back and tells me I am a great young man. Andreja tells her that I am their pronounced adolescent man forever.

I sense Olimpia relax as she comments, "I am so glad finally to hear a woman claim one of my brothers." Ermtraud tells Olimpia if she will change that for women, she will also claim me. Olimpia quickly says women with a happy chuckle. Ermtraud reports that she as well claims me. Olimpia now asks them if she can also claim me until she finds a man to claim her. Andreja reveals to her that they hoped she would stay with them until they figured out how to do whatever they were supposed to do. Olimpia tells us that she would not miss this much fun for anything in the world. The next morning, we take our furs back inside their hut and Daddy asks us for a family meeting before we eat our breakfast. As we sit around each, he asks us if anyone would like to stay in this village. We quickly agree and join our new family for breakfast. Hæge ask my father what our family agreed. Daddy tells him that we would like to stay. Hæge tells us we will examine several available huts today, gather several furs and other things needed to survive here. As I sit beside Andreja, I notice her eyes and cheeks are red. Therefore, I asked her what was wrong. She reveals she was crying because she thought my family would leave them. I kiss her on the cheek and tell her we will stay. Hæge jumps up and yells that according to their village's rules when the boy kisses a girl he must marry her. Ermtraud jumps beside me, kisses me on my cheek, and yells out, "Now he must marry both of us." I stand and confess that our engagement has lasted for almost one day now, and therefore, I am ready to marry. Hæge then sits down, laughs, and apologizes, "Oh, I did not realize the engagement was still on, and was just making sure my daughter and her best friend got the best man." Daddy and Kristoffel begin laughing also as they shake Hæge's hands. Olimpia then stands up and declares, "I also want it to be known the three of them declared that I could keep my little man until they were ready to marry." Hæge looks at Andreja and asks her if this is true.

Andreja stands up and tells her father, "Oh yes, Daddy, because the three of us love her too much, so we are going to keep her, while we can. She is not getting away from loving us."

Hæge begins laughing and tells my father, "These young people have it all planned so perfectly." Daddy agrees. When Olimpia sits down the three of us engaged lovers now jump all over her trying to kiss her everywhere declaring, our love." Kristoffel smiles and tells Hæge, "There is no one else in the world that can teach them love greater than the spirit of love which lives solely in Olimpia." Hæge smiles and agrees that he has never seen one so wonderful with the little people. Olimpia finishes her morning fruits and as she strolls out in the middle of the village children come rushing out to play with her. Andreja, Ermtraud, and I rush to join her screaming that she not start before we join her. Hæge laughs sharing with us, that many parents will have much free time today. Daddy and Kristoffel ask Hæge to explain for about the neighbors that surround his village. Hæge tells us that few are friends in this area and the raids occur when others have a need they must satisfy to live. Hæge tells us the village always puts any extra harvest into the open fields between their neighbors so any who need it may receive. Sadly, this has at times made certain of their neighbors lazy and dependent and when not receiving the same or more than the previous years, they wage war. I tell them that they should save the extra if they must move to a new land. Hæge agrees the village decided during last year's raids never again to share. We understand that we must have a larger Army, yet our numbers are so few. Kristoffel teaches Hæge that it is the numbers who fight that create an Army. Women and men, old and young can fight as a team and with the heart filled with their families love defeat great obstacles. We should begin training and preparing a fighting village immediately. It also would not hurt to domesticate selecting large beasts to transport the village's belongings. Daddy recommended that we see who we have available sixteen and older. We will need the fifteen year olds to watch and care for children under ten.

This leaves the eleven to fourteen-year olds to help the wounded, keep our weapons resupplied, and defend our beasts.

Hæge recommend we do this when all come to eat after they have finished their work. He shall dismiss work for the remainder of this week and will command all to train hard. Hæge confesses that he feels something in the air that is not good for his people. He also believes that something sent us to help them and live with them forever if we wish to do so. He then chuckles as they notice the boys around Olimpia, and girls around Kaus, and I guarded by Andreja and Ermtraud. Once he had directed Kristoffel and my father's attention Hæge commented, "I am sure we could enjoy our future generations with great happiness and peace. I from now recommend that you enjoy a particular courting of our widows. It is so foolish that they live alone, and you live alone. This will not be good for your grandchildren." Daddy told him that, "This is true; however, I first want to get the children settled into their new lives and the village prepared to defend our future babies." Hæge reveals to Daddy and Kristoffel that he tremendously appreciates their loyalty and patience in providing a safer world for our families. Hæge then asks them where our people would go if they had to leave for their survival. Daddy tells him that survival is not required to go east and crossing to the other side of the Cvetka lands that have empty lands. The Cvetka would help us cross because they would be settling in an ally to the far eastern borders, which helps protect them. This also gives them the right to fight and drive these invaders into the great sea. They have few people on their lands, as the number of people living in the entire east is not much. Hæge conveys that this is a new hope for his people. During the remainder of the day, they selected key points to defend and retreating plans if the battle was failing. Daddy tells him that with people, you can fight another day. When you lose too many people, none will stand at the end or at best, a few will live the remainder of their lives miserable and in great pain. Retreating can keep our wives and children from the slaughter of others and therefore is an important skill to have mastered. My father points out that one ridge behind the village slowly rises and about ten minutes' away declines.

The regression provides a place easily to destroy the raiders who would be in the open and has three separate trails as if it were at one time a crossroad. These trails curve as they give this village a chance to cover their tracks, and evade any pursuers, who finally kill our small force at the falloff point. Hæge asks Daddy, how he knows all these things about the land around our village. Daddy tells Hæge that he and Kristoffel had scouted around their village for most of the day the villagers captured them. Hæge reveals how thankful he is that I had such a wonderful angel (Olimpia) in our new family who saved them from making a great mistake. He reemphasizes that they are truly better people, and are no more than trying to destroy any evil that may come to kill them. My father tells them that he understands, it is, time to prepare for tomorrow and forget about yesterday. Daddy then asked for several old feather bags, with either feathers or grass in them. Tonight we would have one group train on archery and another group on throwing spears, while the third group would fight with their hands. They had a few tricks to teach them. All the people trained excellent, as fathers helped their sons, daughters, and wives. The teens molded together training hard. Something about having the males and females working together made it all fun for everyone. The males quickly adapted their styles to help their female counterparts. Daddy stood in front of the village and reminded them that even the strongest male will die unless he has his flanks covered. The stronger, their flanks, the longer they live. We each grabbed the fruit and went straight back to get our furs and feather bags and get to sleep. That night I had a special dream. While walking along a road, alone, I saw a pretty, brown hair girl, I would guess the same age as Andreja and Ermtraud, sitting on a large white rock in the middle of my path. I could see her legs, from her kneecaps down to her feet. Her arms were visible in parts, while other parts had a black transparent fabric draping them. Her top was like one I had never before seen. I could see her sides and her shoulders, as the front of her top was low. She had attractive small flowers in her hair and was looking at something on her left, as I could see, merely the side of her face and head.

What I could see was a gorgeous girl. Now the things I had never seen previously were the long blue feathers that draped from her lower sides and a lot from her legs. She had long smoky white and black feathers springing from her back. I began to walk slower, hoping that she would turn to see me. She continued to stare off with a sad expression to her left. Nevertheless, I maintained my movement toward her, even stepping on branches to create various noises trying to draw her attention. Too soon, I was standing in front of her, and I asked her, "Why do you endure to stare away from me?" Consequently, she moved her face so I could see her. She appeared so sad and helpless; therefore, I asked her if I could be of any form of help. She looked at me and shook her head no. After this, I asked her why she was so sad. She told me that everyone hated her, yet she always merely tried to help people. Next, she asked me where I lived previously. I told her I was from a village called Petenka, yet we are now staying with the people from the village of Bezdroża. Subsequently, she tells me there is no one who lives in Petenka now, for they killed their Spiritual Mothers permitting death to take them, although a few went to seek revenge, yet the Pirate Army killed them all. Notwithstanding; she tells me that she has never seen me in Bezdroża. I told her I just arrived yesterday and that I am now engaged to Andreja and Ermtraud. She gives me a strange stare and then asks, "How many do you intend to marry and is Hæge aware of this?" Now, things are really beginning to be strange for me. She is such a lovely, although sad looking, innocent girl; however, she knows too much about everything. I tell her, "Of course her father knows, after all, who would you think is going to provide us a hut to live in and I a job?" Her voice is so soft and warm, yet her pace is slow as if she owns time and her tone is low, drawing me closer to her to continue our conversation. She continues questioning me by adding, "I did not realize that one person could be engaged with two people. You must be fantastically special." I smile and point to a spot on the large stone beside her and she shakes her head yes. I thereby sit down beside her and tell her, "The village now allows this because death is taking so many of them."

She scratches her throat, takes a deep breath as the wind begins to blow harder and answers in an angry tone, "Death did not take them; their foolishness did. Death has warned them too many times to leave this land, yet they refuse. Death will visit them again in three weeks and those who are still here; they could die at the hands of evil killers from the mountains." I then ask her, "My name is Yakov, what is your name and how do you comprehend so many things?" She reveals to me, "I am Damijana. My job is the saddest in the skies above you. I am the one whom, they send to warn the good people that death is close to take them. Nevertheless, I am also the one who cries over the bodies of the innocent who die, as I did for Answald, Panfilo, Joggeli, Acia, Pava, and long ago Perla, your mother." I ask her, "What did we do wrong? We escaped from a village of evil. For that we had to die?" Damijana looks at me with tears in her eyes and tells me, "That is why cried; at how evil can take so many, through death. I wish that I could warn more. I did warn Joggeli in a dream, yet the next day, he continued as if nothing was wrong. Answald did the same thing. The others were too young to understand. Your mother's body betrayed her, as even death was surprised when they had to collect her." After that, I ask her, "Damijana, are you telling me that Bezdroża is in danger and that we must leave soon?" Damijana repeats, "The longer they stay; the more death will steal during the escape." I stick my hand out, and she places her hand inside mine. Her hand is warm, so I question her, "If I tell them this, how will they realize I am telling the truth?" She tells me to mention her name and to describe me. Damijana also adds, "If you stand and yell out my name three times I will send a wind that will blow down huts until you yell my name three times again, when I will stop. If you ask in your mind for me to help you with the words, I will." She then asks me, "Why are you so willing to trust and believe me?" I told her I just so much want to do something to render her happy and to thank her for the great work she does for us. She reached over and kissed me on my cheek. When she finished the kiss, her giant white stone and she vanished, as I went tumbling to the ground. I knew that I had an extremely important mission ahead of me. The next thing that I remember is Andreja shakes me to wake. She asks me, "Why are you so wet?"

I explain to her that I had a visitor in my dream with a message to our village. Ermtraud rushes me the dry clothes, while Andreja prepares my hair and appearance. She explains that I must tell her father the dream when we eat our morning fruit and meat, because we ate a little last night. I ask her if she wants to see what I dream about first. She tells me that in her village, the man tells his father initially or here her father. As we sat eating our breakfast Andreja, with pride, tells her father that I had a dream about the village last night. Hæge then congratulates me and asks that I reveal this wonderful dream. I reveal to all who are sitting with us, "Last night in a dream, I was walking along a path and noticed a little girl sitting on a large white stone." Andreja's face turns red with anger, yet she holds her peace as I continue, "She had her face turned to the side and looked vastly sad. She was dressed the same and had a few features that are different from ours are. I asked her name and she told me her name was Damijana." Hæge jump to his feet and told me to stop. That making fun of death can curse the village. He did not want me to say another word until their Spirit Man Cornelis had arrived. When Cornelis arrived, Hæge rushed out to brief him. Cornelis came in and sat before me saying, "I will listen to your words, and tell you if they are true." I tell him that he can listen all he wants; however, the words I tell him that Damijana tells me are true. He tells me that Damijana just speaks to him; therefore, my dream is false. He asks me, "Why would she speak to you?" Damijana speaking with my mouth tells him, "For I warned you many times, and yet I solely see death come to take so many from this village as you continue to ignore me. Did not you ignore me when I warned you about the death of your father, mother, and four brothers? I shall no longer speak to those who ignore me." Cornelis looks at me and says, "He has an evil spirit speaking with him. We must cast him from this village." I then stare at Hæge and ask him, "Will you listen to one who ignores the Spirits or one whom Spirits give us our warnings?" Hæge laughing at me asks, "How can I see the Spirits talk with you?"

I tell him that she told me if I tell her name three times she will send a wind to blow down your huts and that when I tell her name three more times she will force it to stop. Hæge then calls for Cornelis and I to stand in front of the people, Cornelis will call her name three times and we will see what happens, and if nothing happens, you may call her name. Cornelis agreed, and we stood before the people. He called her name three times and the wind stopped. I went to call her name and she told me to hold for another minute, she would tell me when. After a few minutes, Cornelis then challenges me. Damijana tells me to call her name. I yell out, "Damijana, Damijana, Damijana." The winds began immediately, blowing hard and knocking down huts, with Cornelis's first. After a few minutes, Hæge tells me to stop the winds. I call her name three times and the winds stops as I call her name the third time. Cornelis tells the people that his command was the one that started the winds and that it just took a little time for him to wake her. I tell the people that Damijana no longer will talk to him because he ignores her too much. Cornelis now becomes angry and tells the people to decide, if they decide him, I must leave and if they pick me he will leave and take all the Spirits that he talks with alongside him. Damijana tells me to say, "If he talks with them, let him talk to them now and show us what wonders they do." Cornelis tells the people that just evil Spirits do the conjectures, not the good Spirits. Damijana orders me to ask, "Do not the good Spirits love more than the evil Spirits? Do not the good Spirits give you your harvests so you may live? Tell us what great works the evil Spirits do?" Cornelis now declares, "The evil spirit gives the boy deceptive words to lead you into its death. I will not debate with an evil spirit. You decide now." The people yell out for Cornelis. I tell them, "Any who are still in this village tomorrow as the Suns are high in the sky shall die three weeks from this day." Hæge now asks my father to take his entire family to his hut before the villagers kill them as evil demons. We go back to his hut.

Andreja follows us, as also a girl named Urška who held Kaus's hand. Hæge orders for Andreja to stay. As she stops, Ermtraud comes running to join me. Her father and brothers chase her and tie her as she is attempting to fight them and drag her back to their hut. When Andreja saw Ermtraud rushing to me, she stopped and returned to me running as fast as her legs could take her. We enter the hut, and Daddy asks me, "What did Damijana say to you?" I told him all that she had said. She also gave me these words, "Damijana tells me that she appeared to you once in the forest, and you listened saving your hunters and to you Kristoffel, she has appeared to you twice, both times saving your hunters." Daddy looks at us. He next orders, "Start packing for we shall leave when I tell Hæge." Andreja and Urška ask me about them and Daddy says, "You are to learn today that when you vow to take a man as your husband you must also follow him. You are welcome, although you must fight the battle with your fathers." Hæge finally returns to speak with us. He looks at me and tells me, "I am so disappointed in you." I tell him that at least I will live longer than he will. Daddy tells him that we are packed, and will be moving out in just a few minutes. Urška now comes rushing in with her bags. Hæge tells her to put away her bags, as she is not going anywhere. Andreja now comes out with her bag and tells her father, "I will go, and you cannot stop me. For if you do, I shall hate you, and fight you for the next three weeks." Next, Andreja's mother stands beside her and tells Hæge that if he tries to stop her, she also will leave. Urška's mother comes in and tells Hæge not to stop her daughter as she is trying to begin her life and not continually kill the people of this village. Hæge next tells them that foolish mothers do not desire daughters. He then looks at us and tells us to leave quickly. Daddy then tells him, "I hope we are leaving in peace; however, I will ask the Jožefa for protection from any who follow us." A few young men stop by, and ask Olimpia to stay, yet she tells them her destiny is which her son and family. We are soon on the path leading to the east. I tell Daddy we must keep walking because many will try to escape this way, and the raiders will seek and kill them. They will search deeper as their hunger to work for death shall be greater.

We continue to walk until we come up against a steep giant cliff of clear stones. There is no way to climb this. I ask Daddy, what we can do. Kristoffel tells us that we can go around the base of this perpendicular mountainside and then work our way through a few passes and return on the above line. It will take a week, yet from above the ridge continues to climb before another great valley. He continues by saying the ironic thing is that they will be on that mountaintop, which is within view, on a clear day, of the village three weeks from today. Damijana speaks in my mind telling me, "You will see those of the village die and hear their screams as the wind will blow toward you that day." I then tell Daddy, "We will see and hear them dying." Andreja consequently, asks me if Damijana likewise visits her. Damijana tells me to reveal to her, "Tonight she will appear in both of our dreams." When we walk through a flimsy pass, between a couple of small hills with rocky tops, Damijana tells me we are to stop and go behind those stony tops for those who wish to kill us follow. I tell Daddy there is a killer behind us, and we must hurry to get through the thin pass and behind the rocky tops, so we can stop them. On arriving, Daddy tells everyone to pick a side and go. Once on top, he orders us to spread out, so we can create a larger ambush zone. He looks behind him and sees about thirty men heading this way with long spears. Daddy afterward warns us that foolish killers' boast spears that will slow down much before they reach us. He will give us the signal. Remember to allow one, injured, to return to the village, and update them concerning this defeat. The defeat was easy, as they had nowhere to hide in our ambush zone. The spears they threw up actually fell back down on them, killing their comrades. We flooded them with arrows as these targets were easy and our arrows grew faster during their flights. With barely five rounds of our arrows, combined with their falling spears we killed them all, except for the injured one. We had injured his arm, and able to surprise him, as we came down around him. Andreja and Urška knew him. They asked him to run back to the village and tell them, that all who leave by tonight will live in a new land. Those who do not will die at the hands of evil. Next, I asked him, "What form of evil tries to protect people from its greatest friend, death? Now go quickly to save those you love."

While sorting the lifeless bodies and taking back our arrows, we added their spears to our weapons. I noticed among the dead Cornelis, with two arrows in him. Daddy also saw him and commented, "It is sad when the blind must lead the blind even to their death. He must have known that if Damijana were to send us into the wilderness, she would protect us. Leading fighters into the mountains to fight with just spears is so foolish." We soon began our journey once again, stopping simply to grab fruit and berries that we along our path. The trees were protecting us from the winds and hot Suns, as we are fortunate to be traveling during the summer season. Occasionally, we pass a small stream and refill our water bags, while soaking our heated feet. It feels to me that even if one were to walk every day of his life, it would unfailingly be the next step that hurts. Either way, something always hurts. Fortunately, this water feels so wonderful that my recollection of this hurt is evading me now. As the evening begins to fall, Daddy leads us to a small area surrounded by rocks and asks us to eat our fruit and go to sleep, because tomorrow will be another day of walking. That night Damijana kept her promise and pulled Andreja and I into her presence. I walked over and sat at her right side. This time she was looking forward. Andreja strangely walked over in front of her, sat down facing her at her feet. Andreja's face was level with Damijana's belly. Damijana leaned over and rubbed her hand in Andreja's hair, telling her, "I wanted to meet you for so long. I hope you find favor with me and forgive me for talking to your mate." Andreja tells her, "How can I not find favor in one who works so hard to save us? If you want my mate, we can share him." Damijana explains to her, "I cannot mate with those who are alive. I selected him because of his hate for death. I hold a little sad news for you Andreja. I cannot forewarn the seeds of those whose parents defied my warning. It is the law of the upper skies. No matter how hard I try, I cannot see in your future. Nevertheless, I can ask you always to stay where Yakov can protect you, and you both should live and be happy for many years. I so much want to be your friends since I can sense a good love between you both. You will meet a Spirit Man in a village one month from here who will marry you. Accordingly, I will tell him to do so in a dream."

Therefore, I asked her if we could stay with her for a while longer and just talk about young people things. She agreed, and began by telling us tales of many wise men, through the ages, who listened to her and their villages grew large in numbers. In each, either the people killed their Spiritual leader, or they died naturally living beyond their promised years. The new ones had to test me by ignoring my warnings. At all times, death won. Andreja complements Damijana on her extreme beauty. Damijana argues that Andreja is the one with the great beauty. I tell them that both are beautiful. They tell me I am foolish and blind. I then ask Damijana how Acia and Pava are doing. She tells me that they are especially happy, so do not worry about them. That is such relief to hear. Andreja then asks how the ones in Bezdroża will die.

Damijana tells her it will not be a pleasant sight, and that she never peeks into the future and witness how death steals the lives of the innocent. Andreja and I tell her we understand, as I wipe the tears from her eyes. Damijana explains that she must return us to our bodies to prevent any damage, and she must finish her work for this evening. We immediately wake up and kiss. Andreja tells me she feels as the most fortunate woman in the entire world to enjoy a husband who the Spirits love. I tell her that Damijana also loves her. Andreja reassures me that she knows this and loves Damijana. I laugh and joke how I cannot escape having two girlfriends at the same time. Damijana tells me, in my head, "Foolish boy, this is because you are so handsome." She scared me when she began with 'foolish boy,' as I thought she was going to slam me. When she finished that phrase with a compliment, all I could do was thank her. The next three weeks passed by slowly, with all the walking and climbing that filled our days. We finally made it to where Damijana told us was the safe spot. The doomsday had arrived for Bezdroża. We watched helplessly, as a band of killers circled their Bezdroża and began their attack. They began by flaming certain huts and killing those who ran out the smoldering huts with their arrows. This was simply their introduction, because they were there to steal and thereby did not want to burn their booty. Their leader told the village that they merely wanted, the plunder.

If all came out, they would keep them against the back rock wall behind the village, and if they promised to stay there after the raiders had collected all they wanted, the raiders would let them live. However, any who tries to hide or to fight, they will rape, or castrate and then burn them on a pole. They next began pounding poles into the ground and collecting the wood for fires. Ermtraud escaped by going out the back of her hut and began running through the woods. She had a long knife with her. As she was zipping through the woods, filled with terrifying fear, she accidentally stepped into one of her village's traps and flung up into the air tied by her feet. The trap also released a few bells, which released loud ringing sounds. Ermtraud, as she was slowly swinging from the rope draws her long knife and cuts the rope that holds her foot. She somersaults through the air and smashes into a tree as a branch stub rams into her chest. Within a few minutes, enemy raiders came to pull her body down and present her as a public torture. Nevertheless, because of the mercies of the skies, they spared her that horrifying torture. Damijana understood that Ermtraud wanted to be with Yakov, yet her family made her a prisoner of death. This is why she allowed death to take her as long as no other hands stole her life. Many among the village felt, as they were resilient enough to outfox these foolish raiders. Maybe, if they formed and fought as one, they could have given the raiders a light surprise. However, by staying separated, they captured them one by one, and had no chance. The raiders raped or castrated based on gender, and then beat them before casting their dying bodies into a burning fire with no hope of help. Those who had surrendered watched this horror slowly unfold before them on this sad hot day of unnecessary death. The truth is they are basing this on an old man's stubborn pride and the people who followed him who not just shared but also cultivated this abysmal end. When the raiders destroyed the village, they made the remaining survivors into slaves, to carry their previous belongings of limited wealth. We watched this horror unfold before us as we cried and shared our expressions of misery for our former friends and their suffering.

I asked Andreja if I were really of such low quality that so many wanted to die rather than follow my words. She told me that if any spoke or thought averse to me, her father once obtaining proof would have punished them. They thought of me the same as, they thought of her. She reemphasizes that is why she stood beside me when I spoke of my vision and why she left everything to follow me. They should have seen that this was a sign of her great belief in me. Urška then adds that they died because of their stubbornness, foolishness, because they did not enjoy mother's, which loved and trusted their judgment. Urška and Andreja hold and cry on each other's shoulders. Olimpia crowds between them and complains, "If you want to be a part of this family, you must also let us share in your grief. We are in this game now for life." With that, Kaus and I joined our girls on sitting on their other side so Olimpia was in the middle. This brought joy to me. The wind was starting to blow the horrific smell toward us, so Daddy said we would pass through the valley tonight in the clean air and cross the next ridge through a nearby pass, which not merely saves time, but also gives us clean air. Urška and Andreja asked if they could share something with the family tonight during our fruit-eating meeting. We decided to eat fruit and berries tonight; for fear that, cooking our game's flesh could cause us to suffer sickness because of what we smelled throughout this day. Before we began to eat, Urška and Andreja stood in front of us and began by thanking us for having them in our family. Daddy told them not to worry about it, because for an unknown reason, since they have been with us, his sons were much happier. They then told us, they wanted to give us their dowry. They unfolded three cloth rags filled with coins, gems, and diamonds, subsequently much that Daddy and Kristoffel asked them how they got so massive of a collection. The girls told us that their mothers gave most of what their fathers had to them.

Then, because Cornelis made such pronounced demand that we must leave, Ermtraud went into his tent and took his great collection. She figured that since the village had paid him to speak with the Spirits, and Damijana told us he had ignored her; he was stealing from the village; therefore, the village should steal back. Ermtraud then gave the collection to Andreja's mother. Kristoffel looks at Daddy and says, "I believe it without any doubts in my mind, because my former wife would have done the same thing for any of our daughters." Daddy looks at Olimpia and says, "If your mother were alive, she would most likely take half of what Petenka had and gave it to you." Olimpia next asks Daddy, what he would have done when he discovered she had executed such a thing. Daddy looks at her and smiles, "Olimpia, you did not recognize your mother. She would have made me not merely help her, but also to carry them for her." Death came and even though warnings went ignored, took away the foolish. Notwithstanding; I do not fear death so much now. I would suppose that Damijana is part of my freedom from this panic. Nevertheless, I enjoy Andreja to help with my hurt and for me to help with her hurt. I can also see how happy Kaus is with Urška, and Olimpia is joyful trying to cement our relationships. Consequently, I think Olimpia believes that once we are settled, she can begin setting up her life. This appears to be different from her earlier plan to set up with Joggeli. Most likely, since we had Acia and Pava, she wanted to give them a better home situation. Because Daddy and Kristoffel were hunters, we could never lock them into being members of a certain village. The remaining five of us represent both Petenka and Bezdroża. The hurt from my walking and previous life is beginning to lose its pain, as a joy and hope for a new tomorrow are flowing in the air just as the flowers in Damijana's hair.

CHAPTER 07

Good-bye father, hello mother

"I believe as if I have known you for a longtime," explains a voice through the foggy air in front of me. I realize who is saying this because her words are the sole ones that echo straight from my ears into my heart. She has molded so quickly with me, almost as two breaths, the first one stopping and blending with the second. It could also be like a cup with water that was half-full. Next, the other half-full cup of water was blended within it. Now, the second half carried with it many elements of the world, more commonly known as dirt and dust. This dirt, which darkened the half-cup, diluted when it blended with the purest water. Yes, the water is still dirty, yet there is enough clean in it to keep the unclean separated. Saying thanks to Andreja is merely the beginning of my eternal jubilees for her. She is what I need. Andreja gave up her world and in faith joined my family becoming one with us. Andreja and Urška appear to blend in so easily and cheerfully. Each time I try to discover what is going on inside her mind, she quickly puts up her defenses and swears everything is so wonderful. I realize she has to hurt, as I had time between my sibling's deaths. However, she watched or even worse heard them cry out in their deaths. I tell her that I appreciate her father is one of the slaves they took away. We were lucky in that they took men, women, and even a few children with them. Daddy tells us that they take the children to keep the parents, because if a parent escapes, their children are automatically tormented to their deaths. I am miserable in knowing that people who are being tortured truly beg for death to free them.

I ask Daddy, why we should build a village when we are just targets for the merciless slaughterers to kill us. Kristoffel tells me the secret is to be mobile and free from your belongings. You can lose your possessions and obtain more in the future. When you lose your life, you sleep in the dirt. I try to picture Andreja's situation. She was the popular girl in the village, and could choose from the best that Bezdroża had to offer. She finds some strangers that her friends want to torture and take as prisoners. Andreja tells me that she felt as part of us the first time she saw us. I enjoy so much how that, when I wallow over Olimpia, she also does. Olimpia will grab her hand and check for dirt under her fingernails. Andreja sits there so proud that she had cleaned them and waits for Olimpia's powerful, "wonderful job my love." I have no concerns that over the future, years that Olimpia will stay with us and be the Queen of our home. Andreja hugs Olimpia so tight that I can see marks on Olimpia's body, yet she smiles and begs her to hug tighter. One is special in my heart. I rush to bed at night to talk with her in my dreams. I ask her why she cannot visit me in the day. Damijana tells me that she is not supposed to be talking with us. She has adopted Andreja in our group as a sister she never had. I asked her one night what I represented, and she told me, "You represent the evil of men," followed by laughing and then continued, "Truly; you stand for my love and hope." Andreja laughs and answers, "I got the best one did not I Damijana?" Damijana responds, "You, without question did, and now we must be careful so you can keep him. If you see him talking to other girls, you tell them that he belongs to you and the death angel and I will visit them with a warning they will never again want to receive." I ask Damijana if that is not too severe. She tells me that, "Andreja can talk to the other girls, and you can talk to the other boys. There will be much less heartache this way." I also ask Damijana if she had anything to do with all the flowers that are blossoming on the ridges we travel. She answers by telling me that our father picked a good time of the year to travel this region, as it gets nasty in the cold months.

Our convoy is settling into its distinctive rhythms now, as Daddy and Kristoffel take turns leading and scouting. Olimpia stays with Andreja and me and rotates to Kaus and Urška when they call for her. Olimpia has been never truly with us when she is beside us, as she keeps one ear and eye scanning our area. She tells me that we have enjoyed our fair share of surprises. We are moving slowly to the high mountains that separate our mountains from the western lands. Daddy passes out some fur strips that we are to tie to our feet because the ground will be cold and slippery. He tells us we will be in the coldest area for a few days and nights. Next, he tells us that when we sleep at night, he does not want to see more than one person in our huddle. We, five young people, are to sleep packed tight boys on the outside and girls crammed in the middle. He does not want to tie our furs into a tent, because the poles will form marks in the grounds for trackers and block our vision of the stars. We must see the moons and stars as they can give us signs of movements in the lower lands. Every sign is a key to our life. Our father is getting much better at sharing his concerns and suspicions with us. We routinely stop during the day and check with each another, and what we saw. He tells us what is on his mind. Daddy is changing our route now and taking us up into the cold ridge, where we can acquire a curvy pass and come back to this area. Nevertheless, this way is much higher on the mountain and in fine position to cross over another ridge that moves us closer to the west. This difficulty in terrain accounts for the main reasons few have ventured to the west. Kristoffel share that he believes a group is about three days behind us. Because we are zigzagging to advance ourselves for a better pass to cross the ridge, we can see if any is following us. I ask my father why anyone would be after us. He explains there are many reasons. One could be that random hunters or scouts are passing through, considering that anytime killers and raiders begin terrorizing their neighbors, tribes begin to relocate. Another reason could be that some of the riders whom captured Bezdroża may have discovered that we have a great dowry and elected to search for it.

The most likely reason is that many of Andreja's old boyfriends are searching for her. Andreja responds casually, "If it is my old boyfriends, then you had better begin producing more arrows, because you have much killing to do." Daddy looks at her, smiles, pinches her cheek, and comments, "We are extremely fortunate to have such fresh blood like you and Urška. You are wonderful blessings indeed." He goes to pinch Urška's cheek and she draws to slap him, saying, "You kiss me like you kiss Olimpia." As he goes to kiss Urška's cheek, Andreja grabs his arm, pull it into an L form on his back, and ask, "Do you have something to say to me?" Daddy clears his throat and winks at me. I am sitting here in shock. Why is she attacking my father? Daddy says calmly, "May I also kiss your cheek?" She releases him and drops in his lap with her cheek in an easy position for him to kiss. Daddy kisses and hugs her tight. Urška complains, "Why did not I get a hug?" Olimpia jumps in and says, "Hay, wait one minute; I did not get a kiss or hug." Andreja leaps up, gives Daddy a peck on his cheek, and dives on Olimpia saying, "I will kiss, and hug you." Confused, I jump on Olimpia also saying, "Me too, save some for me." Daddy motions for Urška to join him, hugs her and says, "Sorry champ." Kaus asks Daddy what happened. I tell Daddy to wait, because I want also to know. Daddy explains that his future daughter-in-laws are claiming their hold on the love and bond in our clan. I ask Daddy how he knew what was on Andreja's mind. Kristoffel tells us that no one will ever comprehend what is on a woman's mind, yet a father will always see what his daughter is thinking. I stare at Kaus and we both say, "Wow," shake our heads and sit down as our brides return to our sides. I ask Andreja how she can express herself so openly. She tells me that every time we try to hide what is inside us, we do other things that bellow our secret for all to hear and see. She must have a father, and therefore, she will work to her death to earn his respect as his daughter. Naturally, she will do what she has to bring honor to me. I tell her to stop that honor stuff, because if I am weak, I need to become strong, and therefore, the more who recognize I am weak the more help I will have.

Anyways, these people grasp everything about me. Andreja adds that soon they will be familiar with correspondingly everything about her. She begs me never to be as her father, but to listen to those who love me. Andreja asks me to tell her about our new homeland. While she is asking, I hear Urška question Kaus if they can join our conversation. Olimpia asks to join us. Urška and Andreja pull her between them and snuggle close to her. Kaus jokes telling us, "Our women will not be cold tonight." Urška and Andreja tell Olimpia that she is going to think as if she is sleeping in the middle of the day during the hot season under both Suns. Olimpia begins to cry, telling us, "I never dreamed my brother's wives would be so wonderful." Urška and Andreja tell her that they are going to care for her the remainder of her days. Andreja after this tells Urška they will have to live with them, because Yakov pledged to care for her from many years ago. Olimpia tells us, "We will all live close enough that when one kicks me into the

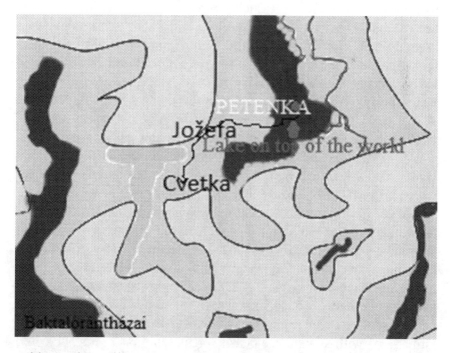

cold, another will save me." Urška and Andreja become angry and scream at her, "Do you think we are that kind of evil people? Do you think our love is fake? We have promised to care, love, and serve you until death separates us."

Olimpia wipes their tears and answers, "Oh; my loves, I was simply trying to cause us to laugh. I would never think anything bad about you two angels. You are my hope for a happy future. My love for you art so great that I shall wait until I marry. I must ensure all my babies are all right. From this day forwards, if you want me to talk with any of you, you must call me mommy. If you wish to live with us, then I am your mother. Never question my faith and love for you." I snuggle close to Kaus and tell him, "These women are strange." He agrees. Andreja declares, "Time to teach these little boys what big girls can do to them." The three of them pounced on us and gave us a solid whipping. It is not fair fighting with the girls because we cannot hit them. I mean, no laws prohibit this; however, our hearts will not permit us. They, on the other hand, go for blood as if they are wild animals. Lucky for us, they love us; therefore, we are receiving the introductory course on how to keep quiet when around them. They slap hard, and then begin to cry, releasing their tears on us as they swoop down to kiss our smitten flesh. I stopped saying, "That is okay," as every time I say it, they slap me again. Kaus and I both are using the completely defeated and without hope. They finally ask us if we surrender. We both quickly plead for their mercy. Daddy and Kristoffel have joined us now as I hear Kristoffel say, "Pawka, those boys will be outstanding husbands." I gaze up at Daddy and ask him if he tells us more about the new lands where we will live. Daddy asks if this would not be better to talk about with our evening meal, because we will have enough time to reach the white lands before dark. Our women dig through our bags and produce a pleasing meal for us. Daddy tells us, "We will be in the mountains for at least one more month. The western sides of these mountains have many large cliffs, and for many are not passable. Do not worry, because we have knowledge of some caves that can take us down to the green lands. We will next travel in the Jožefa lands. Ordinarily, with some large beasts to ride on their backs, we could cross through this land in four months. Unfortunately, once we enter the Jožefa lands we have thirty to forty days until the dark season. I am aware of some thick hilly forestland along the route Kristoffel, and I have selected. This area has many caves. We will work on making a hut within range of a few caves. We should use the caves for cooking the beasts we capture and for cold nights, as the winter months will be following the dark season. Fortunately, for us, these winter months are not as harsh as those in our mountains are. We will travel on the beasts we capture. Several species train easily. The Jožefa use them extensively. They taught me how to capture and train them. We will meet with some of their elders and see what they will let us do. Because we have three women and just two older men, they should agree we are not warriors. We will not tell them that we escaped from great Armies, as to do so can scare them into sacrificing us to their sky masters. We will have many possible places to settle. One thing we have in our favor is the golden hair that Andreja and Urška have. Many of the Spiritual men of these tribes believe the golden-haired women originated in the sky and are extremely rare." I informed Daddy that perhaps Damijana might help us at times. Andreja then asked me if we had told them what she revealed to us last night. I explained to Daddy that with all the things happening today, I completely forgot. I disclosed to our family that last night Damijana told Andreja and me that we had a happy surprise waiting to discover us. She added that this surprise would bring great joy in our futures. Kristoffel asks us; please tell the good news immediately. We need news such as this to give us the extra energy and hope as we struggle through our days. Now, time to head to the white lands. We are currently walking straight up to this somewhat steep hill. Daddy is trailing from behind, covering any tracks we are making, and he is setting a false series of tracks, which lead into a dead-end canyon. I constantly marvel when I watch the way my Father and Kristoffel handle themselves and the surrounding environment. They appear always to be a few steps ahead and continually planning with alternatives. Our group reaches the side path that they selected for us to cross around onto a ledge that drops into a stepping ridge. We will travel this ridge, or precisely about six feet on the smooth slope to its left side.

This is so the moons do not flash our silhouettes for all to see. This side blocks the lights, thus is dark, and helps to camouflage us. We find ourselves tripping into each another often, which is presenting any danger. Instead, it gives us a quick laugh as we help the guilty one back to their feet. The late-night hours are longer than the daytime hours, unless trying to sleep, and then morning rushes to claim a new day. I notice Olimpia and walking close to Andreja and Urška. I can see that they are watching out for each another. Kaus has adopted me this night as we trip over each other in front of our women. Our females' eyes can see in the dark, for when one of us goes down, everyone laughs. We always recognize when one of our females falls, because all three drops. They will not release their sister's hand, instead trying to hold on to her. We had four rabbits stumble in front of us tonight. Kaus simply drops the tip of his spear on them, and gives it a twist. He then flings it towards me as I stab it with my long knife. I would hold him away from me with one hand and use my ax or woodcutter to chop off his head. After that, I hand him to Olimpia, who quickly guts it and then drop him in her meat bag. The rabbits were on the ridge top and therefore, slightly blinded by the night's light. Daddy kept us moving until he found a rare rock stacked holding area. He tells us that legends say these holding areas are the remains of forts, which at one time guarded this area. The rocks are high enough to conceal a camping fire, although we have to put it out in the morning because of the smoke. Kristoffel and Daddy had been collecting wood throughout the night while they were scouting. The girls quickly cook the four rabbits, and a few food root's Daddy found when scouting.

We all ate well. Kristoffel congratulates us and asks us not to catch any more game, as cleaning it is marking our trail. Granted the trail will barely be marked for a few days before nature completely removes their remains, it is a danger. He and our father will catch and clean an assortment of wild game while scouting. I confess that I never thought about it marking our trail; however, with walking on this white land, the red easily can be seen. Daddy also teaches us that not properly concealing the waste parts, such as the chopped head and insides will attract predators, and we do not want them snooping around us. We have another week in this white land, and then we can pass in a small valley that has a pass that leads into the high ridge. That is where we can see if any are following us, as the ridge is also high enough barely to see

Bezdroża. We can see if any others have moved in, and if they are cooking with fire, which will show smoke streams. We continue to travel at night, which Daddy says is more, his preference now. This side of the mountain is unpredictable in that so few travel here, those who do tend to be more volatile. At the end of this boring week, we begin to move down into the valley, which for us is brown land and trees. Kristoffel tells us the remainder of our trip will just include a few days in the white lands and no more than one day at a time. The ridges encompass enough lower trails to support our travel needs. We decided to rest for a few days and give our bodies a chance to thaw. We were not frozen, but merely had the deepest chills in the bones. Kristoffel comes running back down from the lookout point he was hiding calling for our father to join him. He told Daddy what he saw. Daddy looked at us and saw we were all staring intensely, so he told us to put down our gear. When we get to the lookout point, there will be no noise, no talking, and absolutely no movement when at the top. Excitement overwhelms us as we cautiously follow our father. We do exactly what he does.

One ironic thing we did unaware was each of us hit the side of our head as we went pass one of the trees. Before going, the last few feet where we can see out to the valleys below Kristoffel ask us why we did this. Olimpia told him that Daddy did it. Daddy laughs and tells us that he felt an itch under his cap, so he hit it fast hoping to stop the itch. He then looks at us and rebuilds our self-respect by saying he is proud that we executed that move just to be safe. He tells us we obeyed automatically and unconditionally. I was thinking that he must really be impressed because he seldom rattles off such long words. He continues that, "I believe you have the building blocks; we need to produce a wonderful future for you and your families." Lastly, he winks at all three of our women and says, "I want many grandchildren." The girls laugh. Daddy tells us that he will point, and motion where he wants us to go. We take off our hats and crawl slowly to the top. He will motion for us to go beside something, like a rock or small trees. Our entire clan occupied this lookout ridge, and we witnessed something that froze us. There were two old women and a young man, with a beast, with us. Andreja and Urška slid down from their lookout point and then crawled up below Daddy and tapped him on his leg motioning for him to come down and talk with them. Daddy rushed down as so did Kaus, Olimpia and me. We are a united stay together type of young people's group. Urška begins by telling us the older woman who is with the young man looks a lot like her mother and senior brother. Daddy asks her how she knows for sure. Urška tells him that she knows that dress and that her brother smoothed over her to protect her just as that young man is doing. Andreja joins the conversation saying, "The beast they bring is my favorite pet. That is my mother, because I made her that dress." Olimpia asks Urška how old her brother is. Smiling, Urška replies, "He is advanced in years enough to turn your baby making machine on." She then rolls on top of Olimpia and hugging her tells her, "Now you can also have a family." Olimpia smiles and asks her to run this pass her brother. Urška tells her not to worry, he will do what she says or she will give him a thumping he will not forget, then he will do what she told him. Kaus smiles and says, "Great he and I will have something in common, and that is sisters who abuse us." Olimpia pounces on top of him and reminds him he must be quiet so we do not give away our position. She then starts pulling his hair. He is in much pain, yet maintaining his silence. Daddy then motions for her to stop.

Andreja looks at Daddy and says, "Our mothers are widowed now and will be looking for men to own." Daddy smiles and tells her, "Do not worry; we will not have four single elders in this village young lady. I am actually glad she is here, because I did not understand exactly how to tell you, Urška, and my daughter the things a mother is supposed to teach you before you marry." Andreja tells Daddy not to worry, because Olimpia already explained what we had to do if we wanted to reproduce babies. Daddy looks at Olimpia and asks her how she knew this. Olimpia informs him that his wife told him before she died. Daddy smiles and says, "All these years later and Perla is still saving me. She was such a wonderful partner." Olimpia, Urška, and little Andreja squeezed between them, hug Daddy and reassures him everything will be okay. Daddy accordingly looks at Andreja and asks her, "Do you think I could ever love another woman?" Andreja, who can think on her feet, responds immediately, "You love me, do you not?" We laughed at this one and then Daddy responds, "I sure do. I do not have Acia, but believe she helped bring you in our family. One love gone, a new love arrives." Olimpia tells Daddy, "It is the same thing." Daddy then asks Olimpia, "What would my children think if they saw me with a new wife?" Kaus tells our father, "We would be the happiest children in the world. You need a new life, especially since you never left us." Kristoffel joins us and asks Daddy, "Do you want me to bring those widows here, or should I?" Daddy tells him, "I had better had you, because I might screw it up considering how things such as thing always tongue tie me." Kristoffel responds with, "I am gone, and do not worry about those things' old man, the widows will be claiming what they believe is theirs." Urška adds, "If that widow has her son and daughter with her, she will be three times as dangerous." Kristoffel bids us good-bye and yells, "See you all in a week."

I ask Daddy if they are one week from us, and Kristoffel must go to them and bring them back, how is that one week. My father explains that while Kristoffel is going to them, they are coming to him. That will chop off the second week. I find myself once more amazed at how these men can think in the total framework. Daddy tells us he will scout around for a cave we can live in one of the nearby valleys, so we will not be out in the open. Excitement is in the air, because everyone will belong to a pair. Andreja and Urška confess to us that these are not their first mothers, nor are they living with their real fathers. They are all dead. The children rotated many times in their village. Daddy reveals that he knew nothing of all the death in their village. Andreja informs us that they had three villages when she was born. They had a bloody civil war that killed many. Those who remained were too few to ward off their angry neighbors. They had to fight battles for years before they accumulated enough to generate their escape into that last valley. Things had just started to settle until another tribe began harassing them a few years ago. The harassment would include children, beheaded and tied to animals, then released through their common areas. The situation started to become critical when some of the Bezdrożan warriors come to be lost one night and attacked a family belonging to another tribe. Because of that, terror had reigned in their valley. Each day, the families would reorganize based on who was despite everything, living. Andreja reaffirms that love still rule their family relationships. The new parents would rush to their new children as the old, which was dead, could relive once again. This is the reason that their children play each day, and the adults did all the work and protection. Urška explains this is the reason their mothers let them go, because they felt that if this the single time in their young days they found love, then they could not forfeit it. Love and life were like dreams for them, when they awoke, they were gone. I asked them if this type of lifestyle bothered them. Our brides tell us that because all the families lived similar to this, no one knew that different methods were possible. Andreja compares their family culture must like ours. The difference between us is that we did not replace Perla and Daddy always came back.

His departure is compared to death and return corresponding to the arrival of a new father, who trying to capture the life lost during the separation. We must let the dead be the victims and the living the victors. Olimpia asks them what they want from their lives now. They both confess that having their mothers back in our lives will be so wonderful. The hope of having them live in some sort of peace is a dream that has come true. Daddy afterwards tells us that we will still have our battles to fight. We will simply attempt to place ourselves in situations where we will win. Olimpia reports that we have yet to see all the tricks from our Father and Kristoffel. Daddy excuses himself, as he wants to go back up to the lookout. About an hour later, he motions for Kaus to join him. Kaus comes running back to us and tells us that he and Daddy must try to catch Kristoffel that a small group is tracking our newcomers, and then optimistically save them. Kaus orders me to take care of our future mothers. I inform him that he will help me with these mothers; I tried juggling three women before, and I will never try that again. He shakes his head as he grabs his bow and two bags of arrows and zips off beside Daddy. I yell at Daddy; a red rag means trouble, so watch the arrows in the sky. White rag means to wait where you are. Daddy yells back to me, "Got it." Nighttime is quickly approaching, so we position ourselves just below the ridgeline and sleep. We will be peeking down below looking for fires. We see one small one and identify it as the invaders. By watching the shadows as its members pass between the flame and us, we estimate it to be a group of five men. Our defenders have no fires, as they are on the attack currently. When morning arrives, we can see Balderik walking around on the path. He is Urška's brother and must be gathering some morning food for the mothers. Olimpia reports that, by the way, he came out of the ground; they must have slept in a cave the previous night. Estimating from where the flashing fire was last night, the raiders are one day behind them and knowing that Kristoffel takes shortcuts and may barely sleep one hour here and there, he could reach them in two days. Daddy and Kaus will reach them the next day, if Balderik gets them moving soon. They appear to be in no hurry, as Balderik keeps going into the cave with what he gathers, as if he is building up some storage. Our gang, a short while later, could see Balderik and Babali walking with their arms around each other's shoulders. Babali, his mother, appears to be limping. Urška begins to cry, knowing that if her mother cannot walk, they run a great danger of detection and execution. I tell her that it appears the invaders are familiar with this territory as they are staying on the path and moving quickly, without worry of any harming them. We took turns watching, as we could just about follow the raiders and Balderik. Kina appeared briefly in the last afternoon, giving us some relief in that she was extremely cautious. Andreja tells us that her mother is always enormously prudent. All we could do is watch from here, especially as our three rescuers were cautious not to reveal themselves.

Kina and Babali's story was superbly much different. While watching their most-recent orphans depart with their new opportunities to start a fresh life with love, and their mystical association with the Damijana, a spirit whose tales flowed from the elder's mouths in so many legends, they agreed that the truth was with them. They had spent the day of their departure arguing and fighting with their latest mates and with no luck, decided to chase after their young loves. Kina claimed that Andreja had given her something she could not live without having in her future. Her argument with Hæge turned violent as she took a beating before escaping. She rushed to Babali's hut, hoping for some sanctuary that night before leaving the next day. Babali made the same demand on her mate, prior to Kina's arrival. Their fight became so fierce that her son had to save her. Balderik defeated his temporary father and tied him up binding him inside one of their storage containers. That night, the three of them departed. They traveled day and night for three days to ensure their escape was successful. They could not stop after speaking with the lone survivor of the ambush on Cornelis. Regrettably, the constant travel did not appear to move them any closer to us. When they found their first cave to sleep within, they slept for two days. They returned on their journey just to discover a week later that they were on the wrong path. The gang was completely lost, as if there is such a thing as being partially lost. Kina told them that she knew Andreja was going west, so they would use the Suns to help steer them in that direction. They actually had maneuvered themselves to be on a high ridge that gave them a wide view. They saw a deep canyon beside them that had a river flowing through its rock-filled bed. Kina figured that this canyon led to the western lands, as the sister ledge slowly decreased. She figured that it would have to cross our path eventually, as the available paths were extremely rare. It was while walking the ridge they discovered a group of five men, from the raiders of Bezdroża belonging to a clan that call themselves the Agata. When the path they were on crossed with the path the Agata was traveling, they decided to chance it. They were staying in the lead until Babali hurt her leg. This is when they settled into the cave. That night Damijana appeared in their dreams in voice solely and told them about the cave. Damijana furthermore, ordered them to stay in that cave until she told the trio it was okay to leave. They reached the cave and set some special traps in the path ahead of them so when the five attackers pass by them; they would receive a few surprises. The group walked the path and four of them survived the invisible ambush as an avalanche of rolling stones crushed one and banged up a few legs from the others in that death patrol. The survivors rushed the rolling stones rather than running from it as Balderik had hoped. From that point onward, the invaders traveled concealed in the vegetation along the path.

Daddy, Kaus and Kristoffel did not realize the change in plans of the remaining raiders. My father and Kaus were traveling in the vegetation and Daddy's sense in the woodlands. He should be able to maneuver around them; we hoped. Kristoffel omitted his ordinary precaution to run down the path. He more or less figured it was all clean when they went through the first time and because he had spotted no one throughout this evacuation, chose speed over security wanting to save the three future family members. Kristoffel ran head on to three arrows as each raider got a shot at him. An additional arrow barely missed his head. They hit him in both legs and one in his stomach. Kristoffel, knowing that they had him wanting to take at least one of them with him. He pretended to fall down into the vegetation dying. Once inside the vegetation, he crawled to a nearby stone and slowly raised himself. Subsequently, his senses were scanning his area. He saw the direction the arrows came and that two had hit him from the right and two from the left. The four attackers split themselves into two groups of two each. He guessed that they would want to finish off his body. The best chance he had would be to get the two from the other side as they crossed the road. The winds were still now and few birds in the area. His fall into the brush made enough noise to scare the wildlife. Two of the killers crossed the path, and as they approached the middle, Kristoffel hit the first one between his eyes with an arrow. The second man jumped back into the brush. Without warning, he rose and shot an arrow that flung above Kristoffel and into the tree above him. Kristoffel heard a thump and looked behind him to see that one of the raiders was scouting for him in the tree and his comrade mistook him as being Kristoffel and hit him in his chest with an arrow. The man now crawled towards Kristoffel with a knife in his hand. Kristoffel carefully rolled himself behind the nearby tree to have protection from the killers on the other side of the path. As his attacker inched near, Kristoffel grabbed his woodcutter or ax and with his last breathes crushed it into his enemy's head. His hit was extremely fast, direct, and bone crushing that he gave no cries of pain. The enemy on the side of the path remained hidden as he continued unknowingly to track his comrade on the other side of the path. On discovery of his partner and Kristoffel's body, immediately, he called aloud for his comrade on the other side of the path. They verified control of each side and then rushed to see if their comrade, who was lying in the middle of the path was still living. They next, lay the three bodies behind the bush along the path and continued on their mission.

Meanwhile, Balderik when hearing his rock trap release and one man's scream elected to investigate how well his ambush had faired. He rushed to the site, and seeing one still trapped under a large stone used his woodcutter to chop the victim's head. The special thing about these two stones was that they were situated properly on the hill. He simply removed the dirt that held them and then once having the trap door in place below them, filled in the space between with smaller stones. He then repositioned the two large stones on top to keep the pressure on his ambush trap door. He was not the creator of this set up straps. However, he discovered and rearmed them. After reviewing the release, he decided the leave the rocks in the path, as they would force any who was walking to stagger on the remaining special traps. He decided to continue and maybe be some backup for any who might come back to rescue them. He knew that my father was at home in the wilderness. He quickly rushed back to Kina and Babali, grabbed a bag of arrows, and told them he would return within a few days. He favored the right side of the path, therefore, traveled on the fresh brush path to its side. Balderik figured he should be able to handle a retreat ambush. A few hours later, as he continued in the bushes, he discovered Kristoffel and two of the invader's bodies. He knew Kristoffel was a great man of the wilderness, and had sacrificed himself to get two of the raiders. The odds were good now. If he could pluck one in the back, he would be able to secure himself and catch the second one or out wait him until more help arrived sent by his sister. Balderik believed that his sister would not abandon them. It was strategy and luck that would win for them now, yet sorrowfully; neither was on their side this day. Balderik experienced much trouble with negotiating the brush in a quiet fashion. He snapped a few branches and startled a few birds. This was enough to alert the attackers, who were moving cautiously ahead and higher, on the sloping hillside above him. Both invaders hit him in his head with their arrows, and quickly slashed his throat, so they could hope to maintain the wilderness silence. Balderik could get out a yell shake a small tree beside him as his departure from life gift. He could purely pray that it help his rescuers.

Regrettably, Daddy was still too far away. Balderik's dying scream had the opposite effect. It told the raiders that he had to be trying to warn others. The fact that he attacked from behind and Kristoffel had attacked from the front alerted them that there had to be groups both in front of them and behind them. They would continue searching ahead; nevertheless, keep an eye out for anything behind them. The remainder of the day went uncontested; therefore, they slept without a campfire that night, knowing now is the time to exist invisible. Late the following day, their next battle began. They chose to travel beside each other, with one concentrated on behind and the other on the front of them. Daddy and Kaus were walking separately on each side of the path. Daddy first noticed one of the two invaders, as they first noticed Kaus. They were actually trying to position themselves to ambush Kaus. Daddy's arrow hit the nearest raider in his head, which also sent the other one in hiding. Daddy then rose and motioned for Kaus to join him. The remaining raider, now knowing he was outnumbered, shot Daddy in his head with an arrow. If Daddy had been alone or with another hunter, he would not have dropped his guard so fast. He was worried the attacking force also had men on Kaus's side and wanted Kaus to rejoin him for his safety. Most times when hunters are killing together in the wilderness, they both shot at the same time to ensure they get a kill. Notwithstanding; as previous mentioned this time was different. Kaus spotted the second shooter and shot an arrow, which hit the last raider in his chest and sent him to the ground. Kaus rushed to him and slashed his throat. He then went to see if he could save our father. Daddy already died. Kaus stared at his body in disbelief. How could the greatest man of the wilderness now have died? Kaus did not realize what to do. Should he continue and attempt to help Kristoffel or ought he to return and protect Olimpia. He decided that a return was impossible, and that he would stand beside his father's greatest comrade. Kaus continued his side of the path quickly to find Kristoffel. The next day, he noticed the death birds' circle and bushed area on the other side of the path.

Cautiously, he proceeded across the path and noticed some cut branches laying in a pile on the ground. The leaves were decaying, which told him another person had placed the branches there most probable. After moving a few branches, he discovered that a body was beneath it. His heart began to beat rapidly as his sweat dripped as pouring streams from his head. He slowly removed the branches around this bodies head. In this terrible dark place, he discovered the face of Kristoffel. Our clan's two great men now lay along beside the killing raiders. This told him something else, and that was that someone who knew Kristoffel had covered his body with branches, being in a rush to continue. Kaus slowly crawled around the area and located a set of tracks from a Bezdroża adult male who was warrior trained. Bezdrożan warrior shoes had a large X in the middle of their footprint. They designed this, so they could track those lost among them. It was merely one set of tracks. Who from the village would be tracking them? He determined that whoever it was, they either had changed course or were deceased, because he saw no one between Kristoffel and Daddy. Fear gripped his heart the mothers and Balderik were dead. Even if he found them, who would lead our family into the western lands, as now we had no one who had a history with those foreign nations. His life had changed in a way he never expected. Daddy had been the rock we depended on. Never in his life had he felt this alone and afraid. He knew it was time to continue, yet now he would move slowly and be extremely careful. As these raiders had killed Daddy and Kristoffel, he knew they were experienced wilderness men. Kaus was not the solitary one who was filled with fear now in this wilderness path. Kina and Babali were worried because no one had come back to get them. They both felt something was wrong and that possibly at the minimum Balderik needed help. The time arrived that they must get involved with their rescue. They collected some weapons and supplies and began their journey to the west. Slowly, they began their trip. Soon they were in the ambush site of their trap. They decided to move further back on the right side of the path, and this way not be detected by any who was on the path, for those most likely now were to more than likely be the enemy. Their limited experience in the wilderness; however, were not completely lost. One of Kina's temporary fathers as a child was an expert in the wilds and trained all of foster children to survive in the backwoods. They could detect Kaus clambering along and remained out of his sight until he went to pass them. Then they crossed the path to search for a fresh set of tracks marked with their 'X'. The tracks did not contain the 'X' thus could not be Balderik, therefore, they continued up the right path while Kaus traveled down the left path. That night, Kaus decided it would be best if he continued, as he believed himself to be just a few hours from the cave. Meanwhile, Kina had discovered Kristoffel's body, which brought tears to Babali, as she had claimed him as her target mate, forcing Kina to first move on our father. These mothers were actually planning to work their way to be closer to their daughters. Kina and Babali could not bring about fast time on the trail as Babali suffered from a damaged foot. She was hopping most of the way, which is dangerously noisy on the trail. They entertained the notion of separating; nevertheless, Kina rejected this noting that by staying together they would increase their chances of survival and by moving slower, they would be more cautious. Babali hugged her and thanked her telling Kina that she was saving her life. Kina told her that she had a wonderful life to save, as they would someday play with each other's grandchild. They slowly made headway until discovering the bodies of Kristoffel and our Daddy. This puts a great fear in them. Their hope for survival currently depended on their children. Their dreams of a future of love and perhaps some more children now diminished. That naturally depended upon their future mates staying alive, which was now, unknown to them hanging on Kaus.

Kaus continued trumping lightly through the forest, concentrating solely on any movement around him. His path led him straight into the ambushes previously established by Balderik. He had set the traps to cover both the path and the walkways on both sides, in case someone was to bypass his ambush. The side bush traps had spring-loaded small trees tied down with rocks tied to the tree. This would create the effect of being hit in the head with a hammer going three times faster than if hit by a man. Kaus not simply tripped into one of these trees, but when hit by the first tree, he triggered the second tree that bashed him again. He died within minutes, leaving merely half his face recognizable. Kina and Babali arrived within a part of the path that they viewed from the lookout point a few days into the path down the mountainside. Olimpia prepared for a celebration of this advance party, knowing that Daddy and Kristoffel would push the women ahead while they would completely secure the area. They noticed the mothers were walking in each other's arms indicating that one might be injured. Olimpia agreed with Andreja and Urška that they should help the mothers. If danger was in the area, the mothers' security was the paramount issue. We rushed down the path and the next day met them. Hysteria abounded in their initial reunion. The mothers hugged their daughters and leaped around extremely absorbed within their rebounding relationship, leaving Olimpia and myself to search for the men in the clan. Olimpia and I walked about twenty minutes down the path and saw no one. I became weak, suspecting that something could be wrong. Olimpia put me under a tree and told me to keep my long knife in my hand and she would return and ask Kina what she knew. She reassured me that they were most likely securing the mountain for us and doing their normal extensive scouting. We were comfortable with Kina because we were living in her house when staying with Andreja. When Olimpia returned to the reunion point, she discovered all four women sitting on the ground with tears in their eyes. She motioned for Kina casually to slip away and talk with her. Olimpia wanted to understand what and whom she saw on the path and asked her to concentrate on every detail. Kina told her first to join her in her arms. Olimpia was not used to this, yet felt a long lost sensation that had been locked deep inside her since the death of her mother. She now was in a real mother's arms in it had a feeling that was something even she presently discovered she needed. She then acknowledged to finding the bodies of Daddy and Kristoffel and some enemy bodies. They knew that Balderik was ahead of them and hoped that he was here. Someone, most likely one of the enemy had retreated pass them, so they believed the path ahead was clear, as they met no one. Olimpia tells her that Kaus and Balderik are missing. Olimpia motions for everyone to join her. Olimpia explains to us that both Daddy and Kristoffel are dead and that we must go back and find Kaus and Balderik. Olimpia then instructed Urška to care for Babali back at our lookout point and to be extremely careful. Olimpia told them that we would find our men who were still living, and first we had to collect the little boy who just aged twenty years with the death of our Daddy who was waiting just down the trail where she left him. Olimpia was regressing back into her childhood, as two new mothers would nurture our clan. Olimpia so much hoped that we could find the magical brothers, as the number of men in a clan was important in this world. They determined possession, as no society would allow women to live among themselves and ruled by a young boy. They considered this abnormal, dangerous, and not good for our species. Olimpia refused to let this enter her mind at this time. She would find a way to keep us together, even though the 'us' changed almost faster than the days. Notwithstanding; they marched down the middle of the path, not wanting to waste any time, in the event one of the brothers needed our help. We split going down both sides, because the mothers told us they just checked the right side. When we found Daddy's body, Olimpia and I found a nearby partial hole and placed him in it. Once in, we used our axes and loosened dirt to cover him. We hung the two enemy bodies that lay beside him on the ropes they had, tying them to the branches. We then removed their clothing, so when they went to the land of the dead, with this shame they would have stay hidden, as most would laugh at them. As we were hanging them, Andreja came to tell us some more news. They had found some tracks on their side leading downhill. Whoever, and we believed this to be Kaus, had continued the mission alone. This gave us some promise. The next few days we discovered Balderik and Kristoffel's bodies scattered along the path. We gave them their proper beds in the dirt so they could sleep in peace and any enemy bodies that we could shame for them. Olimpia offered to allow all, but for me, to return to the lookout point. Kina refused, declaring that we all live together or die together. She reasoned, if we walk the path of death as one, then we could travel the road of life also united. We continued until discovering the rocks in the road and the dead enemy raider under one of them. Kina warned us to stay in the rocks, because so many other traps were set in this area. As we slowly worked our way through the rocks, I happened to catch a glimpse of someone leaning against a tree. I alerted Olimpia and both Kina and Andreja joined me. Kina told us to stay back, that she had helped set these traps and would find out whom this body belonged. She used her woodcutter to cut and weaken the bent small trees so they snapped releasing the body. After this, she called for us to carefully join her and pull this body back to the path. As we were able to view the side of the face that was not mashed a great wave of hurt knocked Olimpia and me to the ground. We hugged each other as we tried to help each cope with this giant crushing ball of pain was smashing through our souls. Our lives were not supposed to develop this way. Just Olimpia and I remained from a group of destiny seekers. Andreja and Kina struggled to pull his body to a ground free of the traps. Kina was so shocked that the weapon she had fostered to save us was one that killed us. They discovered a sunken area close to one of the large rocks that held the hill in place and began to loosen up plenty of dirt that we could lay over his body when we put it to rest. As Olimpia and I began to pull ourselves back together, Kina told us it was time to put Kaus to rest. We moved his body to the partial hole they found and covered it with the dirt they had loosened. When we were finished, Olimpia recommended that we rest here, and attempt to determine our new plans. Kina asked about going to the new promised land our father told us. Olimpia told her that no other than our Father and Kristoffel knew them. We had no connections and they would treat us as refugees from the mountains, which they did not welcome. Kina next inquired if we knew of any unsettled lands. I told that my father often spoke of the unsettled lands west and south of Cvetka. Kina quizzed me on the one I recommended, the west or south. I told my womenfolk that the trouble with the west was a great dry land had to be crossed and we would have to pass through the hostile Jožefa. Another great problem was that we did not recognize the cave network needed to descend from this mountain range to the hill lands. Our father told us the cliffs were impossible to negotiate without these caves. If there was a way we could go south, we may be able to bypass both and carve out a life for us. Kina smiles and tells us, "I am aware of a way to the south." I asked her how she could be familiar with such a thing, and she explains that they were lost trying to find us and were traveling north on this southern route until they found this path of death. She further explains that it rises high along the southern ridges of this long mountain range. This will give us an opportunity to explore the western lands from the land above us. We would need to start traveling quickly, as we have barely a few months before the winter season and then the dark season will be upon us. She reveals that many hunters had told her of more caves in the mountains than in the lower hills. If they went back and collected the beasts they brought with them and some salt rock, we could have plenty of meat for the winter months. We are not far from the crossing and would merely have to collect Babali and Urška and go on our way. We will need someone to return and get them. I told her we might not have to. I will shoot an arrow to the lookout point with both red and white rags, which will tell them we are safe and they are in danger. If she returns an arrow with a white rag, she is on her way. I shot the arrow up to the lookout point. Soon thereafter, we began to receive arrows dropping down with white rags. We knew another daunting emotional task lay ahead of us. Our group had to tell the beautiful full of hope and enthusiasm Urška that the two remaining men in her life now lay sleeping in the dirt. Oh, the loss of so many nephews and nieces, produced by both was sinking in Olimpia as well, because she sat beside Kina who had also helped to bury her dreams and Babali's dreams. Andreja and I felt guilty that our love was still alive. We agreed that for the next few weeks, we would not glorify in our love, and I would concentrate on Olimpia and Andreja would attend to Kina and allow Urška to concentrate on Babali. Once we had some time and new experiences under our belts then things would settle into our new lifestyle. I knew one thing, that is the wilderness men, and warriors were not going to pass up on Urška. Her beauty was the pride of Kaus and our family. Andreja also has great beauty; nevertheless, to my fortune she is also my age and with me at her side, this should limit the time of their glances. Just to be safe, I will sharpen my long knife on some rocks and keep it in my hand. While waiting for Urška to meet us, we found Kina's beast and packed all the furs and supplies she brought with her. I asked her why she brought so much. She tells me that Babali and she were expecting to win over the hearts of some old wilderness hunters, which can be a tough task. We now waited for them to return. I told the women that I needed to do some scouting to see if we had any more surprises ahead of us. I had no idea what we would do if more killers were to follow us. The last small group put all the remaining men of our clan in the dirt, leaving just me to guide five women, four of them older than I am. I looked for some quick signs and then got back to these older women, considering I felt safer with them around me. We would have to create a new family, and I really could not see any difficulty in doing so, as we were not replacing brothers, uncles, or fathers. We were adding, sisters, aunts, and mothers.

Different names playing the same games; nevertheless, for this challenge, I will need a victory. I realize we must win, or to be more to the point I must win. I lose, and these innocent people suffer. Oh, who has placed this burden on my back? My failure with Acia and lose of Pava should have been enough evidence that I was not created to be around too many women. I figured I have a change with Andreja, because if I tell her, I am too weak to do something; she jumps in and helps me. She is not going to be able to help me now, as with my agreement, the angel Kina must receive care. I always melt her when I call her an angel. The more she begs me not to say it, the louder I say it. I remember the first-time Andreja and I kissed, as it was in front of Kina. That is how she pinned me, as my guard was down, because we were with her mother. I was working hard to occasion a good impression as the last thing I wanted was to have her complain to my father that his son was not a gentleman around women. Thinking again, if I was to receive such a report, it might be better for me if my father obtained it rather than Olimpia. A big combined sister, mother will accept nothing but the best reports of her baby boy with the girls. Acia, Pava, and Olimpia made sure I knew how a girl thinks. I always took the shortcut in deciding what they like. If a boy liked it, they did not. This rule usually kept me from a whipping. I was sitting beside Andreja, answering each question that Kina would ask me, feeling confident that I was gaining her respect. Andreja asks her mother if she can explain what I did to her. Kina asked her, "What has Yakov done to you?" Andreja tells her it is hard to explain that she will instead show her. She gracefully put her left arm over my shoulder. At the point, I am somewhat confused. I never remember putting my arm around her. She has now sparked my interest, as I would like to see what I did. She takes her right hand and squeezes my breast. I think this is so strange. Why would she grip my breast? Girls do not play with boy's breasts, which is why we walk around without shirts during the warm seasons, while they have to wear tops. I never thought that a girl would want to play with something so boring. I just turn and stare at her and ask her, "Why are you playing with my breast?" She reached over and gave me a big kiss, the first one in my life from someone I am not a relation. I tell her, "That was wonderful; maybe someday we can do that again. Now why are you playing with my breast?" She unbuttons her shirt and says, "I am not playing with yours. You are playing with mine, remember?" It then hit me; she was setting me up as an extremely perverted person. I looked at Kina and began crying. That was all I knew I could do, just cry my heart out and maybe hope that in my next life, I did not have a friend such as Andreja.

Subsequently, to my surprise Kina placed her hand on my other breast and massaged it, pressing on my man nipple with her soft hands. Kina afterwards said, "The next time you play with her breast be gentle, and massage it like this." Andreja gave me another kiss and asked, "Do you promise to marry me?" I told her absolutely, anything, just please do not generate any more stories. You are too great of an actor. I have no chance against you. Kina bent over to my side and spoke in my ear saying, "Are you going to promise me something also?" I smiled at her and said, "Absolutely." She smiled and said, "Massage my breasts like I did yours, after all that is no more than fair, please." I looked at her and said, "You both are crazy. You are going to get me burned in front of the whole village by your husband." Kina winked and kissed me on my left cheek while Andreja did the same on my right cheek. Kina then told me, "Son, I would never ever do or say anything bad about you. We love you too much. You must promise at no time to leave us." Tears of happiness ran down my face as I told her I never had a mother say something like that to me. Andreja confessed her love also and added, "Kina is your mother forever Yakov. You can never be free from us." I told them, "I would be scared to realize that two like you were in this world and did not have my love in them." That was the day I fell in love with a real mother, the one who knows her children and can get down in the dirt and play right along with us. Nothing could be better. She never thought for a second that I had abused Andreja. They both worked that accordingly well. Those women could have told me to promise them the universe and I would have done so. They are such pure, defiant, uncontrollable, rule-breaking, law-abiders. How else could I describe them? Kina looked at me, as so much had changed since that day in her home. Kina knew us, gave up such a great title and so many great things to pull a beast into the empty mountains and follow the ones she loved and trusted. She looks at me with those wonderful eyes, which try so hard to hold back the avalanches of terrifying pain and loneliness and asks me, "Yakov, are you scared?" I looked at her and Andreja and said, "I am not scared of anything out there, I am merely scared that someday I might lose on off you angels." They both began to cry and fell into my arms. Olimpia comes in and asks, "Yakov, are you making these kind women cry?" Kina tells her, "Olimpia, how have you got blessed with the greatest son ever to be born?" Olimpia smiles and says to Kina, "He is so wonderful, I believe he deserves two mommies. What do you think?" Kina and Andreja tell her they so much would enjoy this. Olimpia adds, "I made him the man of my life years ago when he demanded that I live with him until I die." I looked at her and said, "I still hold you to that mommy." I am so good inside with two mommies, and my soul mate here for me to hold and love. I recognize I must rise to the occasion. I also understand that all five, it will be five with Urška arrives with her mother, have such great minds, and I believe, that with some help from my recent silent partner Damijana, we will have a chance. I cry out, "Oh Damijana, where have you been?" We were in Kina's cave when I asked this and a light shined in on the dark wall. First, it was white, then it turned red, then it turned maroon, next crimson, afterwards yellow. The voice spoke, "I am aware of the great pain you have experienced with the arrival of so much death. I will promise your five women that while they stay with you, I will fight death and keep life in your bodies. I also promise you that your deaths will not be about torture. Fear not, for when your time comes, I will lead you to death and to your home in the land of the dead. You are my family." I asked Damijana, "I thought you could not protect Andreja?" Damijana flashes an orange light, then green and says, "They had parents who heeded to my warning; therefore, they are now mine, all six of you are mine and death cannot touch you without your will."

Andreja says, "I need a sister, are you acquainted with where I can find one?" Damijana flashes and then answers, "You now have three sisters, including me. Yakov should be so ashamed that it takes six women to force him to behave moral." I glance at her and laugh, "My death will be from my heart exploding trying to give you all the love you deserve. Damijana, we do not grasp where to go and settle, and so many wants to kill us. What can we do?" Damijana answers, "Dumb, dumb, I heard you and Kina's great plan, go with your hearts and understand when you see dead along your paths I was there before you." Kina tells her, "Damijana, we will love you so much, therefore please do not be sad as my daughter told me you were, for I hope you can find many mothers in our new clan." Damijana released a beautiful pink light and said, "I will see you from time to time in your dreams. When you need me, call me. Good-bye, my chosen ones." Olimpia now confessed, "I honestly believed you simply because you said it was so; therefore, I did not care if it was true or not, because such a truth is beyond my comprehension, although incredibly possible in dreams. This was not in a dream today. We truly have an angel to protect us from death." I then reminded the girls that we must listen to what she said. We will die; it is we have the great joy of knowing that we will never die from torture and no matter how we die; she will take us pass the cold grips and chains of death to our eternal place. These are great things to have for peace of mind. I wish she could guarantee that we will always be together; however, we realize that will not be so. That may not be a bad thing, as a few may blend with us who can give you women what you need in life. I for one never want to see Olimpia childless. Kina then tells me, "Yakov, do you want us?" Accordingly, I tell her that, of course I do, and that I never would want to lose any of them, especially my brother's almost wife and her mother as they are now traveling to us. I recommend that we meet them and put them in our group as fast as we can. Olimpia jumps up and orders, "Okay women; you heard our owner." I run over and grab her. As I grab her, she spins around, wraps her arms around me tight, and asks, "Son is there anything that I can do for you?" I go over Kina, Andreja, and her, and say, "Please, do not call me your owner, unless you want others to rush to kill me. You appreciate that when Urška arrives, there will be many men wanting to enjoy that fruit." Olimpia asks me, "Yakov, what do you mean by fruit?" I tell them, "I have no idea, except that many times I heard dad say that about you."

Olimpia looks confused, telling me she never remembers hearing Daddy say that. I tell her that daddies tell their sons some things, which girls do not know. Andreja brags, "I comprehend what they say, because I used to beat up the boys and pressure them to tell me." Kina adds that it is hard for her to believe that her little girl was a boy bully. I remind her of all the times I told her that she was, and how she ignored me. Andreja smiles, chuckles, wink her eye, and then responds, "She knew better than to listen to any such bad things to say about me." Olimpia tells me we are ready to rejoin with the rest of our new family. I ask to speak before we depart. Humbly, I share, "Kina, Andreja, Olimpia as we see our clan has suffered many deaths that require us to shift our relationships until things are settled. Olimpia and I need to grieve the loss of so many, well, in fact, all of our family. Andreja, you and your mother have suffered losses and went from the first ladies to our loved ladies. You need time together so that with Kina and Olimpia strong again, my Andreja and I can begin our family. We understand the grief that Urška will have when she discovers her future husband sleeps in the dirt. She will need to rebuild her life with Babali. If we work with our new partners, we can begin to build a grief-free clan filled with love and respect for each another. Can we do this my love?" Olimpia answers, "Anything for my man?" Kina replies, "Anything for my son?" Andreja responds, "Anything for my slave?" I walk over to her, kiss her smack on the lips, and ask her, "Is that forever, or just temporary?" Andreja asks me, "What do you want?" I tell her, "I was hoping forever." Andreja gives me one of your boy bully hugs and says, "Not a day earlier big boy." Now this made me experience great joy. This was when I passed out our long knives. I had collected all of Daddy and Kristoffel's weapons, and it was time currently to put them in the hands of those who were still walking on this journey. I tell them, "We must now just think of ourselves. If a noise is coming from a friendly force, then it should have sent a signal to tell us. Therefore, if you hear a noise, swing to kill. No prisoners, no being nice. Our time is to kill or be killed. We live today, because those whom we love died for us. We will not die for those whom someone else loves on their behalf. I repeat, do not think, and swing to kill. If you made a mistake, at least we will be alive to debate it for our conscience. The noise will always come from a predator, either man or beast. Okay, time to get the rest of my women."

They always smile when I claim them as my women. At first, I felt rather awkward speaking so dominant; nevertheless, I must now think and act controlling. The stronger I act, the tougher I will be, and the more assurance they will have in following me. I walk about one hundred feet ahead of them, so if any ambushes are set, I will most likely spring them in enough time for the girls to reach safety. Up this mountain hill we go. I can understand all the things' Daddy said to me, and the things I heard him say to Kaus, Answald, or Panfilo. The best information came from when he was talking with Kristoffel. Kristoffel had been exceptionally helpful in the so many stories he had. These were excellent, in that they happened in reality. This gave me insight to the emotions that accompany these events. Late, the fourth day in our return, Urška and her mother appeared before us. We were all so happy. Urška now represents what is remaining of Kaus. Kaus filled his final days with joy and laughter from morning until dawn in his private world he shared purely with Urška. When we first met them, we could merely stand in a line. Someone had to tell them what happened, and that someone was a little boy whom they were desperately trying to shape into a man. I took one glimpse and knew I had another job to do. I looked at Urška and Babali and said, "Sister, mother, we have come to bring you home. Will you please rejoin us?" Urška came over and looked me straight into my eyes. I tried to remain strong, yet tears began to pour from my eyes. She did not say a word. So much beauty now ripped apart on the inside. She put her arms around me and kissed my cheek saying, "Kaus would have been so proud of you today, my brother." Babali hugged us both and revealed to me, "I really could use a strong son like you Yakov." I looked at her and said, "You got it mommy." I then asked them to each hold my hand as we go face the rest of our new family. They walked proud beside me as Babali fell into Kina's arms and Urška into Olimpia and Andreja's arms. I put my arms around Babali and Kina, two fantastically fine and mature middle-aged mothers. I told Babali, "Mommy, now would be a good time to cry. Kina, as with the rest of us, we are here for you. This is your family, now cry mommy." She began to cry, Kina turned into an emotional sponge, as the mother in her took over, and Babali began fighting the battle of pain and misery that raged inside her. Olimpia had already began pumping the well inside of Urška, as Andreja was fighting hard to keep up with removing the tears from her eyes. They vented for about one hour when I told them, "Family, we need to begin our journey to our new land. If we start now, we should be able to reach our campsite from last night late tonight. Now is the time for us to go." My mind was trying to compile how a life of mommies would differ from a life of daddies. Inside me, I knew things would be different, yet they would not be bad. I slowly turned around, leaving my back to them and took my first step on our new journey.

CHAPTER 08

The land of the Gerben

When each tear begins to fall into the clutches of the hidden spiders in my mind as they spin their deceptive silk, trap and toss it into another lost forever section within its torn webs. My tears and thoughts seemingly believe they are matrimonial in that they refuse to separate. I search for my ax in my dreamland to separate these powers of miseries; however, every time I swing, my ax vanishes. I refuse to cease my attempts. If a spider can hide my hope with silk, then why should I fail to uncover it with my enthusiasm and move forward? I fight the desire to surrender multiple times each minute, reaching, deep down, into my special internal fortress that holds my everlasting love for my Daddy. I come charging back swinging my woodcutter sparing no obstacle that dares tries to fuel the next painful attack in my heart. I help no option but to fight this ocean of diversity. Somehow, they placed me in this role to fast as the guardian of our asylum, with five sets of windows that shine into the greatest souls that compose my life. How they follow me with such devotion destroys my faith in the wisdom of the female sector of our species. This is in no way to degrade them; instead, I adore them and strive each breath to exceed what they see in me. The other gender that composes our species must have insights that are still a mystery to any of us who label themselves as males. Our group behaves and thinks differently now. It would be wrong for me to complain, because they just spoil the daylights out of me.

When I reach for something, I can see five of that item coming back for me to choose. This opens the awareness that I am discovering has many favorable aspects. Olimpia had originally paired me with her, Kina and Andreja, Urška and Babali. This flopped during the first few hours on our retreat path. Andreja flowed back to my side. Olimpia understood that she was standing her position, the one promised her. Kina and Babali fell back together, with the lifetime of experiences they could share, to include so many things they understandably did not really want to share with their daughters. The special bonding surprised us as Olimpia and Urška bonded as we never beside seen them share. They were extraordinarily much the same; just we reasoned that Urška was younger. The more I saw Urška beside Olimpia the more I started to doubt an age difference. Olimpia had merely the least age difference between her and Kaus. Our mother later told her this was because our father really wanted a son, so she dropped him four sons in a row, before finishing off with my Acia and Pava. I realize that my claim for them will never disappear, as I see now that Andreja will not diminish her claim for me. Olimpia and Urška discovered that they share so many of the same challenges and loses. Both lost their future mates, home village, and fathers. They both wanted to start their families and once again belong in a relationship that could produce children and a chance to raise them. They wanted what Kina and Babali had lost. Even though Kina had a foster child in Andreja, which to her was the same as blood. She would dash in front of a flying spear to save her as fast as she would a new child springing from her womb. Andreja now had flown from her nest and was setting up her own nest. It would soon be time for her eggs to begin hatching.

None of us counted Kina and Babali out of the race to begin new families. They were strong women, and I would estimate simply about ten years older than Olimpia. These two women had lost their first husbands early in their marriage and sadly lost their babies. Andreja explains that Bezdroża took the children of young widows and gave them to the older, more stable women who could better care for the children. This made these younger, most still healthy, and beautiful able to mate again and with any luck, keep their new husbands and family. Andreja additionally explained that current possession of the children did not grant the foster parents sole custody of these youngsters. Any tribal family could petition their care was better than the guardianship a child was currently receiving and win custody of that kid. This kept the foster or blood parents always striving to provide better for their family. I now understand why Kina and Babali were so close with their foster daughters and placed any family relationship, especially if it could be somewhere other than Bezdroża, as the number one priority. Kina and Babali risked a public beating for their behavior. Hæge and Urška's father decided not to have their wives' beaten, because that would cripple any hope of receiving future children. When Kina and Babali escaped in search of their daughters, they also took with them, their husband's problems, without question for the help of their separated husbands. Kina, who joins this conversation, laughs and states, "The old buzzards most likely got wives the age of Olimpia or maybe even Andreja." Andreja explains that this was the reason she and Ermtraud wanted my engagement.

An engagement would take them out of the pool for whoever decides they want a new wife. I tell Andreja that I do so much yearn for Ermtraud and wish she joined us. Babali blares out, "That is right; you would not be aware of what happened to Ermtraud." Andreja beats me to the punch on this one as our entire small clan stops and piles around Babali. Kina tells me to join them, as she will keep guard. Babali begins by telling us, "Just after your family departed, Ermtraud's parents took her to the middle of the village and beat her. They did this to ward off any attempt from others to take the children under their care. After her beating, they placed her in one of the village punishment rooms. That evening, the guards came to bring her out for another beating when they discovered she was not there. Somehow, she had escaped. Her fears was that her foster parents would never stop searching for her, so rather than escaping on the path you could take; she went the opposite way, hoping to pull any search parties in a direction different from what she truly intended. Forlornly, she desolately fell into one of the villages raiding traps and died instantly. Many surmises that she was going this direction, hoping to make it to stream that passes our village. Here, she could have traveled in the rock beds without leaving the 'X' tracks. Many told us that it was fortunate for her that she died, for if she had lived, the village planned on using her as the example punishment, which would have given the village a chance to show how evil they truly were." Andreja and I hugged each other and began to cry. I should have pushed Daddy and Kristoffel to find Ermtraud and argue to bring her with us. I did not push it because Andreja told me Ermtraud recounted to her that she wanted to stay with her village and not die in the wilderness.

When my mate and I finished our crying and separated Olimpia and Urška surrounded and cared for Andreja as Nina and Babali pinned me. This group is not like any I have enjoyed so far in my life. They are not doing anything new; it is just that they are all doing it so naturally and constantly. I have to describe what they are doing. One thing is that they are not worried about making time. When emotions needed tending, all stop and warmly tends to the emotions. When the boost of knowing that Damijana is a word away, I am beginning to think that if our pace is consistent with that of women, she will not be too disappointed. Anyways, I am so proud of how Babali is improving with her leg injury. Olimpia quickly did whatever she does with injured legs, Urška made her a walking rod out of a sturdy branch and Babali is hoping right along with us, occasionally riding our milk cow they brought with them. I joke with Andreja about selecting a milk cow for a pet. She winks at me and causally narrates, "I have a great attraction for big ugly things." The women in this group all catch this before I do. When I catch it, I wink at Andreja, who is so proud of her joke, and smile at the rest of our group and motion time to walk. We reach our staging cave a few hours into the dark hours. We separate into our pairs and prepare to sleep. Andreja tosses me her furs and hops in beside me. She slides in beside me and immediately begins her sleep. This girl prepares for any move she makes. I peek around at the mothers and sisters. They are in their own worlds, although Olimpia whispers, "Goodnight, Yakov, and Andreja." I say, "Goodnight my mommies." Andreja miraculously awakens and whispers, "Goodnight my loves." I ask Andreja if she thinks we should have someone pulling guard. She tells me, "No, love, for do you see any fireplaces or streams of smoke rising to the sky?" I testified to seeing nothing. Andreja then passes on to me that she tried for years to sneak out of the house and Kina had caught her every time. Nothing gets passed Kina at night. In addition, her milk cow is extremely nervous at night and thus is an excellent warning tool. Kina and Babali share their nighttime blessings and soon we are all fast asleep. Our next morning found us all repacking and looking up our cow. I saw Kina and Babali filling bags with the white stones they were crushing. I asked them to tell me what they were doing. Kina explains to me that they found a scrupulous vein of salt in one of the close by side tunnels. Babali continues by adding, "We need the salt preserve any meat we harvest in the winter months for the dark months, which will be warmer and spoil our meat swifter." Kina tells me that sometimes salt is hard to find. There is no reason not to bring this considering that our cow is carrying it. I smile and say, "Each day I can see more hope in our happy future. I am so lucky to have so many wise women among us." At this time, I explain to my women that I will be walking above them on the ridge above us. If I see any danger, I will come down fast and help prepare for our fight. Andreja wants to go up with me. This creates a dilemma, in that having her with me could interfere with my scouting, yet on the other hand, another set of eyes with me could help keep us alive, at least until I can trust developing my scouting eye. If I tell her no, then there goes my future mate. I smile at her and say, "Good idea, we need to go." Olimpia tells me not to get distracted. I expect for our first two days to be the most dangerous. On this ridge I can see for miles around us, which would give days, if not a week's advance notice for any large movements.

The likeliest danger would be from the small wilderness based, thieves who can hide and almost move invisibly through the forests. The key is that they will be moving and so any disturbances will continue with them. That is how Kristoffel used to discover these small bands. Our clan barely continues this path for one hour and then they shift into the forest, toward our ridge, or should I say a pass ahead of us. Andreja and I study the pass from our viewpoint and soon can track the path they are taking. When they emerge from the forests passing through a small open area, we are relieved. Kina knew what she was talking about, as I can easily see how we shifted from going west, or into the mountains border and are now heading south along the mountain ledge. This ledge will be helpful in that we can get a strong view into the western lands and have plenty of time studying how large their nations are and where the villages are located. Nighttime will be busy, although we will be able to receive our information quickly, especially just after dark. Search for campfires on both sides of us. During the day, explore for smoke streams which most likely will be from hunters or wilderness families cooking their food. Daddy told me that they would find an awkward, easy to block off place, and cook their meat and food, while hiding. When finished, they would collect the cooked food and double time to catch their group who would eat it at another location. We will play with many options in cooking our food. Meanwhile, I believe we will stick with special roots, fruits, and berries. I remember listening to elders talk when I was younger in Petenka that fruit and berries were good food for long hikes, in that they kept your feet moving. We actually made extremely good time and distance our first day on our southern route. I wonder if anticipating a new life in a new world, packed with new things that are pushing us. We could also need these new things to replace the old, which is lost. Andreja and I worked well together on our first day. No one else was with us and we did what we had to do, and appeared to enjoy doing this because we could do it together. As night was arriving,

I sent Andreja down to our family and told her I wanted to scout for the campfires. She told me after finding our clan; she would grab the food and come back to me, so we could eat together before returning. Likewise, this we did. I was hungry, and she brought back more than fruits and berries, but also the other roots that tasted fine. We spotted several large clusters of campfires scattered in the western lands. I felt, as I looked south that we had the distance before finding the open lands. Daddy told me there were large nations of these western lands, so this is not a surprise. I see no campfires in our mountains, as most of my view is north and south. A large ridge that is protruding from our ridge limits my eastern view. I can just hope that many would use that ridge as their border for the west, knowing how giant cliffs provide a wall between the west and the mountain. That would just about make this passageway, or small strip of rocky land of little value and pretty much out of the mainstream passageways. Daddy also told me that few wanted to make any fires along the cliffs for fear the western tribes had secret methods to enter these mountains, and would bring their Armies to clear their border. We are not making fires so we can survive against the killers in these mountains and not because of potential killers in western lands. Besides, I do not want to advertise the rare commodity that composes my clan, and that is beautiful women. I wonder if it is okay that I think of them as beautiful women after all, these two are the loves of my life being Olimpia and Andreja. Urška would have been my sister, with Babali and Kina the wings that hold our love together. I have seen women that I did not consider to be beautiful and of course women who I believed to be beautiful. Babali and Kina compare more with those who I considered beautiful. Strangely, I am the odd one in my family for the first time in my life. Even though, I predominately spent my days with my three sisters, I had three brothers and a father who was my gender. That backup does not exist here; however, I have one of them who are my guardian and mate. Andreja is my shield and key into this circle, alongside Olimpia.

Olimpia's keys open different doors. Her set of key that resemble the ones Andreja gave to me, Olimpia will give to another, when I find them for these women. Andreja and I feel guilty because our love can grow, while all their lives are on hold. They chuckle with me in that being on hold is better than someone holding them against their wishes is. Andreja and I return to the charming camp that the clan set up and fall fast to sleep. We made it through today with no bloodshed. What hits me, as being so ironic is that one small exception almost destroyed our families. I have not seen anyone else so far since all that killing. A small group that appears to be the exception to what this territory is about caused such a shattering blow to our dreams. Our dreams are still alive; it is just that now we do not have any among us who has been in them. Daddy and Kristoffel, had been in Cvetka and Jožefa, and they had a real vision or goal. My goal currently is limited to keep us together and alive, with a maybe at the end of our rainbow. My goal cannot be that far-off base as all the women in this clan are accepting it. I realize one thing from having three sisters, and that is if they did not want to do it, they did not do it. Olimpia and Urška come, join Andreja and I, and begin a normal conversation. Olimpia asks me if she and Urška can scout tomorrow. I grasp that between Daddy, Kaus, and Answald, they taught her much better than they schooled me, primarily because of her age and leadership role in Daddy's absence. I tell my senior sister that is a wonderful idea, and ensure they do not get any facial injuries so I will still be able to marry them to the lucky men. I was going to say victim, as would be expected coming from a baby brother; however, I took one peek at Urška, then glanced back at Olimpia and 'lucky men' came out of my mouth. I just cannot see even chancing saying something that could hurt them. Olimpia smiles at me and says, "I thought you were the lucky man, and anyway, the ridges will give me a chance to search and gather more for us to eat." I tell her, "I am the luckiest man in that I can care for you until Mr. Right drops into your life. Do not have any worry. Daddy taught me what to ask and do when he was preparing for Joggeli. This time, we will not fail, okay champ."

Urška asks what about her. I glance at her and say, "I was getting ready to ask Andreja if I could keep you; however, if she says no, we should start having you also search. Meantime, I will relate to you as I do your sister Olimpia. Now, give me a kiss, and we seal this deal." I got a courteous peck from both of them. This reminded me to ask them how Kina and Babali faired today. They tell me that these women are expert gatherers and can find hidden traps, as they found one today. Olimpia tells me that we need not worry too much about the trap, as it was dreadfully old and may have been part of a defensive network against roaming raiders. I ask Andreja if she will be okay with me going over and talking with our two guardians. Urška asks me not to let them hear me say guardians, as they are additionally hoping to find new mates. I agree and Andreja motions her approval and with our two slightly out of place members, although considering Andreja's and my lack of age, we may actually fit with the out of place members. I ask to examine Babali's leg. They smile and say, "It sure did not take you long to learn where the candy is kept." I explain that I want to ensure the proper. They both laugh and say, "We understand big man; we know." Therefore, I wink at Babali and question, "Now, where is that candy?" Babali asks Kina if maybe they should start wrapping the candy tighter. Kina tells her not simply no, but also absolutely no, as no one else in our clan is, especially Andreja, accordingly. Why should they be deprived of the festivities? Babali, as she is removing the wrapping over her injury smiles and says, "I guess you are right, anyway, if ever a young man deserved the candy it would be our precious Yakov." I told her, "I so much appreciate your words; however, I must concentrate on fighting off all the trouble we will have in keeping the hordes from trying to beat me to that treat." Kina smiles and says, "My goodness, what a fine young gentleman. I understand Olimpia would be so proud if she knew what you just said."

This is when I noticed the other women of our clan were being quiet. This prompted me to say, "Somehow, I suspect that they might already know." I examine Babali's injury, notice no swelling or infection, and tell her, "We can allow this to further air tonight, and Olimpia can investigate this in the morning before we wrap it again." I ask them if they had seen any smoke streams or campfires. Kina tells me she saw one earlier toward the top of our eastern ridge. Nevertheless, it is now long gone. Kina and Babali thank me for saving them. I reach over and give them a kiss and say, "How can I be saving you, when you are in the candy store with the door locked?" Kina tells me, "Son, you must be in the wrong house, because we feel so safe with you in our village that we threw away the locks to our doors." I then confess to them, the candy I was talking about being the mommy candy. Babali asks me if there is any other category of candy. I love the way they all do this to me. Tie my tongue up and have me write 'I am stupid' on my back. I tell them, "I truly do not know, except to say that Andreja told me she would share the secret candy with me after we got married. She told me it would be the best candy I ever enjoyed. I am so curious what she is trying to tell me. Would you have any idea?" Kina looks at Babali and advises them to enter a truce with me. She adds, "The little fellow has Andreja on his side." I snuggle between them and then confess, "I feel so awkward in that you are not much older than Olimpia, yet Olimpia is the lone mother that I ever knew. How can I be the great one you always talk about, while I simply want to ride on your back in a baby suit?" Kina tells me that I am especially natural with this feeling, and they understand. She continues, "The power of life is with those who are the closest to it. Your mother would be so proud when she looks down and sees her baby boy with his 'mothers' reconstructing his shields. Yakov, you are becoming a durable man by building your foundation with strong stones of love and compassion. The more you open yourself, the more of you that others will enjoy. When we hug you and wipe away the tears, we realize that one in our arms is our son and a true man. Have no shame." I thank them both and totally relax as they do their mommy rubs. Something about a woman when they give you their nurturing massage that overrides anything else. It is almost, as if there are special rooms within us, which just they have the keys to unlock.

If these rooms continue to go unlocked, then the proprietor of those chambers is not complete. I wonder if that is why so many killers and raiders fill themselves solitary with evil. Even their wickedness cannot get into these rooms. Notwithstanding; the malice floods the hallways and destroys the internal walls until it controls its dupe. I ask Kina and Babali how they have so much energy after such a long day. Kina tells me, "Son, we could be dying and still find a way to hug our babies." I am; nevertheless, so confused on the inside me, about how I can be a baby and a leader at the same time. I ask them again, "How can you allow me to be a baby in your arms, yet you so quickly follow me trusting me with your lives?" Babali tells me to shut up and move closer to her. She wants to hug me tighter. Kina tells me that one word and just one word explains how this possible and that is, 'mother.' Kina will go, get Andreja, and we will hold our babies tonight. As Kina jumps up, I also attempt to upsurge saying, "Oh, this is okay." Babali swings her legs around to trip me as Kina pushes me back down saying, "Yes, son, this is in order. Please, do not disgrace us." Kina brought Andreja back. Andreja melted into Kina, almost as if they were one. I can see and sense the extension of Kina into Andreja. The sensation of their love is overwhelming. Babali wriggles around some and then repositions me and tells me, "Do not worry son, my body is used to Balderik." Soon she will have me in the peaceful realm of her wings. It feels like every muscle and bone in my body is loose and flexible. My aches and small nagging discomforts are gone. How did she get in me accordingly deep and takes complete control so fast? I realize that by not having a real mother, I may have missed something great. Olimpia was close to this feeling. Nevertheless, she did not grasp how to reach in like this. Babali tells me that once a woman has borne a child from her womb, she receives this gift. I believe this is so wonderful. Babali tells me not to worry, for Andreja will get the gift once we have our first child. Soon, the four of us are off into our dreamlands.

Unexpectedly, I suddenly experience my body tossed into the air. What is happening? I now catch myself rolling on the ground as I see Babali jump. I ask her, "What is going on?" She motions for me to be quiet, picks up her long knife and whispers, "I heard someone move." Unexpectedly, Olimpia and Urška rush to us reporting that they heard people spying on us. Kina and Andreja now have their bows loaded. I ask Olimpia where the last place she heard them. She recounts that they centered themselves about twenty-five feet above us. Urška tells me they heard them first come from the path, and then they have moved themselves into such a good position. I tell my clan to find something to conceal them, preferably behind a tree. We will form a line, with at least six feet between us. They are in a perfect position now to pick us off if that were their desire. Stay protected and we will let them make the first move. Therefore, I will scout above them and see who they are and try to guess what they want. Next, I got into position just before the second moon began to shine. Accordingly, there are merely two men, I would say Olimpia's age. They have their weapons concealed. One of them tosses a rock, and I hear my girls release constrained squawks of fear. They shake their hands in joy, as the other now takes his turn. These two are simply playing with my girls, and I see no large carrying bags, so they must not be thieves, or if they are thieves, they are not that smart. I would guess they are locals, because they are traveling light, and appear to be relaxed, as those who are near their homelands behave. I decide to take a chance and slowly work my way down to them. With my long knife in one hand and an ax in the other, I walk into their camp and say hello to them. They both jump up, still no sign of weapons, as their faces are now red, almost as if they are embarrassed. I ask them if there is anything to do for fun in this area. They motion for me to lower my weapons, which I do as a sign of good faith. The tallest boy introduces himself as Aert and tells me they are from a village called Gerben.

I smile and say, "I must be apologetic; I have never heard of your village." The other boy introduces himself as Carolus and tells me not to be sorry, because many of his neighbors have not heard of it either. Aert assures me that they have no weapons and were just here teasing some beautiful girls. I tell them it has been a long time since I have seen some pretty girls. Carolus alerts me that I am in luck because there is also a smaller one with them. Aert invites me to where he is, so I can see. He tells me to be awfully quiet because they can hear about everything. That is why they had to move so far back up the hill. I take one glance and say, "Oh my goodness, that little one is too beautiful. If I do not get a chance to talk with her, I will die. I am going to go to talk with her." Aert tells me the girls do not like it when you walk into their camp at night. I tell them the way you walk in what makes the difference and that my older brothers taught me many ways to do this. First thing, take off those noisemakers you have on your feet. We need to sneak up to them, and then magically appear. Now, follow me. They did everything I told them to do. Their excitement to meet these beauties had them completely harmless. We lined up so I could walk behind their trees.

I told them that I would go in, take control, and then demand hugs. Carolus tells me that it is impossible for a little guy like me to gain control of these women. This is because they have been watching them most of this day, and these are not simply beautiful women; they are intelligent and appear to be deadly if challenged. I said, "Well, in that situation, I will put my long sword in this side bag and merely control them with my ax." Aert warns me that I am walking into my death. I tell them both to watch and learn. I walk in pass Kina and Olimpia and stop saying, "Women, surrender to me and give me hugs now." My girls dropped what they had and all five flooded around me hugging me. Andreja then asks me, "My love, why are you acting so different?" I tell my girls that I am simply playing a joke on the two spies. I want you to stand in a straight line when I tell you, and I will bring the two handsome young men for you to approve or disapprove. I could see a sparkle glitter in Olimpia and Urška's eyes. Babali asks me, "What about us?"

I stare at her, Kina, and say, "But I need my mommies." Kina reaffirms, "Of course you do, as we need you, right big guy. Now, go get those boys before Olimpia and Urška die of heart attacks." I say okay, and they all move aside from me. As they are moving away, I tell Andreja to take my shirt in a sensual manner. She comes up to hug me, lifts both of my hands, unbuttons my shirt, and works it off while hugging and kissing me. The rest of my women stood clapping. Afterwards, I say now stand in a line while I bring my friends. I go back to get them, and they are both passed out. This forces me to call for Olimpia to give me something to wake them. She rushes me something, with the help of Urška. They glimpse at the boys and confess that they appear strong, and are handsome. Olimpia hugs me and while kissing my head confesses, "I always knew you would take care of me." Urška tells me that, "Tonight. I have carved a special place in her heart." I simply do not want to be the lone boy in our clan. I have Olimpia and Urška go back and stand in the line while I wake up our new captives. As they begin to awaken, they both gaze at me as if I were some sort of god. Aert asks me how I did this. I tell him it is a gift, and you must be able to show the women that you are in control and at the same time, a gentleman who will not hurt them, while they obey you. Now follow me and I will set you up with a girlfriend if that is what you want. Carolus said, "We do, but please not the older ones, okay." I ask them that if I introduce them will they be kind and sympathetic to these girls. They promise with all their hearts. These boys are as desperate as my girls are. They follow me as we walk into the camp. I line them up in front of our girls, point at Olimpia, and ask her, "Which one of these boys do you want to be your man?" Olimpia points at Aert and asks, "Is it okay if I pick you?" Aert drops to his knees and begs, "Please pick me." Olimpia rushes to Aert and they embrace, then move to another tree and begin talking for the remainder of the night. I point at Urška and ask her if this young man would be acceptable. Carolus drops to his knees, as his face turns red as he stares at Urška. She smiles and says, "Sure, if he has me." Carolus shakes his head rapidly. I tell her to get to him before he passes out again.

She rushes to him, helps him stand, and then they find them a tree, as a safe distance from us and begin their talking. Andreja and I get our mothers and relocate to a more private place, considering our show is no longer simply for future mothers. The four of us finish the night sleeping like baby bears. Our new couples were still talking nonstop in the morning. I could tell that they had not slept. There is no way they can walk all day without rest. I tell Kina we will be staying here today, as I do not want any of my people to get hurt, maybe get into a fighting situation, and have to battle for their lives. Kina tells me this is a wise choice, as it will also give Babali a chance to nurse her leg. Olimpia joins me now and with a great smile on her wonderful face asks me what our plans are for today. I tell her we can rest here for another day. She tells me that Aert and Carolus have invited us to their village, which is no more than one hour ahead on our trail. Their homes are inside some caves, which are inside the sloping ridge beside the trail. Olimpia adds that he told her they have plenty of extra food we can eat. I ask her how soon she thinks we should go. She tells me we should leave now, as she is hungry for something besides fruit and berries. I agree with her and tell the rest of the gang we need to prepare to move out. Consequently, with Andreja at my side, I explain our possible new fortune with the mothers and we scramble to load up our cow. Soon, we are on the road once more. I can sense Olimpia and Urška's hearts beating with their new joy. The boys appear to be well behaved. It gave me some extra peace in that I believe I saw the true side of them in their camp. That side was not bad, somewhat playful, but not dangerous. I would be scared to death if I placed one of my women in a dangerous situation. I believe my girls will enjoy their playful side. I go to scout for us and zip up the left side. Aert tells me it would be better for us if I scouted on the right side, as it slopes much higher and I will be able to see much further. The right side slopes down into a valley not far ahead. I thank him, as Andreja and I ascend the steep hillside to near the ridge top.

His recommendation did prove to be correct. Granted, he was on this path before, just as Daddy has been so many places during his journeys. We soon arrive in front of his caves. He takes us all to a small gorge hidden by dropping from within the ridge. We wait, as soon they come out, with three old ladies who bring us some food and sit to chat with us, while the boys take Olimpia and Urška inside the cave. I ask one of the old women, while eating some delicious soft meat, why they took two of my clan in the cave. The old woman apologized and said if they were my women, she would go in and bring them outside the cave. I told her that I introduced them to Aert and Carolus. I was just worried about their safety. The three women assure us that no one will hurt, or even touch those beautiful women. Kina compliments them on the meal they are sharing with us. Something about the food of these people tells so much about them. Notwithstanding; a great method to learn about the Gerben is to ask them; therefore, I work these gentile and kind women to discover what they are about, "First, I am so thankful to you wonderful, kind, and special hosts. Aert told me you are the Gerben tribe, in which he confessed to me that I was not the lone one who were not aware of what appears to be wonderful people. This is a special treat for us as death has chased us into so many miserable chambers of tears. We would really enjoy knowing more about your people, as I hope you can appreciate we worry so much about our sister's welfare." The woman smiles at me and says, "For the individual young man in your clan, you appear really to care about those who are sharing your life. We are a boring and simple people. We gather or hunt what we need to survive. Our families are the cores of what we are. The love of our children surpasses any other joy we seek. Our families stay within themselves, merely sending out the sons to find mates. I have grieved for Aert and Carolus for some time now, as they have not been fortunate enough to find a possible mate. Our elders almost passed out when they saw the beauty and charm of the two 'goddesses that you let walk in with our poor humble sons. We do not realize how to thank you for such great kindness."

Kina asks if they have any older men around her age that need wives. They tell her that most men in their society commit suicide when their wives die, and the wives go to the brothers if their husband dies. This keeps the blood in the same families and prevents families have children from other bloodlines. Right or wrong many argue about this; nevertheless, it has been our way for so many ages and works great. I tell the women that, "The important things for me are that my sisters are loved and live within a place of love and safety. How do we defend ourselves from all the horrible thieves and raiders that roam this area?" They explain to me that, "Our tribe has no weapons and has never lost a battle. The cave networks that we live within allow us to exist in many places where no others can travel, such as so many plateaus above on ridges completely sealed by impassable cliffs. When others attack our village, we regress deeper inside our caves, beyond the ambush areas we have established. No one has yet to pass the first ambushes, let alone they are four to five ambushes thick. You may visit here anytime for the rest of your life and find your sisters and their children healthy, happy, and loved." The way she said that introduced a scary thought into my mind. I would now be living without Olimpia, for she has worked so hard and deserves this life. I cannot guarantee her that she would be alive one hour down our path. Andreja and I will never leave our mothers and will keep them with us until some lucky men win them. An elder man comes out and motions to Kina for us to go inside now. The women glare at Kina and ask her if we are ready to enter. Kina tells her, "You have to ask my man." Babali and Andreja jump on my sides. The elder man now walks up to me and sticks his hand out, and we shake. He asks me, "Would you please bring these lovely women in with you, so we can talk and maybe even have a festival tonight?"

I tell him, "I would not miss this for the world, my angels, follow me inside here." One old woman asks me, "Young man, why do you have them follow you?" I tell her, "Because their safety is my responsibility." She smiles, in fact, all three of these women beams and asks, "May we follow you also?" Babali tells them, "If you want to see without a doubt you are going somewhere safe, jump in with us." The elderly man walks beside me comments, "Son, it is always a great feeling when you can contribute to the safety of those whom, you love." I tell him, "A feeling meriting and dying for." He grins and adds, "Also, a feeling worth living to receive." We walk into a large dark empty cavernous space. I ask him where my sister is. He tells me to follow him. This is an open area, which strangers sometimes will camp. They maintain this place as a decoy area. We continue to walk to the far back, and then we enter another area that they have flames burning that do not make smoke. They tell me it breaths special air. I do not worry so much about the details; the children are playing around them, accordingly, and if they were not worried about it, then why would I worry. We continue to walk through some special tunnels and enter a huge room with many people sitting at tables and one large table in front. The elder man guides us up to this table. A man, wearing a special robe tells me, "These two fine beautiful women say they cannot marry unless you give this permission. Is this actual?" I peek at him and say, "If my sisters say it, then it is true, for they are not liars. They are vessels of great purity and love." The man quickly qualifies his statement saying, "Oh my; I never would accuse them of being liars. Never would I even dream such a terrible thought. Do you give your consent?" I tell him that I must first hold them and speak with them. He looks at me and says, "You may only when you give your consent." At this, I turned and began to walk away, motioning for my women to follow me. The man stands up, and demands that I stop. I continue to walk. He then asks me, "Where do you go?" I stop and turn around and declare, "I came in peace believing you received my women in peace. You now refuse to give them back to me, so I shall leave in the peace I came, and will return with my long knife and kill all who refuse to return my women."

I continued to walk. Just as I was to enter the open entranceway, Olimpia calls out to me, "Brother, do not leave without me." Urška is behind her screaming the same words. My women now pull out their knives and stand firm with me. The man with the elegant robe comes running out to me, "Please stop young man; you have your sisters." I walk over to him and tell him, "I have my sisters because I will kill to protect them. Their hearts and dreams are for me to ensure they find." The man asks me what he can do as a token of peace. I ask him to give me his robe. He takes it off and hands it to me. Next, I borrow Kina's knife and cut the robe in two. I glance at him and tell him, "Your foolish pride will kill many of your people. This robe makes you think with an evil heart." At this time, many people come over to stand behind us, all hugging my women, and smiling at me. He asks me if we can try this one more time. I agree, saying, "My father told me that forgiving will create more happiness rather than hating." I just need to bring something extra with me in case your memory fails you. Subsequently, I walk over to my belongings that I had left on the cave's floor and pull out my long knife, putting it at my side. I ask the many people who are with me please to make sure my sisters are safe. Olimpia leaves with them, as my elderly man once again guides us to the table. I stand in front of the table. The man, without an elegant robe tells me, "I have been told by two incredibly wonderful women that they may just now be given in marriage by you. I ask you, will you give this in marriage?" I answer, "Honorable leader, I must first speak to my sisters. Please send them to me." Olimpia and Urška come walking out to me. I open my arms and they begin to run as we embrace so hard. I ask them, "My sisters, my special love, do you want these marriages and is love in your hearts?" They each stare at me and swear, "This is our wish." I give each a kiss and ask them to stand one on each side of me. I gaze to the table and ask, "Who do I give these angels?" Aert and Carolus both stand up and face me. I ask them, "Will you promise me that you will love these special angels, care for them, take no other woman to be your wife, and protect them until death takes one of you?" They both promise me loud and clear. I glare at the main leader and say, "I give my blood to Aert and Carolus, that they may have love, children, and happy families for the remainder of their lives."

Now, all in the room began to cheer. The leader stood up, came out to me, and shook my hand, telling me that my sisters will live great lives. He motions for Aert and Carolus to join us. I glance at Aert and say, "Oh, by the way, not at any time, let a little boy join you to gaze at girls, okay." They both laugh and reassure me that will be a memory they shall never forget. I glance at Olimpia and say, "My love, how can I live without you?" Olimpia tells me that I will do fine, "For she sees before her the strong man she raised and who kept his promise to her." We kiss and I hug Urška telling her also that I will always love her. I tell Carolus and Aert that I must take my three women and go while I can. They shake my hand feeling how hard this is. Aert asks me, "How can you thank a man for giving up so much?" I tell him, "By loving what he surrendered to another." We exit out of this large group. On our way to the entrance, some people call for us to stop. They guide us to a special tunnel and begin to give us supplies. The elderly woman tells me that they are giving us special foods they created for when they went on long exploring trips in the deep caves. It appears to be extremely compact, yet expands when mixed with water. This is interesting, indeed a fascinating discovery. We load up our cow, who is even looking better. A regular man tells us he cleaned our cow and gave him some special foods for her health that would help her produce more milk for us. One of the men also gave me a copy of a map they had made by sewing color threads into plain garment strips. They explained a few areas where it would be better for me to backtrack through a few passes and cross the obstacle from behind in the lowlands, afterwards follow a new pass back up into the mountains. I told my three remaining women, "We need to get a few hours from this point and later take a comfortable break and figure out what just happened here." Babali comments how happy the girls looked. I agreed, and showed her the map saying, "Look for the blue dots. Those are the places where we may find a few men for you two. We will stay together until our first break, after that Andreja, and I will return to scout."

Our first break arrives, and we guide our cow off the path into a small ravine that we discovered. I sat on the ground, and it hits me that Olimpia is gone from my life now. This is painful, as I have never been so frightened. Being afraid does not cut it any longer. Constantly telling these poor girls that I am afraid is not going to cut it anymore. I shall no more complain and no more whine. They asked me if I would give them Olimpia and Urška. I asked my girls if this is what they wanted, and they told me it was. I feel fine in that I could get the boys into our camp, introduce them and like a burning fire, they bound themselves forever. If I had any brains, I would have stayed with them during the cold and dark months that will be on us soon. To my consolation, they did put many marks on this map of places I should spend the winter and dark months. Kina comments on how lucky the girls are to be in such a family oriented clan. We agree that anywhere was better than Bezdroża. Kina tells us she came from a village way north of here. Notwithstanding; I stare at her and ask her if she wants us to take her back. She tells me that she never wants to go back there. That was why she and three friends ran away. I ask her to tell us about this place.

Kina begins by saying, "The name of my home village is Ewout. The people were normal, and lived ordinary lives. The exceptions are that all the men hunted, and all shared the game. That was good. Our troubles came later when a species of extremely big bears, who could change back and forth from their human forms, moved between the sea and us. The bears would eat so many fish, that we had simply to depend on the fish that lived in local small lakes, and for capturing large beasts, as one could feed our village for maybe two days. We never kept meat under salt because they thought that would curse it. Like every place I have lived, we too had our Cornelis. His name was Gerben. He was not like the other men in our village, for he hated girls. He claimed that they were a curse to torture the men. No matter how hard he would try to get us all banished, the men in the village would not give up their wives and daughters. My father was a quiet man and never was involved with much in our house. He would visit, determine what we needed, and bring it to us. He was a wonderful provider. Our mother loved him. They barely spoke and never yelled at each other. She would tell him what she wanted, and he would get it, if it were available. He never forgot anything, and sometimes would bring an item home; we had requested many months earlier. We liked that about him. He was the first person, other than my mother, that I could trust. Mommy told us once that our Daddy had some head problems, and that grandmother was so much better at controlling this difficulty. Many times, he became sick for a long time. During these times, grandfather would collect our food and supplies for us. Our father made sure his family had the physical things to survive. We never noticed accordingly, what we were missing until our friends began inviting us to their homes to play. This is the sad part of life, in that it is that one piece of the link, which breaks and destroys the entire chain. I have always thought back to those days and have shame for the way I thought. The lone blessing is I kept my mouth shut. The reason I had to leave was partially from this. The lunatic, Gerben convinced all in our village that if we sacrificed a three-year-old girl each season, the spirits would protect us from some of the evil spirits. He was the one who could pick the child. Gerben hated our home as my father had seven daughters. With our father gone most of the time, this left eight women alone. Gerben believed that we could create much evil if no man was there to control us. He took two of my sisters and sisters from three of my friends. Sometimes, he would take the little girl early and put her in a cage for the village to witness each day for a month. This was a cruel and terrifying experience for a young child. I joined with my three friends, and we carefully planned to kill Gerben. We waited until he was asleep. Afterwards, we slowly crawled into his hut from a small opening created earlier. I was the lucky one that could cut his throat. We subsequently put papers all around his room and afterwards set his bed on fire. He used to mess around a lot with fire in his hut, claiming it allowed him to see into the spirit worlds. These made it appear as if he was trying to conjure up this strange spell and that a few of his papers caught fire while he slept. We walked carefully out of his front door and unlocked the cage the little girl was in and brought her with us. I raised her in Bezdroża."

Andreja asked her, "Mommy, what happened to her, because I never remember you raising a little girl?" Kina points at her and confesses, "Andreja, that little girl is you." I asked Kina, "How did you escape?" Kina tells us, "Our village was not far from a big stream. We went to the stream and ran, or swam if we could, for many days until we passed four villages. After the fourth one, we went to land and kept walking south for what felt as an age of moons. I finally ran up on Bezdroża where Hæge discovered me. We later married and told everyone that I had found this baby. I was still a virgin, in which of all demons, Cornelis verified. Thereafter, no one ever questioned what I said about our little girl." I ask her, "What happened to your three friends?" Kina explains, "We divided after the fourth village, knowing that most would ignore a woman passing through; however, four women would draw too much attention." I laugh and say, "To think that I tried to move five women through their lands." They all laugh, and Kina says our situation is so different because we have such a fierce leader. I ask where she gets the fearless. Babali asks if she can answer this one by saying, "Last night, you went into the dark, knowing that danger was around us and shortly thereafter return with them in peace as they are now your brothers. Today, you demanded to see Olimpia and Urška refusing to give them away in marriage, until you knew for sure it was their will. You cut in half the prized robe of their great leader. Do not ever tell us you are not fierce. Do you understand?" I glance at her and say, "Young woman; an attitude like that is going to cost you extra kisses and hugs." Babali laughs and says, "Son this is a debt I hope to pay on frequently." I tell her I consider forward to a great time with all three of my remaining family. Therefore, I tap on Andreja's belly and say, "I need to get us in our new home, so we can start pulling little babies out of there." She agrees.

Her life means something extra for me now. That beast would have crucified her if Kina had delayed her revenge. We are going to relax here and get needed rest, although we did not do many physical things, we were involved in many stressful things. My question for this clan currently is, "Should I had stayed and shared in the ceremony with Olimpia or was I right to escape?" We agree it would have been better to stay for a few days; however, having so much love you recognize escape is the solitary way, you can give the loved one what she needs is not completely bad. Unexpectedly, we hear the people walking on the path. I have the girls each drew their bows, but not to fire until they can see the face of the target, because we are still close to the Gerben, and they could be bringing us something. The travelers pass by in front of us, and our bows drop, as we rush to them. Olimpia and Urška with their husbands are with us. I ask them, "Why are you here?" Olimpia answers, "Because you left me." I hang my head down and say, "Yes; we just agreed that may not have been the right thing to do. I was afraid of what I would do when faced with knowing you were lost forever." Olimpia pats my head and replies, "I understand you inside and out. I understand; however, that is not why we are here this day. You are all in danger. If you continue now on your path, you will not be able to find shelter for the winter, and will be unprotected during this deadly season. We are here to guide you to safe shelter for both the winter and dark season. We must prepare for a long series of fights with the mountain dark and winter beasts." I glance at Aert and say, "Show us the way." He is now my oldest brother, so I am quick to put the reigns in his hands. Aert tells me, "Oh no, I do not want to take your position from you." I rebuke him, "Aert, wake up; you are married to my oldest sister/mother. In addition, this is your territory. It is time for us to work in one direction with one leader who can save these wonderful women. You have Carolus and me, now we need to prepare against those things that Olimpia told me."

Aert said, "Okay; Carolus and Urška will scout today, while Olimpia and I try to explain the highlights of what we need to do and brief you on special things we need our scouts discover." Kina asks what she, and Babali may do. Aert tells them just to stay looking beautiful. I peep at him and say, "Oh come on, give them something hard to do." We laugh at this one and then prepare to continue our trip. Carolus tells us that wall all should carry our long knives. They brought some extra. There are many snakes in this next region, so when we see one, you must strike it immediately. Legend claims the snakes can hear each other's death hiss, and this hiss will force them to retreat. If they give their hiss of potential food available, many will attack. This is why they kill them on sight. Save their bodies, as they do make for good eating. He explains that we must watch our cow, as the snakes will sneak into our packages and wait for us to unload them. Once they grasp their spring can whirl them to us, they will strike. They regularly strike at the first possible opportunity. He continues that they always stay on the path and walk on rocks. Their tales warn of curses to those who walk on the open ground and just permit intruders to pass through on the path or sleep on the rocks. He will show us one of their temples, which is no more than a few hours ahead of us. The mountainsides are active this season, as the leaves and brush cover all that they can, including the life that bustles beneath it. The range of noise increases as we move south and make it harder to detect enemy activity. Aert tells us that few could ever survive this path the first time. I remember Daddy always preferred the northern areas because he said they were quieter. Having our newlyweds with us is special. The way they behave, as couples are so impressive. If Aert or Carolus point to do something, Olimpia or Urška will get it. They do not base this action on who asked for something, but about whom is the closest to fulfill it. Urška and Olimpia work together to keep their men happy. Aert and Carolus are just as ambitious to please their women, as either will strive to help to protect and care for my sisters. Kina tells me this is because they are young in their relationship; it will wear down for most men.

Andreja reminds her that even Hæge always was looking to do things to please her. Kina smiles and says, "Like I said, most men. There are exceptions, such as Hæge and our Yakov." Andreja calls her crazy and informs her that I will be lying around each day telling everyone else what to do. Babali and Olimpia jump into the conversation claiming that Yakov has too many mommies to behave like that. Andreja stands her ground and claiming this is why Yakov will be such as that. I laugh and pat her but saying, "Get to work old woman." Andreja spins around and tries to grab me. I take off running as our convoy stops and each takes side routing for a victor. I am able to keep ahead of her for a while, then as we are getting too far in front of our group, so I turn around and zip past her. Ordinarily, I would have tried to spin around in the forests that border the corridor. However, we must stay on this path to prevent the curse. I appreciate Andreja understanding this, as she actually offers no resistance to me as I pass her. She even gives me my three-foot lead and then the race it on once more. This is one of so many things that I enjoy about her; she will attempt to play fair, unless involved in a real fight and like a wonderful member of our clan, fights to win. As we become back within view of our clan, I fall to the ground surrendering. She pounces on me. Once securing her control, she grabs my hair, and orders me to shout that I surrender. I immediately yell in surrender. She then demands that I scream I love her. I call out that I love her. Andreja goes for one more that gains cheers from our clan, as she demands that I roar out, which she claims to be the most beautiful and lone woman for me. I bellow out these words. Andreja tells me she will release me and that I am to hug and kiss her. She releases me, and I hug and kiss her. We hold hands as we return to our clan. Andreja was smart enough to figure that with the locals, Aert and Carolus with us, we could have this play time. When we return to the camp, Kina begins teasing, "When are you both going to take the oaths?" I tell her, "As soon as possible." Kina continues, "I think you really meant what you were saying while Andreja was on top of you."

I shake my head yes, while Aert tells us, "Of course he did, because Andreja is the best woman that he will ever find for him." I walk over and shake his hand. Andreja is blushing her face red, and this is rare, because it is tough to get one over on her. Babali alerts everyone, "Andreja is in love as well. This is the best news that our new family has released." Andreja tells everyone that it must have been obvious. Olimpia tells her that it is not real until you confess it before others. She also tells us they may have a surprise for us after our evening meal, which will also be a celebration. I tell them, "We should celebrate your bonding, as they are official." Olimpia recommends that we hold off on the bonding's celebrations until we find a way to bond Andreja and me. I tell her that probably would be best. Olimpia tells Andreja and her man to get up front and lead the way for us, while they protect the mothers. We jump to the front and while holding hands lead our convoy that is beginning to flourish again down this path. I am comforted to recognize that this path does not seem worn. Aert tells these lowlifes, use this path extensively during the winter months when so many of the northern lands scavenge anything south of them. They treat the southern lands as having no worth, and take everything they can grab with their hands. Providentially for us, they usually do not hit these lands until the middle months in the cold season. Some are so famished that they stay too long and then end crawling back to their homelands, or for a few odd ones crawling over the cliff into the western lands to their immediate smashing death. I ask Aert, "Everyone knows the winter months are bad, why they not prepared during the summer months?" Aert looks at me and asks if we prepared. I point to our cow. He then asks, "What if someone stole your cow?" I inform him, "I would be dying, and because that is the single way that they will get this cow." Aert reveals, "Yes, my brother you would be dead. I might be better for us if we found a safe place for the winter, would you agree?" I smile and report to him, "My brother this is why we follow you." Aert smiles and says, "Kiss your Queen and move on to our next place."

Andreja shares our kiss and our feet begin to move once again. A few hours later, Aert tells me to stop and follow the small side path to my right. We walk this path for a short distance when it ends with a strange looking something in front of us. I ask him, "Aert, what is this?" He tells us it is an ancient temple called Klavdija. Here we can walk on the ground and around the temple, both inside and outside its nature coated walls. He shows us a specific curtsy, and we repeat the particular words to avert any misfortune. Andreja steps on something, looks down, and comes rushing back to me. Aert changes his recommendation to stay on the rock stones, because there are many bodies of those who tried to do evil to this temple. Andreja is shaking her head yes to me, so I realize she stepped on a body. That is the unique thing about dead bodies, no matter how many, you have seen, each one has the same terrifying message, 'your time will come.' This building (?) stands as high as the surrounding trees. The lower section is as a square stone, yet maybe two-hundred times larger. The front top of this square stone has what looks like a giant trunk of a tree, being round and massive. The outside is completely verdant with vegetation, as even the large entrance above the square stone has green vines dropping in front of it. The top of this structure had a great assortment of trees growing above it. There is a series of small flat stone ledges, which circle the lower section, from the ground to the entrance providing a doorway. This place blends into the forest so effectively, looking as if it has been here for a long time. We walk around the outside in amazement. Never before in our lives have we witnessed such a structure. We walk up the stone ledges being enormously careful, as the stones are loose and finally arrive at the entrance. The inside is dark as a night without stars. The air smells fresh inside and is not a muggy smoldering hot I would have expected, especially as it is sealed. The inside feels comfortable. I ask Aert how this can be, and he explains the Gerben believes this place is alive and can breathe as we do. Even in the cold of winter, when we walk inside, the warmth brings us peace.

The divine law is that no one may sleep over night inside this temple, because, if you do so you will be vanished from existence. Not even the dirt or insects may stay inside for the night. Insects and birds may never enter. Whey they try; they hit an invisible wall that spins them around to the ground. We come inside, and then go down to the large dark room where we think for a while. We have the listening time, as many have claimed to receive messages. Our legends claim many messages that revealed events that have saved many lives. We claim this as, 'the temple of no lies,' as even my father claims once to have received a warning here. Andreja asks if we can try to receive a message. Aert teaches us that we must all confess to believe, 'the spirit of Klavdija speaks the truth.' We affirmed. We held hands and remained silent. I felt so at peace in the tranquility that radiated from this room. After about twenty minutes, a large purple ball appeared before us and began to spin. Our eyes opened as each froze in place. I do not even think our hearts were beating. The middle part of the purple ball became white as we now witnessed a group of elders, who was a shiny silver trimmed in gold. Their heads appeared like diamonds with long white hair that flowed behind them. A voice began speaking. It was not simply one speaking, as they would change speakers even in the middle of their words. One powerful mind with so many faces was now before us. They began, "Welcome to our home oh faithful ones. We will do you no harm, so do not fear us. Our news for you art beneficial, as with your blessings and exceptional mission. A special spirit protects you, which has great love for you. This spirit tells us many pronounced things about you. That is one of the important reasons, which we speak before you today. We would recommend that our children now bond with our strangers stayed beside these strangers as they venture to their new homelands in the south. Blessed you will be, if you do this. It is time that we begin to spread our seeds among the other lands before the great Armies take such opportunities from us. We need an opportunity for us to get our seed into the greatest who will ever spread love and morality in this world. Which among you art called Yakov?"

I stood up and confessed to be Yakov by saying, "I am the little boy who is called Yakov." I definitely wanted to make sure they knew I was still young. Fear raced through my heart these legends may have portrayed me as being much greater, or the village leader was seeking revenge through his spirits. Then the voice of a female spirit spoke, saying, "However, you are a cute little boy." Olimpia, Kina, Babali, Urška, and my Andreja began laughing as women do in their special manner. The voice continues, "You also appear to be special for the women among your clan. This is accordingly important for us as we have a great mission that just a man who has the love inside him these women respect can perform our mission and who walks with spirits." Olimpia now stands before these spirits and asks, "What mission do you wish for my son?" The voices ask, "Are you the wife of Aert?" Aert stands, genuflects, and answers, "She is oh great ones." The voices then cheer saying, "Then Yakov is a son of the Gerben." I spoke with pride, "Yes; I am the son of the Gerben." Olimpia came beside me and we hugged as I told her, "I shall always be your son, because you are my greatest love." The voices then asked us to watch a vision of what happened to their chosen one. It began with a man and a woman, both exceptionally clean and elegant standing in front of a large crowd within a giant building. The music was lovely, and all the people were so happy. A loud voice cried out, "Behold your King and the new Queen of love." The vision continued showing how she worked so hard helping the poor, and everywhere she would go; the masses would follow her. She ended each day kissing and hugging the children of the poor who were following her. The people chanted, "Queen Jolana Queen of Love," throughout the night. Her Kingdom had no more than a few isolated cases of poor people, as those people stayed in their homes as the neighbors cared for them. The poor who followed the Queen were from neighboring Kingdoms, who suffered from the atrocious wars. Her Armies pleaded with her to deny these people sanctuaries. She refused to allow suffering if she could help them. When they came into her Kingdom, she could help them. She respected the sovereignty, although questionable, of her neighbors, thus she would not invade them.

Her Kingdom prospered, over these exact lands as she built the temple you now stand. Each night, before she rested, she filled her prayers with pleas for a child. One day, while she was in her elder years, her medical men told her that she was with a child. This was the greatest news in her life, as she ordered a great celebration for her entire Kingdom. Not all who heard this news was pleased. During her long reign, she had helped many who had escaped from evil hateful slave masters. Once a slave entered her Kingdom, she declared them free and would not return them, or allow the master to harass them. She ordered slave owners executed at once after proven guilty. This deep hatred among the immoral masses who wished her dead began to attract evil spirits, who found these evil people obedient servants. Even the wicked spirits knew they could never touch her, for all love protected her. During all her great works of love, then she left the King alone, allowing him to rule his Kingdom. He began to hate her, claiming she loved the people more than him. This was the opportunity, which vice had waited so many years to come. They corrupted many of the King's advisors with false riches. These immoral advisors deceived the King into expanding his Kingdom for his new son that would be born soon. The King sent his untrained Armies into battles. His wicked neighboring Kingdoms united and destroyed all his Armies and then invaded this Kingdom, killing all in their path. Some righteous men of the temples helped the Queen escape, refusing to help the King. Queen Jolana refused to leave her husband, thus the medicine men gave her an herb that put her into a deep sleep. The temple elders hid her in some of the nearby caves until she tried to give birth to her daughter, 'Ráðúlfr', or called by many, Wise Wolf.' During the delivery, something happened in the spirit world as the evil spirits tried to capture her spirit from the righteous spirits. During the battle, something destroyed Queen Jolana's body as the baby entered our world. The baby was born with no life. Queen Jolana took the Wise Wolf's spirit with her to the land of the dead. The evil spirits that sought to kill this child are now captured and being punished, never to be free again. The great spirits of justice have declared that Ráðúlfr be awarded a life, as this is her creation right. She was born into a kind family who loved her with all they could give her. A new form of evil decided to exact revenge and killed this family. They tried to kill young Ráðúlfr; however, the wolves freed her. She has remained with these wolves and is a fierce dangerous fighter. We were given the right to send one boy, her age into the deep, deadly southern lands to free her and bring her back to us, where she will rule as Queen. We beg that you save the Gerben royal blood so our people may continue to live in love and peace. If we do not get our Queen, the wicked will get her and curse the Gerben people. Will you do this great deed for us?"

I asked them, "What will happen to my mothers, sisters, and wife?" The spirits answered, "We shall take them to your modern homeland and help them build their new homes. It is at the time you will be bonded to the special Andreja whose love you hold so dear to your heart." I ask another question, "How can I fight all the evil, which doubtlessly will certainly try to prevent me?" They answered, "We will work beside Damijana, as all the great spirits that rule have commanded death not to touch you or your clan." I pick up my sword and ask another question, "As you understand the ways of boys and girls in that each girl will like a different kind of boy. No boy could have the love of all the girls. What will I do if Ráðúlfr refuses to join me?" The female spirit chuckles, "Do not speak of her loving you, or Andreja will not permit you to attempt this mission, as is her right according to the laws of love. We wish that you gain her trust, that she will have faith in you and your ability to protect and guide her. She trusts no person. We hope for you to rebuild that trust." Kina now spoke to the spirits, saying,

"There is none other than Yakov, who could do such a great thing. Ráðúlfr will follow him."

Andreja declares, "If she does not follow my Yakov, I shall search for her and knock some sense into her failing brain." Urška and Babali, while holding hands add to the endorsements, "Our Yakov can do this even if he has no words, for his eyes will melt even the wildest female beast." Olimpia kisses me on my head and adds, "When you bring her back, you will be able to take care of me for the remainder of our days as you wish, my son." The spirits spoke to me again saying, "We believe you can do this, just as those who appreciate you believe. What do you say?" I ask the spirits, "Will you continue to talk to me and warn me if evil tries to cheat in this mission?" The spirits confess to us, "Yakov, we are coming into this fight with you to fight. Our days of kindness and mercy will return when our Queen is once again on her throne." I looked at them and asked another question, "Do you truly believe I can do this for your wonderful people who are now my family?" They returned with an instant reply, "There are one thousand spirits in our number in this council. There is not one spirit that doubts your success." I saw so many lights begin to flash inside this great ball. I knelt to my knees and looked at Andreja, who shook her head yes. Next, I glanced at Olimpia, who also shook her head yes. Finally, I looked at the spirits and said, "Begin preparing the throne for your returning Queen. Tell me where to go to when to do our will." The spirit answered, "There is one who wishes personally to give you this knowledge. We will see you whenever you call for us. Simply call for 'Love,' and we will be there." The ball vanished as our room was once more dark. Aert began to cry. Olimpia inquires, "Why do you cry?" Aert explains, "My father spoke so often that someday a great, mighty one, who did not understand the fear, who could defeat any mountain that stood before him, and had faith of iron would use love and purity to defeat the extreme evils and bring our Queen back to rule us. Ráðúlfr is a word I have never before spoke or heard. We merely recognize her as 'Wise Wolf.' The legends say that when the phenomenal great one, whom even death would fear, would bring her back and reveal her name. We must never again tell her name until Yakov tells her Kingdom when he returns her to his throne."

He now looks at Andreja and reports, "You will be the first couple bonded by our Queen." He joins Carolus as they salute me and Aert says, "I pray the great spirits forgive me for thinking this old prophecy to be a tale of foolish elderly men. Our fresh Queen will build our land into a considerable place for lovers and families. We will serve you for the remainder of your days in our new blessed home in the southern lands, where our children will be blessed." I thank them and then begin to drift inside my mind. How did I get myself into such a dangerous situation? When will I ever learn to say no? As I ask this question a bright white-light flood this large room. The light begins to change into many colors. I recognize who this is, and I will confess that I so much want to see her. She now focuses her light on the back wall of this huge temple, accordingly I walk forward and drop to my knees while I await for her to appear. A giant white rock begins to rise out of our floor. The rock has three large seats cut into it as she begins to descend through the roof. I gawk back at Andreja, who rushes up to my side. We now stand up and begin to walk to our seats on each side of our wonderful love. Carolus cries out for us to be careful. Andreja looks back at all their scared faces and yells out, "Do not fear; this is the one who holds our love." As we sat down, Damijana descended to stand before us. She bows before each of us and then shares a kiss with each of us before she sits. Kina cried out when Damijana stood before Andreja, "Please do not hurt my baby." When she saw Damijana bow to her, and kiss her hand before sitting next to her asked, "Who is this great one that they appreciate so well?" Olimpia says, "She is the reason we still live; she is the angel who warns of death." Damijana begins by saying, "All who are with us; I ask that you have no fear. Today is a pronounced day for me, as my pride for my Yakov and Andreja are as great rivers that take all the water from the endless seas. I have come to promise all here that Queen Ráðúlfr in this temple will marry Yakov. So I will not be considered the strange woman among this clan, I also will declare my love for Yakov and Andreja." Damijana looks at Andreja and continues, "I so much envy you Andreja and at the same time certify that you, and Yakov belong as one. You both are my hope and now my greatest pride. I owe so much to you Andreja, for it was my desire to have you as a sister who forced me first to speak with Yakov. I knew that he would be faithful and bring you to be at his side when we met."

I next confessed to Damijana, "That was consequently, extremely difficult because of your extreme beauty." Damijana agrees, "That is what makes a few men great and others weak, for you fought the temptation, in your desire to provide a more caring love for the one who promised to be yours." Andreja joins in, "To imagine, today I had to chase him and struggle, using all the force my poor frail body could spare and yet remain alive, to make him promise to love and care for me." Damijana chuckles with all the others in attendance and then adds, "I saw that; nevertheless, I would bet all that I have that you could have received those promises from him with much less force." Andreja laughs and confesses, "I agree; a simple smile or wink would have compelled him to fall before me declaring his love to be forever and true." I then add, "I think you can have even received my vows with much less force than a wink or smile." We next join our hands and rest them on Damijana's knees. She comments, "Oh the great feeling of so much love flowing in such warm bodies is a blessing that I cannot put into accurate words. I have placed your mission in your mind. You will understand how to get where you must, to save the Queen. Remember, death may not touch you, so do not obey the laws you now obey. If you wish to cross one ridge to the other, do not fear the cliffs. Jump into the air, for death cannot touch you. Walk on the raging waters and through the fires, for death cannot touch you. Do not fear long knives or duck from arrows, for death cannot touch you. Yakov, tell me what I just told you?" I smile and kiss her saying, "I can kiss you anytime I want to, because death or Andreja cannot touch me." Damijana looks at Andreja and chuckles, "Can you believe a Kingdom depends on the lover boy here to bring back their Queen, not raped? Are we not sending the wolf after the lamb instead of the lamb after the wolf?" Andreja laughs and says, "Why not? The poor girl is entitled to a challenge. Since she lives with wolves now, she should be able to recognize him easily?"

Damijana looks at me and says, "If you need me call me. That I demand from you. You will allow me to serve you. Do you understand young man?" I shook my head yes and then told her, "I guess now is the time for hugs and good-byes?" Damijana qualifies this, "What about the hugs, and the 'I shall returns'?" I shake my head yes. Damijana looks at Andreja and informs her, "If you want to see what your man is doing, call for me, and I will show you through a vision." Damijana calls the rest of our clan to join us. The woman walks over to Olimpia and gives her a tremendous hug congratulating her on doing such a great job in raising her son. Damijana thanks Nina and Babali for their great support in what she labels, 'My most loved couple.' She thanks Urška for all the wonderful things she has done for her family. Damijana finishes her introductions by thanking Aert and Carolus for supporting their wives and agreeing to move to the southern lands. She authenticates that this clan will need their help to remain alive. Damijana looks at me and informs me, "You may begin once you are finished saying good-bye to these wonderful people." She sits back in her seat and vanishes slowly. Now comes the hard part, the convincing them that I shall return.

CHAPTER 09

Staging for the Search

I am staring at five sets of milky sad eyes, as my lone consolation is the excitement in Carolus and Aert's eyes. This just about causes me to think they do not want me around, yet I understand them too well. They want me for the great advice that I give them on getting girlfriends, or in their cases, mates. My women appear as if their insides our exploding in agony. I glance at them and ask, "Why do you seem so sad; I am doing what you asked me to do?" Andreja responds by telling me, "We understand that Yakov, now we are living with the pain of knowing that when you go to save the Queen, you must leave us. This is the hard part about giving what you love for your village. I believe that we hoped to forgo this for specific later time when our village had developed." I glimpse at them and respond, "I can tell you one truth that few can ever refute, and that is the beauty of each of my five women is far better than the beauty of any Queen. The best blessed me. Aert and Carolus are wonderful brothers, whom I recognize will share great memories with our clan, throughout the many years ahead on our journey, for the remainder of our days. I have faith that they will provide greater care and protection for the mothers of our new clan. Remember, I will return." I hugged each one in such different manners. During the time, I was in the arms of Kina and Babali, I truly felt as a child from their wombs. They have a maternal grasp. Never could I deny that this grasp can drop the strongest son to the ground in tears begging to stay within this bosom. Mothers have been painfully sending their sons into the unknown since the birth of a family unit. I cannot conceive the feeling of creating from within, just to fear having the body return to sleep in the dirt. Notwithstanding many never received the bodies of their lost loved ones.

I think of how Petenka and Bezdroża saw themselves slaughtered by death. These mothers watched what they created to be destroyed. The extraordinary special thing about Kina and Babali is how one minute they appear as helpless old fools, yet the next minute can give an order that we will obey. When they give us their serious stare, we are on our toes, waiting to do what they say. Kina and Babali have made me a part of them. When they hug me, I am actually visiting the part of me; they have kept. I wish that they were small enough to put in my pocket, if that were the case, they would never be free from me. I must continue with the part of themselves; they welded inside my heart. The amazing thing is that they are the perfect age to be my mother, yet younger than would qualify as Olimpia's mother. Babali is Urška's appointed mother and had devoted herself, while in Bezdroża to be the intimate and the perfect mother of both Balderik and Urška. Urška has shared so many stories with us about the never-ending work that Babali did to make sure they had the best care and love. She did not swamp them with things; she gave up every spare moment of her life just to mother them. I can see why the band that recognized the morality of escaping from Bezdroża would have her and her children firmly under her wings. As Urška smiles, Babali will also smile. When Urška cries, Babali wipes the tears. When Urška's stomach is about to ask to be fed, Babali hands her the food. I can see completely how Babali knows Urška's body just as Kina knows Andreja's body. My additional pride comes in the way Urška and Andreja treat these old nagging women. They place them on a great pedestal and strive with all they have to lift them into the highest places of honor. Aert,

Carolus, and I have established our degree of honor for them in the same manner. We compliment these mothers from dawn until dusk and always do as they suggest.

Kina has, at times, called me foolish for obeying her, and is fixed in that we never obey them on the things of men. When danger comes, they stop and stare at Aert, Carolus and I. Olimpia has the place within me that she created and sealed with her love. Andreja has commented so many times, about how I change when Olimpia is near us. The change is always in the highest form of honor for Olimpia. I can beg these women not to do something, and if Olimpia does it in front of me, I will be begging her for a kiss and hug before she is finished. My defenses against Olimpia were never given birth. Granted, Olimpia would not at any time openly defy me, for her goal has always been to develop me into the kind of leader she believed I was. This is why this mission means so much to me. When I have successfully finished it, she will have such great pride. We discussed so many times how our mother-son relationship was different, yet still realistic. Granted, I did not come forth from her uterus. The blood in this relationship comes from the fact that we came from the identical womb. The same mother created us in her womb. The final stamp of authority as my mother came from the promise that she pledged to our mother. Our mother asked her to take me as her son. When mommy was fighting for her last few breaths, Olimpia promised her that her babies would be the same as her babies. Things do not always work out the manner originally planned. However, when the one who was our mother, knew death was at her door, she transferred her babies to one of her babies. I do not understand how powerful this transfer is physically; nevertheless, I do comprehend how powerful this transfer is spiritually. Nothing can shake it piously. This must be why she has returned with her mate. We must be together. Her voice rings through my mind just about every time I see something or go to do something. I hear her voice to give me permission or a warning. She worked hard giving all to Acia, Pava and I, while adding support to Kaus, Answald, and Panfilo. How she did it; I will never understand. She had her post in our family, as even Daddy and Kristoffel honored it. The next two of my women are the extremes.

I call them my women, because of my commitment to them. Their lives are my responsibility. It does not matter if I wanted for this; by the custom of our world, shared by every village or tribe I have ever known, I am responsible. Just if they did not have those milky eyes. The final two Andreja and Urška. Andreja is my mate for life; we are to be and will always be one. Urška is the widow of my brother. She passes on to me. Kaus's promise passes to any other remaining males in his clan. My problem with Urška was her majestic beauty. I was fortunate that she shared her true beauty with me. She laughed and played when I was around and spoke to me as if I were Olimpia. Urška is an expert prankster and keeps everything around her from being bored. It is great that we have Aert and Carolus in our family currently and they share my responsibility for Olimpia and Urška. The key point is that they are still my blood and as such my responsibility. Aert and Carolus are fine with this, as the same rules apply in their village. A brother may never abandon his sister. This custom evolved to combat the abuse of women by their mates. When the brother attempts to save his sister, with her consent, the village will side with the brother. This is a good rule, for no child should ever be helpless when he or she witnesses his mother suffering abuse. Aert and Carolus are exactly subservient to our women as I am. We want our women to experience the value we place in their thoughts and part of our life. Our philosophy is not radical or even considered strange. More fathers share our view than those who do not. Most do not belong with primitive tribes who suffered from particular mutations that created them distinctive. Although created distinct from us, if our hunters see them abusing their female members, these hunters will attack. This is simply the way of the wilderness. This is one of the few ways, in which those who believe they are moral supporting each other. Conversely, the malicious people rejoice in this abuse. Our sole consolations are that even the vicious hate and kill the wicked. Those who are of the same unjust heart today will share the hand who will strike the just tomorrow. Foolishly, they call too many brothers.

I feel so blessed that I have escaped those who are malicious, even though this road has covered itself with the blood of those

I love. Their blood forbids me from turning back. Their blood demands that I care for Olimpia and the others who have melded into our clan. Another great consolation that I have for this mission is that spirit of love has requested and selected me to do this work on their behalf. This work is their work, and I would hope never to believe it is my work. If I see a cliff and deny death will realize that I have jumped, I must believe these great lights protected me, and it was not the certain power of my wisdom, which saved me. Those times will come and then go; the important issue is the Queen returns to her throne that has been vacant for too many seasons. I am now beginning to walk away and soon am out of their sight. Our separation and my journey of a few steps are in progress. If they were a few steps or a few thousand steps apart, the same end is true. We are not together and cannot touch each. The arms that held me just a few breaths ago, no longer hold me. The next time they hold me will be when the Queen is within their vision, unless by the magic of Damijana. Naturally, I am not traveling the path we were previously walking. Now, I am traveling as a scout would travel. Alone and quiet I slide through the wilderness, the difference since I will have no clan to join in the evening. Each time I see a pretty flower I think about Andreja and Olimpia. A few times, I almost picked one, placing it in my pocket to adorn with them on our reunion. The obstacle I face in picking them now is that their beauty and life will vanish during the upcoming freezing and dark seasons. A feeling inside me calls that I move forward every minute of daylight until the cold season forbids it. I wonder whether the wintry season will permit me to travel any. The one thing that I do know, that as I have never been in this part of our world previously, I will depend on the lights to guide me. If I leave a cave and travel during the cold season, I will have to believe they are aware of another cave on the path. Part of me does not expect many tribulations to get the Queen, as I am alone and flexible and easy to cloak.

The trouble will begin removing her from wolves, which can be feisty and deadly if they wish to be and actually dragging her back. It is difficult to survive in the wilderness when making much noise. I thought about maybe devising a method, which I could constrain her and carry her; however, I find myself still extremely far from developing into a man, and I cannot see me being able to carry a girl all this distance. I am, nevertheless, at the age where the girls are physically more developed. This is why Andreja can tackle and constrain me. Men do not win in this process, as when we are younger, the larger girls thrash us at will, yet when we get older and much stronger, to prove we are kind and gentle; we let our now smaller women flagellate us at will. I love it when Urška's face turns and she dives for Carolus. He tries will all he has to escape her, most times without success. The few times he was successful, Olimpia tripped or ambushed him. The sole factor of mercy on their souls is these older girls do not like to hit little boys and tend to provide additional moral support. I, for one, appreciate the special merciful feature they share, because, if even the big girls went around whopping me, I would be terrified of girls forever. Therefore, my safety valve that Andreja will not destroy me is that Kina or Olimpia would jump in and save me. Boys, girls, how could it ever be more difficult? Knowing all this, I agree to go alone in an unknown wilderness, a search for a half wolf girl my age, and bring her back. Possibly progress is merely possible through fools as myself. Staying in the safe area will never expand it. If we want the secure areas to be larger, we must move out into the unsafe areas for the conversion. Too much comfort accordingly turns into discomfort. Blending a number of challenges in with the comfort creates a stronger comfort, one in which discomfort finds distasteful. Oftentimes, I wish I could remember so many more things' Daddy told me. Most of what I recite that he supposedly taught is from what Kaus and Olimpia have shared with me. Daddy always told us that there was so much more in the wilderness and other lands he did not have the time to share with us, and we did not need to grasp, as it would never concern the world we lived.

He never talked about going south, as all his tales concerned the northern lands. I wonder how he could have passed the challenge of going to the southern lands. To think he would always go just one-way, especially with the cliff wall that blocks so much of the western lands, or at the minimum the extremely limited access to the west, as he had discovered a passageway through the caves so he could explore Jožefa and Cvetka. He talked about open land below

Cvetka; therefore, I wonder why he would not have explored for a mountain passage to this land, as a mountain passage would be more in line with his familiarity and expertise. I never gave this any mind, until now, that I walk along this never-ending divide from the mountains and western lands. I appreciate this has a crossing entryway, in that my feet are to lead me to our lost Queen. Because the evening is rapidly ending, I search for somewhere to eat the roots and fruits I collected throughout the day and sleep for the night. I spot a few trees, and as I walk under them, I can see in all four directions, and the eastern side has a moderately deep cliff in front of it. This allows me to guard my north and south. I am not all that much worried about the north since I have walked through it this day. I lay down facing the mysterious south and lightly crunch my roots and fruits as darkness now covers this land. I reach over to hold Andreja, because she gets angry if I do not. However, I cannot find her to touch. Then it hits me; she is not here, as neither are Olimpia. Bizarrely, my mind lost track of where I was. It must have been the lying down that confused me. I had, within such a short period been able to shift my nighttime sleeping partner from Olimpia to Andreja. My entire existence had its nights, shared with a loving support, although I had shifted from protected by Olimpia to protecting Andreja. The emptiness that flowed through my heart now is from the lack of one to protect. A part of me is missing as this is totally disrupting me. Finding myself beginning to fall apart, I quickly start the fight to hold myself together. This fight is harder than originally projected; nevertheless, it continues. In delight, I finally pull my disturbed mind back together by telling myself that I am a young man and must be strong. I can no longer be the little boy who clung to the one who acted in the role of my mother nor the one I later substituted in her place. I toss and turn attempting to find a new way to merge my body with the ground instead of my comfort partner.

Even though my partners had bones, they also had muscles, which provided me a little relief from the unyielding ground and bones. I harshly lie looking to the south as the first moon begins to shine through the clouds. Something begins to move in front of me. It is a black covered in fabric from a round head-like top to a bend with a small circle, which resembles a kneecap. A prolonged pole with a bent extensive blade appears, as having six fingers to grasp it at the base of what I would have considered its head. I call out, "Who goes there?" I struggle to make the tone appear relaxed and of exploration. A large black raven appears toward the end of his long blade that appears to extend into the clouds, as I cannot witness its end. The voice asks me, "Why do you walk along the southern path?" I speak back, "If you were from the spirits that lead me, you would know." He questions once more, "Why do you walk along the southern path? Is there one you search for?" I answer in return, "Why do you not listen to the answer I gave you?" This spirit replies, "Do you not see my long knife?" I lift my long knife and respond, "I see it, as it can be of little value to save yourself. You can see that my long knife is a better cutting tool when we fight, as we will unless you go back to the ugly place that you came from." I stand while this thing sits down on something beside it. Walking toward it, a voice warns, "I would not move closer if I were you." As it talks, a body of a sleeping woman appears with her hands forming an 'X' over her chest. I do not recognize her face, knowing I have never seen her before this. The voice asks me, "Do you understand who I have beside me?" I truthfully answer, "I realize not who she is." He tells me, "She is the Queen you seek." I peek at her, noticing that her hair is black and tell him, "If I seek a Queen that you now possess, then in the morning I will return south. Notwithstanding if you have not what I seek, then in the morning I will go south once again." I moved toward him swinging my long knife. He quickly vanished, taking his partner with him.

I truly hope my guess is correct, in that I simply saw blond or brown hair on all the Bezdrożans that I was in contact. I wonder now how he could believe I was seeking a Queen; notwithstanding, he apparently does not recognize this Queen, or she would be a blonde-haired woman, as he also does not understand my mission, or the Queen would have been living. I might have given away too much information when I said the spirits of the lights, as he was clearly from the dark. The one thing I realize is that I am not alone, as something wishes to stop me, though they may not realize why. It could be nothing more than a path spirit that haunts all who travel this path. I slowly fall to sleep after discovering how to ignore the small noises that were alarming me in anticipation of another visitor. Once in my sleep, a favorite friend appears before me. Damijana applauds me for a victory over a dead spirit. I ask her who the woman who slept was. She tells me the woman was barely one who slept in the land of the dead. She continues to tell me that I will have more visitors and to be careful what I tell them. They will use this information in their attempt to cause me to fail in my mission. I ask her how Andreja and Olimpia are doing. She tells me, that outside missing me, they are doing fine, and they have great faith in me. Morning arrives speedier than I wanted it to do so. I do not complain, as with my first night, I may wish for the days to grow longer. I will enjoy no such fortune, as the cold months will be soon with their longer nights, until the black month arrives with no light. Fortunately, our 1,000-day year merely has about seventy-five dark days sandwiched with ten other seasons. Enough about this world's seasons, as even the children from our world understand the seasons. The night world has so many mysteries such as how our three moons change in the light they share. A few shine as a lighted circle, while other times they appear as a half-lighted circle, and other times, they were light such as a banana. Sometimes, they show no light. I am confused on how they have such power, considering our Suns always shine as a circle in the daytime hours. Someday, I hope to comprehend what the little white dots that paints our nighttime sky and where they go during our daytime hours. We also have many lights that are smaller than our moons and much larger than the bleached dots.

Now is the time to stop thinking about things that have no value in my life, and move these feet south to something that can create meaning in my life. The journey of my first full day begins. The one thing that I am noticing is the further south I go, the fewer leaves the trees have shed. This helps me move quieter, as fewer leaves crunch under my feet and give me a little additional cover, making it tougher for scouts who are on other ridges to spot me. I, of course, have a harder time seeing them. There is actually no need to see them, long as they stay on their ridge, we will do fine. The grass has completely overtaken my ridge's path in so many spots. This is extremely encouraging in that it provides evidence that few ever travel this path. I get a feeling that most used the second ridge in this area. Oddly, I see numerous footprints on the side of the ridge I am scouting. These prints move in both directions; thereby, they are as hunters looking for their prey and taking it back with them. I can just guess they are coming from the south, as these tracts were not on this ridge side yesterday. I may actually have one or two visitors after all. I thereafter decide to travel the path below, as it appears to be where no one walks and gives me the choice of a ridge on both sides to escape. As I am on this ridge, I can just escape to that path, as my western side sealed with a death trap from a cliff too far to jump down. I will walk about ten feet above the path on the eastern side. They should allow me to monitor the eastern ridge and have enough space to retreat if the western ridge shows activity. The strategy is so hard to develop when fighting an unknown and unseen enemy. The two Suns are high in the sky now, forcing me to stay under the trees while I walk. It is not good to be out in the open where the Suns, when directly above, can burn with much more ease. Without warning, the sky grows dark and nighttime is on our land. I am aware enough to recognize that when the Suns are high above us, that much more daylight is ahead. This could be a surprise storm, yet the rains are pouring slowly with no winds. Suddenly, a full moon appears in the sky to my right. I gaze around and can see no other moons.

I see no stars and see the dark clouds must be working extremely hard to block the Suns. If it can block the Suns, then there should be no moon. At any rate, it is larger than normal. If anything, this moon could work to my benefit. My path is no longer made of grass and is now such as a few paths were in Petenka. The stones covered those paths. These paths have perfect rhombus sides. I have never even heard of stones such as these. On the road now appears my dark visitor. This time, he has two ravens and chained to a pole with a light on top of it. The light reminds me of the ones the Gerben use in their caves. For this visit, dark man has no peoples' hands, but hands such as the feet of his ravens. There is enough space for me to walk along the western side of the path, under the light and one raven, easily within a strike of dark man's claws. This must be a test of my confidence and courage. I begin walking. Dark man warns me that if I try to pass him death will take me. That was exactly what I needed to hear, thereby I walked pass him, saying nothing. I pretended as if he did not exist and continued walking on the stone ground until I was completely in the dark, except for the moon, which appeared to move with me, allowing me to see the basic highlights of this stone road. I hear a smashing sound and a raven's cry as in serious pain. Dark man screams out, "Why did he not see me?" Apparently, he became so angry that he killed one of his birds. I have a solid weapon against him, so long as he does not actually swing that knife that runs from the top of his tall cane across his head. The light is no slowly returning, as does this path. I am now walking on the top of a ridge, which is not the western one I was traveling. As I continue to walk, the Suns once return and the path changes from the stone road to a well-worn path. Somehow, I am lost. The best I can figure from seeing two ridges to my west is that someway the stone path was a bridge that moved me across the valleys to this ridge top. The trees are much different on this ridge and all that I can see to the east. There is an extremely high ridge to my east, with snow covered treeless land. This will work to my benefit, as now the west will be my danger point of entry. This ridge has many bald spots, where nothing grows.

I see nothing crossing over it. Therefore, I will stay in the evergreen trees that surround these open areas. We have a few of these evergreen trees in our wilderness. Notwithstanding we do not have so many and nowhere do they dominate as I see. They appear to be spaced enough to allow me to pass through them. The next two weeks go by smoothly, although I now find myself forced to hunt smaller animals for food, as the evergreens do not have any fruit. The ground is dead, dry dirt, or sand that I heard filled the shores of the great seas. The sand holds no grass or vegetation, so roots do not exist. As the available game draws to nothing, a voice inside me tells me to eat the cones that cover the ground of these evergreens. At first, the taste was dreadfully strange; however, I could take away that deep hunger that was beginning to slow me. The third day of the cone diet found me feeling extremely energetic. Enhancing this joy saw the ridges before I begin to level. I take advantage of this leveling by crossing back to the western most ridges. On arriving, I discover a shocking change in the layout of this area. The giant protective cliff is now a sloping ridge, which declines into the western lands, allowing access in both directions. This explains why I was two ridges east and should return quickly. The days are beginning to cool down, as I understand the cold season shall fall on me soon. I must go east and hope to find various shelters. It appears as if cones will be my lone food for both the cold and dark seasons. Because they cover the ground, I can crawl in the dark and find them. Another alternative is if I find a cave, I can pack it with enough cones to keep me alive, just selecting the cones that are not within crawling distance from the cave's entry. Turning, I begin to walk back to my ridges as I stumble into another surprise. As I stop and gaze around me a group of men surrounds me. They all are wearing special garments made from a green fabric, color almost matching the evergreens. This would make them hard to detect. Four of them point their spears into my neck, as another removes my back bag and takes my long knife. Next, they tie my hands and then a rope around my neck.

They lead me to the west, which for me is much better than the east, although both ways will put me in harm's way. This may give me a chance to learn more about the Cvetka. I ask them if they are the Cvetka. The one who walks in front of us comes back to me and hits me in my mouth. He declares, "If you recognize who we are, then why you were in our lands?" I tell him, "You are confused and come across stupid. I was in the mountains, which do not belong to the Cvetka." He tries to kick me; however, I jump to my side and swing my leg up kicking him as he falls before me. The other men begin to laugh. He comes back to my face and says, "This is not finished. Once we have you in our territory you will be our captive and spend your remaining days in a prison." I reply, "You are correct in that this is not finished, for when I have my hands untied, I will beat you down and prove to your people that you are a weak woman. I will find you, as a sissy hiding behind a tree begging for your mother to save you." He walks back to me and hits me in my face once again. I yell out to his men, "See; he merely hits a man who is bound. Would he hit me if someone untied me? I tell you no, for he is a coward and can just fight as a woman would fight." One of his men screams out, "Then we shall untie your hands, so he can shut your mouth." Their leader, Asmus speaks, "We will not untie him, as our laws declare he may merely be untied once inside his prison. You who cry for him to be unfastened, I should also tie and place you in prison for becoming weak by his words. I will spare you, as you will now hit his face many times so we could convince him to shut his mouth." The man came before me and began hitting my face. Subsequently, I heard him say, "I am so sorry," as he continued to hit me. I decided to shut my mouth, as this man did risk prison to provide me with a fighting chance, and if I were in his position, I would be hitting as well. A voice inside me gives me a warning saying, 'you must learn to be quiet when you cannot protect yourself.' I whisper in my head, "It would have been better to receive this warning before my deeds." We travel the rest of the day. They beat a long knife into the ground and tie my head hardly any feet from it. Next, they put a man on each side of me and a man sleeping crossway at my feet. The remainder sleeps in a circle me. I have no expects escaping until I hear from Damijana.

Something else I noticed is that once we entered Cvetka, we did not proceed straight. We walked in a southwestern direction, moving into their territory, yet at the same time moving south. I can almost see the logic now. They are feeding me something except evergreen cones as I am once again in the rich forests. The brush is exceptionally high in that it takes two men who cut constantly in front of us. I can hear the streams flowing close to us. The long leaf packed tree branches block the moons from shining through. The ground is softer than the mountains and thereby easier to sleep. When morning arrives, a few of the men take me to a nearby stream and allow me to clean myself and run the cool water over my face. This water feels wonderful, as I currently lie parallel on the stream's rocks soaking my feet at the same time that I douse my head. They tie my neck rope to one of the trees beside the stream as all the captors now play in the stream. My nose picks up the smell of meat cooking on a fire. A short while later we walk back to where we slept where I now see a large campfire with much meat cooking on it. Besides the fire, is much meat already cooked lying on a piece of fabric. The man who beats my face tells me that they do not waste meat from a killed beast, and will cook it, and we will eat it while continuing our march. Long marches go better when eating plenty of meat and a selection of fruits. I marvel at the fireplace, as we seldom had fireplaces because of the danger in an enemy discovering our location. This tells me that they are completely comfortable in the lands we now travel. I have seldom heard of mountain people raiding the western lands, even though I have never been this much south previously. My father was at no time this far, as he would have told us about a way to cross into the Cvetka lands without having to find a cave to bypass the uncompromising cliffs. Any thinking of escape would be foolish now as we are, or should be, in the freezing season with the dark season soon arriving. I ask one of my captors about the bitter season approaching. He tells me the cold season is not as harsh in the southern lands as it is in the northern lands. They seldom get a solid freeze to slow the vegetation.

This is why they must continually cut the brush as we walk through this wilderness. The brush tapers back a bit as we continue our trek. We continue as we soon enter an area with little vegetation. We have been slowly walking upwards for about one day. One of the men pointed to my left and reveals to me, "That white is where you were. This section of our journey molds closer to the mountains with our flat land to your right. We use this land for our war training, so we can fight hard and strong against you evil ones from the mountains." I ask him, "Why do you say the immoral ones from the mountains?" They all stop, and we sit in a circle. The leader gives each of us a large piece of meat. They begin their story, "Many ages ago; large Armies from the mountains came into this land, and began to kill many of our people, taking their lands. We tried to make peace with them and share these lands, yet they refused and continued to attack, invade, and kill all those they could discover. Eventually, all our tribes united and began a large war against them. We fought hard and drove them back to the mountains: however, sadly had to face the fact there could never peace among our nations. Our Armies, therefore, continued this fight until destroying all who they found before them. We vowed that any in the mountains we catch would be either killed, enslaved, or be forever in our prison. All villages in the bordering northern villages have received our warnings through the release of beaten prisoners." I tell them that I am from a village now destroyed, close to the giant Lake on Top of the World. Their leader declares to me, "You could not have made it that far without the help of several tribes. Someone has helped you, and they would have warned you." I tell them that my mission is to bring back one who lives in the lands below Cvetka. This is the reason my search for a passageway to these lands followed routes that avoided the Cvetka. My father told me the Cvetka were at war with the Jožefa; therefore, I reasoned that my interference from the Cvetka would be limited. The leader tells me that I see much about the Cvetka that we have not shared. You should not be aware of these things. He wonders if a spy is among their nation warning the wicked mountain tribes. I tell him to relax; my father was a hunter and a friend of the Cvetka.

One of the captors explains to the leader that both the Jožefa and Cvetka use the hunters to exchange messages, as a treaty from the ancestors forbids them from entering each other's lands. Their leader looks at me and smiles, "Fortunately; we have no treaty with the mountain tribes." I turn my head to the mountain ridges between my homelands and I. Curious; I ask why this semi barren land has so few trees. They begin laughing and respond that they removed the trees to allow earlier detection of invasions from the mountains. The one thing they recognize is the mountain people do not want to travel over uncovered land. They left minuscule patches of trees on this side of the ridges that would entice the mountain invaders into entering small groups, which the defender could destroy with ease. I explore out over this death trap once more knowing what they say to be true. I now turn to the Cvetka side and see low hill forest lands. This appears to be the perfect land. It resembles the flat lands scattered throughout the peak ridges where I live. I find myself astounded by the visible diversity from the crests of the mountains to the flatter low lands of Cvetka. They now lead me into the low-lying flat lands as we continue southwestern. We continue to walk for another complete rotation of the moon's lights. I am aware that it must be deep into the cold season and that Andreja wrapped tight in furs in a hidden cave sleep most of her days. The intense cold takes away any desire to be active. This means that I should be able to get the Queen back way in time before the next cold season, with ten seasons to travel. The mountains are now elevated, however, surrounded by giant cliffs. These men explain that most of the ridge that divides Cvetka from the mountains from these points southward enjoys protection once again by cliffs. The cliffs appear so different from this side. They provide a strong sense of protection. I see many green grasslands in this area. This is where the large wild beasts graze. I witness a sizeable herd come rushing by us. The men shoot their arrows high into the sky ahead of the herd. The arrows drop, a few hitting the backs of a few animals.

This forces them to fall and receive additional injuries from the animals behind crossing over them. Afterwards, they go over and find two injured animals. Using ropes, they pull them up and by hitting with a stick force them to walk with us. The men explain that once these animals are back in a village, that village will secure them and feed on them when needed. I ask them if these animals make it to their village. They tell me no, that is why they give them to the next village. This is the custom for all who injure animals. It rewards those who live closest to these beasts and helps remind themselves that as one people, they are bonded. We continue walking until the evening is on us. Soon I can see what appears to be a hut made from stone. I ask them why they created these huts from stone. They explain the stones last so much longer and that their people keep their villages in one place, never moving them as the mountain people do. As we enter this cluster of many stone huts, the guards move away from me, motioning that I walk in front of them alone, yet still tied around my neck with their long rope. It appears as if they are parading me in front of the people who are gathering on both sides, and hiding the beasts behind them. I am puzzled about why they are doing this, until they begin to hold small stones up and throw them at me. I will not give them the satisfaction of seeing me afraid. I simply jump ahead or back occasionally so all the stones thrown will hit those on the other side. Most of the stones hit those on the other side, as fortunately, for me; they are not great throwers. I laugh when I see one hit. Often, I will fake that I am running toward one of the sides, and they scatter. Nevertheless, a few of the stones hit me and hit hard. Otherwise, most did not hurt as their children and women are among the throwers. I stare at them and yell out, "Someday; we will rape your women, sacrifice your children, and destroy all your men after they carry all your possessions back to our giant cities that hold our many Armies." Shortly, thereafter, we arrive at a large stonewalled place. The gates open and they guide me inside to what is as a smaller village in this village. I see no people in here, as all is quiet, as not even the birds enter now to sing.

They take me into a stone building now and in here lock me into many chains. Many men sat on the other side of a large table staring at me. One speaks, "Young man, tell us your name so your fellow prisoners will recognize who you are?" I respond, "Oh kind gentleman, do not concern yourself with such trivial things, as I will be glad to tell them my name." The man did not like this answer, notwithstanding continued to his next question. "Your captors tell me that you claim to be aware of the Cvetka and Jožefa through your father. Is this statement true?" I answer, "Yes, however, he was mistaken about which people were good and were bad?" This man, finding it hard to hold his peace explains, "If you give me his name, I will send it with my reports to our northern leaders, and if they recognize the name, they will send back orders for me to release you." I tell him, "His name is Pawka, the friend of Kristoffel the hunter." I turn my head to the leader of the captors that brought me here and smile, then flash my eyes as full of revenge. One of his guards comes up to speak in his ear. He writes something on a piece of wood and gives it to him. The guard departs. The man continues, "You spoke of many Armies to defend the mountains. Why have they not yet attacked?" I tell him that, "Indeed there are many Armies, which will pass over the mountains from the eastern lands to the great seas, and from the northern tribes that settle along the great rivers. They had no interest until the Jožefa showed them your great riches. Now, the mountain people will join the great White and Pirate Armies and destroy all until they find all the great riches that you are hiding. In fact, I saw two great Armies forming at the Lake on Top of the World on my way to join with my bride." I could sense a little uneasiness as the fools who were so hungry for the unknown they would believe anything. I stood strong and relaxed as if I knew victory would be mine, as actually I did know. They held their faces and told the guards to take me to my new home. Down into a deep hole they threw me and I crashed into the dirt falling quickly into a deep sleep. I awoke a few days later completely hungry as if I had been starving. I looked around this large hole and instantly discovered I was not alone. Peeking down at my body, I noticed someone had taken my wrapping furs. This was not good, as there were women down here as well.

Nevertheless, as I glance around at them, I notice everyone is without garments. However, they all appear calm. I see an elderly man, and I ask him who took my garments. He chuckles and answers, "The same who took our garments. They do this, so we can see each's whip marks and will be less liable to escape. You may relax, as you will be here for a long time. I was your age when they brought me." I began to reason that as nervous and inquisitive as our captors were, and quickly willing to act as our friend, they would put a spy among us. I would suspect the spy to be a female so as not to draw many suspicions. The part I do not understand is if they beat their own women. There are about three men to each woman, so it should not be too hard to investigate. I notice the women do not hang around each, yet instead appear to collect their private herds of men. This will be a challenging investigation to say the least. I must be careful the women do not get spooked and alarm their protectors. I begin by telling them, "My fellow countrymen, do not fear, for we have many Armies preparing to march just after the dark days. They want plenty of days with lights, so they can have the Cvetka slaves carry the great riches that they plan to bring back with them. When they arrive, it is important that we have those who are sickly, weak, or have too many whip marks with many scares to go first. The Eastern Armies plan to bring many new roots to help with these scars. I will need your help to assign each position, so those of us who are strong can help guide these Armies to those we wish avenged. These will be beaten in burned in front of the children, before executing them." A woman asks why the innocent children must suffer. I explain to her that, "These children will hold memories of a nation that no longer lives and may someday try to rebuild it. No new-generation blood will remain living. This is the rule of the Eastern Armies, and the Mountain Armies must comply or the Eastern Armies will avenge us as well." I asked if they had an appointed leader. They all pointed to one they called Coosie. He introduced himself to me. Then he turned around to set back down in his seat. I noticed he had no whiplashes.

This was fantastically interesting, as this would make sense in that he would be the first, so they would have their spy always in place. I asked Coosie if he helped me assign a number to each of their priority in care. He motioned for everyone to stand for inspection. All who we inspected had lash marks, although no woman had more than three. I asked Coosie why no woman had greater than three. He tells me that one of their gods forbids any woman from being given more than three lashes. I ask him why a god would make such a rule. He explains that according to what the guards told him, the gods considered any woman a potential mother for one of their sons or daughters. I decide to play this down by saying, "I remember my father telling me of many tribes that hold the same belief. It almost makes one believe these gods appeared in more than one area." Coosie appears to take this with a lump in his throat. I realize the Cvetka is extraordinarily possessive of their gods. This is a dreadfully convincing sign of his true loyalty. He tosses me a loop and adds, "My mother was a Cvetka and refused to talk about her gods with my father. I have longed frequently in my life to learn as much about them as possible. When we are free, I believe that a trip to those tribes you speak of would benefit my curiosity greatly." I ask him why he would not ask one of the slaves we bring with us. He explains that just as his mother, that slave would at no time talk. The lone reason that the guard spoke to him was that he believed we never would see our freedom. There is a certain element of truth in what he says. He then tells me to put his name last, as he has no remaining visible lashes. When they switched to the cutting whips, he knew and obeyed every rule without challenge. Coosie claims he is the proof that if you obey, you will never pay. I realize that he has made many good points that create doubt in me, and there is no way to select from any woman, who accepts assignment here; she would have to agree with the three lashes. It will be hard to tell, which received harsher whippings without knowing when each arrived. Coosie would know; however, if he were the spy my asking him would set off too many alarms and destroy my bluff of Armies arriving. I will have to be patient, as the dark season is close enough to waive any escape attempts. After this, I will keep to me and be quiet.

We have all agreed on our rescue numbers. The guards ring a special bell, and all the prisoners lie on the ground on their backs. I do the same; the single exception is that I keep an eye on what they are doing. They bring in stone plates, filled with food, with cups of water and place them in front of each. No one moves; therefore, neither do I move. The prisoners wait until the guards are all-out, and the door locked before slowly returning to a sitting position and beginning to eat. Not all the plates have the same food. A few eat just meat, others simply vegetables. The meat is also unlike on a few plates. I ask Coosie why the plates are different. He explains, "The Cvetka prides themselves in feeding those who may not hunt extremely well. They strive to tailor our plates to the eating habits of our homelands. Certain here cannot eat vegetation, while others cannot eat meat, and yet although others eat barely certain meats. They even attempt to adjust for those who eat less and those who eat much. We may change our diets at will. They will adjust the food based on behavior, as if one attempts to escape; we go hungry for three long days. The one who attempted to escape usually is found deceased the second day, and once found dead, our food restored. We have a simple rule, if you attempt to escape, make sure you escape, because you may at no time evermore live among us again. Furthermore, never move when they are in our cage. You might as well learn their laws as any Armies will not arrive until after the black season." I tell him not to worry about the dark season, because the cave tribes have lights that burn from the air deep within the caves. These lights shine long and strong. They will turn the darkness into light for these Armies. Coosie now shares with me that unfortunately the lights do not shine long and strong in this hole. This is why we go to sleep after our final meal of the day. The dream world is where we live. I notice that a few puts their stone plates with food remaining on it at their feet in the walkway. They consequently, position all the remaining plates and cups at the door. Soon, we fall fast to sleep. Before dozing off, I ask Damijana if she appears in my dreams tonight. She agrees and off to sleep, I go. She appears on her large white rock. I walk up to sit beside her when noticing that I still am not wearing my garments.

I ask her, "Damijana, at least I could have garments in my dreams. Would not this be just?" Damijana confesses to me that she likes me better without garments. It takes away a bit of my feistiness. I tell her that I did not realize she was like this. She complains, "You did not seem inhibited when inspecting all those women for whip marks." I told her that was a part of my mission to save the Queen. Damijana next remarks, "Anyway, Andreja said I could." I ask her, "Oh; you mean you asked her?" Damijana tells me, "Well, not yet, but I might if you want me to do so." I answer, "Damijana; you understand I had no choice and that these guards will beat me severely. Any ways, I am afraid to talk with anyone, as I believe a spy is among them." Damijana now smiles. I ask her what she is making her smile. She tells me that knowing I can think and shut my mouth at the same time. She continues, "You are correct in suspecting Coosie. I will keep you here until after the dark days are finished. Each day, you must exercise. Simply explain to your mates that the people in your family become obese easily unless they exercise much. I will give you two special friends, which will first slowly have to wean off their puppies. A few, I will give diseases, which shall justify their shift to your camp. Each one will be at near death, and you will save them, causing them to pledge their lives to you. Vida is the name of the first one, and she is a great explorer of the seas in the southern lands below the Cvetka. When you capture the Queen, you may not return the way you came. The Cvetka will kill you and all in your group. Instead, Vida will take you to the sea, and her brother will help her sail her boat to the southeastern shore, where you will climb back into your mountains and deliver the Queen to her throne. Špela is as a sister to the wolves and she will help you get to the Queen and calm her enough to pull her from the wolves. You must grasp the Queen will be wild and Špela will slowly distill her dying wolf side, as you and

Vida will bring back her woman and social personalities. Meantime, we have the dark season to cement your relationships, so you must first show yourself to be kind, gentle, strong, smart, faithful, and dependable. Oh, I do not realize if we could ever persuade one about these attributes, let alone convincing two strange women."

I wink at her and say, "I convinced you and Andreja, did I not?" Damijana winks at me and answers, "That you did my Angel. You three must resolve never to talk aloud about this mission until I have freed you. I shall speak to each in your minds and gave you simple questions and answers so you will realize I have spoken to all you." I ask her why we can never even whisper this. She tells me that, "There is nowhere in the prison where a whisper cannot be heard by many. The Cvetka offered great rewards for information about those attempting to escape. Never say anything that would sound as if you are unhappy. They will burn fires to keep you warm during the coldest times, and provide you people to be with, and plenty of quality food during the icy months. Yakov, it is much better than alone in a cold cave eating pine cones." I tell that she speaks the truth and reaches over to give her a kiss, first warning, "Keep your hands where I can see them." Next, I kiss her and thank her for helping me, as, in reality, she has no obligation to help me find a Queen she never knew. Nevertheless, she grabs my hair with her hands, shakes my head, and says, "Why do you take all the fun from me?" I while looking shy, confused, and innocent answer, "Andreja." Damijana responds, "Darn, why do I have to love both of you so much?" I tell her, "Because you are the Angel, Who Warns of Death." She answers, "Oh, okay. Lover boy, please walk softly and carry a flexible stick. I hate watching you beaten for doing the things I asked you not to do. Is this fair enough?" I limply walk over to her and stand in front leaning forward. She quickly gives me an amiable hug. I think to myself how she surely must be a special spirit in that she can provide warm hugs. I can sense the optimism in her growing as she finishes by saying, "I am so lucky that you wish to be the good strong young man whom Olimpia raised, Andreja will always love, and I yearn to save." I reached for her hand and holding it said, "I promise." The next place that I find myself lying is in a large wilderness of fruit trees and hearing

Acia and Pava playing. They both come running to me as Acia says, "Yakov, they are letting us play with you while you are in prison."

They both are my age now. Thank something somewhere, as all three of us are wearing white robes. I could never live down the humiliation of standing without clothes in front of my little sisters. I ask Pava, "Do you why Pava?" She answers, "Something to do with you being innocent and on a mission of righteousness." This was so special to talk with Pava as I would Andreja. I respond, "Mission of Righteousness; I am simply trying to pull a half wolf woman from the wolves and bring her back to rule people she does not even know. What good thing could come from this?" Pava tells us that indeed something great will come from what I am doing. I gaze at my sisters and ask, "What; please share this news with me?" Acia walks over to me and speaks, "First, my brother; I must apologize for the way I treated you during my final days. I am so ashamed. Please, will you forgive me?"

I respond, "My love; I cannot forgive you, as I never considered what you did was wrong. I hurt you, and we at no time showed you how to deal with the same hurt that was crippling me. I wish you could have lived longer so I would have been able to crawl forever, if need be, to regain your love." Acia looks at Pava and speaks, "I knew there were many more reasons we love him so much." Acia turns back to me and continues, "Your words are so much appreciated my eternal brother. Back to your question, your mission is critically important, in that the history of much of this universe is at stake." I glance at Pava and grin, "Like the universe depends on what I do. That is one method to make a boring mission sound challenging." Pava now continues, "The wolves are not part of our world. An evil force planted them long ago chancing that Queen Jolana, being curious would chase the pretty dogs to play with them. Once she went into the woods, the entire pack surrounded her and in their mouths took her to their secret den. Here they have kept her for almost twenty years. When the father of time discovered this evil deed, he tasked us to find one who could deliver her. We recommended you, our fearless brother." I responded, "Oh no, once again the women in my life have put me in a situation I cannot bear." Acia replies, "You will bear it brother, for you are not alone. Love will be beside you. You will stand on the tallest mountaintop of the Gerben lands and raise their new flag, which we will give you at the appropriate time." I stare at Acia and ask, "Where did you learn that big word?" They smile and giggle. I say, "Good, there is still the girl in you both. Okay, you have explained to me that this little girl should not have grown up with the wolves. I agree; however, I also recognize that our world has many young girls, so what is special about one who is extremely lost in the wilderness?" Pava reveals to me now, "She can mate with both spirits and people. No other will ever be created on Lamenta to do this." I stop her, "What is Lamenta?"

Acia contributes, "The name of the world you live?" Pava jumps back in, "As Queen, she will bear many sons. Most will have her prized warriors as fathers. Nevertheless, her first son will be from a great spirit, and his name shall be Ewoud, which means law and power. It is critical that his father is from the land of the dead. From his seed, shall be the Tamarkin nation, who will live along the southern sea. This nation will give birth to one who her father calls Khigir. She will be the mother of the lineage that will produce a great King, who will rule or control all Lamenta. He shall also influence a demon Queen into a path to her greatness, saving many galaxies. His most famous achievement will be destroying the last evil empire ever to kill so many and rule Lamenta." I tell my sisters, "I do not realize for sure if this true; nevertheless, if my sisters believe it to be true, then it is true for me. I have no concern with all the future events, as my sole concern is in saving this Queen and returning her, so I may be once again live with Olimpia and Andreja." Pava and Acia hug me and tell me how happy they are that I am with Andreja. I ask them if they recognize Andreja. Acia tells me, "My brother, we have been with you for such a longtime. I believe you recognize us by another name." At this time, Acia turned into Damijana and Pava into a white giant stone. Damijana asks me, "Please do not be angry with us; we did not understand of any other way to relax and desire us." Damijana fades backward to Acia and the stone to the rear to Pava. Acia subsequently adds, "We take turns being Damijana." Then a brick hits me. They saw me nude. I ask them, "Why did you keep me unclothed when I appeared before you and after that delight in it?" Acia later giggles and replies, "Brother, did you not forget that Olimpia always bathed us together and nude?" I tell her, "Acia, we were children subsequently; this is now as I am more developed as you both know." Pava afterwards retorts with, "Brother, did you not forget that we are dead and our bodies' rot in the dirt? We can see all who live nude, and none will ever give us joy, as those things are no more for us. I did get joy from seeing you in that you are healthy and should be able easily to bring joy to Andreja. Do you understand?"

I smile at them and ask them, "Can you do the genial hugs again?" Acia and Pava rush around me, and I can sense my flesh has become warm and relaxed. I then tell them, "I care not what you see in my flesh, I have a greater fear now of you not being with me. You are my sister for eternity, and that mean we have the same blood. To suffer no shame around those who are not my blood and yet experience shame to those who is my blood is wrong. I am so proud that you recommended me for this mission, and now that you are a spirit, I will understand my true fears as does Olimpia and Andreja. When I go to fall, help me stand again. I plead that you are free inside me, as I never want a thought in my head that my two sisters of love do not know." Acai tells me that they will not leave me until they bring me to live with them for eternity. I think, "How can this not be the greatest news ever in my life?" I drift into a dreaming sleep and then awake in the morning abundantly confused. Maybe my dreams someway blended themselves, as I am having trouble believing Acia is really Damijana. It just does not add, yet at the add time does not take away any part. I wonder why my sisters would be involved in the rescue of this Queen, even though they explained how they became associated. That said; they were constantly on the verge of reviewing anything that was happening, no matter if dangerous or boringly safe. They kept me on my toes, because I had Kaus and Olimpia are watching me and always asking what my sisters were doing. Fortunately, for me, they were never angered because my sisters were playing in the dirt, as we pretty much lived in the dirt. There was something about digging a hole and finding buried things, which was disappointingly almost invariably a rock, except sometimes a bone. Several exceptional memories are flooding me; however, the most special is at peace with Acia. This is why that dream must remain true, even if it is the death of Damijana. If I recognize my sisters, Damijana will return at times. She is a birth of their constructive creativity and a channel to react with me with a wider range of freedoms. Because they apparently understand their roles, I have not lost anything, but instead gained a large part of my early childhood. It was so strange talking with them as if they were Andreja's age.

As I am finishing our morning meal, Coosie comes over beside me and informs me that a guard told him they had to do various special community work on a nearby village and that our prison would have few guards. This may be our greatest opportunity yet. I asked him, "What about the, 'I will never live again in this prison if we are caught'?" He tells me that we should have six of his trusted friends in this group. I ask him when this guard shift takes place. He tells me in a few weeks. Okay, reality check, guards is not going to another village in the deep of winter, and six people will not keep their mouths shut. Equally, a guard is not going to tell about a temporary draw down. Therefore, I play this like a bait trap. I tell him the guards beat me rather hard on our trip here and that I had been on the tough move before that, trying to resettle my family and from the western mountain lands further north before the giant wars, by it keeping me in a position to return to low bountiful land. I have been living from pinecones. I need to eat this good food and exercise, so I can rebuild myself and be able to escape back into the mountains before these invading Armies recruit me. I ask him to keep me posted as any changes take place. I now walk away with a slight limp, as if I am trying to hide it. It is important that he think I am still searching, yet thinking for of a rush from an impending invasion. My goal is now to find Vida and Špela. I would like to realize who they are, so I can plan when and where to put my best shows. I attempt casually to avoid Coosie, yet he continues to show up in so many places. My first break comes at our evening meal, in that today they gave us each bread roll with the meal. I heard one man say, "Hey, Vida, do you want my roll? What about trading a roll for a role?" She stands up, walks over to him, and kicks him in his face. This knocks him to the ground. She kneels beside his face and starts hitting him repeatedly, as her harem continuously chant, "Go Vida, go." A short while later, the guards come running inside to her group.

She stays where she is. The guards investigate what is happening. The men around the pounded man inform the guards telling them what happened. They take the man with the beaten face, bind him, and against all the resistance he can release, carry him out of our cage. I am rather curious about what happened. An elderly man who is eating beside me explains that any solicitation of women for sexual purposes is punishable by death. I tell the old man, whose name is Gijsbert, which anyone could see that was a pun on words, and merely a joke. Gijsbert, defending Vida, tells me that he hindered her honor and image of chaste by those words and the females must hold a firm line on such behavior, or they could become the victim to unmerciful continual rapes. I tell Gijsbert that based on our situation. I can understand this. Likewise, I plan to stay clear of them. Gijsbert warns me to always be as kind and a gentleman around them, and if they speak courteously, speak the same manner in return. If they speak angrily, apologize and back away from them. Usually, once they have their space you will be okay. Gijsbert adds that he always stays quiet when one is near us. We will not sleep after our meal tonight, as they will take us all in the open area, and we will watch that man's execution. The Cvetka believed in rapid executions. They herded us to the open area as they have a huge stone that they have bent this man over and strapped down with ropes. A guard, which is holding a large ax, swings chopping off this prisoner's head. A few guards quickly toss the body to a chained lion attached to the rock walls. Gijsbert tells me this is the single way to leave this prison, and that is inside the belly of a lion. I notice everyone is standing in a long line with Vida first facing all in the line. Gijsbert tells me we must now all tell her, "You are honorable and chaste and shake her hand. Make sure you shake her hand gently and respectfully." Soon, I am in front of her and tell her she is honorable and chaste. She tells me, "Are you new, for I have not seen you before." I answer, "Yes, Vida I am new here." She then asks me how I knew her name. I tell her that I heard that terrible man call her name. She looks at me and says, "I will need another man in my harem. Do you wish to join?"

I tell her, "Vida, I so much want to; however, I am still suffering from the adjustment living here and really must pull myself together first. I do hope you remember your invitation when I find myself." She smiles at me and says, "I never forget someone I like." I smile and then exit from her presence. Standing in front of her was accordingly hard as her beauty exceeds that of Urška. She has all the female body features that appear in perfect condition. Looking over at the lion, these pleasurable memories flee from me. Gijsbert shows me around our smoke packet prison. There is a rotating team, which works by keeping the body wastes collected and moving out. They appoint others in a morning raffle to help them. I am aware that those days will not be pleasant. One day while standing beside a tree, I notice a large spear come flying inside our walls. The spear is heading toward Vida. I rush to her and just in time deflect the spear. It hit the man beside her, as she is unharmed. I go over to see if the man is going to make it. Unfortunately, he is already dead. Just then, the gates come flying in and several warriors come running toward us and grab the spear. The warrior looks at us and says, "We are sorry." They pick the dead man up and drop him off in front of the lion. That fast, and the memory of his life is finished. Vida notices my hand, his cut and grabs it. She sees a long cut along my arm, then confesses, "I did not recognize if you touched the spear or not." I told her, "All I could do was to deflect it from you." Vida calls for Coosie to bring her several bandages and cut string. She cleans my wound and sews the deep part of my cuts back together. The sewing hurts worse than the cut; however, I must give the impression of being strong, so I pretend it does not hurt. She stops halfway and tells me, "Look here boy; it is okay to show your pain. I am not the evil, just scared. Therefore, do not be afraid of me." I smile at her and say, "I am not frightened of you Vida, just what this place can do to you. I hope you understand this." Vida asks me why I saved her. I told her, "Because you have been friendly to me." Vida looks at me with a serious stare and says, "For a strange reason my impression is as if I recognize you. Have we met before?" I told her, "No we have not. I so wish we would have, for if we had either would be here now. Because I would never have allowed you anywhere that was safe."

She smiles and confesses, "I believe you. Your eyes have so much truth in them, and I enjoy having them examine me." I smile at her and slowly slide out of her presence. A few do later, she walks pass me with her plate and tosses me a roll and jokes, "I save all my rolls for you smiley boy." I freeze, as not to make the slightest movement, more for fear that they will punish her. Gijsbert cautions me to warn Vida the guards do not care the gender of those they feed to the lions. I give him a serious smile, and slowly walk over to Vida. As she sees me approach her, she motions for her men to make room next to her. She signals for me to sit down beside her. I sit beside her as she begins to become excited. Notwithstanding I motion for her to calm down and inform, "Oh Vida, please act sad as the guards enjoy killing women, and I must have you in my future. Do you understand, or to save myself much pain, maybe you would enjoy me hitting one of the guards?" She smiles at me and apologizes. Vida confesses, "I am so enormously sorry; it is that you not simply appear like my brother, but you act exactly like him. My brother is my life." Tears begin to fall from her eyes. The surrounding men appear to relax now, as they do not perceive me to be a hierarchal threat in their little harem. I tell Vida, "All right, princess, you relax and stay calm, I will be keeping an eye on you, so please do not hide from me." Vida smiles at me, and promises, "Okay, boss." I return to sit beside Gijsbert. He tells me I did a great job, and that we must be careful for Vida that her harem does not get jealous and report her. She continuously watches us, as I finally wave for her to come over to us. When she drops before us, she asks, "How can I serve my master?" I point to Gijsbert and he tells her, "Daughter, please hold your joy of this young man who is willing to die for your safety. If those men in your harem suspect you like this boy more than them, they will report him with lies, and he will die. It is good if you have enthusiasm for him, as no woman should need to live without that excitement. While we keep you alive, opportunities will arise. Okay princess."

She agrees and goes back to her group. She has now settled down going about the business in her group. That night while I sleep, Acia appears and congratulates me for finding Vida. I tell Acia that Vida actually likes me. Acia purrs up and beginning to roar says, "She had better like my brother." I tell her, "It is not so much like that, I mean something like the way you like me." Acia smiles and says, "That is good, is not it?" I tell her, "She has to keep it calm and we will have to find a way to thin out her and Špela's harems, as these men become too jealous and will cause deadly trouble with the guards." Acia tells me that while Pava is introducing herself the Špela, she will visit Vida. Subsequently, I ask her what Pava is asking Vida. She tells me that, "Pava is giving a brief introduction and telling her that she will be going on an important mission with Vida with one man from the prison. She will not tell your name and explain that she will realize my name before their freedom. Nonetheless, I just told her about dropping her harem and to hang with Vida." Acia tells me that she will make rotating from each become sick, have an accident, argue with the guard and many other actions that will cause them to die, as we still have plenty of time. Acia tells me she is going to see Vida, and for me to stay out of trouble. She also adds the next time they appear it will be as Damijana so for me to get my kisser warmed. I peek at her and wink. She departs with her 'funning' grin. Acia appears in Vida's dream. Vida is dreaming about watching the boats sailing in the sea. Acia comes floating down from the sky beside her on the shore. Acia introduces herself and explains the spirits will need her to do a special mission with a woman called Špela and the one she claims is her brother. She also adds that her men will begin to die and not to worry about this. This must be, consequently allowing her to plan with her brother. Vida next asks how they will get out of the prison. Acia tells her not to worry, for we will free you without harm. Acia adds, "Never speak of this nor allow others to speak of this. When the dark days begin, I will bring you into each another's mind where the three of you may plan in secret. Oh, by the way, the boy who you believe is your brother is indeed my brother and we, my sister and I, will be glad to share him with you. I sense goodness in your soul."

Vida asks, "How will I recognize you have talked with the others?" Acia replies, "When you ask them who sent you, they will say Acia." When you find Špela, say to her, "Pava is a kind person, would you agree?" She will see that I sent you." Vida asks, "Who is Pava?" Acia tells her, "My sister spirit who is talking with her now. You will meet her soon enough." The next day, her men were on a work patrol moving large stones. One of the levels to rock the stone back and forth broke, as one of her men fell under the stone dying immediately. Vida rushes to help soothe the man, to no benefit as he dies before she arrives. Coosie offers to give her another man. Vida turns down the offer, citing, "The pain is too great when one dies. Any ways, is it not foolish to hunger for power inside this place?" Coosie accepted that and moved on to his next problem. I glance at Vida and she asks me, in front of all, "Who sent for you?" I tell her, "Acia." Vida then looks around and answers, "I see no one here named Acai. Good bye." She did a fine job acting on this one. Now, the lone thing is to find Špela. I realize that Vida will be looking for her, so I will stay back. The clue I have is that because one died from Vida today, one from Špela will die tomorrow. There are not too many that die here from prison conditions. Therefore, when one does, and no warriors are involved, they try to conduct a mock trial. We are extremely lucky that they do feed and force us to maintain the proper sanitation. The next day, I receive somewhat of an inconclusive challenge. Two men die of two different harems. I see both female leaders. One is sort of on the male acting rough and tough side, while the other acted with me feeling and precaution. I will guide Vida to her first, as the other one I cannot really picture on a mission to save a Queen, unless we must pass through the Armies. After I get my evening meal, I sit beside Vida, as many men who are not in her harem are offering their condolences, especially with the loss of two men in two days. I tell her that I think our lost friend may soon bring her men to eat. The single men eat first, and the harems pass through.

I estimate that about ten have passed by, with twenty more to go. Fortunately, they move through quickly. When I see the one, I suspect to be Špela. When the female we believe to be Špela returns pass us with her food Vida asks, "Pava is a courteous person, would you agree?" The woman looks at her and me and winks saying, "Mates, that I would agree. Would both of you like to join me in the back with my boys where we can eat with each other and tell these tall or funny tales to each?" I gawk at Vida and say, "Of course we would enjoy such a treat to appreciate a friend of Pava and Acia." Špela smiles and says, "They are your sisters, no doubt by the way you speak of them." Špela and Vida put me between them. They do this because Špela does not want her men around me and that Vida has no fear, as she will sacrifice in a minute one of her men that even talk with another female. She tells us, "Business, nothing personal." Špela looks exceedingly similar to Urška. I once thought Urška had a unique appearance, yet now I am finding that many women have similar facial features. Either way, they are all beautiful. I consider myself lucky in that aspect. Špela begins her story by saying, "I am from Jožefa, and was taken prisoner by Cvetka raiders who killed my family, burned our country home, and brought me and our domestic animals back as booty. The slave market was slow that day, so the raiders dumped me into prison and left. They will not sell slaves when the market is low, in that they vow to keep the value high. The Cvetka government buys prisoners, and as we do here, makes us work for hire. When each prison leader discovered I was Jožefa they would send me to a prison further south, until I arrived at this prison. I loved your story about the Jožefa preparing to invade. They will never invade. Nonetheless, I enjoy watching these warriors sweat. I have always been more of an animal person than the people person has. I try hard to treat my men kindly, and I hope the three of us become great friends."

I smile at her and tell Špela that we will become great friends and that our days will be many. We stare now at Vida who prepares to tell her story. She reveals that, "I was married to a wonderful man and we had three children. As Špela, we lived in the countryside, enjoying our long family hikes packed with so much family time. One sad day a small band of thieves came to hang our children while we were trading for the food. My husband grew angry and went to punish them. I waited for one season and he did not return. Then, one day I went searching for him. One week from our home, I found him, hanging from a tree with his mouth tied shut and severely beaten. My first thought was to avenge; however, a group of men stopped me and promised to catch the killers and bring them back for justice. They did bring them back to us for their judgment. The next season they brought the men back in chains. I followed them to the place where the local people were gathered and we enjoyed the executions extremely. They put on an excellent painful show for us. Afterwards, I went back to my empty home, selected a few items, and planned to travel back to my childhood home. I discovered from a few travelers who told me that if went south, I could bypass the cliffs and travel the ridge. I traveled the ridge and to my misfortune captured by my own people. They refused to accept that I was from one of their northern territories. These captures brought me here, where I await the day to avenge them."

I sandwich our conversation with, "Those avengers will arrive someday to free us. You may be one of the lucky Cvetka that they spared." Accordingly, I understand that while I continue to preach the salvation is coming from outside, the guards will not give our talk any consideration. As their men continue to die, soon Vida and Špela just have half their harem remaining. They ask Coosie if they can disband their harems, and go under the care of Gijsbert and myself. They claim to think that they are unlucky, or maybe even cursed. Coosie reveals to us that the prison never designed the harem system. Therefore, he sees no reasons they cannot leave their harems. Vida explains to him that the men will try to cause trouble for them. Coosie provides us an option; he will take Gijsbert and myself as his head administers, and ask the guards to declare Vida and Špela as under their protection. We agree after I explain to my group that we are never to speak aloud about our activities, so it would be better for the closer that we are under their noses. As a result, they will see what we are doing and not try to guess or anticipate which, if they do wrong can accidentally put them in our path. At first, I did not completely understand why Coosie wanted both Gijsbert and myself. Gijsbert reveals to me that Coosie is doing two things at once. First, he knows these women hang around us too much, and as such, if they are cursed, we belong to him and not the cursed women. Second, the closer that he keeps them to himself, the nearer we will remain from our own free will. Third, he does truly value our skills and believes that as the prison runs better, he will receive more benefits. Gijsbert confesses that he does not worry about Coosie receiving rewards, as he always shares with all equally. Gijsbert continues to claim that Coosie knows he is a sharer and most likely reads me as one. Coosie notices the girls sleep between Gijsbert and me. He tells us not to worry about holding hands, laughing, and talking with each, as the men are under his umbrella and the women under the guard's umbrella. I ask Coosie if the guards will ever want a favor from Vida and Špela. Coosie tells me that he will not tell the guards, and no prisoner will be stupid enough to ask the guards. They will punish any who did severely, as the Cvetka had serious rules about male interactions with female prisoners. If they ask him, Coosie would simply tell them he felt their lives were in danger, and that is why the three of us protect them. We stay tight with each other, as our group of four appears to have bonded fine. Vida and Špela have opened so much, as they help Gijsbert and me on our daily missions. Coosie never says anything about them tagging along after us.

No guard gives one of our females a task in this prison, as they are merely here to remind us that we are different and provide an opportunity to give pleasant things too. The guards also do not want to deal with any favoritism charges, so they simply pretend as if our females do not exist. Vida and Špela can therefore roam around the prison at will. This gives us flexibility in our operations, which still have yet to begin. Acia holds our first of many mind meetings. Gijsbert is our confidentiality gauge, as we say nothing about our missions around him. Vida and Špela also rotate daily who works with whom. This way, no bonding accusations can arise. Vida, Špela, and I appear before Damijana tonight. This was the first time they met Damijana, so we had a little fun. I ran over and jumped on her lap. She wraps her arms around me and starts smooching me saying, "Do you have my love for me big boy?" Next, she looks at Vida and Špela and complains, "Who are these women with you? Are your sisters trying to make me angry again?" I run my hand through her hair and tell her, "Oh Damijana, these are my friends, and they are incredibly sympathetic to me. They are going to help me find the Queen." Damijana then waves for me to sit in the seat beside her. She has carved out two more seats so I invite Vida and Špela to sit in them. The white stone or Pava reforms itself, so we face each. Damijana then confesses to Vida and Špela that she knows their name and the great mission that we are preparing so we may save the Queen. She also tells these women that they must begin exercising their bodies. She explains to them, "Vida and Špela I recognize it is hard for you to exercise your bodies in front of so many men, who become excited every time you move your bodies. During the day, when the men are working, you can sneak to the back of the empty prison and exercise. Correspondingly, when you follow Yakov on one of his out of camp assignments, you may find various opportunities. We are in our first twenty-five days of the dark season. I have traveled into the future a brought back the night glasses that will enable you to see in the dark, enough to hunt and travel. Accordingly, she gave us each pair of these things and showed us how to rest them on our nose and hook them to our ears." This was so strange, in that we could see in the dark.

Damijana retrieved the night glasses as that is what she called them revived the light that was previously around us. I have a special series of small trails and streams that you will use in the last twenty-five days of the dark season, as no warrior will be able to find you. As we know, they will not attempt to search for you until the Suns wake up again. I have noticed three men who have been spying on you. They will not wake up tomorrow. Notwithstanding please be careful. We are so excited about how you three are bonding so well. When you have the feisty Queen, your teamwork will prove to be challenging. I figured that we could have selected relax time and allow you three to become closer. I asked Vida to take my seat so I could sit closer to them, as Pava shifted our seats making it easier for us to talk. Damijana excused herself, telling us she had important work to finish. This was the first time we could talk freely. We began talking about so many stupid and funny things. It was delightful to relax and have fun, something we were quickly forgotten to do while in prison. These women behaved as children with me, or at the minimum boy meets girl phase. They ganged against me in attacking me and trying to pull me down to the ground. I gave them just enough challenge to bring out the fierceness in them before surrendering. Their confidence is important in our mission and most likely will be used in situations they will save my life. There is something special about the pride that shines in a woman, or group of women, who defeat their male challenger. Now comes the checking me over to make sure they did not hurt me. As I am the sole male part of this mystery of the gender's game we are playing, I tell them that they did not hurt me. However, when I go to stand, I do so with a slight limp, as if I am hiding it. They catch it and come running to me begging for forgiveness. I decide that because this is our first game I will tell them I will forgive them, and continue to walk away with my limp and pretending to hide the pain.

As they rush to each side of me to help me walk, I grab them and start running with one in each hand. They start to scream as I tell them, "I got you this time." They are both yelling that I did not play fair. I stop and slowly release them. Unexpectedly, we rejoin in a large hug and for the first, time kissed each other on our cheeks. We are still too afraid to be alone with just one other. As we walk back to our rock seats, I can sense the energy in these women as they are expecting our future freedom and enjoying our current freedom. Something about the reintroduction of freedom changes everything. This may turn out to be the motive we have in obtaining the Queen's freedom and ours in the process. We are now in the final stage before our big mission. This is our purpose, and our purpose is beginning to escape from the dark and shine in front of us.

CHAPTER 10

Discovering Wise Wolf

I find myself doing two things I never dreamed of doing in this prison. The first thing is hitting, although not hard, a woman and living through it. The second thing is to hear a woman grunting. The additional thing is why I had to execute the first thing. Špela and Vida had been exercising like maniacs. They took what Damijana told them to heart. I tell these women repeatedly that they do not have to carry me. They waited until the dark season took effect before placing ultimate emphasis on their physical conditioning. I continually beg them to be careful, because I am so afraid that one of these men will inform the guards for a reward. It is accordingly much easier for crimes to occur during this season. They leave the prison gates open in the dark season as dogs, the quiet, sneaky ones that kill with one bite, roam outside our walls. Fortunately, they do not come inside our gate. I continually hope that they remember this. So far, they have not entered. The Cvetka is exceedingly efficient during this season, as we eat bread and grains, as meat is extremely rare. I do not mind that, as we never ate meat during the dark season, as we could never tell if the animal was clean enough. The air is chilly now, as the freezing days pass us, yet the warm days are still in our future. The drizzling rain each day keeps the ground soggy and packed with footprints, thereby making it extremely difficult to pinpoint where we are in this crowded prison. Špela and Vida are good about keeping us all packed tight and not miserable with the chills. Each night is so long, as it is so hard to calibrate time and even to remember what life appeared like. Dark voices with no eyes or body to add to it forces our imaginations to aid with communication. This, more instances than not, distorts our messages, creating much confusion. Most times, we just ignore each. Špela and Vida are extremely proficient at getting their message through to me.

They have no qualms with biting, kicking, hitting, and yes, hugging just to keep me on my toes and from hiding from them. Acia and Pava tell us in our dream tonight that we have one more week, and then we will walk out the front gate. They will open the gates and silence anyone who tries to stop us. Acia will put them to sleep, to include the dogs, and then erase this event from their memory. Pava will remove our scent from the prison so the search dogs will have no scent to track. Actually, she is going to put the scent of the prison warden's wife in our area, so the dogs will rush to his house and try to capture his family. This will discredit the dogs, and have these dogs removed, giving us more time as new ones given to our camp and their deployment delayed until they learn the landscape. Vida complains to Coosie that she and Špela want moved to a corner with me so the men do not realize where they are. Gijsbert and Coosie are involved in many camp activities, therefor if they were with us, most people would recognize where we are located. Auspiciously, another female who has slowly become friendly with Špela and Vida has offered a little protected territory behind her harem. The other women no longer consider Špela and Vida as threats, nor enemies as they previously felt defined their relationship. This makes it easier for us to keep a low profile and so harder for Gijsbert to track. We still love Gijsbert; it is that especially during this dark season Coosie is with him constantly. If we have any chance of making more distances before these guards learn of our escape, we must stay far away from

Coosie. Vida's female friend is training her men well to cover for us. We hang around ourselves and as quiet as possible. Most of our talking is in our nightly dreams as we rehearse our escape plan in detail systematically. We never speak about it, as Acia is afraid evil spirits may be monitoring us. Neither she nor Pava spoke about it anywhere, other than to speak openly about trying it two years from now. They closely check that any information about the Queen. Špela and Vida voices have changed from harsh around me to sister style tender. I am proud of them, and how they gave up their little kingdoms, and risk horrifying torture if our mission fails.

They have my back, and I have theirs. They chase me and try to tickle me until I cry when I ask them if I can have their fronts. That is when they tell me the solitary funny boys, they are like the ones who are laughing. They can be so much fun. To meet such great people while here is a precious gift. I seldom think of Olimpia and Andreja any longer. I believe reintroducing Acia and Pava in my life fulfilled that empty place. We sat beside each while the guards' stops in front of us while they are walking pass us, stopping our hearts. They get that cheap thrill of scaring the women. Špela and Vida always give them a show that keeps them moving on to other adventures. The two halves of the nights are quiet now, as any noise alarmingly amplifies itself. Acia tells us that we are to tell Vida's friend that tonight we must join Coosie for an extra mission until the dark season leaves us. We will actually begin our casual escape after the morning meal. Acia gave us our night glasses. Therefore, we will be capable to see where we walk and be able to see where the others are walking. We can see them, before they hear us and slip to the side trying to stay on the paths, so we do not make noise by stepping on branches. The first few hours were a little tricky, yet we walked as if we were anxious. Too much was at risk for our comrades and us. Acia ordered that we do no thinking as this could alarm our enemy spirits. Once they discover we can see in the night, they would begin watching us intensely. Špela, Vida, and I were becoming afraid of any spiritual battles. We do not understand this land, because of that all the noises constantly fill the air. The darkness has covered our world long enough to take the snap out of any vegetation and instead of the bursting aroma of vegetation, the stale smell of dying brush.

The strongest memory that I have as a child was how the constant light rain, without the light to take away the moister and instead allow it to accumulate brought back to life so many seeds. As if they understand when the Suns are returning, the sprouts are usually well on their way to take whatever they take to make them green and tough as the hungry world waits for them to develop. Pava started something new with us in our dreams, and that was teaching our group personal songs from our childhoods. This has opened us open to each of our partners sharing our feelings in this fresh approach. The sweat that pours from our shaking bodies as all this dark tension and not knowing what is going to happen in our lives is as a breath of refreshed life. We are slowly beginning to move to a rhythm. We talk openly in our dreams about our days in the Cvetka prison. I was fortunate in that my time, there was not as long as these women, nevertheless. We constantly talk about Gijsbert, who became as a father to us and share our complaints about Coosie, who unfairly catches all the blame for that prison's hardships. We continue to treat each day as if it was the day of our escape. My mind maintains to deny how easy they walk through us. At first, I was confused why no others leave until I remember that they cannot see in the darkness, and punishing a mistake is a painful death. Without seeing where we walk, this place would be nothing more than solid walls. We have traveled for three weeks now. I notice the hills are much smaller and streams slightly growing wider and deeper. We have not heard or seen any other people for a while. Previously, we could see a few campfires at night, yet in the last few days we have merely seen one. This could be that we are between villages, or we can have made it to the southern Cvetka lands. Acia and Pava now worry about how we will react as the smaller days begin to appear starting next week. The Suns start by giving us almost one hour of daylight, which increases each day until the sixtieth to ninetieth days and the start of the growing seasons. Acia and Pava are going to acquire visible spiritual forms and walk with us. We can see and talk with them, yet cannot touch them. They will stay in this limbo, so they can monitor the spiritual realm for us.

We have enough distance in our escape that we can make it to the sea before any of the Cvetka warriors could apprehend us. Acia believes that they will not send any warriors over their border, in that they do not have a good relationship with their scattered neighbors in this region. Pava explains that twice in this region's recent history, the southern villages have united and destroyed everything in Cvetka they could find. This was to avenge Cvetka's scattered raids. Because of the bitter ongoing war with the Jožefa, Cvetka has moved their southerly villages toward the central part of their nation and now use the southern portion of their nation for hunting game and as a buffer zone in case of a surprise attack. I can just hope that ultimately, mountain Armies will also invade Cvetka. I will ask the Queen if she commands this eventually, so the ridge lands may be safe for those who live in the mountains. I am still puzzled how Daddy could get along with them and now wonder if they would not have led us into a prison instead, especially after they no longer needed Daddy's missions. We are planning our first light celebration, which is a popular custom of our world. This signifies that we have survived the cold, dark, and new life is in the front of our futures. Nevertheless, I cannot think of ever experiencing such a great opportunity to celebrate. The Suns slowly coat the sky red and shades of orange. Nonetheless, I gawk around and see these four angels sitting with me in our pleasant garments that Acia gave us. A key event, which is now taking a rear fireplace, is that my mission is once more progressing. We are moving ahead. Notwithstanding I essentially did not lose any time from my original estimations. Travel during the winter and dark seasons were not originally included, and if any lucky traveler had, it would never be equal to one entire month of dark season travel, which was traveling with extremely limited security interruptions. My mountain voyage was one eye forward and the other looking backwards. Špela and Vida constantly badger my sisters about our childhood adventures. Acia and Pava relentlessly paint me in the best light, as if I never did anything wrong.

I repeatedly tell Špela and Vida that my sisters are stretching the truth, and not to fall for the lies that I am not harmless. Vida walks pass me and orders me to shut up, as she knocks me to the ground. I sit back up and ask her, "Honey, why did you do that to me?" Špela now promises, "If you will call me honey, I will hit you as well." Vida answers, "To see if you are harmless. You are a peaceful bird." I tell her, "Our Olimpia taught me to be compassionate to those who are mean to me." Špela questions, "Then why were not friendly to the guards?" I snap back with a smile, "Because they were not mean to me." The rains are beginning to pour for short periods now, instead of long slow drizzles. The extended cloudless cover has returned much of the night-lights. Acia explains with visions about the stars, planets and the source of the lights that reflects from our moons. It just does not make sense to me, how little balls can spin around each other in such a great emptiness. I will have to consider that she may be lying to me or trying to prank me. Even though this may be the situation, it does not affect the small part of this world I exist. We pass a few huts built in a tucked away valley today. Vida asked Pava if we could see the people. Pava put them to sleep for us and we, yes Špela and I followed her, went into their structures. The first was the largest. As we entered, it had one large open area, which the family was sleeping. This is a sizeable family as we counted nine bodies. They sleep under what Acia called blankets. These were large square cloths made from fabric. We always slept wrapped in our furs. They had the little bags packed with feathers that Andreja introduced me. Vida never saw these bags previously. It also does not appear that they wear much clothing, enough to conceal their differences. Špela teases me that because of this I would hate living here. I simply tell her that if they had such a blessed body like hers and went to fake squeeze her breasts. She did not move or jump back in defense or even hit me as I considered might be one of the outcomes. This event caught the eye of Acia, Pava, and Vida. Women notice things such as this, especially when two bears a responsibility to protect me as my sisters. Quick fun, no one laughed, move on to the next situation. Vida withdrew more toward Acia and Pava after this event and Špela tugged closer behind me.

I had no reason to think anything was different as groups always form into subdivisions, and Vida is the explorer with Pava and Acia controlling the unexplored. Špela is more of a dependant type, and prefers male company to female company. Vida lost her family, so I think that too much time around me could be stirring up those painful lost memories. We do notice the gown customs hanging from their walls. Acia tells us they have cultural celebrations according to the tales of their gods and legends. These alternate much among the homes in this area, not so much different as each appears to incorporate all these figures, simply emphasizing specific ones or events. They also have large containers, not made from wood as is our cups and plates. Pava tells me they produce their crazy water in these substantial vats. They have plenty of spears, bows, and different cutting tools. Acia explains that these people grow much vegetation for trading in the large markets about one day walking. I ask her why they would carry vegetation one day to trade it. This must be too much work for so little to trade. She explains that they have large wooden wagons pulled by their domestic beasts. Next, she takes us to where this family keep their animals. They had cut down long, thin tree trunks and tied them to posts encircling these animals. This allows them to graze freely within this area. I like this in that they do not have to break their leg or legs, which I always felt sorry for them afterwards. They also have a structure these creatures can stand under while it is raining. A few of these buildings hold the grains. Acia had to teach me concerning how they store, and then take it to market. Our prison, fed us grain; however, they further processed it for our final consumption. These people, to a certain extent, can produce everything in their small living area. I tell Pava that this family does not appear to have mobility as an option for their defense. She agrees the Cvetka posed fantastically few threats in these areas. We must still keep moving and be careful, as I did run my mouth a lot and thereby may motivate the Cvetka to offer a greater reward for my capture.

Moreover, I embarrassed them by bringing two women with me, which hurts the Cvetka prison warden's pride and makes him appear too foolish and weak even to keep women under his guard. I ask Pava to scan and see if any is following us and getting dangerously close. Pava looks alarmed and confesses that three are riding the Cvetka fast beasts or horses and barely about one day behind us. I stare at Acia and complain, "Come on sisters; I am counting on you to keep us posted on our situation. Is there anywhere we can get them from their horses and kill them, while taking the three horses?" Acia tells us to explore in the tool house and collect three spears and three bows with plenty of arrows. We will create a mess inside this tool building so these farmers can take an inventory and replace their missing weapons. She will do this later this month when all being well, we are on the sea. Tonight the raiding guards will tie their horses and sleep around a campfire. Acia will put them into a sleep when we will fire our arrows into their hearts, cut off their heads, and collect their supplies. To my great joy, the warrior is shot is the one who was the leader who captured and tormented me on my way to his prison. He died without his sickly grin and is no longer laughing at me. We do as Pava tells us; however, she wants us to put the horses in with the farmer's animals. They can use these horses taking their produce to market. This will also help prevent them from discovering our footprints and warning their neighbors. She recommends that we continue to walk, as we are not far from the Queen's last known den, and the horses may spook the wolves, or at the least make them extremely hungry. I ask Acia if she knows where the Queen is. They tell me that they only have a few scattered reports and that since a Queen is divinely appointed they do not have to power to find her. She must give her permission to be found, and most likely does not even recognize she is lost. I glance at Vida as if to wonder if we are missing any more special little details such as this. Glancing around our area, I notice the freedom in our low jagged horizon. The most distinct difference is that it is just one horizon and not horizons (ridges) stacked on one another rising to the sky.

Acia and Pava take Špela and begin scouting for wolves. Since the moons have yet to become bright, they are not howling and therefore, not as easy to find. Špela traps two rabbits, spreads their blood over the ground in two areas, and waits in a tree above her trap. When the wolf bites the rabbit, she will release a branch that will drop a wooden box that she has above it. She hopes to trap a wolf, and then we will tie two leases to his or her neck and pull snugly apart so the wolf will not be able to bite one of us. Špela will try to calm the wolf and make friends with it as she has so many times in her homeland. Vida and I stroll around the countryside looking for streams, or anywhere with many wolf prints. She tells me that many from her village do not like wolves as many suffered harm from them. I realize that we always avoided them if possible. The ones that stayed in our area were more precarious as the terrain made it difficult for them to support large groups. These lowlands permit the wolves to travel in larger packs. Špela catches two wolves her first night trying. Now, the tricky part and that is getting the leash on them. Our wolf catcher takes the first wolf, a male and ties him standing his back against a tree. She next takes a small rope and ties a tight knot around the scrotum. Špela explains this is to dry the tentacles. They shall falloff in one week with no bloodshed and mean to reduce the kill instinct and aggressiveness in this animal. The female, unfortunately, will need a destructive surgery. She has the female tied with two ropes, and her jaws tied shut. Špela also covers this animal's eye. Next, she breaks one of her legs, and after that she then begins removing female parts through tubal ligation of the animal. I ask her why she broke one of the legs and then bandaged it. Špela tells me this is to prevent her from trying to escape with her insides still healing. She blindfolded the animal so it would not recognize who operated on it. Vida asked her how she knew these were the alpha male and female of the pack. Špela said she did not realize for sure, the male procedure was not that hard on him; however, she felt it was important to make sure this female did not breed and stayed beside this male for protection against an angry female alpha wolf who wants to impregnate another ovary. By keeping the male tied with his back to the tree, she hopes to rub his belly quite a lot over the next week to solidify the taming process. I ask her what good these wolves are if they are not the ruling pair of the pack.

Špela reminds me that all the wolves of that pack want to hang or run together and the alpha or master wolves would not be involved with raising or attending to non-wolf life-forms such as our Queen. She has us feeding them carefully, as food must be ground and slowly pressed through between their teeth, as their jaws must stay tied closed. Špela continues to work hard on the animals each day, as Acia and Pava are watching where the wolves roam. As a treat, Vida and I massage Špela each night, and stroke her hard with compliments about her wonderful work. Špela makes me promise to do this every day when entering the sea part of our journey. Vida tells her she gets me for that entire trip. I remind them that I do need a little time with my sisters during that part of our trip as well. They all glare at me as if to say, "We will see." One would think that all the time I have lived under the umbrella of women whom would have noticed this. Perhaps I was always used to it, thereby thought it to be normal. This is not to say that it was abnormal, because it is from hearts, and when the heart wants something and strives hard, even playing by the rules such as marking her territory than no wrong is present. In this part of our search, Špela is the heart and the body of our game, especially as we are transferring our search with the help of the subject species. All this attention to the wolves has taken away any appetite for meat, and instead inflamed joy in the new fruit trees we are finding. Bananas, pineapples, oranges, to name just a few of the budding trees that are overflowing here. The apples are much larger and so many types. Pava tells me the initial round of fruit will be ready to pick in just a few weeks. The mild cold season and warm, dark days, coupled with the massive light that is beginning to appear now, and rich soil are speeding the first round along quicker. These favorable conditions also kept much of the fruit that was on the ground or trees unpicked or eaten by the birds available. Vida swore never to eat another pineapple after this period. I told her we were lucky the lone thing available was not pinecones.

The three weeks we gave the, she-wolf to heal also provided us a few exploration opportunities. We elected to avoid campfires, so no one would locate us during the dark hours as with the female wolf not mobile, we were stuck here as well. Vida gets me off alone tonight, and asks if we can have a serious talk. She begins by asking me if I think that she or Špela would ever be able to love and have families again. I ask Vida, "Vida, do you love me?" She tells me that she loves everything that I am, and for what I do with her spirit. Vida loves the way she trusts and believes in me. She is afraid to invest anything deeper in me for fear that death would take it away from her. I kiss her on the cheek and tell her, "Vida; you already love once more. Families are not something you decide to obtain at a market; they are a garden of people that you plant yourself. Accordingly, is there a fear the seeds will not grow or that a storm will destroy your garden? Of course, there is such a fear, and love will make you take that chance. You just relax woman, because both you and Špela are diamonds in the rough. Could I ever find myself in love with either of you? Yes, I could because, you cannot live this hell, we have and not be bonded. I actually understand the day we depart will be hard." Vida asks me, "Is there one you are promised to?" I answered, "Yes. Consequently, although much has happened and will continue to happen until we get the Queen back on her throne that sometimes now I do not understand for sure. Additionally, having Acia and Pava back in my life is so confusing, even though I recognize that when the Queen is safely within her throne's seat, they will be no more, and then Damijana will return." Next, Vida tells me that she does have feelings for me, as I am the rebirth of a brother. She warns that Špela has deep feelings for me and has staked her claim on me, a claim that she, Acia, and Pava respect and acknowledge. I ask Vida why a woman can stake the claim such as this. She tells me that I could have staked it first, and they would have stepped aside as well. Špela gets the claim because they can see in her eyes that she is willing to make all the sacrifices to make it work. She also begs me not to tell Špela that she told me. I tell her that Špela would make a wonderful wife, and that we must deal with that situation when the time arrives.

This is not the type of world, even if escorted by spirits, to take any future event as guaranteed. The one thing I do grasp is that I will not hurt my women, and when the woman gives her heart to me, I refuse to break it. I fear that you and Špela have placed too much comfort in my morality as a man. If you both simply knew how hard, it was not to hold you in love while we were in the prison. There were times when I could just cry in pain on the inside. Vida reveals to me that I was not the sole one to suffer such as this, for both her and Špela at times wanted to tie me to a tree, write their names on me, and kill to the death any other woman who dare investigate me. I smile, saying, "I would have never known that." Vida smiles and says, "We were afraid that we no longer could show a man, how we felt in matters of love." I explain to her that in the prison, no one could. I believe that after rebuilding our fundamental emotions, the rest will be reborn naturally. I tell her that we now have two choices, one is to stay here and kiss all-night, and the other is to return to our gang. Vida winks at me, and smiles, sharing, "That is easy; we will kiss all-night." I tell her the thing I love the most about her is the way she can fight off the lustful temptations. She smiles and replies, "Like the urges I get to bite your ears," and begins to move her mouth toward my ear. I jump and begin running back to camp begging for help. As I rush in, Špela, Pava, with an alarmed Acia asking me what is wrong. I tell them that Vida is going to bite my ear and that someone must save me fast. Špela chuckles, "Darn, you have been a good boy once more." I give her a fast kiss and say, "Sorry girls," and dash behind Špela continuing, "I appreciate you will save me, I hope." Vida comes strutting into our camp cheering, "Špela, I got him to fall for you, yeah." Špela snickers, "Not fall for me this way." Vida responds, "Oh, sorry loves. Anyway, to all those great hearts packed with love in my wonderful family, Good night." We found happiness in the acknowledgment that a family existed once more, and we were a part of this family. Even Pava and Acia are slowly molding into this new association. We did not linger on Olimpia or Kaus much lately, as our current events and the 'love affair,' occupy a lot of our talks currently. They orchestrate the 'love affair,' in my absence, as my return elicits snickering and sweet grins supplemented by winks. Our wolves are now exceptionally calm and the center of our social activity. We feed them, clean and constantly pet them.

The food keeps them at peace with us. Vida throws sticks, and they retrieve them. I may be the singular one hypnotized by this; nevertheless, it is a new experience for me. The male has taken custody of Špela. I may solely approach with her consent, and she does all the touching. At night, a wolf who we call Wolf sleeps beside Špela and the female wolf, who we call Howl sleeps on the other side of Vida. They tuck me in the middle, which means any attempt for me to go somewhere requires Vida or Špela's consent. Acia and Pava ignore our wolves as they shy away from spirits. The wolves appear purely to accept as true what they smell. They cannot smell spirits, so simply walk pass them, although with a little precaution. One thing I see for sure now and that is if any raiders were to capture Špela or Vida they must fight theses wolves to get them. This creates jubilant peace in these women. Their confidence and courage are laying a foundation that I hope will stay with them even when the wolves leave. I say when the wolves leave because they will never mate again with their wolf at their side, as these wolves would tear their mate apart. For this stage in our mission, they are essential. Wolf and Howl permit me to pet them, while holding Špela or Vida's hands. They will also retrieve sticks for me, if their masters stand beside me. Today, we loaded our back bags, and with our two new friends, started searching for Wise Wolf. It did not take long for them to pick up a scent, as Acia and Pava, has seen a pack flash through hereabout one week ago. Acia tells us the wolves made a circle through a nearby low valley just two days previously. She guides us to this area, and soon their ears are up and pointed, and we run to keep up with them. We continue south until what Acia claims is one day to the sea, and then we shift west. As we cannot keep up with Wolf and Howl running all day, we leash them and walk briskly behind them. We initially had a little fear that they may not take us to their pack, just simply get us close, and then leave us.

This does not appear to be the case. This worn path can just be so through an excessive use; therefore, several grazing herds must also travel it. Most likely, this is the grazing herd's path, and the wolves travel it looking for any stragglers or other easy kills. We get our big break about one month into this season when we see specific part footprints of a person. Oddly, as Vida, tries to get the wolves to focus on these footprints, they ignore her. Fortunately, for us, the footprints stay with the wolves, so we are still on the right tracks. Acia and Pava provide us our next big break. The wolves began to double back through a nearby series of low forest covered hills. This puts us right behind them. We decided to track at night also as the moons were shinning much light during these few nights, so we had to take advantage of this.

Then it happened, and my reaction was not what I had expected. I saw the Queen I had searched for, the reason that Andreja was not at my side each night, and Olimpia was not guiding me during my days. She froze when she spotted us as well. She wore a torn dress, which we believe she took from one of the nearby families in this area. Acia also suggested that our Queen may have found a dead woman, and took her dress, as she needed something for the chilly nights. She wrapped her hair was around the neck as like a rope. She stood and faced us standing on her toes and surprisingly upright instead of on all fours as the wolves. We knew this was her style from the month of tracks we had tracked. Her face, covered in dirt, as was her legs and arms. This had to be her preference, as the daily light rains kept us clean. She must have used the rains to get wet and then roll in the dirt. Queen Jolana or as Acia calls her Wise Wolf and Pava calls her Ráðúlfr locked her eyes on me if to dare me to even think of capturing her. I stop for a moment and ask Acia and Pava what is this woman's name. Pava tells me that her name in the current Gerben language is Ráðúlfr, which means Wise Wolf. Jolana is the name who floated into the legends and is her official Royal name, which means violet flower or the wildflower found in the wilderness. I told Acia it was time for me to take this Queen back to her home. As I walked toward her seven wolves went to attack me.

Wolf and Howl jumped on me fighting to keep the wolves from tearing me apart. Wise Wolf made a howling sound, and the wolves ran back to her, as she climbed up, the tree beside her and began jumping from branches to the next tree. She vanished as fast as she appeared, leaving me in shock lying under Wolf and Howl. Vida and Špela came rushing to me. They helped pull, me up as I stood facing them and my sisters, all four giving me a strange look. I immediately ask them, "Why am I getting the Olimpian look?" Olimpia would always give me a strange gazes before she let me have what was on her mind. They gawk at me and shake their heads. I order them, "Now stop shaking your head at me, and tell me what strange thing has invaded the minds of the women who surround me?" Vida, who is never afraid to tell me what is on her mind begins laughing, "Špela hates you now the Queen has an interest in you." I stare at them and say, "I could not be that lucky that a woman who is interested in me would climb a tree and jump from branches to another tree to escape from me. What is wrong ladies, except for Vida, why are not the other three of you jumping from the branches above?" Acia reports, "Because as spirits, we never learned how to climb trees." I glance at her and report, "Come on sister; I was being sarcastic and talking foolish, the same as you four. The four of you always think with the same mind, which is one filled with absolute foolishness." Špela tells me to be quiet, or she will sick Wolf and Howl on me. I then add, "You are right Špela; Wise Wolf did spare my life at the last possible moment by calling back her attack force." Vida tells us, "More like that was her defense force." Špela adds, "Wise Wolf must have read your mind." I said, "If she read my mind, she would have seen a serious scrubbing in her near future." Pava laughs and adds, "Yes, brother, anything to get her dress removed." I gaze at her and say, "I am going to tell Olimpia that you have a dirty mouth."

Acia, while Pava is giving her innocent appearance ask me, "Now, do you think she would believe such an angel as Pava would say such a thing?" I then recommend, "We need to figure out how we can trap her and get her away from those wolves." Špela adds, "We will have to capture her in a tree and draw the wolves away from that tree." Špela suggests that once we tie Wise Wolf in a tree, she will make Wolf and Howl give their distress howls, which will pull the wolves away from the Queen. Accordingly, I quiz Špela on how she plans to distress Wolf and Howl without hurting them, because they saved my life today, and I would suffer badly if we hurt them. Špela smiles and looks at Acia and says, "A spirit could put a vision in front of them that would scare them into a loud howl without any physical damage." Acia confirms this and the puzzle now is how to tie Wise Wolf in a tree. While tracking her the next day, Špela notices that she now walks in the middle of the path, as if she wants us to track her. The pack is moving slower. I tell them this is because she is being much more precarious. The theory holds true for a few hours until something hits me in my head as I walk under a tree. I glimpse up and there she is staring at me. Nevertheless, instead of taking a serious teasing from the women who live merely to harass me, I simply wave at her and continue walking. Considering our first meeting, I made a move for her and scared her, I hope that by posing as no threat she will become more relaxed and appear once more. After all, she appeared today. That was our second encounter, which lasted for about two hours. Ráðúlfr leaps from branch to branch staying one tree behind us. I wave at her when Vida and Špela are not looking. Surprisingly, her pack of wolves is not following her. They most likely tune themselves to a special howl that she calls out with when in danger. The next day, I try to sneak with us a few meat strips that we feed to Wolf and Howl. Our two pets follow so close that many times I find myself tripping over them. Vida and Špela become extremely suspicious, so I confess to them, "I am expecting and planting meat strips in the trees so Wise Wolf will begin to include trees in her search." Vida pulls me to the side and asks, "Could it also be that she has been tracking us in the trees?" I come clean and ask her not to tell everyone else, thereby not creating any unnecessary friction. Vida smooches me on my cheek and explains, "That is why I kept quiet. I will promote this today at lunch and start selecting the meat strips for you to plan to make this official."

I acknowledge her as a saint. Vida then confesses the teasing they were giving to me was not to hurt me but to make me deem special. I admit to her that I am not ready to tease or joke about certain things around my little sisters. This is when Acia appears beside me and tells me, "You no longer have younger sisters, an older brother, so you must learn to treat us as you would Olimpia." I tell her that I think catching the Queen will be easier than doing this. Pava appears beside me, and then appeals, "We will help you big boy, okay sweetie." I glance at her and ask, "When will you both turn back into my little sisters?" Acia says, "When you no longer like women?" I laugh and finish this with, "I guess that will be a long time, right?" This is going to be so difficult for me, yet I must realize that my little sisters sleep in the dirt, and these are their mature spirits, as I most likely is not fair for me to grow into an adult, and they be frozen as infants. During the remainder of our morning walk, Špela kills three more rabbits and at our lunch, we share one and half another, while she separates the others into three piles, giving me one for Wise Wolf as she keeps two for Wolf and Howl. She will carry their portions, thereby keeping them away from me. These also keeps Špela closer to her, giving me more flexibility. I continue to plant rabbit meat in the lower branches as Wise Wolf continues to follow us. I notice that she is moving closer now that Špela nor anyone or wolf around me. The third day of this I tried something new. I sat on a branch as she jumped into this tree above me. She slowly worked her way down to me. I opened my bag, put a piece of meat in my hand, and held it out for her. She calmly took it, went one branch above me, and began tearing the raw meat apart and ate it. I had wanted to cook it; however, Špela said not to, so I feed this to Wise Wolf raw. After she has taken a few bites, I slowly work my way out of the tree. While standing on the ground I wait for her to finish eating the piece and then begin walking once more.

By now, Špela has filled Vida into what I am doing, and she is trying to help me as much as she can. While the Queen was eating today, I could pet her dirty shabby hair. Before doing this, I sat on the ground below her and petted Wolf and Howl as they ate from my hands. I am impressed with how fast she learns and can apply what she saw. She witnessed me feed and pet Howl and Wolf, and I surmise believed the method I use in feeding my wolf friends. I lightly touched the top of her head, slowly moved my hand about two inches, and then ploddingly pulled my hand back. The next day, she surprised me in touching the top of my head and pulling her hand back. I smiled at her and then continued as if nothing had happened. That afternoon I slipped while walking, requiring Špela help me walk. Wise Wolf came flying down the path behind us leaping on Špela scratching and biting at her. I yell no to Wise Wolf as Wolf and Howl come also to protect her. Wise Wolf stops, and then stares at me while I am waving no. Next, I point my hand to a tree and motion for her to leave. As she gets a few steps away, I stomp the ground as if to chase her. She leaps into the tree almost in one solid move. I now begin to tend to Špela's wounds as Vida joins us. Acia and Pava prefer not to be visible to Wise Wolf, as we fear it could scare her back into her pack. We decide that two days henceforward, I will make my neck rope attempt. I want to use the rest of today and tomorrow to calm her. Notwithstanding

I believe that by having Vida and Špela come to underneath the tree and call for me will be a solid way to distract Wise Wolf. This is the feminine friction thing, so tells me that Wise Wolf does not appear comfortable around female people. I tell Vida and Špela to come underneath the tree I am in beside Wise Wolf and to lie on the ground and do several strange things while making specific peculiar noises. This should not cause her to become threatened, and I hope will confuse her. If I can confuse her, I can drop my noose around her head. I have the other end tied to the tree with solitary enough to allow her to drop to the ground. She is staring at Vida and Špela and actually chuckling at them. I must give Špela credit in her knowledge of the wolves. I get the noose over Wise Wolf's neck and then immediately start to touch her hair. She ignores me.

The hair she has wrapped around her neck is concealing the rope, so I slowly tighten the noose and then grab hold of her hand as we jump. I pretend as if I lost my balance, just in case. We go to the ground, and the noose held tight. Špela rushes over, stuffs a piece of meat in her mouth, and then blindfolds her. I am holding her and humming as I often do when sitting in the tree with her. Vida ties her feet as Špela ties her hands. Wise Wolf spits out the meat, and I rush a thick piece of garment into her mouth and then wrap a heavy piece of fur around her bottom face to hold the gag in her mouth. We continue to double and triple tie her arms and feet as she has a tremendous kick and swing. We are less than one day from the sea; therefore, Vida rushes ahead of us to prepare our ship. Last week, she slid away from us for a few days, met several sea people, and bought us a respectable medium-sized ship with the gold we took from the prison and the precious gems we took from certain of the Cvetka public statues during our escape. Acia and Pava had prepared it, so we simply had to grab the trading stones and return to our escape. Even though it is late on this day, we will walk all-night and be at the sea mid tomorrow morning. It takes longer to walk at night, especially as we appear like kidnappers, even though we are just that. We are lucky to meet with Vida in the morning. She guides us to our ship.

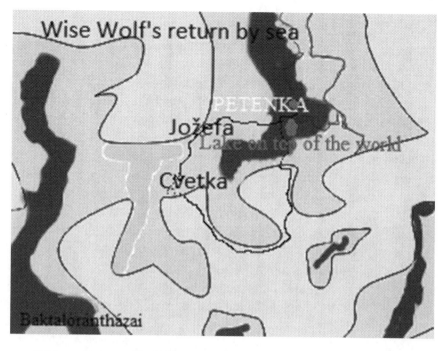

Vida recommended that we train Wise Wolf while on our ship because she will not jump off the ship and into the sea, especially once she learns that we are eating fish consistently, and she needs us to get her the fish. Vida was also able to find a refined gown for the Queen, which we will not put on her until we hit the shores of our mountain peninsula. For now, we have a bikini on her. Acia jumped into the future and brought this back for us. She also brought back a selection of chemicals we will use to scrub her. It will take much work and now with just Špela and myself as Vida is working this sailboat. We keep the Queen blindfolded until we are out of sight of any land. This will prevent her from knowing how far she is from the land. Next, I pull the fur out of her mouth and then secure her bottom jaw to her chest, so she cannot bite. While still blindfolded, we rip off her ragged dress and put the bikini on her. She does not like this, as I can expect there will be many things she is not going to like over the next three months while we sail around this peninsula to ours. Our first bathing session worked considerable fighting spunk out of our Queen. Keeping her hands and feet tied, while also blindfolding her, I jumped into the water holding her. As she resisted, I simply let her go. She wiggled and splashed a little, and then I reached over and pulled her to me. Securing her with one arm, I used the other to start working off the dirt. Once I began to hum, again, she calmed down. I would release her and start to drift away from her. She was industrious in working her way back to me and bumping my arm with her head. I decided to take a chance, remove her blindfold, and jaw strap down. I slowly stuck my finger in her mouth and ran it across her tongue. Afterwards, I released her and moving away from her spun around and motioned for her to come to me. She came to me, and I hugged her humming while petting her hair. Thereafter, I sunk in the water in front of her, touching her belly, waist, and legs as I worked my way to her feet and untied them. I then worked my way back up here, and afterwards, I surfaced with my arms straight up pointing to the sky. I opened my arms slowly drifting away from her. She used her legs to move to me, and I gave her a big hug and smile. Moreover, I hummed again. This is when our bag of tricks Queen really surprised me.

She asks me, "Why do not you talk to me like you do the other women?" I glance at her and smile confessing, "We did not realize you could talk. Why did you wait until now?" She smiles and says, "Because with my feet untied I can catch you if you try to get away from me." I tell her, "We are going to have a variety of fun on the ship. I will completely untie you. You will then jump on me, and we will start kissing. That is when I want you to ask for more. Do you understand how to kiss?" She tells me she watched her parents a couple of times until they caught her and began to lock her in her bedroom. I agree to give her a lesson. Afterwards, she tells me that licking is so much better. I smile and say, "Sorry, you are not a wolf any longer Wise Wolf, okay." She agrees. I spin her around and begin to untie her arms. The first act with her free hands is to hug me. I ask her why she likes me. She explains that she felt sorry for the way our women in this group treated me. I explain to her that she will have to be genteel to the others as well. She reluctantly agrees. I give her a smooch and tell her not to worry, because sometimes it is, likewise, hard for me. I apologize for talking so low about her all this time. She confesses not to remember she could speak until blindfolded in this water. Her father was the one who taught her to swim by diving into the stream with her. I take her and put her on the deck calling out for my partners to help me, because I think, I drowned her. Vida tells us not to worry, for she can breathe life back into her and begins what Acia calls cardiopulmonary resuscitation (CPR). About the second breathe Wise Wolf slaps her, and demands that she learns to kiss from me. Vida and Špela are now in a state of shock, stuttering to each other. Vida jumps up and starts cheering. Špela screams at me, "How does the Queen understand how you kiss?" Wise Wolf tells her, "From watching you and him kiss so much." Acia and Pava appear and ask me, "When were you two doing this?" I told them, "When my little sisters were not watching." Wise Wolf appears frightened now.

I tell her it is okay, no one here will hurt our Queen. Wise Wolf asks us to explain this Queen thing. After we explain it, she declares that she will not return to be a Queen to these people that had abandoned her. I try to explain to her that they did not abandon her, which is why they sent us. Now the easy gains have turned into hard losses. If she refused to take her throne, I will have failed my mission. Špela joins Vida and me as we explain to her the terrible prison, except for the food; we had just escaped from to find her. We explain how hard it was, even with spirits helping us. Špela tells her that Queen or no Queen, we are going to make her come across like a woman. Wise Wolf asks me if I want her to appear like a woman. I explain to her that I really think she looks special and wants the men to long after her. She argues that I am the sole one she trusts, as I could go inside her and pull back the little girl tucked inside her. Acia laughs while Pava comments, "He does appear to be able to explore inside a woman and pull out a little girl." I explain, to deaf ears, that it is hard to see the woman when you merely comprehend the little girl. Wise Wolf then questions, "Oh, you knew me when I was a little girl?" I tell her, "No, my Queen, I was talking about my angry sisters." Anyway, you decide, do you want these appealing women to clean you or this tired inexperienced man to clean you. She smiles and looks at Špela, Vida, and comments, "My answer is the same as would be Špela and Vida's, and I want the experienced man who is trying to trick me." I am convinced the spirits gave all women this genetic tool. They can detect when a man does not want to do something, and then tell him you want him to do it. Špela and Vida hand me the chemicals and say, "Do a good job lover man." I give them as nasty look, for to say such a thing before a helpless Queen is so ignorant. I scrub her extremely gently and systematically. I do not care how foolish Špela and Vida have to be, I am going to bring the true royalty out of her. I explain to her that we cannot take her to her kingdom, unless she gives us permission. She asks me if any on this ship is her subjects. I tell her that we are not; however, my sister and mother and oldest brother's widows did, and I hope to find husbands for two mothers who are part of my clan that I must forever care for from her kingdom.

She tells me that if she were ever to set on that throne, this would be one of her most important missions. I tell her, "See, you are a Queen of love as was your great mother who worked so hard to care for your people." Wise Wolf next asks me, "Why then did she have wolves raise me?" I tell her there are many awful spirits in these lands and that twice they tried to stop me when I came for her. Continuing, I explain to her how bad things happen to everyone in our search for our lives. I lost three brothers, a father, and the two sister spirits on this ship since leaving my village at the beginning of this mission. Wise Wolf begins to cry, saying how remorseful she is that I have suffered. I ask her if she is so sorry that she would let her people serve her and have back their Queen. She milks her eyes on me and then tells me she will think about this. As if every minute must be accounted for my turbulence, a storm begins to rock our ship. Vida asks for my help in taking down the sails. The higher that I get on our flimsy sail poles, the harder that the wind blows. I yell down for Acia to make sure undocumented visitors are not supplementing this. Vida likewise, struggles hard as we get the sails down and take them below deck, which for this ship is crowded. As Vida enters, Špela begins to dry her. The Queen does, similarly for me. She tells us both that she was worried for our safety. Wolf and Howl join us, so we may pet them. They are sensing our hands detecting if we are worried. We both must have sent the correct vibes because these two vicious land creatures return to sleep in their corners. Pava returns to tell us the storm will be rocky most of the night; nonetheless, we are in no dangers. She shows us how to bait our fishing lines and drop them into the sea. This way, when we are awake in the morning, we will be able to retrieve them, maybe have thirty, and fish to eat tomorrow. Afterwards, we pull out our furs and prepare to sleep this rocky night. Ráðúlfr, as also the rest of us, is scared this night. The going up and down and sideways, never knowing for sure who you will be sleeping on the next minute is nerve racking.

Each of us worked hard to keep Wise Wolf, Wolf, and Howl calm and shortly, although not soon enough; the storm calmed and daylight came. Even though I cleaned Wise Wolfs hair, the next morning Vida and Špela complained that they needed to braid her hair in piggy tails. After doing so, both Acia and Pava agreed, and even our Queen liked it. Being outnumbered and knowing that I would be in serious trouble, unless I wholeheartedly agreed, I agreed. I hope that Vida and Špela take a more active interest in Wise Wolf. I explain to Wise Wolf that no one knows a woman better than other women do. We have no desire to hurt her; in fact, her kingdom has Armies that are dedicated to save their Queen. She begins crying and telling us, she does not understand how to be a Queen. I tell her not to worry about it, because they will appoint elders to help her to be a Queen. I then pinch her cheek and tell her, "Honey, you get to be the boss and tell everyone what to do." Next, she tells me that, "The wolves I lived with had two bosses, one male, and the other female. The male could have any female he wanted, and likewise, for the female in her choice of partners. I will make you the male boss so you can have as many women as you want." Špela tells her that I cannot be the boss man because I am from another kingdom. Wise Wolf looks at me, and I shake my head saying, "Sorry, honey, she is telling the truth." She looks at us and crying says, "You are all going to leave me. I forbid it." Vida volunteers, "I will be one of your chamber maidens if you want me." Wise Wolf asks, "What is a chamber maiden?" Vida tells her, "I will stay in your palace private rooms and help you every day, so you will never be alone." Špela jumps in and likewise volunteers. I then tell her, "See, you already came up with two chamber maidens who are not from your kingdom to help keep you happy and safe. You are awfully lucky." Wise Wolf then yells at me, "Why did you have to take me from the pack that protected me? I was free to run from tree to tree and had no worries. Now everything is strange. Why did you have to take my freedom? You kidnapped me." I reach out to hug her. She takes one step toward me and stops about one step from me. I start thinking about what we did, and now I wonder if we did the right thing. It is her life, and she was protected and happy. I gaze at Vida and Špela and ask them, "Do you remember what our prison life was like? Is it fair that we take away her freedom?"

The three of us stand around Wise Wolf, and I tell her, "My love, we will take you back to your freedom. Vida, we need to turn around." Wise Wolf tells us to hold on for one minute and asks, "Are you sure, you will give me back my old home?" The three of us shook our heads yes. Wise Wolf looks each of us in our eyes and then asks, "If you were me, what would you do?" I tell her that I am not her. She has a voice inside her to tell her what to do. She looks at Vida and Špela and they confess, "You are your own person, and must do what you believe; however, we can merely dream of knowing a Queen, let alone ever being one. Royalty is special blood. Those incredibly few that were blessed to be born with it are too great to depend on our counsel." Vida continues, "Did you envy the boss female of the wolf pack that protected you?" Wise Wolf looks at me and reveals to me, "I will do what you tell me to do? What must I do?" I motion with my fingers for her to move close to me, and then I hug her tight before confessing, "The girls are right; I have no right to tell you to take or advocate your throne. The spirits gave it to you. If you asked me yesterday, when I thought, you wanted it, I would have told you to take it. Accordingly, do what your heart tells you to do. Your heart pumps Royal blood, as ours does not. Give us your command." She looks at Vida and declares, "Take me to my kingdom, and if you three want to keep your heads, make me into Queen." She smiles at me and says, "A Queen that is not pregnant." Vida laughs, "Ha Ha. She busted you." I add, "Wow, that Royal blood kicked in fast. Why did you change your mind Wise Wolf?" She tells me, "I did not change my mind. I made up my mind, using my free will and not as a prisoner." Špela and Vida looked at me, as we knew Wise Wolf was so true in what she had just told us. She was her Queen as well. Afterwards, I help Vida put the sails back in place, and we retrieve our trout lines and all the fish on our hooks. A few slipped out of our hands and landed on the deck. Wolf and Howl gobbled them up quickly.

Vida and I went down into the eating part under our deck that had a small fireplace. We started the fire and began cleaning and cooking the fish. The parts we did not want, such as the heads Wolf and Howl gobbled down completely. They are so full that they barely made, it back to their corners to sleep. After we finished all our cooking, we carefully put the remaining hot coals into certain large bowls and dumped them into the sea. Notwithstanding I go to our deck and invite our two other women down for our first meal today. Vida had selected leaves that she told us might last three days under the deck. Nonetheless, she recommended that we eat them quickly. She adds as well that we will be making land stops every two weeks. Here we will search for fresh leafy vegetables. We will also hope to find other good things to eat. I ask her if she thinks this is wise. She tells me, "If we want to deliver a beautiful Queen and two chamber maidens, afterwards it is extraordinarily important." Wise Wolf then asks us, "Chamber Maidens are high positions, as solely you three here will ever be permitted to enter." Vida asks, "Why just the three of us?" Wise Wolf answers, "Because you three were willing to give me back to me, therefore, you can be with me." Špela then complains, "You are going to let that cunning wolf near your bed chamber?" She smiles and says, "Why should I worry about something such as that, for if the three of us cannot control him, well, after that he belongs in my bed." Vida subsequently laughs and says, "Aman to that oh great Queen." Špela looks at her and with a stunned appearance agrees, saying, "That is so true." Consequently, I begin to become suspicious about how something just yesterday would rip us apart with her mouth is now answering these questions as a real Queen would be expected to do. It in the same way hits me that I have not seen my sisters recently. I excuse myself explaining that I need to find my sisters. On the deck, I call out to them, and they appear. I ask them, "Where were you?" Pava tells me, "Brother, we have other works we must also do. We can watch you in the sea with ease. Why did you call us?" I tell them, "The Queen has for a particular strange reason, completely developed from an animal to a Royal Highness is a matter of a few short minutes. I am curious to how this is possible."

Acia tells me, "She was always a Queen raised by her mother until her death and then her mother's spirit until the evil spirits took control of her turning her into a beast. We have completely destroyed those spirits, and her mother is with her conscience to help her be Royal." I tell my sisters that this story continues to get more interesting each day. Last night, I scrubbed her with the chemicals you gave me seeing all parts of her. Today, I am afraid to breathe around her because of her powerful Royal radiance. I fear that she will remember how I touched her yesterday and become angry." Pava tells me not to worry; they with the Queen Mother watched me in detail. Afterwards, the Queen Mother complimented them on the honorable work and sacrifice I had made for her daughter's continued honor. Acia then adds, "Come on, do not you think they have medicine men who care for them? Accordingly, think about the Queen Mother as she bore Wise Wolf. Sometimes we must do things through whoever is there to do it. The good lost from not doing them outweighs the bad for doing it." I tell them that from what I see now, it is an honor to be around her. Consequently, Pava tells me the Queen does have a deep love for me. I ask her what I should do about Andreja. Acia asks me, "Which do you want?" I tell her, "I want to keep my promise to Andreja." Pava tells me the Queen will be okay and is a strong person with Royal blood. Acia tells me it is more like she knows you can be trusted even with her life. I invite my sisters to meet the Queen. They drift downstairs with me, as the conversation among the girls gets interesting as they are stuck. The Queen tells my sisters that she is trying to think of a great title or position for me. Acia asks, "What about King?" Wise Wolf says, "He knows what must be done to get that title. Nevertheless, I suspect his heart is walking in the mountains with his clan." Pava asks her, "Queen, how does that bid with your heart?" Wise Wolf answers, "It is foolish to grieve over the loss of something that was never yours, is it not?" Acia and Pava smile and glance at me and reply, "Yes, our brother, the true Queen is here with us." Wise Wolf looks at them and asks, "Are you going to give me a serious realistic title?" Acia smiles and asks her in return, "What title would a Queen give a man who has saved and protected her life?" Wise Wolf looks at Vida who tells her, "Honorable Queen, you would make him a Queen's knight? It may not be the night you originally hoped for; however, it is a knight."

Wise Wolf looks at me and declares, "I declare you to be the highest of my Queen's Knights." She then looks at Acia and asks, "Is this legitimate?" Acia tells her, "Oh mighty Queen, if you say it, it is legal." Acia then looks at me and declares, "Daddy and your brothers will be so happy when I tell them about this great honor." Wise Wolf currently gives a new order, "Listen to me now, until we land on the shores to travel the mountains, we are all equal on this boat, so someone must assign me specific work to do, or you will see me become extremely angry." Vida asks her if she would like to help her clean Wolf and Howl's contributions and then wash the floor with her. Wise Wolf walks over to her and kisses her telling her thanks so much. To work they went. Špela tells me, "We have a Queen with integrity and true honor." I agree completely. Špela now asks me if we can go to the deck and talk about that special someone in my mountain clan that she was never told existed. I told her that we had many things to talk about and currently a real Queen to escort. We will have plenty of time to heal the hurts within us, now is not the time to jump overboard, but to hang tight for today and fight for tomorrow.

CHAPTER 11

Return to Olimpia

B y including the deck, our medium-size ship is large enough to give us each small space. Wise Wolf rotates among us having developed a special relationship with each. She relies on Vida for her social and survival skills. Špela avoids the rational and performs as the expert on the side of love. Wise Wolf uses me to test and corroborate what they say. Extremely weird, it cannot be true unless a woman teaches it and not real, unless a man verifies it. Wise Wolf is indeed the great Queen, her people appreciate she is. Each day with her radiates her greatness. The three of us find ourselves trying to elevate her highest yet she continually humbles herself around us. This is driving us crazy. I cannot sit down while a Queen is dressed in her bikini, which the further I forbid her to wear the more she appears in it. As if, I have the power to forbid a Queen. The one power she has is her absolute stubbornness. She will do what she wants to do, and I can testify to my life that her Kingdom will do as she commands. The floors in her private chambers will be the cleanest in her Kingdom, and merely those on this boat will ever realize who cleans them. She knows the price of life, how to exist with danger surrounding her and to depend on others for protection. Špela, Vida, and I now laugh about the prison days, as Wise Wolf grills us on every detail. Because of Wise Wolf, we can claim those days as ours. They are no longer days of suffering to save a lot Queen.

They are days of honor we endured before receiving permission to serve her needs. Wise Wolf is a character indeed. She enjoys using me to practice all the things related to the relationship of the genders, enjoying my intense shyness, as a Queen is more than one hundred sisters and mothers packed into one. She teases me endlessly, in which I struggle until the dreamtime when I laugh myself into great pain. Wise Wolf continually stresses that by knowing how to crawl low and hide high, one can stand strong in the open. Living with wolves, she would comprehend this. Constantly, she compares her life with the wolves against her throne. Špela, Vida, and I envy her life with the wolves, almost wanting to find us a pack of wolves. Even so, we must settle for Wolf and Howl, who have turned into loyal friends for us. Wise Wolf asked if she could have them stay with her. We agreed wholeheartedly. She is not going to hide her past, nor, as seems, allowing others to hide it. Wise Wolf tells us that her parents planted her in that garden, so she could live and someday return and for us to explain how her parent's love and deeds could be wrong. We cannot. I remember when I told her that her pride in whom, she is the willpower that she is. She calmly told me to shut up and sit down while she practiced the new kisses that Špela taught her. To make it fun, she called for Acia and Pava to watch. I was so humiliated; however, the power in her kisses began to overwhelm me. After that, she asks Acia and Pava how I did. They confessed to see well. I asked her, "Queen, how can you expect me to do great when you invited my sisters to watch?" She laughs and reveals, "Oh, I just invited them in case you became overwhelmed, after all, my Kingdom does not want to receive a pregnant Queen." Acia becomes angry, and in my defense claims that her brother would never do such a thing. I confessed to Acia that the Queen had great reason to be precarious. I looked at Wise Wolf and report, "Be careful, playing with fire will get you burned." She smiles, points at my sisters and replies, "Not if you keep two buckets of cold water nearby." I often worry that she puts too much confidence in me. Either way, we are allowing her to shine off her fine points before we finish our sea part of this mission. We understand that once on land, we will need to concentrate more on our security. Our vegetation stops have gone well. Acia and Pava tell us where to stop, and they have placed us in the right location saving days of searching.

The peacefulness of our journey evaded one hurdle. We were sailing in the middle of the sea, attempting to make sure that no one saw us. The natives in this area, though scattered, do not cross this sea. Instead, they stay close to the peninsula's land, fearing monsters live in the middle. I also hold this belief; however, Vida wants to cross over to last peninsula in our journey. She insists on avoiding any possible contact with the Cvetka, or their collaborators who may be in the slave business. The eastern mountain ranges do not reach the sea. This permits the tribes on the lowlands of the far east to enjoy free access to Cvetka. Greedy traders would sell their mothers, if allowed. Vida has planned our trip with a heading close to the eastern tip of this peninsula. She plans to cut due west about one day from the shore. We will continue due west for two days and then hit the shore running. She has selected one of the shorted green land crossings that led to certain excellent passes that will get us into the highlands with a few days. We will be in the mountains for barely two weeks. As we were making our crossing, Acia warned Vida that we must take down our sails while a small group of five ships passes. We will be safe, while we anchor where we are. I help her pull down the sails, and we drop both our anchors. The ships pass by us, taking about two hours. We waited until Acia said they were well gone. We had to depend on her, as they were too far away for us to see. Vida, Wise Wolf, and me put the sails back up and retrieved our anchors. We were soon on our way, as we grabbed an oar to make our ship faster. I asked Acia to explain to me what this concerned. She tells us that small groups of ships are beginning to sail from the other large continent on Lamenta. They come here to plunder all they can steal and to take slaves back to build their Empire. They will lose a great battle to our Queen when they try to invade her lands. Our Queen's Armies will drive them into the sea and sink their ships as they try to escape. Because of Wise Wolf's great victories, that Empire will declare her mountains cursed. I then walk over and curtsy to her kissing her palm. She yells that she cannot accept victory for a battle she has yet to fight. That night she had a dream that a treasure chest came down from the sky into a cave in her Kingdom.

She was to find this treasure chest before meeting her people. When she awoke, our Queen revealed this dream to us. I knew that she had not been in these mountains since being a child. Wise Wolf claims she has been in this cave before and can remember the land the surrounds it. We ask her to give us a detailed description of this place. She explains it in detail, to include the ridges that surround it. If this place is real, we can find it. Acia and Pava recognize nothing of the treasure chest when I ask them about it during their afternoon visit. My sisters tend to shy away from me and spend more time with the women on this boat. They are not the little babies whom I used to play. Now, they are grown women themselves. Therefore, I have adjusted to their new age and personalities. In a way, I am happy they are adults and can think as adults. I do not have to worry about their safety, even though I see nothing about the land they live. At least, I can take joy in that they helped me on this large long mission. Acia similarly confessed that they were not Damijana, as, they merely then told me, that so I would be comfortable with them initially. I asked Pava if she knew where Damijana was. She did not realize where Damijana was current. Acia eases me by reporting that Damijana did understand about their assignment to help bring me home. I felt guilty for enjoying the fact that Damijana would reenter my life when my sisters left. I am happy about this. Sometimes, trying to make something into what it destroys was what it genuinely was. Rather than destroying my memory of my smaller sisters and replace, those with what they now are will not work for me. I understand that all in my family who live in the Land of the Dead are different presently. I also realize that I am not supposed to grasp this until I live with them as well. Therefore, I will have two sets of memories for my sisters, which are the set that we lived on Lamenta, and the set that brought back the Queen. They came to do a mission, and they have done it well. For this, they deserve congratulations. I sit daily thinking about the love on this boat for me. Then I consider how I must return to Andreja and walk away from it. My mind battles me daily on where I belong.

I am a Queen's Knight, therefore I should belong in her service, yet I did promise myself to Andreja. Andreja should not have to suffer for insisting that I do a deed of honor. Špela is wonderful about searching for me on this ship and then invading my privacy. Now, I find myself looking forward to her attacks. She can read me somehow. I asked her how she could read me so easy. She told me it was because I was an open book for her. She did not have to read because my heart was yelling it out for her to hear. That made, sense to me, in that my heart would be trying to get me into trouble. Špela has done me right with my personal information that she holds. She does share it with the Queen and Vida, explaining that we have done too much together not to share ourselves. This I cannot deny. Think about all that time we lived unclothed among so many other prisoners and the way the Queen ate as wolves. Why would we be not bond? We are new people on this boat presently and even at that, we are still changing. When the Queen makes me angry about her absolute insults and retaliation or arguments on everything I say. I walk away simply finding my love for her burning harder. Špela confides in me that she shares the same frustrations. We do not resist or even attempt to slow her down because we want to have a Royal personality that can think through the actions of others.

Our evenings were, for the most part, peaceful. Everything must have its exception, as did our serene evenings. One evening, while looking over the peaceful sea, with the moons at half-light, and the large planets reflecting their lights on us, we could see enough to avoid surprises. I still find confusion in my mind about all this solar system functioning as Acia and Pava explained. If these large planets and moons are reflecting light from the Suns, or if they are generating lights from inside their balls, we gain light. I have not figured out how our world can generate light inside; it appears just to be able to receive the lights and deny them. Dark means rest for me; therefore, when the dark arrives, it brings peace for me. Wise Wolf began our conversation by asking questions about babies. This was a touchy issue for Špela and Vida; nevertheless, they shared their experiences with her. A white light took over our sky. I saw six large dark birds exploding through the sky. It appeared as if they were raining black eggs all over the land. The dark man reappears with his woman. This time the lights reflect his open chest and the woman's neck and side of her face. They are wearing red garments. The female wore a garment highlighted with ruffles. She braided her hair as the Queens, except she stuffed her piggy tail on our side in her ear. We could not see her other side. Someone sewed her mouth with lengthy, at least two-finger length, threads. The surrounding sky was in complete dark chaos. It walked from the sea onto our ship's deck; we sat around acting mild. Acia tells me in my mind to remain calm. The women are watching me, and I try to appear as being bored. He stops in front of me and asks, "Is this who you seek?" Acia takes my mouth and says, "Oh Fata Verde, when will you learn that fools should never hold women?" He drops the women as she instantly turns into black birds and flies away. Fata Verde asks me how I recognize his name. I, or Acia through me, tell him, "All the virtuous spirits of the skies are now preparing to take your prisoners and set them free unless you promise never to leave your prison once more." He answers, "No one can force me to do what I wish not to do." At this time, Acia and Pava both struck him hard with lightning. His garment burned as he leisurely walked back to the sea. He explains to us that he has decided to change his mind and slowly sinks into the water. Acia and Pava appear as Acia thanks me for allowing her to use my voice. Vida then complains, "Darn, I thought our man was finally getting strong again." I motion for her to come to sit beside me, nevertheless; she declines. Wise Wolf jumps up and proclaims, "I will," and before I could make any motion, she was beside me. She stares at Vida and Špela and tells them that we have seen the work tonight of a true Queen's Knight. They reluctantly agree as I do my fictitious gloat. Vida then asks, "Who is Fata Verde?" Pava says, "Oh, he is someone whom no living person would ever dare make angry, for he will seek his revenge." My face turns pale as I begin to shrink. Špela says, "Oh, do not worry, for a Queen's Knight has no fear, right Yakov."

I remain silent as I stare at Pava. Acia subsequently tells us, "Oh, do not worry, for he did not see your faces. Anyone who is kind to me all the way back to the Kingdom will remain disguised." This means that my final memories of being among my younger, now grown, the sisters will be those of total servitude. The little runts always did figure a way to get over on me. Pava further explains how Fata Verde is one who guards a gateway to the evil dead. He enjoys torturing them and is always looking for virtuous souls to steal. She was surprised that he did not put up a bigger fight, and believes he might still be hanging around, so she is going roughly to snoop. Later, that night we heard a selection of serious thunder and saw lightening that lit up our entire sky. Shortly after that, she returned and revealed that Fata Verde had decided in favor of returning to the other side of Lamenta, where the wicked people were more plentiful. Our curiosity now flared, as we had always merely heard of the Land of the Dead, never knowing that they segregated the evil ones. This brought joy to us, since we could comprehend how to avoid going to that part. Acia told us not to worry, for we would never go there. Just those who live in evil go there. I asked her, "What is wrong?" Pava tells us that evil includes for now such things as raiding and looting for personal gain, killing innocent people, and hurting guiltless people for pleasure. One additional thing she augmented was helping evil spirits with your own free will. Špela then looks at me and tells me, "You will go there, because you hurt me with your own free will." I deny this and tell her she should never say such things. I then turn my head to Pava and ask her, "Am I in any sort of trouble over Špela?" Pava shakes her head now and tells Špela to be extremely careful when making jokes about whom is evil and who is not, for we are not the judges. I was so thrilled that finally it was, may be three against two in this argument, with one of my two having firsthand knowledge. Usually, it is four against one. It also hits me the Queen volunteered to sit beside me and defended me. That is two good deeds from these monsters in one day. At least tonight, when I go to sleep, I will not think like Wolf and Howl stuck in a corner with no one bothering them. It honored me that Acia picked me to do the talking even though Fata Verde came straight to me ignoring the other women surrounding me.

He was extremely shocked that I knew his name. I guess that takes all the fun out of being sneaky and trying to hit an easy target. As I lie down tonight, I find three women snuggling close to me. My defeat of Fata Verde apparently took the spunk from their defiance. Actually, with the thought that he could return someday, I am not going to gloat over this victory, nor attempt to add to the uneasiness they are trying to hide from me. They are easier to protect and find in an emergency the closer that they are, so I gain particular peace of mind from this new sleeping arrangement. Additionally, I notice the Queen takes my stronger right side as Špela takes my left side. Vida protects the Queen's other side, so all is well. We enjoy protecting the hidden treasure that we were so lucky to discover. Close to one hour before dawn, another light began to shine in our room. This time it was a woman who appeared to resemble Vida and the skull at the top of a male body beside her. The woman has a coating of blood covering the left side of her face below her lower lip. Her chest was soaked in blood as was his. There was a large gush of blood squiring between their heads. We could not identify the source. Blood was also pouring into the man's left eye. The top of the male's bony skull had a light reflecting from it. The light fully lit the woman's face, as if to make sure we knew whom she was. Vida saw this and at once began crying. I was waiting for Acia to take my mouth and calling for both her and Pava in my head; nevertheless, they remained silent. The single defense, I knew to execute now was to remain quiet and to wait for their first move. After appearing, they stopped and at the present simply stare at us. To me, it is important to appear peaceful and tranquil. I enjoy the way they are simply watching us and while they keep their blood to themselves and do not attempt to add ours, we will appear undisturbed. My women are staring at me and I easily motion for them to remain calm. Notwithstanding, there must be a message to this. If it were from evil, I am sure my sisters would have warned me or be here fighting beside us.

I motion for Vida to begin. She shakes her head no and scoots behind me. Surprisingly, she fits, although the Queen and I have a new leg stretching between us as also Špela and I enjoy another leg between our sides. I can sense Vida's heart beating against my back. She is not sweating much; therefore, I do not believe she feels fear but just sadness. I take a chance here to speak, as all speaking flows from my mouth. The Queen and Špela are each gripping one of my hands and Vida has my body frozen in place with her legs and arms. This is why I prefer to have selected men on my trips with me. Women just want to argue all the time about how much stronger and wiser they are, yet when the real test comes, they are looking for protection. Either way, these three are special, so I will protect them. I begin by introducing myself, "Hello Vida, my name is Yakov, and my sisters and I are bringing a friend back to her home. How may I help you tonight, in peace I hope?" The voice responds, "Yakov, we come in peace. May I ask which your sisters are among us?" I tell her, "Because you come in peace, my sisters sleep. Please ask several more questions, as I would hope we can learn so much more about you and you about us." The woman replies, "We do not understand why we are here before you. A force told us our answers were with you with our questions." Now, I am aware of Vida and the other two relaxing some; nonetheless, they are still holding their secure positions. I study her and smile, "I am sorry that my voice is all you can receive, since my friends are holding me tight." They behave much in the same manner as any other woman who enters their bedroom when their Knight of love is with them. Nevertheless, I really would like to hear your questions. I see no reason I cannot strive to help you find your answers. The first question she asks is, "Do you realize what happened to my three children? I have searched for them sense, escaping a brutal raid on our home. While searching, I found my husband, and I hope you can witness that he is not in a good way." Acia finally breaks her silence and tells me that their spirits are lost. We must pull the woman's spirit back into Vida, and release the husband's spirit, as his flesh is no longer awake. In my head, I ask her how she is doing this. She tells me not to worry, for she will guide me. I respond by first clarifying with Vida, "You speak the truth, as I do realize where your children are. They are doing so well, and have many to care for them. They cry for their father and cheer for your victory."

Vida the spirit asks, "Where are they?" I tell her they are in the bright light that has been guiding you since we were lost so far. I ask her, "Vida, please examine your husband and ask me what you see?" She reports to me that she sees much suffering; nevertheless, as his wife, she will save him." I pore over the husband and ask him if he knows where they are. He tells me that they are in the Land of the Dead, and that he told his wife this many times, yet she does not believe him. After this, I reveal to him, "You are the husband, and must free your wife for me have Vida's body behind me as she has not yet been called to the Land of the Dead. He looks over at me and says, "I see that you speak the truth." I now focused on Vida the spirit telling her that her flesh may die unless her spirit is made completely again as one. Two spirits cannot exist as this is a glitch in the death process, and she is holding her children's father from them. She must let him go free. My Vida now calls out, "Vida, please save us." Vida, the spirit releases the hold she has with her husband. The light immediately pulls him into it. My Vida has currently worked herself free and is walking toward the spirit Vida when a new vision freezes them both. We can be their three children rushing to their father, who now has a new body and is free from the blood and the skull. We can hear their cheers plainly and see the joy. I reach my hand out for Vida the spirit and while holding my Vida I ask them, "What you say we give those children a strong, loving mother, whom they may watch with pride?" My Vida opened her arms as the split part of Vida's spirit made her spirit complete once again. Vida is complete once more. Her milky eyes are glowing at this time, and I tell them, "Špela should rejoice that you were separate, because, if she were to be competing in a new race, we understand Vida would win by miles." Wise Wolf adds, "I have no idea what happened here. The lone thing that I understand is that my Knight may have a hard time breaking free from me. No Kingdom would want to see their Queen crying and begging in the street for one man."

Vida laughs and asks her, "What makes you think that Špela and I would not be beside you also begging?" She laughs and reveals, "You two do not matter, as you will be in my chamber with me always anyway." Špela then complains, "You mean we have to listen to you moan while you are making princes and princesses?" Wise Wolf laughs and says, "Do not forget, you may have to bring me water if I were to become thirsty during such a pressing session." I gawk at her and yell, "No," as everyone pauses believing me to be angry. I continue, "I drink merely Royal wine, not water." Wise Wolf winks at me and says, "I do believe you might be a bit of a challenge, yet, please remember that it is the end of the race the winner is declared, and you will win with me." She is so clever with her words and now lays them out to include both, her and me as winners. Am I to stand up and tell her that I will not be a winner? I think not. I merely reply, "Oh Queen, while you are as well a winner, then everyone wins." For once, I also have Wise Wolf thinking. This has turned out to be an interesting day. I ask my women, "Angels, when do you think we will ever talk to the living again?" Each one tells me that they hope soon because depending on me is so scary. I smile and say, "Okay, any who did not wish to depend on me, may sleep on the other end of this deck. Those who wish to continue depending on me may sleep on this side." No one went to the other side, yet each gave their little, 'we are puppies' expressions and pried a little of my fur from me. They covered themselves fine, and my sole chance of warmth is to call for Wolf and Howl. They both respond to my call and jump on me. They are warm indeed, and heavy. The difficult part is how they keep licking my face. For a few strange reasons, they do not believe me when I tell them the faces of our women would taste better. It must be those chemicals, which Acia and Pava brought them. They sit around for hours playing with that smelly junk. I often believe that is why Wolf and Howl sleep in their corners away from those chemicals. I am interested in knowing what my perfectly licking, and by then soaked face will appear as in the morning, as the darkness in this deck now has my women sleeping as if babies.

I behold the world that surrounds us now unable to say that because I do not see anything, there is nothing, as something continues to appear. It would be so foolish to believe that just I had the solutions, yet not foolish to think that we have the solutions. Therefore, I can merely hope that someone in the 'we' I am part of at the time has the answer. Our special clan shares, one love and that is the love of our new freedoms. Wise Wolf will be ruling those who do not want to be free from her, even though they do not discern her. We, which serve her on this boat recognize one thing, and that is she will be more than they could have ever dreamed to set on a thrown over her Kingdom. Špela, Vida, and I all share the belief the mountains will grow stronger with her ruling the Armies that serve her. She searches deep for answers as our recent experience with Vida proves. First, she quizzes Acia who explains to her the point of death when the spirit leaves its body. So many forces are at play as many things are going in all directions. The one force that controls everything is love and sometimes when the love is intense, the separations do not go as they should go. In Vida's situation, a part of her spirit, grabbed a hold of her husband and embraced on, preventing him from entering the light. The blood still flowed because she would not accept the death. Fortunately, enough of her spirit remained in her body to keep her flesh from going to its sleep. The determination in her eyes would not let go until she realized the welfare of her children were at risk. Therefore, she released her husband who reunited with their children, and she rejoined with her soul. Acia also revealed that she placed many happy images of her children in the Land of the Dead now secured by their father. Wise Wolf wanted to understand more about the mother-child relationship. I told her my mother died when Pava was born, and therefore, I never knew her. This is why Olimpia plays such a large role in my life. Wise Wolf tells me she believes this reason is why I tend to bond easier with mature women. I told her that she might be right, as I am not going to get into a habit of telling a Queen, she is wrong, although I should say more about the enduring strength of the women that surrounded me and the too frequent deaths of the surrounding men.

Wise Wolf complains that she has never been a mother. Špela tells her the time to complain about such a thing is after having the child and not before it, as the process it has a way of nullifying complaint. I tell her, "Wise Wolf, you are the Queen and the Queen is the mother of all in her Kingdom." Wise Wolf next argues this is why she needs to get how to be a mother. Špela tells her that no woman gets, practice of being a mother before actually receiving her baby. The baby teaches the mother as her Kingdom will instruct the Queen. A Queen will learn how to experience her people and search for how to care for them. Do not worry if you do not know, for this is why those from the sky appoint Royalty, as they will help the Queen. Wise Wolf complains how we keep telling her little extras the closer that we get to her Kingdom. I glimpse at Acia and confess to hear that same complaint given by others on this mission. Acia tells Wise Wolf not to worry. Her mother is in her heart, and shall guide her. Wise Wolf wonders how a mother can live in her daughter's heart. Špela tells her not to worry, for someday she will live in her daughter's hearts. Wise Wolf at once responds, "See, I told you guys, there was a lot to this being a mother thing than you are sharing with me," as she gives me a mean look. I gaze at her and reply, "Look here woman; I cannot be a mother. Do you want me to teach you why?" Špela slaps me and says, "You have to teach me first." Wise Wolf looks at both of us and complains, "Yes, you can play, because everyone will not be asking you the questions." Špela tells me, "You need to give the Queen a calmer kiss. Your kisses are fantastically successful in putting women to sleep." I glance at her and smile while asking Acia, "Sister, when will Fata Verde be visiting again? I think this time he may not leave empty-handed." Špela runs over and kneels before the Queen, begging her, "Please, my Queen do not let Yakov have me killed, for I want to live to serve you." Wise Wolf looks at me angrily and says, "You are spared my sister." I gaze at them and said, "Vida, will you join me on the deck?" She agrees and I quickly help her up and complement how soft her hand feels. She asks me if I am okay.

I tell her loudly, "Oh Vida, I am always okay with you." We walk onto our upper deck, she asks me again, and I explain that Špela and the Queen are playing games with me, and my dependence on them. Vida chuckles, "Oh; I thought it might be something serious." The rains began to fall once again. I laugh at Vida and the comment the sky must not think this important either. Vida invites me to her planning area, where she tries to determine where we are. This is on the upper deck under a cloth roof; she erected if of rains. She can see enough of the sky to make her marks of where the stars, planets, and moons are. From this point, she estimates where we may be. She scratches her head, swears, throws a few things, and then confesses that she believe we are here as she makes an X on her map drawn on the deck. She looks confused, so I ask her if everything is all right. Vida complains that her numbers and marks are slightly wrong. I asked her if she considered all the sleep she enjoyed today while the Queen and Špela were abusing me. Next, she sighs, saying that would account for it. She continues with confessing that someday she knew I might be good for something, yet she could never figure out why. I examine her and say, "Okay, Queen and Špela, you can take a break." She kisses me on my cheek in her own special mommy way and says, "At least with me you understand I mean it." I glance at her flabbergasted. She punches me in my side and says, "You realize you could never live without me do not you?" I smile and confess. She has such a wonderful personality, especially now that I understand what she was dealing with. I recognize the power of her strong brown eyes; I saw today that no other set of eyes should ever overpower. I grasp the Queen and Špela appreciate her internal power, as neither complained when she brought me to the deck. Vida did not miss this neither as she now asks me why they consented so easily. I brushed it off by explaining that after all those hours of badgering me; they felt bad in not allow her various fun. I continue by adding, "Even I did not realize you would come out hitting so hard."

She hugs me and says, "You are special on this ship as it is not often that three women who want to be mothers can enjoy one little boy such as you." I believe that my brain is now getting the message to let this slide, because Vida is loaded with the hard shots today. She asks me to help her turn the sails, as it is, time to head west for a few days. Acia now recommends that we start swimming with Wolf and Howl, so we can rebuild our strength for particular mountain climbing once more. Pava informs Špela and the Queen, who at once removes her gown appearing in her bikini that she loves so much. The Queen appears before me and asks Vida if I am still pouting. Vida asks her if she has been mean to our special man. The Queens assures her that she would always be caring to me and looking at me asks me if I forgive her. Špela accuses the Queen of cheating by asking him while wearing her bikini. Vida reveals to the Queen that all men will forgive any woman who is wearing a bikini. The Queen then chuckles and concludes, "I take it afterwards that we are all forgiven." I stare at them and confess, "Sure, for whom am I to break traditions." Pava inquires that she never knew of such traditions in the mountains. I tell her that is because the mountains do not have seas. Špela chuckles while saying, "Oh where would the logic of men be if it were not first released on their younger sisters?" With her having said this, I jump into the sea with Wolf and Howl closely behind me. Our three bikinis quickly fall under the surface waters as we begin working our muscles in the mountains ahead. After a few hours, the winds begin to pick up once more; therefore, we board our ship, lift the anchors, and head west. Vida saves us a little sea time by putting more of an angle in our northern shift. The last day on our ship was filled with joy and singing. We were extremely jubilant once more to live on land, even though we had been so happy to live on the sea at first. The land was growing larger before us each hour at present. Although our journey had been shorter when compared to other segments in our lives, we now bonded completely. The Queen no longer depended strictly on me, yet openly on all of us. She leaned without even giving concern if we were there to stop her fall. She laughed that she would prefer to fall alone than to stand without us. I asked her so many times why she forced herself to depend on us. Wise Wolf would stare me down with that Royal glare and say, "Why not."

I stopped asking the next question, "Do you want to stand without us?" Wise Wolf always said, "No." Špela reminds us that she is a Queen and can say no. We envy her for that power. The way she says 'No' with so much authority and relays the point that a yes will not be forthcoming is Royal indeed. I will have trouble going back into the real world where it is possible to change a 'no' into a 'yes' and of course, all the agony that goes with orchestrating such a change. Our Queen requests that Špela and Vida once again tell their mating stories. She stops the stories and asks why Špela and Vida did not have the same mate. She understands the need for more mothers because human women most usually merely produce one child per gestation, a species weakness that she adds will always make it impossible for humans ever to rule Lamenta, yet she is confused with the need for so many fathers. She asks Špela and Vida if they came from different regions. Acia intervenes and tells her that in most humans on Lamenta came from a race called the Planters almost 1,000 years previously planted by one of their seeded couples. Other children, the Planters planted much earlier in other parts of the skies have also sent small colonies. One important value has always been that each child or family has a set of parents. Sometimes, after large wars in which many men died, exceptions developed. The rule of thumb has always been to keep the women reproducing as often when possible. Recent events in the mountains will require adjustments the species construct when needed. The Queen stops her and says that it is better to have the strongest male father all the children. This will create a stronger species. Pava explains that such reproduction practice with humans creates the reverse effect. The offspring was born deformed in the future generations. The sole way to offset this is by adding more mates to choice. This is why it is so important that many humans wonder to new areas until the population grows large enough to remove this breeding curse. I then asked, "Is this why the boys must find fresh wives or not return?" Acia asks me how I knew this. I told her, "Olimpia and Kaus's widow found their husbands because this rule." Acia smiles and asks me why I have not spoken much of them. I told her, "Honey, I appreciate they are wonderful men and friends of mine as I was the one who introduced them, yet since then I have been searching for Wise Wolf. You should have no fear, for at present that they have a wonderful Queen; your sister will survive a great life."

The muscles in our bodies are all now tight with our swimming, so we decide to stay on our ship for a few extra days and swim not as hard hoping to revive our sore muscles and enjoy quite a few more fish before returning to eating mountain food. The mountain fish do not taste the same as the sea fish. The sea additionally offers such a wide choice. We choose to eat no more than fish and to swim for these days and as well discuss the obstacles that may be ahead of us while we still have Acia here. Wise Wolf shifts off the subject by wanting to understand why she cannot see or hear her mother while she is talking to her, yet we can see Acia and Pava. Pava explains the original destiny was not to bring Wise Wolf back to her Kingdom, yet the pleas from so many of her Kingdom forced a method created. Without direct supernatural powers, this method came into existence. We borrowed and returned the night glasses created by a future Empire. We still required them, allowing us to walk across the lands and fight any predators or other humans. The selected warrior to perform the Search for Wise Wolf was I. I had to move from Petenka to the Gerben. This journey, without supernatural powers beyond what was available for all, took the lives of many people while also hitting my family extremely hard. Since Acia and Pava died of this process, they were allowed to return and help save their remaining brother. Wise Wolf apologizes to me for the loss my family has suffered. I tell her that if my family met her, just as Acia and Pava, they would all agree the sacrifice was extremely worthy, especially when they learned about the lives changed and saved. Future lives saved to create a feeling of toil completed for the just, yet the current lives of those who did the saving beat loud drums that drown any dream of silence. Temptations and questions of any reality to the mission's claims abound, working so hard to trip the one who is marching to a higher cause. Eyes in the sky will fail to protect the feet on the surface.

I pride our group for not acknowledging these great salvation claims other than to accept them as being true. Wise Wolf won us with her humble and giving attitude. She has always refused us when we requested to put her on a pedestal. Instead, she would jump below us serving with her heart. Her pride in those she claims as friends melted our hearts. We truly love this special person as she has proven to us what a real, Royal being concerns. She proves that a Queen, who loves her people, will earn their affection and honor. We are the ones who boast of pride, never Wise Wolf. Špela, Vida, and I dream of serving her ensuring she gets the greatness that was meant for her. Špela reveals to us that when the Queen's Kingdom receives her, we will fall to the side. Wise Wolf heard this and became extremely angry. She cried out to us, "What sort of monster do you take me for? Have I not already declared Špela and Vida as my chamber maidens? Did not I appoint Yakov as the Queen's Knight? What more do you desire, tell me and I will make it so? How can I ever gain your trust and faith?" I told her, "We recognize your heart as being greater than the angels of love, yet we also understand the greed of those who hunger for the power of others." Wise Wolf then asks me, "With this understanding, why do you ignore my begging you to be my King? Is not this, the same as feeding me to those whom, you believe that would destroy me?" I see her and say, "Oh Queen, if you just knew how I dream to be your King, yet I am a slave to a promise to another. She gave me to save you, how can I punish her by casting her aside?" Wise Wolf responds by declaring me a man of great honor, and that she will reward the one who sleeps alone now because of the price to gain her freedom. Špela confesses to the Queen that her complaint about others taking their Queen away from them was from the pain of not having her love exclusively. Wise Wolf then asks us, "How can one take the love from the Queen for her chamber maidens? Will not you be the solitary who sees that I am simply mortal like all others?" Vida adds, explaining to Wise Wolf that she is not, nor ever will be merely humanlike all others.

Wise Wolf then apologizes to us for not being able to prove to us that she is simply a person, if not at the same time lower coming also from a family of wolves. I correct Wise Wolf by explaining that even the wolves, how kill people fell in love with her. No one can ever defend against her love. She corrects me, "Except for the one I want, is this not true Yakov? Oh, whom are we fooling, except for the one we want? Is this not true, my friends?" Špela, and surprisingly Vida, both agree. I inspect Vida and confess, "Vida, I did not realize that you also care for me." She looks at me and confesses, "Even for a creep, you tend to grow on a person." I kiss her while acknowledging that I have never been so happy when someone calls me a creep before in my life. Acia reappeared before us and gave Vida a magic eye that could see from far distances. She called it a telescope and told us that when we went ashore, we would be traveling for two days across wide-open green lands in which many tribes used as trading routes. She warned that female slave trading was extremely profitable, because a healthy woman could bear many children. Next, Pava appears and recommends that we use certain of the deck floor wood to make added arrows, and that we use the sails to make lighter blankets and dull fabrics to wear. Vida worried about taking down the sails. Acia explains the sails can be seen from afar, and that without the sails, they will be able to hide so much better while they continue to rebuild their muscles through swimming and eating sea fish. Pava continues to stress the need to do all cooking at night, as the smoke is hard to pinpoint from the sea, as many will mistake it as fog. Acia also reveals that Lamenta is preparing a wonderful gift for the Queen's first steps back on land. Pava reports that various previous Kingdom spirits have told her Kingdom that she is awaiting to go ashore and will soon come to regain her Kingdom once more. Two weeks later, we agreed that our bodies were toned enough to begin the march toward our new home. We packed our back bags with cooked fish, loaded our arrows, and began to paddle our small ship to the seacoast. Mystery overshadowed us, as the land, we approached was not green, but instead coated with so many other colors.

This resembled the mountain place that Olimpia once took us that had so many flowers. The wind was blowing from the land to the sea, thereby causing the beauty not to be the sole wonderful thing to tantalize our senses. The fragrance was so overwhelming, throwing us onto our deck with illusions of love tingling all internal senses. One view of Wise Wolf with these aromas flooding our minds released our love. To any colors lay before us. We could see red, purple, yellow, white, and every color between them. A few were the shape of Cvetka coins, others the shape of balls and still others the silhouette of flames. The women from this ship hit the shore running in excitement, while I did as Acia had requested and beat large holes into the bottom floor. This was to prevent this ship from sailing again. I believe this was correspondingly to force us into the mountains. These mountains rose calmly in our horizon. It would take a few days to reach these giants. From here, they appeared as peaceful small hills. The girls are now picking blossoms and tucking them into their hair. I dare not just give flowers to precisely one, yet I, likewise, dare not give any blooms. I elected to pick three of each of the three different types I collected. In this fashion, I would offer each choice of three. Even though their heads were flooded with the plants, they had already chosen, they each took the three I offered, unable to decide. I knew that Olimpia invariably loved flowers; however, I always thought this to be a strange aspect of her personality. Nevertheless, I never expected that Špela, Vida, and Wise Wolf would all be this fanatical over these flowers. They do not even complain about the flying insects that can sting with great pain, as I do. They ignore them. I give them the reverence their destructive power in entitled. I so often wonder why the spirits that created us made simply the men intelligent. I naturally keep this thought private, as these three would fight, without rationality of course, even if they thought I was thinking such a thing. What makes matters worse is how they can detect one of my weaknesses too easily and bring it to my attention. Even adding greater insult to this dilemma is that something made them smaller than their male counterparts were.

Like all the other males who live under these conditions, I will have to adjust, considering that I do prefer to have them as a company, compared with the alternative of having merely male counterparts. The warmth of the land is refreshing, as I believe it will take a little time before I can work all this dampness out of my body. Accordingly, I notify this clan that we must head for the mountains if we wish to remain alive. I fake a startle, as if I heard a noise. The three of them huddle me again, "Well, old man, must we wait the entire day for you to start moving?" I ignore them and begin walking. I can hear that they are tagging within an arm's reach of me. Within the hour, we have passed all the flowers and now walk among high grass. I take out my long knife and sense the ground before me, wishing to avoid any snakes who love the sun bathe in the tall grass. The mountains continue to grow before us. I notice the pass is to our left; therefore, I shift our journey to the left. I do worry about hitting it perfectly, as we can climb the ridge between the pass and us and then take the pass. I simply wish to decrease the time in this grassland, and the left angle will not put us in that much of an additional threat. The mountains are still waiting to turn its vegetation to green, as I can; nonetheless, see white that is frozen ice from the winter and dark seasons. Nevertheless, the streams appear to be flowing again, so the ice is melting slowly each day. We stop to eat select fish when I inform the girls that we should continue to walk in the dark, as the land is flat and open. The sooner we get between the trees, the safer we will be. We will be able to catch up on our sleep once we are in the pass that awaits us. The three of them agree, even though I can tell they are getting tired. I further tell them, "If anyone feels their body is becoming injured, let me know. We are not in such a danger that we must destroy ourselves." They each promise to do so. I recognize that they will not; therefore, I must devise a way to monitor them, even in the dark. My women are stubborn little creatures, sometimes going to the extreme. This is one of the occasions where I find myself having much respect for them. They have a greater desire avoiding danger. These girls would too easily sacrifice themselves evading it. This is one of those times, which I must provide the leadership, and take care of them.

One method I always had success with when caring for Acia and Pava was to hold hands. They will not let go of one another. Therefore, as one lags, she will pull all of us back. This is when I understand to act calm and move slower. Whoever claimed these women did not have pride must have grown around just men. It is how I handle that pride, which determines how smoothly evens flow. The mountains are now close enough to us to block much of the moonlight and the stars. This is making it harder for me to navigate. I realize to move toward the giant blackout out mass before us. My concern is that I could be shifting too much to the left. To offset this I put Špela to my left and Vida with Wise Wolf to my right. This should keep me on the correct path. Soon, it becomes apparent to me that we will not reach the mountains before daybreak. I also fear that if we sleep the entire day in the open, danger would be able to sneak up on us. Therefore, we must get certain of our sleep in during the night and hopefully; the daybreak will wake us, and we can continue toward our pass. Notwithstanding I tell our gang my reasoning, and that we should rest a little now, as the risk of injury currently outweighs any gain. They agree, and the four of us huddle up and quickly fall to sleep. Our first day from the ship was a long one, as so many bad events could have taken us yet they did not. These women are nervous, as they are not beating me with insults. They are showering me, with compliments, and requests on how they can obey me. Obeying me is what they consider avoiding that pain. There is a bit of truth to this. That is why I take this extremely seriously. It seems as if forever since I have heard from Acia and Pava. I could wonder no more if it is time for Damijana to reappear. Before lying down to sleep, I have us plant many arrows, tip up, in the surrounding grounds. I hope that if someone is trying to sneak up on us, he will meet one of these arrows and make enough noise to alert us; they are attempting to ambush us. Surprisingly, as the sun came up, so did these women. The three of them woke me first thing. We ate a handful more of our fish and began walking once more. While eating our fish, I noticed Wild Wolf as she had a far-off stare into the mountains. I asked her if everything was fine.

She told me that it was, because she had never seen mountains before and had a quiet voice inside her informing her that this was her true home. I told her that these mountains were dreadfully large and long. There are so many worlds in these wonderful mountains. I confessed to her that it had been a while since I was at my home. The Suns were now reflecting from her hair and shinning from her cheeks. Once again, I realized what beauty was among us, as even Špela and Vida as well resembled angels. I have been so concerned with their safety that I had not given much attention to what I was saving. Subsequently, I wondered how her people would see her. I knew that they would review us to see how we treated her. All their claims of wanting their Queen would boil down to how much honor they were willing to give her. I called our gang together and explained to them that it was how we treated our lovely angel her people would regard her. I conceived an idea. We would jump to attention and give her the honor she deserved. Wise Wolf objected to this, until both Špela and Vida told her it must be this way. Wise Wolf began crying saying that she could not watch us humble to her. We explained once again that she must do this and simply to see our tremendous love pouring out of her. She is the greatest Queen that we have ever known, okay, she is the sole Queen we have ever known, yet putting that aside, we believe she is Royalty and that her people must treat her as such. She reluctantly agreed, as both Špela and Vida put their pressure on her to do so. She could wiggle around me, but not her chamber maidens and accepted that we knew, best. We had shifted more during the night than I had projected, yet not too far. Within a few hours, we are at the mouth of the pass. Green trees, budding plants, and large leaves are covering the landscape. As even to a greater benefit, I can see a small path. This suggests to me that life abounds in this area. I would expect these grazing animals would use this to feast on the green lands below us. My feet step on the first mountain rock for what seems to be ages. Could I finally be back into the lands that I have spent most of my being, which lives within? It sure feels like it.

I see how Wise Wolf is touching the trees as if something deep inside her is crying for its freedom as well. She looks at us and I smile, saying, "You think you could do us all a favor and zip up the tree and tell us if you see anything around us?" She smiles and up the tree she goes, laughing all the way. Špela, Vida, and I congratulate her more for the joy we are experiencing and watching her have so much fun once again. As I am watching her, two other females appear beside me. I scan them and say, "Acia and Pava, we believed that you had forgotten us." Pava explains that they will be with me for one more day, and then they must give me to another that will protect us. I tell them that I need my younger sisters more than I need protection. They explain that they as well need me more than to protect me; however, certain powers control these things and they accepted something instead of nothing. Looking, at Acia I confess that this Search has preoccupied me, taking me away from my true concerns. I then asked Pava if we could talk in our heads. My first question was how those in our family were doing in the Land of the Dead. Acia tells me that our father, Kaus, and mother stay together, while our other two brothers hang together or pester them. Next, I ask my sisters if they knew why I felt so empty after they died. Pava smiles and tells me it was because I loved them too much. You have greater compassion and capacity for love. I never thought so much about love previously. I understand that Olimpia had built a caring person within me and that is not bad. When the time comes to kill, I can do so. This is why Špela is behind me during times of her fear. Notwithstanding they touch peace with me throughout the peaceful times, which is why they are comfortable to tease and play with me. Acia explains that this is a great type of relationship to be a member. If they need something or if I need something, we have the foundation to discuss this.

Our group is beginning to show independent life once more. They have been scrounging the vegetation all-day, collecting what they believe will add to our midday and evening meals. I have learned to compromise on the longer meals, as it gives them a chance to shine and contribute to our mission.

The three of them work accordingly hard together for these meals, and even I must confess ads considerable to our days. I am so much more energetic and alert while following their program. Nothing adds to the chilling sounds of the wilderness such as the laugh of gainfully employed women. Because my perceptions of Acia and Pava have matured, they flow right in line with Špela, Vida, and Wise Wolf. Wise Wolf now blends perfectly with them, as each order they give she responds wholeheartedly. They behave as sisters and not as a Queen to her chamber maidens. We value our Queen's happiness more than a few old customs written for other people living in other ages. Wise Wolf understands that we will just permit this when she is alone among us. She is willing to compromise with us; therefore, we have no excuse for failing to make conciliations alongside her. Who knows, maybe someday she will make worthy servants from us. The one who determines if our service is compliant is our Queen. When these women are playing, laughing, enjoying, while working so hard, they pull me into their world. Acia and Pava sit beside me as Acia asks me, "Why do not you join them and have fun with them?" I tell her because of fear. I have never truly been able to share myself with anyone, as she should know. The fear of a mistake takes away any joy of a temporary satisfaction. Acia tells me that she overreacted with me, and yet I still pulled myself through, so why not try once more. I told her that I did and that is why I rush back to Andreja. Acia warns me never to give up today for what may be in the future. She continues that these three stood beside me and followed my lead. This is too much to throw away. Your visitors will arrive soon, so now is a good time to set on the rock above us and gaze out over the land we have crossed. I accept this offer and jump onto the rocks above us. The view is overwhelming, to such wonder that I call my partners to join me. They quickly assemble to food they have prepared and join me. We spread out the vegetation and fruits, and eat while absorbing this wonder. We can see the sea and its sapphire rippling waves. Behind it are the shades of blue, purple, and orange sky. I notice the shoreline here has many large rocks projecting from the water. Vida tells me that her map showed these rocks, and that is why she took us to shore before lining up with the pass.

What boggles my mind is how flat the sea is, when compared to these mountains we shall be entering. Špela tells us that this reveal to her the green lands were once a part of the sea. I compliment her this analysis. These women are smart, a fact I could never deny. Nevertheless, in all the time, we were on the sea we did not behold a view such as this. I am still amazed how Vida used the stars and one or two other pointers across this vast emptiness. I wonder whether humans will someday travel these large seas as we cross the lands during our lifetime. Wise Wolf begins singing a song in which we jump in and join her. We left the security of the vegetation below us to stare out into the open world behind us. We held each another's hands while we sang. A hold attempts to deny that we may someday go our separate ways. Acia and Pava each gave Wise Wolf their curtsies. She looked at this in disbelief, asking if they were going to leave us, as tears flowed down here angelic cheeks. They told her that another who would be with her all the remaining days of her life was soon to arrive. Wise Wolf asked them for a way to determine if this agent was dependable. They tell her that from my mouth will come the determination. Wise Wolf replies, "If my King says they are good, then I give no refusal." This brought a special feeling of joy in my heart, for she is always so willing to place her life in my hands. I tell Acia and Pava, "They had better be virtuous or they shall return with no one." Acia tells me that within the hour, my replacements will be here. I glare at Špela and Vida as the tears now flow down their cheeks. Špela, I say, "Have no fear my hearts since I will never allow anything less than an angel to care for you." Pava chuckles and then respond, "Then angels, it shall be." We return from the solitude offered on this rock to our fireplace below to prepare for tonight's feast and celebration. While we worked for this event, I heard footsteps approaching. Quickly, I ushered my women to their safety simply leaving me standing with Acia and Pava at my sides. It felt good that they stayed beside me and removed any fear that tried to deceive my mind. Soon four images began to appear.

Suddenly, one of them yells out, "I see Yakov." They flood on us within an instant and I see before me Olimpia, Aert, Carolus, and Urška. They surround me jumping over me as we crash into the ground. Olimpia stops and asks me, "My son, who is within those two lights?" I answer, "Mother, do you not understand your children." She falls before them crying, "I think I know. It is the fear that they may not be who I wish them to be." Acia and Pava answer her, "We are who you wish us to be." Both of their lights descended into Olimpia, as her face glowed a new light. Aert, Carolus, and Urška ask me, "Yakov, who is in those lights?" I tell them, "Her lone sisters." Urška answers, "Is it Acia and Pava, whom she talks about daily?" I shake my head yes. Carolus now adds, "I thought we came to find our Queen." I tell them, "Your Queen is here as well. Do not you think the spirits would not send the greatest from them to end the Search for Wise Wolf? I could at no time think of any greater spirits than the sisters of Olimpia." Urška responds, "That would be a truth that could never be disproved." I tell Olimpia to go on the rock in the sky above us and she may see her Queen later this evening. Her time with Acia and Pava is important because tomorrow they will leave. I glance at Wise Wolf, and she shakes her head yes and motions for Olimpia to depart. Špela and Vida jump to my sides and I say, "Aert, Carolus, and Urška, behold your Queen." As I say this Špela, Vida, and I curtsy as Wise Wolf stands up. We have prepared a special gown for her to wear. They sewed this garment, while we were in the sea. As she stood up, the Suns reappeared pouring their lights on her. Aert, Carolus, and Urška immediately hit the ground screaming out, "Long live the greatest Queen of the Gerben." When they finished saying this, the Suns gave up their light as darkness now reigned around us. Aert declares, "Surely this is our Queen, and she has returned to take back her Kingdom." Wise Wolf goes to each one and hugs them kissing their cheeks requesting, "And will you take me to my people?"

Aert and Carolus promise, "Not even our deaths will prevent us from serving our great Queen." Wise Wolf then declares, "I have brought from the wilderness, my two chamber maidens, and our King." Urška tells her, "Whosoever you say is they shall be." Wise Wolf afterwards reveals to them that Yakov has spoken so much about those whom, he loves. She then asks, "Where is the one called Andreja?" Urška reports that no one knows where Andreja is, for she has departed from the Kingdom. They plan to share all the details with me with Olimpia returns. Because she is also my mother, she has this right. Wise Wolf and I agree. Wise Wolf asks Urška by whispering in her ear, if she thinks the news will make me happy. Urška whispers back to the Queen that she thinks it may hurt him. Wise Wolf walks to me and asks, "My King, when you hear this news will you promise to be in my arms, so we may receive it as one?" I curtsy to her and tell her; I will love to be in her arms, yet fear I may not be able to break loose from them. Wise Wolf asks me, "Why would you want to be free from my arms? Do you hate me that much? Have not I always assured you that what I have is yours?" I hold her and for the first time I realize she wants to be in my arms. I never took this seriously before. Wise Wolf is, without question, the greatest available bride. We will have to work out particular boundaries with our chamber maidens, as they are a part of us. Urška tells the Queen of all the things her Kingdom is now doing. They are building homes and villages as they now prepare to move from the caves. Wise Wolf tells her that all great changes for people must take time, and that she would prefer to keep the children and old people safe in the caves until they can fight the current tenants in these lands. She hopes that extremely little bloodshed, and that no person, friend or foe, should lose his or her dreams. Urška, Aert, and Carolus listen intensively in amazement. Aert tells them that our new Queen is truly wise. I tell them the Queen has amazed me with so many pronounced ideas that I see a great future for the Gerben, as she is they, and they will be her. Olimpia returns with Acia and Pava. I ask her why she has returned quickly. Olimpia tells me that she must give me bad news. I set myself as Wise Wolf sits in my lap as Špela and Vida crowd in on my sides. Olimpia smiles at me and says, "My son; I am so amazed at the loyalty of the women who are with you." Špela tells Olimpia,

"We would give our lives for him under any condition." Wise Wolf adds, "I would not simply give my life, but also give my Kingdom for the one who searched for, and found me." Olimpia kneels before me and wraps her arms around both the Queen and me. She asks the Queen forgiveness. Wise Wolf tells her she has done no wrong and that once she knows I am safe; she will give me to my mother.

Olimpia begins her story, "Yakov, we heard so many terrible tales about how you were taken prisoner. One warrior saw them beat you. He watched them put you into a Cvetka prison, one in which no one ever escapes. We knew that if you escaped, others would suffer great punishments for your actions. I, therefore, told Andreja that you would at no time escape, because my son would never hurt innocent people. Andreja went to the Gerben temples and cried both day and night for your return. She refused to eat. Aert gathered a few of his friends and took her prisoner, forcing food inside her. The value of a barren woman in Gerben who is from another tribe is priceless. I interviewed over 1000 warriors who wanted to care for, and marry her. In the middle of the dark day's season, we selected one man. The priests, after long debate, declared you died, which also destroyed our Search for Wise Wolf. She refused to let you go, and as such refused to sleep with her husband. Therefore, we force the consummation of her marriage. When she became pregnant, she began to give up hope of your return. Two months into her marriage, with her husband's child inside her, we received word that you had not simply escaped, but found Wise Wolf and was bringing our hope back to us. She tore off her clothes in the middle of the high open area in the caves and fell to the ground begging that someone would kill her. When all refused, she tried to kill herself many times. This forced our tribe was forced permanently to tie her hands, so she could do no harm to herself. The head chief then ordered her husband and her to flee for their lives, as all believe you will seek revenge." Olimpia now handed me her long knife and said, "If you must seek revenge, subsequently you must first kill me, for I lost faith in you. As I have seen all in my family go to the Land of the Dead, I believed you cheated to get there before me. I beg that you kill me first." She then tore a hole in her dress exposing her swollen belly. Špela asks Olimpia, "My mother, are you with child?"

She looks at Špela and tells her, "Yes, Aert and I are expecting our first son, whom we were to name Yakov, because he is the greatest love in my heart."

I threw down the long knife and told Olimpia, "I would die 1000 deaths before I ever inflicted any pain on you. I worry so much about Andreja, as I can never have joy in my life knowing she suffers." Next, I asked Wise Wolf, what I should do. She stands up, looks at me with her Royal stair, and declares, "The first thing you must do is stop refusing to be my King. I demand that you take me as your wife and allow me to love you until we join Acia and Pava." Everyone around us stood up and curtsied Wise Wolf, remaining bowed as no one would move. I then ask Wise Wolf, "What shall we do with your chamber maidens, whom I also love?" Wise Wolf tells me, "I demand that you never stop loving them, as neither shall I ever stop loving them." I looked at Wise Wolf and asked, "How does one marry the Queen?" Wise Wolf stood up and looked at each of us, and then she declared, "I declare Yakov to be my husband and the keeper of my chamber maidens. Is there any who will challenge this?" Olimpia and Urška both spoke, saying, "None will ever challenge the Queen and our King." Olimpia looked at me and said, "Wow; my son is a King." I looked at her and asked, "How can this be so easy?" Olimpia tells me the Queen rules by divine right, and the stars obey her commands. She clarifies, "Yakov, you are married, and you are my King." Aert and Carolus both bow to say, "Long live the King of the Gerben and all the princes whom, he shall give our Kingdom." Wise Wolf looks at me and then tells Olimpia, "Two of you must rush back to my Kingdom and order that Andreja and her husband return to my Kingdom. I will not have my children, especially daughters who are pregnant, roaming in unprotected lands. I give Andreja the title of Protector of the Queen's Family. Armies shall obey her, as my husband, and I will consult with her each day. The chamber next to me is for her family, for her children will play with mine. Her lack of faith caused her to lose the husband whom I found. She needs not to suffer any longer."

Wise Wolf cut off a handful of her hair and tore a piece from her gown wrapping her hair. She gave this the Aert and Carolus and told them to give it to the high priest as this being her divine order. She further ordered that every one of her Armies join in this search. Wise Wolf's final argument was, "Andreja lost her life in the search for me, and she will be given a new life as a reward. Her sacrifice is the 'Sacrifice for the Search of Wise Wolf,' Aert asked her if she needed more men to protect her. She looked at him and said, "I have the King to protect us. I am in the arms that will guide me until I return to the Kings and Queens in the Land of the Dead. Now, go quickly." Wise Wolf currently lies in my lap as a child would. She looked at me and said, "I hope that you will be pleased with the love that I have for you." I grab hold of Špela and Vida's hands and say to her, "Our Love will live forever as a part of me rejoices in that we may keep it." Vida looks at the Queen and complains, "Oh no, does this mean I have to love him as well?" Wise Wolf looks at her and says, "Yes, if you want to keep your head." Vida then says, "I guess a little foreplay would be worth keeping my head. Here, Yakov, you may play with my toe." I peek at her and say, "Wise Wolf," as Vida qualifies her invitation, "As a starter my master, please enjoy what you wish." I gaze at her and say, "You know; I always did fancy your wonderful hugs." Vida smiles and reports, "Thank the heavens, he remains housebroken." I believe all within miles could hear us laugh on at this. I continue by reporting to our Queen, "As there is just one Wise Wolf, there are simply one Špela and no more than one Vida." Urška looks at me and says, "Did you forget about me?" I considered both her and Olimpia and said, "Certain loves have a solid foundation inside that I identify to belong to me. I do hope that my mother and Urška will stay in my heart." Olimpia then laughs and says, "Even though you refused to kill me, and now I must bear a son, who has your name, I guess I can forgive you." I looked at Olimpia and reply, "As usual; you continue to bear the greatest burdens."

Olimpia and Urška fall on the ground beside us, as we are but one combined flesh. Wise Wolf then says, "I truly sense as a part of a family now." I thought for a minute as Acia and Pava stood before me and said, "This is a moment in the Search for Wise Wolf that will never end in my heart." After a short time, Olimpia stood up and said, "I need to bid my farewells to the greatest sisters, I could ever be blessed to have." Olimpia, Acia, and Pava depart for the high rock. Urška goes to stand up as Špela grabs hold of her and asks, "Where are going?" Urška tells us that she does not belong to us, nor does she belong to Olimpia, so she will find a comfortable place and sleep alone. Wise Wolf looks at her and questions, "Why would my daughter say she does not belong to me. Tonight you will sleep with us." Urška bows and lays down beside us as this day almost ends for us. Wise Wolf looks at me and then reminds me that this is our wedding night and the King has specific official work to do before the Suns rise in the morning. This night, I found Wise Wolf. The Search for Wise Wolf is complete, as now her people grasp her. She has given herself to be known by a man, the one whom, she made her King. Wise Wolf has begun the great work that her ancestors always gave the highest Royal responsibility, and that is to ensure her seed travels through time. Her seed will change the universe and history. Except for Wolf and Howl, there can be no peeking, or spying, as they guarantee our Royal privacy. Wise Wolf prepares the garden to cultivate this seed. Good night, as our tomorrow will be great in that we have our Wise Wolf.

INDEX

P

Q

R

S

MAPS INDEX

Lamenta

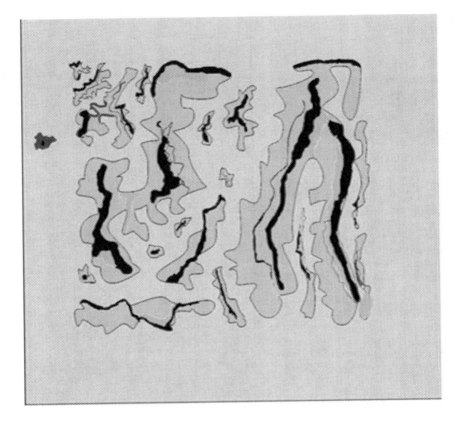

Earth vs. Lamenta

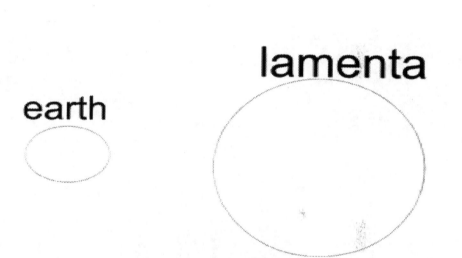

LAMENTA MOONS

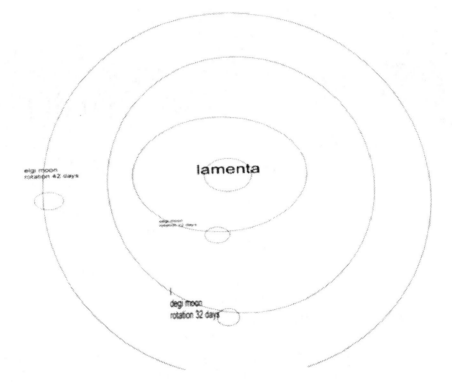

TWIN SUNS

INNER SOLAR SYSTEM

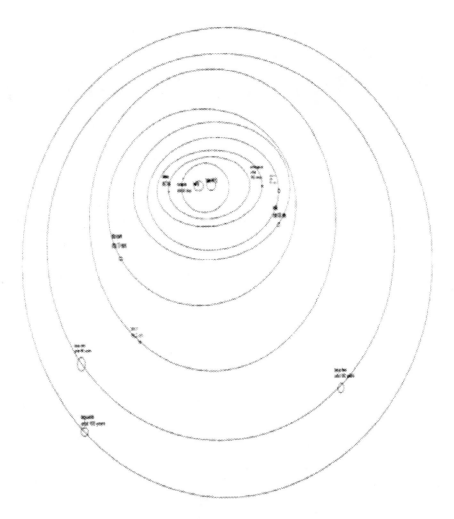

COMPLETE SOLAR SYSTEM

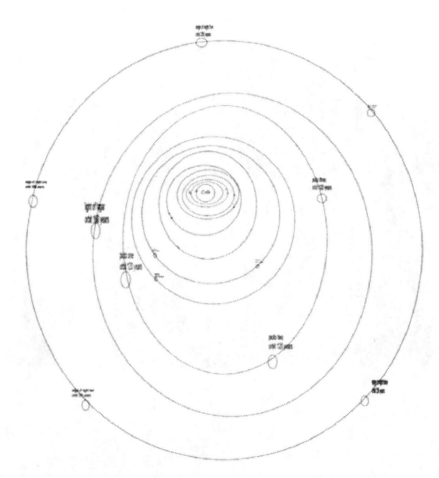

PETENKA
LAKE ON THE TOP OF THE WORLD

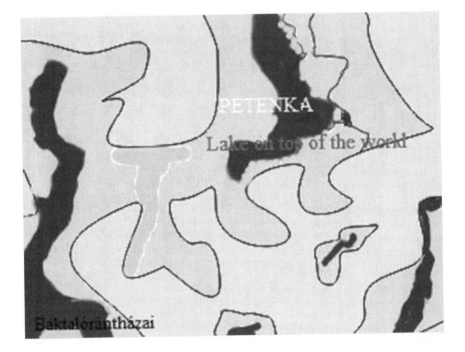

JOŽEFA
CVETKA
ARMIES MEET FOR GREAT BATTLE

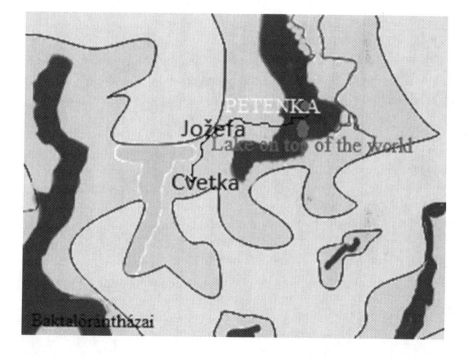

Wise Wolf's Return by sea

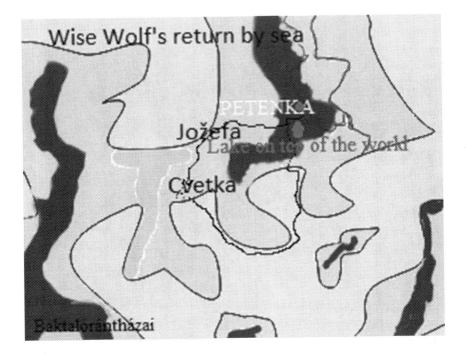

The adventures in this series

Prikhodko, Dream of Nagykanizsai

Seven Wives of Siklósi

Passion of the Progenitor

Mempire, Born in Blood

Penance on Earth

Patmos Paradigm

Lord of New Venus

Tianshire, Life in the Light

Rachmanism in Ereshkigal

Sisterhood, Blood of our Blood

Salvation, Showers of Blood

Author Bio

J ames Hendershot, D.D. was born in Marietta Ohio, finally settling in Caldwell, Ohio where he eventually graduated from high school. After graduating, he served four years in the Air Force and graduated, Magna Cum Laude, with three majors from the prestigious Marietta College. He then served until retirement in the US Army during which time he earned his Masters of Science degree from Central Michigan University in Public Administration, and his third degree in Computer Programing from Central Texas College. His final degree was the honorary degree of Doctor of Divinity from Kingsway Bible College, which provided him with keen insight into the divine nature of man.

After retiring from the US Army, he accepted a visiting professor position with Korea University in Seoul, South Korea. He later moved to a suburb outside Seattle to finish his lifelong search for Mempire and the goddess Lilith, only to find them in his fingers and not with his eyes. It is now time for Earth to learn about the great mysteries not only deep in our universe but also in the dimensions beyond sharing these magnanimities with you.